Praise for

THE LOVE HYPOTHESIS

"Contemporary romance's unicorn: the elusive marriage of deeply brainy and delightfully escapist. . . . *The Love Hypothesis* has wild commercial appeal, but the quieter secret is that there is a specific audience, made up of all of the Olives in the world, who have deeply, ardently waited for this exact book."

—*New York Times* bestselling author Christina Lauren

"Funny, sexy, and smart. Ali Hazelwood did a terrific job with *The Love Hypothesis*." —*New York Times* bestselling author Mariana Zapata

"This tackles one of my favorite tropes—Grumpy meets Sunshine— in a fun and utterly endearing way. . . . I loved the nods toward fandom and romance novels, and I couldn't put it down. Highly recommended!" —*New York Times* bestselling author Jessica Clare

"A beautifully written romantic comedy with a heroine you will instantly fall in love with, *The Love Hypothesis* is destined to earn a place on your keeper shelf."

—Elizabeth Everett, author of *A Lady's Formula for Love*

"Smart, witty dialogue and a diverse cast of likable secondary characters. . . . A realistic, amusing novel that readers won't be able to put down." —*Library Journal* (starred review)

"With whip-smart and endearing characters, snappy prose, and a quirky take on a favorite trope, Hazelwood convincingly navigates the fraught shoals of academia. . . . This smart, sexy contemporary should delight a wide swath of romance lovers." —*Publishers Weekly*

TITLES BY ALI HAZELWOOD

• • • •

The Love Hypothesis
Love on the Brain

LOATHE TO LOVE YOU
Under One Roof
Stuck with You
Below Zero

LOVE
on the
BRAIN

ALI HAZELWOOD

JOVE
NEW YORK

A JOVE BOOK
Published by Berkley
An imprint of Penguin Random House LLC
penguinrandomhouse.com

Library of Congress Cataloging-in-Publication Data

Names: Hazelwood, Ali, author.
Title: Love on the brain / Ali Hazelwood.
Description: First Edition. | New York: Jove, 2022.
Identifiers: LCCN 2021053843 | ISBN 9780593336847 (trade paperback) |
ISBN 9780593336854 (ebook)
Subjects: GSAFD: Love stories.
Classification: LCC PS3608.A98845 L69 2022 | DDC 813/.6—dc23
LC record available at https://lccn.loc.gov/2021053843

First Edition: August 2022

Printed in the United States of America
1st Printing

Title page art: space icons © kosmofish / Shutterstock
Book design by Alison Cnockaert

To my Grems. [Insert DolphinBoob.gif]

1

THE HABENULA: DISAPPOINTMENT

HERE'S MY FAVORITE piece of trivia in the whole world: Dr. Marie Skłodowska-Curie showed up to her wedding ceremony wearing her lab gown.

It's actually a pretty cool story: a scientist friend hooked her up with Pierre Curie. They awkwardly admitted to having read each other's papers and flirted over beakers full of liquid uranium, and he proposed within the year. But Marie was only meant to be in France to get her degree, and reluctantly rejected him to return to Poland.

Womp womp.

Enter the University of Krakow, villain and unintentional cupid of this story, which denied Marie a faculty position because she was a woman (very classy, U of K). Dick move, I know, but it had the fortunate side effect of pushing Marie right back into Pierre's loving, not-yet-radioactive arms. Those two beautiful nerds married in 1895, and Marie, who wasn't exactly making bank at the time, bought herself a wedding dress that was comfortable enough to use in the lab every day. My girl was nothing if not pragmatic.

Of course, this story becomes significantly less cool if you fast forward ten years or so, to when Pierre got himself run over by a carriage and left Marie and their two daughters alone in the world. Zoom into 1906, and that's where you'll find the real moral of this tale: trusting people to stick around is a bad idea. One way or another they'll end up gone. Maybe they'll slip on the Rue Dauphine on a rainy morning and get their skull crushed by a horse-drawn cart. Maybe they'll be kidnapped by aliens and vanish into the vastness of space. Or maybe they'll have sex with your best friend six months before you're due to get married, forcing you to call off the wedding and lose tons of cash in security deposits.

The sky's the limit, really.

One might say, then, that U of K is only a minor villain. Don't get me wrong: I love picturing Dr. Curie waltzing back to Krakow *Pretty Woman*–style, wearing her wedding-slash-lab gown, brandishing her two Nobel Prize medals, and yelling, "Big Mistake. Big. *Huge*." But the real villain, the one that had Marie crying and staring at the ceiling in the late hours of the night, is loss. Grief. The intrinsic transience of human relationships. The real villain is love: an unstable isotope, constantly undergoing spontaneous nuclear decay.

And it will forever go unpunished.

Do you know what's reliable instead? What never, *ever* abandoned Dr. Curie in all her years? Her curiosity. Her discoveries. Her accomplishments.

Science. *Science* is where it's at.

Which is why when NASA notifies me—*Me! Bee Königswasser!*—that I've been chosen as lead investigator of BLINK, one of their most prestigious neuroengineering research projects, I screech. I screech loudly and joyously in my minuscule, windowless office on the Bethesda campus of the National Institutes of Health. I screech about the amazing performance-enhancing technology I'm going to get to build for none other than NASA astronauts, and then I remember that the walls are toilet-paper thin and that my left neighbor once filed a formal complaint against me for listening to nineties female alt-rock without headphones. So I press the back of my hand to my mouth, bite into it, and jump up and down as silently as possible while elation explodes inside me.

I feel just like I imagine Dr. Curie must have felt when she was finally allowed to enroll at the University of Paris in late 1891: as though a world of (preferably nonradioactive) scientific discoveries is finally within grasping distance. It is, by far, the most momentous day of my life, and kicks off a *phenomenal* weekend of celebrations. Highlights are:

- I tell the news to my three favorite colleagues, and we go out to our usual bar, guzzle several rounds of lemon drops, and take turns doing hilarious impressions of that time Trevor, our ugly middle-aged boss, asked us not to fall in love with him. (Academic men tend to harbor many delusions—except for Pierre Curie, of course. Pierre would never.)

- I change my hair from pink to purple. (I have to do it at home, because junior academics can't afford salons; my shower ends up looking like a mix between a cotton candy machine and a unicorn slaughterhouse, but after the raccoon incident—which, believe me, you don't want to know about—I wasn't going to get my security deposit back anyway.)

- I take myself to Victoria's Secret and buy a set of pretty green lingerie, not allowing myself to feel guilty at the expense (even though it's been many years since someone has seen me without clothes, and if I have my way no one will for many, many more).

- I download the Couch-to-Marathon plan I've been meaning to start and do my first run. (Then I limp back home cursing my overambition and promptly downgrade to a Couch-to-5K program. I can't believe that some people work out *every day*.)

- I bake treats for Finneas, my elderly neighbor's equally elderly cat, who often visits my apartment for second dinner. (He shreds my favorite pair of Converse in gratitude. Dr. Curie, in her infinite wisdom, was probably a dog person.)

In short, I have an absolute blast. I'm not even sad when Monday comes. It's same old, same old—experiments, lab meetings, eating Lean Cuisine and shotgunning store-brand LaCroix at my desk while crunching data—but with the prospect of BLINK, even the old feels new and exciting.

I'll be honest: I've been worried sick. After having four grant applications rejected in less than six months, I was sure that my career was stalling—maybe even over. Whenever Trevor called me into his office, I'd get palpitations and sweaty palms, sure that he'd tell me that my yearly contract wasn't going to be renewed. The last couple of years since graduating with my Ph.D. haven't been a whole lot of fun.

But that's over with. Contracting for NASA is a career-making opportunity. After all, I've been chosen after a ruthless selection process over golden boys like Josh Martin, Hank Malik, even Jan Vanderberg, that horrid guy who trash-talks my research like it's an Olympic sport. I've had my setbacks, plenty of them, but after nearly two decades of being obsessed with the brain, here I am: lead neuroscientist of BLINK. I'll design gears for *astronauts*, gears they'll use in *space*. This is how I get out of Trevor's clammy, sexist clutches. This is what buys me a long-term contract and my own lab with my own line of research. This is the turning point in my professional life—which, truthfully, is the only kind of life I care to have.

For several days I'm ecstatic. I'm exhilarated. I'm ecstatically exhilarated.

Then, on Monday at 4:33 p.m., my email pings with a message from NASA. I read the name of the person who will be co-leading BLINK with me, and all of a sudden I'm none of those things anymore.

"DO YOU REMEMBER Levi Ward?"

"*Brennt da etwas*—uh?" Over the phone, Mareike's voice is thick and sleep-laden, muffled by poor reception and long distance. "Bee? Is that you? What time is it?"

"Eight fifteen in Maryland and . . ." I rapidly calculate the time difference. A few weeks ago Reike was in Tajikistan, but now she's in . . . Portugal, maybe? "Two a.m. your time."

Reike grunts, groans, moans, and makes a whole host of other sounds I'm all too familiar with from sharing a room with her for the first two decades of our lives. I sit back on my couch and wait it out until she asks, "Who died?"

"No one died. Well, I'm sure *someone* died, but no one we know.

Were you really sleeping? Are you sick? Should I fly out?" I'm genuinely concerned that my sister isn't out clubbing, or skinny-dipping in the Mediterranean Sea, or frolicking with a coven of warlocks based in the forests of the Iberian Peninsula. Sleeping at night is very out of character.

"Nah. I ran out of money again." She yawns. "Been giving private lessons to rich, spoiled Portuguese boys during the day until I make enough to fly to Norway."

I know better than to ask "Why Norway?" since Reike's answer would just be "Why not?" Instead I go with, "Do you need me to send you some money?" I'm not exactly flush with cash, especially after my days of (premature, as it turns out) celebrations, but I could spare a few dollars if I'm careful. And don't eat. For a couple of days.

"Nah, the brats' parents pay well. Ugh, Bee, a twelve-year-old tried to touch my boob yesterday."

"Gross. What did you do?"

"I told him I'd cut off his fingers, of course. Anyway—to what do I owe the pleasure of being brutally awakened?"

"I'm sorry."

"Nah, you're not."

I smile. "Nah, I'm not." What's the point of sharing 100 percent of your DNA with a person if you can't wake them up for an emergency chat? "Remember that research project I mentioned? BLINK?"

"The one you're leading? NASA? Where you use your fancy brain science to build those fancy helmets to make fancy astronauts better in space?"

"Yes. Sort of. As it turns out, I'm not leading as much as *co*-leading. The funds come from NIH and NASA. They got into a pissing contest over which agency should be in charge, and ultimately decided to have two leaders." In the corner of my eye I notice a flash of orange—Finneas, lounging on the sill of my kitchen window. I let him in with a few scratches on the head. He meows lovingly and licks my hand. "Do you remember Levi Ward?"

"Is he some guy I dated who's trying to reach me because he has gonorrhea?"

"Huh? No. He's someone I met in grad school." I open the cupboard where I keep the Whiskas. "He was getting a Ph.D. in engineering in my lab, and was in his fifth year when I started—"

"The Wardass!"

"Yep, him!"

"I remember! Wasn't he like . . . hot? Tall? Built?"

I bite back a smile, pouring food in Finneas's bowl. "I'm not sure how I feel about the fact that the only thing you remember about my grad school nemesis is that he was six four." Dr. Marie Curie's sisters, renowned physician Bronisława Dłuska and educational activist Helena Szalayowa, would never. Unless they were thirsty wenches like Reike—in which case they absolutely would.

"*And* built. You should just be proud of my elephantine memory."

"And I am. Anyway, I was told who the NASA co-lead for my project will be, and—"

"No way." Reike must have sat up. Her voice is suddenly crystal clear. "*No way.*"

"Yes way." I listen to my sister's maniacal, gleeful cackling while I toss the empty pouch. "You know, you could at least pretend not to enjoy this so much."

"Oh, I could. But will I?"

"Clearly not."

"Did you cry when you found out?"

"No."

7

"Did you head-desk?"

"No."

"Don't lie to me. Do you have a bump on your forehead?"

". . . Maybe a small one."

"Oh, Bee. Bee, thank you for waking me up to share this outstanding piece of news. Isn't The Wardass the guy who said that you were fugly?"

He never did, at least not in those terms, but I laugh so loud, Finneas gives me a startled glance. "I can't believe you remember *that*."

"Hey, I resented it a lot. You're hot AF."

"You only say so because I look exactly like you."

"Why, I hadn't even noticed."

It's not completely true, anyway. Yes, Reike and I are both short and slight. We have the same symmetrical features and blue eyes, the same straight dark hair. Still, we've long outgrown our *Parent Trap* stage, and at twenty-eight no one would struggle to tell us apart. Not when my hair has been different shades of pastel colors for the past decade, or with my love for piercings and the occasional tattoo. Reike, with her wanderlust and artistic inclinations, is the true free spirit of the family, but she can never be bothered to make free-spirit fashion statements. That's where I, the supposedly boring scientist, come in to pick up the slack.

"So, was he? The one who insulted me by proxy?"

"Yep. Levi Ward. The one and only."

I pour water into a bowl for Finneas. It didn't go *quite* that way. Levi never explicitly insulted me. Implicitly, though . . .

I gave my first academic talk in my second semester of grad school, and I took it very seriously. I memorized the entire speech, redid the PowerPoint six times, even agonized over the perfect outfit. I ended up dressing nicer than usual, and Annie, my grad school best friend, had the well-meaning but unfortunate idea to rope Levi in to complimenting me.

"Doesn't Bee look extra pretty today?"

It was probably the only topic of conversation she could think of. After all, Annie was always going on about how mysteriously handsome he was, with the dark hair and the broad shoulders and that interesting, unusual face of his; how she wished he'd stop being so reserved and ask her out. Except that Levi didn't seem interested in conversation. He studied me intensely, with those piercing green eyes of his. He stared at me from head to toe for several moments. And then he said . . .

Nothing. Absolutely nothing.

He just made what Tim, my ex-fiancé, later referred to as an "aghast expression," and walked out of the lab with a wooden nod and zero compliments—not even a stilted, fake one. After that, grad school—the ultimate cesspool of gossip—did its thing, and the story took on a life of its own. Students said that he'd puked all over my dress; that he'd begged me on his knees to put a paper bag over my head; that he'd been so horrified, he'd tried to cleanse his brain by drinking bleach and suffered irreparable neurological damage as a consequence. I try not to take myself too seriously, and being part of a meme of sorts was amusing, but the rumors were so wild, I started to wonder if I really was revolting.

Still, I never blamed Levi. I never resented him for refusing to be strong-armed into pretending that he found me attractive. Or . . . well, not-repulsive. He always seemed like such a man's man, after all. Different from the boys that surrounded me. Serious, disciplined, a little broody. Intense and gifted. Alpha, whatever that even means. A girl with a septum piercing and a blue ombré wouldn't conform to his ideals of what pretty ladies should look like, and that's fine.

What I *do* resent Levi for are his other behaviors during the year we overlapped. Like the fact that he never bothered to meet my eyes when I talked to him, or that he always found excuses not to come to journal club when it was my turn to present. I reserve the right to be angry for how he'd slip out of a group conversation the moment I joined, for considering me so beneath his notice that he never even said hi when I walked into the lab, for the way I caught him staring at me with an intense, displeased expression, as though I were some eldritch abomination. I reserve the right to feel bitter that after Tim and I got engaged, Levi pulled him aside and told him that he could do much better than me. Come on, who *does* that?

Most of all, I reserve the right to detest him for making it clear that he believed me to be a mediocre scientist. The rest I could have overlooked easily enough, but the lack of respect for my work . . . I'll forever grind my axe for that.

That is, until I wedge it in his groin.

Levi became my sworn archenemy on a Tuesday in April, in my Ph.D. advisor's office. Samantha Lee was—and still is—the bomb when it comes to neuroimaging. If there's a way to study a living human's brains without cracking their skull open, Sam either came up with it or mastered it. Her research is brilliant, well-funded, and highly interdisciplinary—hence the variety of Ph.D. students she mentored: cognitive neuroscientists like me, interested in studying the neural bases of behavior, but also computer scientists, biologists, psychologists. Engineers.

Even in the crowded chaos of Sam's lab, Levi stood out. He had a knack for the type of problem-solving Sam liked—the one that elevates neuroimaging to an art. In his first year, he figured out a way to build a portable infrared spectroscopy machine that had been puzzling postdocs for a decade. By his third, he'd revolutionized the lab's data analysis pipeline. In his fourth he got a *Science* publication. And in his fifth, when I joined the lab, Sam called us together into her office.

"There is this amazing project I've been wanting to kick-start," she said with her usual enthusiasm. "If we manage to make it work, it's going to change the entire landscape of the field. And that's why I need my best neuroscientist and my best engineer to collaborate on it."

It was a breezy, early spring afternoon. I remember it well, because that morning had been unforgettable: Tim on one knee, in the middle of the lab, proposing. A bit theatrical, not really my thing, but I wasn't going to complain, not when it meant someone wanted to stand by me for good. So I looked him in the eyes, choked back the tears, and said yes.

A few hours later, I felt the engagement ring bite painfully into my clenched fist. "I don't have time for a collaboration, Sam," Levi said. He was standing as far away from me as he could, and yet he still managed to fill the small office and become its center of gravity. He didn't bother to glance at me. He never did.

Sam frowned. "The other day you said you'd be on board."

"I misspoke." His expression was unreadable. Uncompromising. "Sorry, Sam. I'm just too busy."

I cleared my throat and took a few steps toward him. "I know I'm just a first-year student," I started, appeasingly, "but I can do my part, I promise. And—"

"That's not it," he said. His eyes briefly caught mine, green and black and stormy cold, and for a brief moment he seemed stuck, as though he couldn't look away. My heart stumbled. "Like I said, I don't have time right now to take on new projects."

I don't remember why I walked out of the office alone, nor why I decided to linger right outside. I told myself that it was fine. Levi was just busy. Everyone was busy. Academia was nothing but a bunch of busy people running around busily. I myself was super busy, because Sam was right: I was one of the best neuroscientists in the lab. I had plenty of my own work going on.

Until I overheard Sam's concerned question: "Why did you change your mind? *You* said that the project was going to be a slam dunk."

"I know. But I can't. I'm sorry."

"Can't what?"

"Work with Bee."

Sam asked him why, but I didn't stop to listen. Pursuing any kind of graduate education requires a healthy dose of masochism, but I drew the line at sticking around while someone trash-talked me to my boss. I stormed off, and by the following week, when I heard Annie chattering happily about the fact that Levi had agreed to help her on her thesis project, I'd long stopped lying to myself.

Levi Ward, His Wardness, Dr. Wardass, despised me.

Me.

Specifically me.

Yes, he was a taciturn, somber, brooding mountain of a man. He was private, an introvert. His temperament was reserved and aloof. I couldn't demand that he like me, and had no intention of doing so. Still, if he could be civil, polite, even friendly with everyone else, he could have made an effort with me, too. But no—Levi Ward clearly despised me, and in the face of such hatred . . .

Well. I had no choice but to hate him back.

"You there?" Reike asks.

"Yeah," I mumble, "just ruminating about Levi."

"He's at NASA, then? Dare I hope he'll be sent to Mars to retrieve *Curiosity*?"

"Sadly, not before he's done co-leading my project." In the past few years, while my career gasped for air like a hippo with sleep apnea, Levi's thrived—obnoxiously so. He published interesting studies, got a huge Department of Defense grant, and, according to an email Sam sent around, even made *Forbes*'s 10 Under 40 list, the science edition. The only reason I've been able to stand his successes without falling on my sword is that his research has been gravitating away from neuroimaging. This made us not-quite-competitors and allowed me to just . . . never think about him. An excellent life hack, which worked superbly—until today.

Honestly, fuck today.

"I'm still enjoying this immensely, but I'll make an effort to be sisterly and sympathetic. How concerned are you to be working with him, on a scale from one to heavily breathing into a paper bag?"

I tip what's left of Finneas's water into a pot of daisies. "I think having to work with someone who thinks I'm a shit scientist warrants at least two inhalers."

"You're amazing. You're the best scientist."

"Aw, thank you." I choose to believe that Reike filing astrology and cristallotherapy under the label "science" only slightly detracts from the compliment. "It's going to be horrible. The worst. If he's anything like he used to be, I'm going to . . . Reike, are you peeing?"

A beat, filled by the noise of running water. ". . . Maybe. Hey, you're the one who woke me and my bladder up. Please, carry on."

I smile and shake my head. "If he's anything like he was at Pitt, he's going to be a nightmare to work with. Plus I'll be on his turf."

"Right, 'cause you're moving to Houston."

"For three months. My research assistant and I are leaving next week."

"I'm jealous. I'm going to be stuck here in Portugal for who knows how long, groped by knockoff Joffrey Baratheons who refuse to learn what a subjunctive is. I'm rotting, Bee."

It will never cease to befuddle me how differently Reike and I reacted to being thrown around like rubber balls during childhood, both before and after our parents' death. We were bounced from one extended family member to another, lived in a dozen countries, and all Reike wants is . . . to live in even *more* countries. Travel, see new places, experience new things. It's like yearning for change is hardwired in her brain. She packed up the day we graduated high school and has been making her way through the continents for the past decade, complaining about being bored after a handful of weeks in one place.

I'm the opposite. I want to put down roots. Security. Stability. I thought I'd get it with Tim, but like I said, relying on others is risky business. Permanence and love are clearly incompatible, so now I'm focusing on my career. I want a long-term position as an NIH scientist, and landing BLINK is the perfect stepping-stone.

"You know what just occurred to me?"

"You forgot to flush?"

"Can't flush at night—noisy European pipes. If I do, my neighbor leaves passive-aggressive notes. But hear me out: three years ago, when I spent that summer harvesting watermelons in Australia, I met this guy from Houston. He was a riot. Cute, too. Bet I can find his email and ask him if he's single—"

"Nope."

"He had really pretty eyes and could touch the tip of his nose with his tongue—that's, like, ten percent of the population."

I make a mental note to look up whether that's true. "I'm going there to work, not to date nose-tongue guy."

"You could do both."

"I don't date."

"Why?"

"You know why."

"No, actually." Reike's tone takes on its usual stubborn quality. "Listen, I know that the last time you dated—"

"I was engaged."

"Same difference. Maybe things didn't go well"—I lift one eyebrow at the most euphemistic euphemism I've ever heard—"and you want to feel safe and practice maintenance of your emotional boundaries, but that can't prevent you from ever dating again. You can't put all your eggs into the science basket. There are other, better baskets. Like the sex basket, and the making-out basket, and the letting-a-boy-pay-for-your-expensive-vegan-dinner basket, and—" Finneas chooses this very moment to meow loudly. Bless his little feline timing. "Bee! Did you get that kitten you've been talking about?"

"It's the neighbor's." I lean over to nuzzle him, a silent thank-you for distracting my sister mid-sermon.

"If you don't want to date nose-tongue guy, at least get a damn cat. You already have that stupid name picked out."

"Meowrie Curie is a great name—and no."

"It's your childhood dream! Remember when we were in Austria? How we'd play Harry Potter and your Patronus was always a kitten?"

"And yours was a blobfish." I smile. We read the books together in German, just a few weeks before moving to our maternal cousin's in the UK, who wasn't exactly thrilled to have us stay in her minuscule spare room. Ugh, I hate moving. I'm sad to leave my objectively-crappy-but-dearly-beloved Bethesda apartment. "Anyway, Harry Potter is tainted forever, and I'm not getting a cat."

"Why?"

"Because it will die in thirteen to seventeen years, based on recent statistical data, and shatter my heart in thirteen to seventeen pieces."

"Oh, for fuck's sake."

"I'll settle for loving other people's cats and never knowing when they pass away."

I hear a thud, probably Reike throwing herself back into bed. "You know what your condition is? It's called—"

"Not a condition, we've been over—"

"—avoidant attachment. You're pathologically independent and don't let others come close out of fear that they'll eventually leave you. You have erected a fence around you—the Bee-fence—and are terrified of anything resembling emotional—" Reike's voice fades into a jaw-breaking yawn, and I feel a wave of affection for her. Even though her favorite pastime is entering my personality traits into WebMD and diagnosing me with imaginary disorders.

"Go to bed, Reike. I'll call you soon."

"Yeah, okay." Another small yawn. "But I'm right, Beetch. And you're wrong."

"Of course. Good night, babe."

I hang up and spend a few more minutes petting Finneas. When he slips out to the fresh breeze of the early-spring night, I begin to pack. As I fold my skinny jeans and colorful tops, I come across something I haven't seen in a while: a dress with yellow polka dots over blue cotton—the same blue of Dr. Curie's wedding gown. Target, spring collection, circa five million years ago. Twelve dollars, give or take. It's the one I was wearing when Levi decided that I am but a sentient bunion, the most repugnant of nature's creatures.

I shrug, and stuff it into my suitcase.

2

VAGUS NERVE: BLACKOUT

"BY THE WAY, you can get leprosy from armadillos."

I peel my nose away from the airplane window and glance at Rocío, my research assistant. "Really?"

"Yep. They got it from humans millennia ago, and now they're giving it back to us." She shrugs. "Revenge and cold dishes and all that."

I scrutinize her beautiful face for hints that she's lying. Her large dark eyes, heavily rimmed with eyeliner, are inscrutable. Her hair is so Vantablack, it absorbs 99 percent of visible light. Her mouth is full, curved downward in its typical pout.

Nope. I got nothing. "Is this for real?"

"Would I ever lie to you?"

"Last week you swore to me that Stephen King was writing a Winnie-the-Pooh spin-off." And I believed her. Like I believed that Lady Gaga is a known satanist, or that badminton racquets are made from human bones and intestines. Chaotic goth misanthropy and creepy deadpan sarcasm are her brand, and I should know better than to take her seriously. Problem is, every once in a while she'll throw in a crazy-sounding story that upon further inspection (i.e., a Google search) is revealed to be true. For instance, did you know that *The Texas Chainsaw Massacre* was inspired by a true story? Before Rocío, I didn't. And I slept significantly better.

"Don't believe me, then." She shrugs, going back to her grad school admission prep book. "Go pet the leper armadillos and die."

She's such a weirdo. I adore her.

"Hey, you sure you're going to be fine, away from Alex for the next few months?" I feel a little guilty for taking her away from her boyfriend. When I was twenty-two, if someone had asked me to be apart from Tim for months, I'd have walked into the sea. Then again, hindsight has proven beyond doubt that I was a complete idiot, and Rocío seems pretty enthused over the opportunity. She plans to apply to Johns Hopkins's neuro program in the fall, and the NASA line on her CV won't hurt. She even hugged me when I offered her the chance to come along—a moment of weakness I'm sure she deeply regrets.

"Fine? Are you kidding?" She looks at me like I'm insane. "Three months in Texas, do you know how many times I'll get to see La Llorona?"

"La . . . what?"

She rolls her eyes and pops in her AirPods. "You really know *nothing* about famed feminist ghosts."

I bite back a smile and turn back to the window. In 1905, Dr. Curie decided to invest her Nobel Prize money into hiring her first research assistant. I wonder if she, too, ended up working with a mildly terrifying, Cthulhu-worshipping emo girl. I stare at the clouds until I'm bored, and then I take my phone out of my pocket and connect to the complimentary in-flight Wi-Fi. I glance at Rocío, making sure that she's not paying attention to me, and angle my screen away.

I'm not a very secretive person, mostly out of laziness: I refuse to take on the cognitive labor of tracking lies and omissions. I do, however, have one secret. One single piece of information that I've never shared with anyone—not even my sister. Don't get me wrong, I trust Reike with my life, but I also know her well enough to picture the scene: she is wearing a flowy sundress, flirting with a Scottish shepherd she met in a trattoria on the Amalfi Coast. They decide to do the shrooms they just purchased from a Belarusian farmer, and mid-trip she accidentally blurts out the one thing she's been expressly forbidden to repeat: her twin sister, Bee, runs one of the most popular and controversial accounts on Academic Twitter. The Scottish shepherd's cousin is a closeted men's rights activist who sends me a dead possum in the mail, rats me out to his insane friends, and I get fired.

No, thank you. I love my job (and possums) too much for this.

I created @WhatWouldMarieDo during my first semester of grad school. I was teaching a neuroanatomy class, and decided to give my students an anonymous mid-semester survey to ask for honest feedback on how to improve the course. What I got was . . . not that. I was told that my lectures would be more interesting if I delivered them naked. That I should gain some weight, get a boob job, stop dying my hair "unnatural colors," get rid of my piercings. I was even given a phone number to call if I was "ever in the mood for a ten-inch dick." (Yeah, right.)

The messages were pretty appalling, but what sent me sobbing in a bathroom stall was the reactions of the other students in my cohort—Tim included. They laughed the comments off as harmless pranks and dissuaded me from reporting them to the department chair, telling me that I'd be making a stink about nothing.

They were, of course, all men.

(Seriously: why *are* men?)

That night I fell asleep crying. The following day I got up, wondered how many other women in STEM felt as alone as I did, and impulsively downloaded Twitter and made @WhatWouldMarieDo. I slapped on a poorly photoshopped pic of Dr. Curie wearing sunglasses and a one-line bio: *Making the periodic table girlier since 1889 (she/her)*. I just wanted to scream into the void. I honestly didn't think that anyone would even see my first tweet. But I was wrong.

> @WhatWouldMarieDo What would Dr. Curie, first female professor at La Sorbonne, do if one of her students asked her to deliver her lectures naked?

> @198888 She would shorten his half-life.

> @annahhhh RAT HIM OUT TO PIERRE!!!

> @emily89 Put some polonium in his pants and watch his dick shrivel.

> @bioworm55 Nuke him NUKE HIM

> @lucyinthesea Has this happened to you? God I'm so sorry. Once a student said something about my ass and it was so gross and no one believed me.

Over half a decade later, after a handful of *Chronicle of Higher Education* nods, a *New York Times* article, and about a million followers, WWMD is my happy place. What's best is, I think the same is true for many others. The account has evolved into a therapeutic community of sorts, used by women in STEM to tell their stories, exchange advice, and . . . bitch.

Oh, we bitch. We bitch a lot, and it's glorious.

> @BiologySarah Hey, @WhatWouldMarieDo if she
> weren't given authorship on a project that was
> originally her idea and that she worked on for over
> one year? All other authors are men, because *of
> course* they are.

"Yikes." I scrunch my face and quote-tweet Sarah.

> Marie would slip some radium in their coffee. Also,
> she would consider reporting this to her institution's
> Office of Research Integrity, making sure to
> document every step of the process ♥

I hit send, drum my fingers on the armrest, and wait. My answers are not the main attraction of the account, not in the least. The real reason people reach out to WWMD is . . .

Yep. This. I feel my grin widen as the replies start coming in.

> @DrAllixx This happened to me, too. I was the only
> woman and only POC in the author lineup and my
> name suddenly disappeared during revisions. DM if u
> want to chat, Sarah.

> @AmyBernard I am a member of the Women in
> Science association, and we have advice for

situations like this on our website (they're sadly common)!

@TheGeologician Going through the same situation rn @BiologySarah. I did report it to ORI and it's still unfolding but I'm happy to talk if you need to vent.

@SteveHarrison Dude, breaking news: you're lying to yourself. Your contributions aren't VALUABLE enough to warrant authorship. Your team did you a favor letting you tag along for a while but if you're not smart enough, you're OUT. Not everything is about being a woman, sometimes you're just A LOSER 💀

It is a truth universally acknowledged that a community of women trying to mind their own business must be in want of a random man's opinion.

I've long learned that engaging with basement-dwelling stemlords who come online looking for a fight is never a good idea—the last thing I want is to provide free entertainment for their fragile egos. If they want to blow off some steam, they can buy a gym membership or play third-person-shooter video games. Like normal people.

I make to hide @SteveHarrison's delightful contribution, but notice that someone has replied to him.

@Shmacademics Yeah, Marie, sometimes you're just a loser. Steve would know.

I chuckle.

@WhatWouldMarieDo Aw, Steve. Don't be too hard on yourself.

@Shmacademics He is just a boy, standing in front of a girl, asking her to do twice as much work as he ever did in order to prove that she's worthy of becoming a scientist.

@WhatWouldMarieDo Steve, you old romantic.

@SteveHarrison Fuck you. This ridiculous push for women in STEM is ruining STEM. People should get jobs because they're good NOT BECAUSE THEY HAVE VAGINAS. But now people feel like they have to hire women and they get jobs over men who are MORE QUALIFIED. This is the end of STEM AND IT'S WRONG.

@WhatWouldMarieDo I can see you're upset about this, Steve.

@Shmacademics There, there.

Steve blocks both of us, and I chuckle again, drawing a curious glance from Rocío. @Shmacademics is another hugely popular account on Academic Twitter, and by far my favorite. He mostly tweets about how he should be writing, makes fun of elitism and ivory-tower academics, and points out bad or biased science. I was initially a bit distrustful of him—his bio says "he/him," and we all know how cis men on the internet can be. But he and I ended up forming an alliance of sorts. When the stemlords take offense at the sheer idea of women in STEM and start pitchforking in my mentions, he helps me ridicule them a little. I'm not sure when we started direct messaging, when I stopped being afraid that he was secretly a retired Gamergater out to doxx me, or when I began considering him a friend. But a handful of years later, here we are, chatting about half a dozen different things a couple of times a week, without having even exchanged real names. Is it weird, knowing that Shmac had lice three times in second grade but not which time zone he lives in? A bit. But it's also liberating. Plus, having opinions online can be very dangerous. The internet is a sea full of creepy, cybercriminal fish, and if Mark Zuckerberg can cover his laptop webcam with a piece of tape, I reserve the right to keep things painfully anonymous.

The flight attendant offers me a glass of water from a tray. I shake my head, smile, and DM Shmac.

> **MARIE:** I think Steve doesn't want to play with us anymore.
>
> **SHMAC:** I think Steve wasn't held enough as a tadpole.
>
> **MARIE:** Lol!
>
> **SHMAC:** How's life?
>
> **MARIE:** Good! Cool new project starting next week. My ticket away from my gross boss.
>
> **SHMAC:** Can't believe dude's still around.
>
> **MARIE:** The power of connections. And inertia. What about you?

SHMAC: Work's interesting.

MARIE: Good interesting?

SHMAC: Politicky interesting. So, no.

MARIE: I'm afraid to ask. How's the rest?

SHMAC: Weird.

MARIE: Did your cat poop in your shoe again?

SHMAC: No, but I did find a tomato in my boot the other day.

MARIE: Send pics next time! What's going on?

SHMAC: Nothing, really.

MARIE: Oh, come on!

SHMAC: How do you even know something's going on?

MARIE: Your lack of exclamation points!

SHMAC: !!!!!!!!11!!1!!!!!

MARIE: Shmac.

SHMAC: FYI, I'm sighing deeply.

MARIE: I bet. Tell me!

SHMAC: It's a girl.

MARIE: Ooooh! Tell me EVERYTHING!!!!!!!11!!1!!!!!

SHMAC: There isn't much to tell.

MARIE: Did you just meet her?

SHMAC: No. She's someone I've known for a long time, and now she's back.

SHMAC: And she is married.

MARIE: To you?

SHMAC: Depressingly, no.

SHMAC: Sorry—we're restructuring the lab. Gotta go before someone destroys a 5 mil piece of equipment. Talk later.

MARIE: Sure, but I'll want to know everything about your affair with a married woman.

SHMAC: I wish.

It's nice to know that Shmac is always a click away, especially now that I'm flying into The Wardass's frosty, unwelcoming lap.

I switch to my email app to check if Levi has finally answered the email I sent three days ago. It was just a couple of lines—*Hey, long time no see, I look forward to working together again, would you like to meet to discuss BLINK this weekend?*—but he must have been too busy to reply. Or too full of contempt. Or both.

Ugh.

I lean back against the headrest and close my eyes, wondering how Dr. Curie would deal with Levi Ward. She'd probably hide some radioactive isotopes in his pockets, grab popcorn, and watch nuclear decay work its magic.

Yep, sounds about right.

After a few minutes, I fall asleep. I dream that Levi is part armadillo: his skin glows a faint, sallow green, and he's digging a tomato out of his boot with an expensive piece of equipment. Even with all of that, the weirdest thing about him is that he's finally being nice to me.

WE'RE PUT UP in small furnished apartments in a lodging facility just outside the Johnson Space Center, only a couple of minutes from the Sullivan Discovery Building, where we'll be working. I can't believe how short my commute is going to be.

"Bet you'll still manage to be late all the time," Rocío tells me, and I glare at her while unlocking my door. It's not my fault if I've spent a sizable chunk of my formative years in Italy, where time is but a polite suggestion.

The place is considerably nicer than the apartment I rent—maybe because of the raccoon incident, probably because I buy 90 percent of my furniture from the as-is bargain corner at IKEA. It has a balcony, a dishwasher, and—huge improvement in my quality of life— a toilet that flushes 100 percent of the times I push the lever. Truly paradigm shifting. I excitedly open and close every single cupboard (they're all empty; I'm not sure what I expected), take pictures to send Reike and my coworkers, stick my favorite Marie Curie magnet to the fridge (a picture of her holding a beaker that says "I'm pretty rad"), hang my hummingbird feeder on the balcony, and then . . .

It's still only two thirty p.m. Ugh.

Not that I'm one of those people who hates having free time. I could easily spend five solid hours napping, rewatching an entire season of *The Office* while eating Twizzlers, or moving to Step 2 of the Couch-to-5K plan I'm still very . . . okay, *sort of* committed to. But I am here! In Houston! Near the Space Center! About to start the coolest project of my life!

It's Friday, and I'm not due to check in until Monday, but I'm brimming with nervous energy. So I text Rocío to ask whether she wants to check out the Space Center with me (No.) or grab dinner together (I only eat animal carcasses.).

She's so mean. I love her.

My first impression of Houston is: big. Closely followed by: humid, and then by: humidly big. In Maryland, remnants of snow still cling to the ground, but the Space Center is already lush and green, a mix of open spaces and large buildings and old NASA aircraft on display. There are families visiting, which makes it seem a little like an amusement park. I can't believe I'm going to be seeing rockets on my way to work for the next three months. It sure beats the perv crossing guard who works on the NIH campus.

The Discovery Building is on the outskirts of the center. It's wide, futuristic, and three-storied, with glass walls and a complicated-looking stair system I can't quite figure out. I step inside the marble hall, wondering if my new office will have a window. I'm not used to natural light; the sudden intake of vitamin D might kill me.

"I'm Bee Königswasser." I smile at the receptionist. "I'm starting work here on Monday, and I was wondering if I could take a look around?"

He gives me an apologetic smile. "I can't let you in if you don't have an ID badge. The engineering labs are upstairs—high-security areas."

Right. Yes. The engineering labs. Levi's labs. He's probably up there, hard at work. Engineering. Labbing. Not answering my emails.

"No problem, that's understandable. I'll just—"

"Dr. Königswasser? Bee?"

I turn around. There is a blond young man behind me. He's non-threateningly handsome, medium height, smiling at me like we're old friends even though he doesn't look familiar. ". . . Hi?"

"I didn't mean to eavesdrop, but I caught your name and . . . I'm Guy. Guy Kowalsky?"

The name clicks immediately. I break into a grin. "Guy! It's so nice to meet you in person." When I was first notified of BLINK, Guy was my point of contact for logistics questions, and he and I emailed back and forth a few times. He's an astronaut—*an actual astronaut!*—working on BLINK while he's grounded. He seemed so familiar with the project, I initially assumed he'd be my co-lead.

He shakes my hand warmly. "I love your work! I've read all your articles—you'll be such an asset to the project."

"Likewise. I can't wait to collaborate."

If I weren't dehydrated from the flight, I'd probably tear up. I cannot believe that this man, this nice, pleasant man who has given me more positive interactions in one minute than Dr. Wardass did in one year, could have been my co-lead. I must have pissed off some god. Zeus? Eros? Must be Poseidon. Shouldn't have peed in the Baltic Sea during my misspent youth.

"Why don't I show you around? You can come in as my guest." He nods to the receptionist and gestures me to follow him.

"I wouldn't want to take you away from . . . astronauting?"

"I'm between missions. Giving you a tour beats debugging any day." He shrugs, something boyishly charming about him. We'll get along great, I already know it.

"Have you lived in Houston long?" I ask as we step into the elevator.

"About eight years. Came to NASA right out of grad school. Applied for the Astronaut Corps, did the training, then a mission." I do some math in my head. It would put him in his mid-thirties, older than I initially thought. "The past two or so, I worked on BLINK's precursor. Engineering the structure of the helmet, figuring out the wireless system. But we got to a point where we needed a neuro-stimulation expert on board." He gives me a warm smile.

"I cannot wait to see what we cook up together." I also cannot wait to find out why Levi was given the lead of this project over someone who has been on it for years. It just seems unfair. To Guy *and* to me.

The elevator doors open, and he points to a quaint-looking café in the corner. "That place over there—amazing sandwiches, worst coffee in the world. You hungry?"

"No, thanks."

"You sure? It's on me. The egg sandwiches are almost as good as the coffee is bad."

"I don't really eat eggs."

"Let me guess, a vegan?"

I nod. I try hard to break the stereotypes that plague my people and not use the word "vegan" in my first three meetings with a new acquaintance, but if they're the ones to mention it, all bets are off.

"I should introduce you to my daughter. She recently announced that she won't eat animal products anymore." He sighs. "Last weekend I poured regular milk in her cereal figuring she wouldn't know the difference. She told me that her legal team will be in touch."

"How old is she?"

"Just turned six."

I laugh. "Good luck with that."

I stopped having meat at seven, when I realized that the delicious *pollo* nuggets my Sicilian grandmother served nearly every day and the cute *galline* grazing about the farm were more . . . connected than I'd originally suspected. Stunning plot twist, I know. Reike wasn't nearly as distraught: when I frantically explained that "pigs have families, too—a mom and a dad and siblings that will miss them," she just nodded thoughtfully and said, "What you're saying is, we should eat the whole family?" I went fully vegan a couple of years later. Meanwhile, my sister has made it her life's goal to eat enough animal products for two. Together we emit one normal person's carbon footprint.

"The engineering labs are down this hallway," Guy says. The space is an interesting mix of glass and wood, and I can see inside some of the rooms. "A bit cluttered, and most people are off today—we're shuffling around equipment and reorganizing the space. We've got lots of ongoing projects, but BLINK's everyone's favorite child. The other astronauts pop by every once in a while just to ask how much longer it will be until their fancy swag is ready."

I grin. "For real?"

"Yep."

Making fancy swag for astronauts is my literal job description. I can add it to my LinkedIn profile. Not that anyone uses LinkedIn.

"The neuroscience labs—your labs—will be on the right. This way there are—" His phone rings. "Sorry—mind if I take it?"

"Not at all." I smile at his beaver phone case (nature's engineer) and look away.

I wonder whether Guy would think I'm lame if I snapped a few pictures of the building for my friends. I decide that I can live with that, but when I take out my phone I hear a noise from down the hallway. It's soft and chirpy, and sounds a lot like a . . .

"Meow."

I glance back at Guy. He's busy explaining how to put on *Moana* to someone very young, so I decide to investigate. Most of the rooms are deserted, labs full of large, abstruse equipment that looks like it belongs to . . . well. NASA. I hear male voices somewhere in the building, but no sign of the—

"Meow."

I turn around. A few feet away, staring at me with a curious expression, is a beautiful young calico.

"And who might you be?" I slowly hold out my hand. The kitten comes closer, delicately sniffs my fingers, and gives me a welcoming headbutt.

I laugh. "You're such a sweet girl." I squat down to scratch her under her chin. She nips my finger, a playful love bite. "Aren't you the most *purr*-fect little baby? I feel so *fur*-tunate to have met you."

She gives me a disdainful look and turns away. I think she understands puns.

"Come on, I was just *kitten*." Another outraged glare. Then she jumps on a nearby cart, piled ceiling-high with boxes and heavy, precarious-looking equipment. "Where are you going?"

I squint, trying to figure out where she disappeared to, and that's when I realize it. The equipment? The precarious-looking equipment? It actually *is* precarious. And the cat poked it just enough to dislodge it. And it's falling on my head.

Right.

About.

Now.

I have less than three seconds to move away. Which is too bad, because my entire body is suddenly made of stone, unresponsive to my brain's commands. I stand there, terrified, paralyzed, and close my eyes as a jumbled chaos of thoughts twists through my head. *Is the cat okay? Am I going to die? Oh God, I* am *going to die. Squashed by a tungsten anvil like Wile E. Coyote. I am a twenty-first-century Pierre Curie, about to get my skull crushed by a horse-drawn cart. Except that I have no chair in the physics department of the University of Paris to leave to my lovely spouse, Marie. Except that I have barely done a tenth of all the science I meant to do. Except that I wanted so many things and I never oh my God any second now—*

Something slams into my body, shoving me aside and into the wall.

Everything is pain.

For a couple of seconds. Then the pain is over, and everything is *noise*: metal clanking as it plunges to the floor, horrified screaming, a shrill "Meow" somewhere in the distance, and closer to my ear . . . someone is panting. Less than an inch from me.

I open my eyes, gasping for breath, and . . .

Green.

All I can see is green. Not dark, like the grass outside; not dull, like the pistachios I had on the plane. This green is light, piercing, intense. Familiar, but hard to place, not unlike—

Eyes. I'm looking up into the greenest eyes I've ever seen. Eyes that I've seen before. Eyes surrounded by wavy black hair and a face that's angles and sharp edges and full lips, a face that's offensively, imperfectly handsome. A face attached to a large, solid body—a body that is pinning me to the wall, a body made of a broad chest and two thighs that could moonlight as redwoods. Easily. One is slotted between my legs and it's holding me up. Unyielding. This man even *smells* like a forest— and *that mouth*. That mouth is still breathing heavily on top of me, probably from the effort of whisking me out from under seven hundred pounds of mechanical engineering tools, and—

I *know* that mouth.

Levi.

Levi.

I haven't seen Levi Ward in six years. Six blessed, blissful years.

And now here he is, pushing me into a wall in the middle of NASA's Space Center, and he looks . . . he looks . . .

"Levi!" someone yells. The clanking goes silent. What was meant to fall has settled on the floor. "Are you okay?"

Levi doesn't move, nor does he look away. His mouth works, and so does his throat. His lips part to say something, but no sound comes out. Instead, a hand, at once rushed and gentle, reaches up to cup my face. It's so large, I feel perfectly cradled. Engulfed in green, cozy warmth. I whimper when it leaves my skin, a plaintive, involuntary sound from deep in my throat, but I stop when I realize that it's only shifting to the back of my skull. To the hollow of my collarbone. To my brow, pushing back my hair.

It's a cautious touch. Pressing but delicate. Lingering but urgent. As though he is studying me. Trying to make sure that I'm all in one piece. Memorizing me.

I lift my eyes, and for the first time I notice the deep, unmasked concern in Levi's eyes.

His lips move, and I think that maybe—is he mouthing my name? Once, and then again? Like it's some kind of prayer?

"Levi? Levi, is she—"

My eyelids fall closed, and everything goes dark.

3

ANGULAR GYRUS: PAY ATTENTION

ON WEEKDAYS, I usually set my alarm for seven a.m.—and then find myself snoozing it anywhere from three ("Raving success") to eight times ("I hope a swarm of rabid locusts attacks me on my way to work, thus allowing me to find solace in the cold embrace of death"). On Monday, however, the unprecedented happens: I'm up at five forty-five, bright-eyed and bushy-tailed. I spit out my night retainer, run into the bathroom, and don't even wait for the water to warm up to step under the shower.

I am *that* eager.

As I pour almond milk on my oatmeal, I give rad Dr. Curie the finger guns. "BLINK's starting today," I tell the magnet. "Send good vibes. Hold the radiations."

I can't remember the last time I've been this excited. Probably because I've never been part of anything this exciting. I stand in front of my closet to pick out an outfit and focus on that—the sheer *excitement*—to avoid thinking about what happened on Friday.

To be fair, there isn't much to think about. I only remember up until the moment I fainted. Yes, I swooned in His Wardness's manly arms like a twentieth-century hysteric with penis envy.

It's nothing new, really. I faint all the time: when I haven't eaten in a while; when I see pictures of large, hairy spiders; when I stand up too quickly from a sitting position. My body's puzzling inability to maintain minimal blood pressure in the face of normal everyday events makes me, as Reike likes to say, a syncope aficionado. Doctors are puzzled but ultimately unconcerned. I've long learned to dust myself off as soon as I regain consciousness and go about my business.

Friday, though, was different. I came to in a few moments—cat nowhere in sight—but my neurons must have still been misfiring because I hallucinated something that could *never* happen: Levi Ward bridal-carrying me to the lobby and gently laying me on one of the couches. Then I must have hallucinated some more: Levi Ward viciously tearing a new one into the engineer who'd left the cart unattended. That had to have been a fever dream, for several reasons.

First of all, Levi is terrifying, but not *that* terrifying. His brand is more kill-'em-with-icy-cold-indifference-and-silent-contempt than angry outbursts. Unless in our time apart he's embraced a whole new level of terrifying, in which case . . . lovely.

Second, it's difficult, and by "difficult" I mean impossible, to imagine him siding against a non-me party in any me-involved accident. Yes, he did save my life, but there's a good chance he had no idea who I even was when he shoved me against the wall. This is Dr. Wardass, after all. The man who once stood for a two-hour meeting rather than take the last empty seat because it was next to me. The man who exited a game of poker he was winning because someone dealt me in. The man who hugged everyone in the lab on his last day at Pitt, and promptly switched to handshakes when it was my turn. If he caught someone stabbing me, he'd probably blame me for walking into the knife—and then take out his whetstone.

Clearly, my brain wasn't at her best on Friday. And I could stand here, stare at my closet, and agonize over the fact that my grad school nemesis saved my life. Or I could bask in my excitement and pick an outfit.

I opt for black skinny jeans and a polka-dotted red top. I pull up my hair in braids that would make a Dutch milkmaid proud, put on red lipstick, and keep the jewelry to a relative minimum—the usual earrings, my favorite septum piercing, and my maternal grandmother's ring on my left hand.

It's a bit weird to wear someone else's wedding ring, but it's the only memento I have of my nonna, and I like to put it on when I need some good luck. Reike and I moved to Messina to be with her right after our parents died. We ended up having to move again just three years later when she passed, but out of all the short-lived homes, out of all the extended relatives, Nonna is the one who loved us the most. So Reike wears her engagement ring, and I wear her wedding band. Even-steven. I shoot a quick, uplifting tweet from my WWMD account (Happy Monday! KEEP CALM AND CURIE ON, FRIENDS 👩🏻‍🔬👩🏻‍🔬👩🏻‍🔬👩🏻‍🔬👩🏻‍🔬) and head out.

"You excited?" I ask Rocío when I pick her up.

She stares at me darkly and says, "In France, the guillotine was used as recently as 1977." I take it as an invitation to shut up, and I do, smiling like an idiot. I'm still smiling when we get our NASA ID pictures taken and when we later meet up with Guy for a formal tour. It's a smile fueled by positive energy and hope. A smile that says, "I'm going to rock this project" and "Watch me stimulate your brain" and "I'm going to make neuroscience my bitch."

37

A smile that falters when Guy swipes his badge to unlock yet another empty room.

"And here's where the transcranial magnetic stimulation device will be," he says—just another variation of the same sentence I've heard over. And over. And *over*.

"Here is where the electroencephalography lab will be."

"Here you'll do participant intake once the Review Board approves the project."

"Here will be the testing room you asked for."

Just a lot of rooms that will be, but aren't yet. Even though communications between NASA and NIH indicated that everything needed to carry out the study would be here when I started.

I try to keep on smiling. It's hopefully just a delay. Besides, when Dr. Curie was awarded the Nobel Prize in 1903, she didn't even have a proper lab, and did all of her research out of a converted shed. *Science*, I tell myself in my inner Jeff Goldblum voice, *finds a way.*

Then Guy opens the last room and says, "And here's the office you two will share. Your computer should arrive soon." That is when my smile turns into a frown.

It's nice, the office. Large and bright, with refreshingly not-rusted-through desks and chairs that will provide just the right amount of lumbar support. And yet.

First of all, it's as distant from the engineering labs as possible. I'm not kidding: if someone grabbed a protractor and solved for x (i.e., the point that's farthest from Levi's office), they'd find that x = my desk. So much for interdisciplinary workspaces and collaborative layouts. But that's almost secondary, because . . .

"Did you say *computer*? Singular?" Rocío looks horrified. "Like . . . one?"

Guy nods. "The one you put on your list."

"We need, like, *ten* computers for the type of data processing we do," she points out. "We're talking multivariate statistics. Independent component analysis. Multidimensional scaling and recursive partitioning. Six sigma—"

"So you need more?"

"At the very least, buy us an abacus."

Guy blinks, confused. ". . . A what?"

"We put five computers on our list," I interject with a side look at Rocío. "We will need *all* of them."

"Okay." He nods, taking out his phone. "I'll make a note to tell Levi. We're heading to meet him right now. Follow me."

My heartbeat accelerates—probably because the last time I saw Levi my brain confabulated that he was carrying me *An Officer and a Gentleman*–style, and the previous came on the tail of a year of him treating me like I'm a tax auditor. I'm nervously playing with my grandmother's ring and wondering what disaster of galactic proportions this next meeting has in store for me, when something catches my eye through the glass wall.

Guy notices. "Want a sneak peek at the helmet prototype?" he asks.

My eyes widen. "Is that what's in there?"

He nods and smiles. "Just the shell for now, but I can show you."

"That would be amazing," I gasp. Embarrassing, how breathless I sound when I get excited. I need to follow through with my Couch-to-5K plans.

The lab is much larger than I expected—dozens of benches, machines I've never seen before pressed against the wall, and several researchers at various stations. I feel a frisson of resentment—how come *Levi's* lab, unlike *mine*, is fully stocked?—but it quiets down the instant I see it.

It.

BLINK is a complex, delicate, high-stakes project, but its mission is straightforward enough: to use what is known about magnetic stimulation of the brain (my jam) to engineer special helmets (Levi's expertise) that will reduce the "attentional blinks" of astronauts—those little lapses in awareness that are unavoidable when many things happen at once. It's the culmination of decades of gathering knowledge, of engineers perfecting wireless stimulation technology on one side and neuroscientists mapping the brain on the other. Now, here we are.

Neuroscience and engineering, sitting in a very expensive tree called BLINK, K-I-S-S-I-N-G.

It's hard to communicate how groundbreaking this is—two separate slices of abstract research bridging the gap between academia and the real world. For any scientist, the prospect would be exhilarating. For me, after the mild shitshow my career has put up in the past couple of years, it's a dream come true.

All the more now that I'm standing in front of tangible proof of said dream's existence.

"That's the . . . ?"

"Yep."

Rocío murmurs, "Wow," and for once doesn't even sound like a sullen Lovecraftian teenager. I'd tease her about it, but I can't focus on anything but the helmet prototype. Guy is saying something about design and stage of development, but I tune him out and step closer. I knew that it'd be made from a combination of Kevlar and carbon fiber cloth, that the visor would carry thermal and eye-tracking capabilities, that the structure would be streamlined to host new functionalities. What I did not know was how stunning it would look. A breathtaking piece of hardware, designed to house the software I've been hired to create.

It's beautiful. It's sleek. It's . . .

Wrong.

It's all wrong.

I frown, peering closer at the pattern of holes in the inner shell. "Are these for the neurostimulation output?"

The engineer working at the helmet station gives me a confused look. "This is Dr. Königswasser, Lamar," Guy explains. "The neuroscientist from NIH."

"The one who fainted?"

I knew this would haunt me, because it always does. My nickname in high school was Smelling Salts Bee. Damn my useless autonomic nervous system. "The one and only." I smile. "Is this the final placement for the output holes?"

"Should be. Why?"

I lean closer. "It won't work." A brief silence follows, and I study the rest of the grid.

"Why do you say that?" Guy asks.

"They're too close—the holes, I mean. It looks like you used the International 10–20 system, which is great to record brain data, but for neurostimulation . . ." I bite into my lip. "Here, for instance. This area will stimulate the angular gyrus, right?"

"Maybe? Let me just check. . . ." Lamar scrambles to look at a chart, but I don't need confirmation. The brain is the one place where I never get lost. "Upper part—stimulation at the right frequency will get you increased awareness. Which is exactly what we want, right? But stimulation of the lower part can cause hallucinations. People experiencing a shadow following them, feeling as though they're in two places at the same time, stuff like that. Think of the consequences if someone was in space while that happened." I tap the inner shell with my fingernail. "The outputs will need to be farther apart."

"But . . ." Lamar sounds severely distressed. "This is Dr. Ward's design."

"Yeah, I'm pretty sure Dr. Ward knows nothing about the angular gyrus," I murmur distractedly.

The ensuing silence should probably tip me off. At least, I should notice the sudden shift in the atmosphere of the lab. But I don't and keep staring at the helmet, writing possible modifications and workarounds in my head, until a throat clears somewhere in the back of the room. That's when I lift my eyes and see him.

Levi.

Standing in the entrance.

Staring at me.

Just staring at me. A tall, stern, snow-tipped mountain. With his expression—the one from years ago, silent and unsmiling. A veritable Mount Fuji of disdain.

Shit.

My cheeks burn. Of course. But *of course*, he just caught me trash-talking his neuroanatomy skills in front of his team like a total asshole. This is my life, after all: a flaming ball of scorching, untimely awkwardness.

"Boris and I are in the conference room. You ready to meet?" he asks, his voice a deep, severe baritone. My heart thuds. I rack my brain for something to say in response.

Then Guy speaks and I realize that Levi isn't even addressing me. He is, in fact, completely ignoring me and what I just said. "Yep. We were just about to head there. Got sidetracked."

Levi nods once and turns around, a silent but clear order to follow him that everyone seems eager to obey. He was like that in grad school, too. Natural leader. Commanding presence. Someone whose bad side you wouldn't want to be on.

Enter me. A proud resident of his bad side for several years, who just renewed her housing permit with a few simple words.

"Is *that* Dr. Ward?" Rocío whispers as we enter the conference room.

"Yup."

"Welp. That was *excellent* timing, boss."

I wince. "What are the chances that he didn't hear me?"

"I don't know. What are the chances that his personal hygiene is very poor and he has huge wax balls in his ear canal?"

The room is already crowded. I sigh and take the first empty seat I can find, only to realize that it's across from Levi. Awkwardness level: nuclear. I'm making better and better choices today. Cheering erupts when someone deposits two large boxes of donuts in the center of the table—NASA employees are clearly as enthused by free food as regular academics. People start calling dibs and elbowing each other, and Guy yells over the chaos, "The one in the corner, with the blue frosting, is vegan." I shoot him a grateful smile and he winks at me. He's such a nice guy, my almost-co-leader.

As I wait for the crowd to disperse, I take stock of the room. Levi's team appears to be WurstFest™ material. The well-known Meatwave. A Dicksplosion in the Testosteroven. The good old Brodeo. Aside from Rocío and I, there's one single woman, a young blonde currently looking at her phone. My gaze is mesmerized by her perfect beach waves and the pink glitter of her nails. I have to force myself to look away.

Eh. WurstFest™ is bad, but it's at least a small step up from Cockcluster™, which is what Annie and I called academic meetings with only one woman in the room. I've been in Cockcluster™ situations countless times in grad school, and they range from unpleasantly isolating to wildly terrifying. Annie and I used to coordinate to attend meetings together—not that hard, since we were symbiotic anyway.

Sadly, none of my male cohort ever got how awful WurstFest™ and Cockcluster™ are for women. "Grad school's stressful for everyone," Tim would say when I complained about my entirely male advisory committee. "You keep going on about Marie Curie—she was the only woman in all of science at the time, and she got two Nobel Prizes."

Of course, Dr. Curie was *not* the only female scientist at the time. Dr. Lise Meitner, Dr. Emmy Noether, Alice Ball, Dr. Nettie Stevens, Henrietta Leavitt, and countless others were active, doing better science with the tip of their little fingers than Tim will ever manage with his sorry ass. But Tim didn't know that. Because, as I now know, Tim was dumb.

"We're ready to start." The balding redheaded man at the head of the table claps his hands, and people scurry to their seats. I lean forward to grab my vegan donut, but my hand freezes in midair.

It's not there anymore. I inspect the box several times, but there's only cinnamon left. Then I lift my eyes and I see it: blue frosting disappearing behind Levi's teeth as he takes a bite. A bite of *my* damn donut. There are dozens of alternatives, but behold: The Wardass chose the one I could eat. What kind of careless, inconsiderate *boob* steals the single available option from a starving, needy vegan?

"I am Dr. Boris Covington," the redhead starts. He looks like an exhausted, disheveled ginger hard-boiled egg. Like he ran here for this meeting, but there are five stacks of paperwork on his desk waiting for him. "I'm in charge of overseeing all research projects here in the Discovery Institute—which makes me your boss." Everyone laughs, with a few good-natured boos. The engineering team seems to be a rowdy bunch. "You guys already know that—with the notable exception of Dr. Königswasser and Ms. Cortoreal, who are here to make sure we don't fail at one of our most ambitious projects yet.

Levi's going to be their point of contact, but, everyone, please make them feel welcome." Everyone claps—except for Levi, who is busy finishing his (*my*) donut. What an absolute dingus. "Now let's pretend that I gave an impressive speech and move on to everyone's favorite activity: icebreakers." Almost everyone groans, but I think I'm a fan of Boris. He seems much better than my NIH boss. For instance, he's been speaking for one whole minute and hasn't said anything overtly offensive. "I want your name, job, and . . . let's do favorite movie." More groans. "Hush, children. Levi, you start."

Everyone in the room turns to him, but he takes his sweet time swallowing *my* donut. I stare at his throat, and an odd mix of phantom sensations hits me. *His thigh pushing between mine. Being pressed into the wall. The woodsy smell at the base of his—*

Wait. *What?*

"Levi Ward, head engineer. And . . ." He licks some sugar off his bottom lip. "*The Empire Strikes Back.*"

Oh—are you kidding me? First he steals my donut, and now my favorite movie?

"Kaylee Jackson," the blonde picks up. "I'm project manager for BLINK, and *Legally Blonde.*" She talks a bit like she could be one of Elle Woods's sorority sisters, which makes me like her instinctively. But Rocío tenses beside me. When I glance at her, her brows are furrowed.

Weird.

There are at least thirty people in the room, and the icebreakers get old very soon. I try to pay attention, but Lamar Evans and Mark Costello start fighting over whether *Kill Bill: Vol. 2* is better than *Vol. 1*, and I feel a weird prickle in the center of my forehead.

When I turn, Levi's staring hard at me, his eyes full of that something that I seem to awaken in him. I'm a bit resentful about the donut, not to mention that he still hasn't answered my email, but I remind myself of what Boris just said: he's my main collaborator. So I play nice and give him a cautious, slow-to-unfurl smile that I hope communicates *Sorry about the angular gyrus jab*, and *I hope we'll work well together*, and *Hey, thank you for saving my life!*

He breaks eye contact without smiling back and takes a sip of his coffee. God, I hate him so—

"Bee." Rocío elbows me. "It's your turn."

"Oh, um, right. Sorry. Bee Königswasser, head of neuroscience. And . . ." I hesitate. "*Empire Strikes Back.*" With the corner of my eye I see Levi's fist clench on the table. Crap. I should have just said *Avatar.*

Once the meeting is over, Kaylee comes to speak to Rocío. "Ms. Cortoreal. May I call you Rocío? I need your signature on this document." She smiles sweetly and holds out a pen, which Rocío doesn't accept. Instead she freezes, staring at Kaylee with her mouth open for several seconds. I have to elbow her in the ribs to get her to defrost. Interesting.

"You're left-handed," Kaylee says while Rocío signs. "Me too. Lefties power, right?"

Rocío doesn't look up. "Left-handed people are more prone to migraines, allergies, sleep deprivation, alcoholism, and on average live three years less than right-handed people."

"Oh." Kaylee's eyes widen. "I, um, didn't . . ."

I'd love to stay and witness more prime Valley Girl and Goth interaction, but Levi's stepping out of the room. As much as I loathe the idea, we'll need to talk at some point, so I run after him. When I reach him, I'm pitifully out of breath. "Levi, wait up!"

I might be reading too much into the way his spine goes rigid, but something about how he stops reminds me of an inmate getting caught by the guards just a step away from breaking out of prison. He turns around slowly, hulking but surprisingly graceful, all black and green and that strange, intense face.

It was actually a thing, back in grad school. Something to debate while waiting for participants to show up and analyses to run: *Is Levi actually handsome? Or is he just six four and built like the Colossus of Rhodes?* There were plenty of opinions going around. Annie, for instance, was very much in camp "Ten out of ten, would have a torrid affair with." And I'd tell her *Ew, yikes*, and laugh, and call her a traitor. Which . . . yeah. Turned out to be accurate, but for completely different reasons.

In hindsight, I'm not sure why I used to be so shocked about his fan club. It's not so outlandish that a serious, taciturn man who has several *Nature Neuroscience* publications and looks like he could bench-press the entire faculty body in either hand would be considered attractive.

Not that I ever did. Or ever will.

In fact, I'm absolutely *not* thinking again about his thigh pushing between my legs.

"Hey." I smile tentatively. He doesn't answer, so I continue, "Thank you for the other day." Still no answer. So I continue some more. "I wasn't, you know . . . standing in front of that cart for shits and giggles." I need to stop twisting my grandmother's ring. Stat. "There was a cat, so—"

"A cat?"

"Yeah. A calico. A kitten. Mostly white, with orange and black spots on the ears. She had the cutest little . . ." I notice his skeptical look. "For real. There was a cat."

"*Inside* the building?"

"Yes." I frown. "She jumped on the cart. Made the boxes fall."

He nods, clearly unconvinced. Fantastic—now he thinks I'm making up the cat.

Wait. *Am* I making up the cat? Did I hallucinate it? Did I—

"Can I help you with anything?"

"Oh." I scratch the back of my head. "No. I just wanted to, ah, tell you how excited I am to collaborate again." He doesn't immediately reply, and a terrible thought occurs to me: Levi doesn't remember me. He has no idea who I am. "Um, we used to be in the same lab at Pitt. I was a first-year when you graduated. We didn't overlap long, but . . ."

His jaw tenses, then immediately relaxes. "I remember," he says.

"Oh, good." It's a relief. My grad school archnemesis forgetting about me would be a bit humiliating. "I thought you might not, so—"

"I have a functioning hippocampus." He looks away and adds, a little gruffly, "I thought you'd be at Vanderbilt. With Schreiber."

I'm surprised he knows about that. When I made plans to go work in Schreiber's lab, the best of the best in my field, Levi had long moved on from Pitt. The point is, of course, moot, because after all the happenings of two years ago happened, I ended up scrambling to find another position. But I don't like to think about that time. So I say, "Nope," keeping my tone neutral to avoid baring my throat to the hyena. "I'm at NIH. Under Trevor Slate. But he's great, too." He really isn't. And not just because he enjoys reminding me that women have smaller brains than men.

"How's Tim?"

Now—*that*'s a mean question. I know for a fact that Tim and Levi have ongoing collaborations. They even hosted a panel together at the main conference in our field last year, which means that Levi knows that Tim and I called off our wedding. Plus, he must be aware of what Tim did to me. For the simple reason that everyone knows what Tim did to me. Lab mates, faculty members, janitors, the lady who manned the sandwich station in the Pitt cafeteria—they *all* knew. Long before I did.

I make myself smile. "Good. He's good." I doubt it's a lie. People like Tim always land on their feet, after all. Unlike people like me, who fall on their metaphorical asses, break their tailbones, and spend years paying off the medical bills. "Hey, what I said earlier, about the angular gyrus . . . I didn't mean to be rude. I wasn't thinking."

"It's okay."

"I hope you're not mad. I didn't mean to overstep."

"I'm not mad."

I stare up at his face. He doesn't seem mad. Then again, he also doesn't seem not mad. He just seems like the old Levi: quietly intense, unreadable, not at all fond of me.

"Good. Great." My eyes fall to his large bicep, and then to his fist. He is clenching it again. Guess Dr. Wardass still dislikes me. Whatever. His problem. Maybe I have a bad aura. It doesn't matter—I'm here to get a job done, and I will. I square my shoulders. "Guy gave me a tour earlier. I noticed that none of our equipment's here yet. What's the ETA for that?"

His lips press together. "We are working on it. I'll keep you posted."

"Okay. My RA and I can't get anything done until our computers arrive, so the earlier the better."

"I'll keep you posted," he repeats tersely.

"Cool. When can we meet to discuss BLINK?"

"Email me with times that work for you."

"They all do. I don't have a schedule until my equipment arrives, so—"

"Please, email me." His tone, patient and firm, screams *I'm an adult dealing with a difficult child*, so I don't insist further.

"Okay. Will do." I nod, half-heartedly wave my goodbye, and turn to walk away.

I can't wait to work with this guy for three months. I love being treated like I'm a piece of belly button lint instead of a valuable asset to a team. That's why I got a Ph.D. in neuroscience: to achieve nuisance status and be patronized by the Wardasses of the world. Lucky me for—

"There's one more thing," he says. I turn back and tilt my head. His expression is as closed off as usual, and—why the hell is the feel of his thigh in my brain again? *Not now, intrusive thoughts.*

"The Discovery Building has a dress code."

His words don't land immediately. Then they do, and I look down to my clothes. He can't possibly mean me, can he? I'm wearing jeans and a blouse. *He* is wearing jeans and a Houston Marathon T-shirt. (God, he's probably one of those obnoxious people who post their workout stats on social media.)

"Yes?" I prompt him, hoping he'll explain himself.

"Piercings, certain hair colors, certain . . . types of makeup are unacceptable." I see his eyes fall on one of the braids draped over my shoulder and then drift upward to a spot above my head. As though he can't bear to look at me longer than a split second. As though my sight, my *existence*, offends him. "I'll make sure Kaylee sends you the handbook."

". . . Unacceptable?"

"Correct."

"And you're telling me this because . . . ?"

"Please, make sure you follow the dress code."

I want to kick him in the shins. Or maybe punch him. No—what I really want is to grab his chin and force him to stare at what he clearly considers my ugly, offensive face some more. Instead I put my hands on my hips and smile. "That's interesting." I keep my tone pleasant enough. Because I am a pleasant person, dammit. "Because half of your team are wearing sweats or shorts, have visible tattoos, and Aaron, I believe is his name, has a gauge in his ear. It makes me wonder if maybe there's a gendered double standard at play here."

He closes his eyes, as though trying to collect himself. As though staving off a wave of anger. Anger at *what*? My piercings? My hair? My corporeal form? "Just make sure you follow the dress code."

I cannot believe this chucklefuck. "Are you serious?"

He nods. All of a sudden I am too mad to be in his presence. "Very well. I'll make an effort to look *acceptable* from now on."

I whirl around and walk back to the conference room. If my shoulder brushes his torso on my way there, I am too busy not kneeing him in the nuts to apologize.

4

PARAHIPPOCAMPAL GYRUS: SUSPICION

MY SECOND DAY on BLINK is almost as good as my first.

"What do you mean, we can't get inside our office?"

"I told you. Someone dug a moat around it and filled it with alligators. And bears. And carnivorous moths." I stare silently at Rocío and she sighs, swiping her ID through the reader by the door. It blinks red and makes a flat noise. "Our badges don't work."

I roll my eyes. "I'll go find Kaylee. She can probably fix this."

"No!"

She sounds so uncharacteristically panicked, I lift an eyebrow. "No?"

"Don't call Kaylee. Let's just . . . knock the door down. Count of three? One, two—"

"Why shouldn't I call Kaylee?"

"Because." Her throat bobs. "I don't like her. She's a witch. She

might curse our families. All our firstborns shall have ingrown toe-
nails, for centuries to come."

"I thought you didn't want kids?"

"I don't. I'm worried about you, boss."

I tilt my head. "Ro, is this heat stroke? Should I buy you a hat?
Houston's much warmer than Baltimore—"

"Maybe we should just go home. It's not like our equipment is
here. What are we even going to do?"

She's being *so* weird. Though, to be fair, she's always weird. "Well,
I brought my laptop, so we can— Oh, Guy!"

"Hey. Do you have time to answer a couple of questions for me?"

"Of course. Could you let us into our office? Our badges aren't
working."

He opens the door and immediately asks me about brain stimulation and spatial cognition, and over an hour goes by. "It might be
tricky to get to deep structures, but we can find a work-around," I tell
him toward the end. There's a piece of paper full of diagrams and
stylized brains between us. "As soon as the equipment arrives, I can
show you." I bite the inside of my cheek, hesitant. "Hey, can I ask you
something?"

"A date?"

"No, I—"

"Good, because I prefer figs."

I smile. Guy reminds me a bit of my British cousin—total
charmer, adorable smile. "Same. I . . . Is there a reason the neuro
equipment isn't here yet?"

I know Levi is supposed to be my point of contact, but he's currently sitting on three unanswered emails. I'm not sure how to get
him to reply. Use Comic Sans? Write in primary colors?

"Mmm." Guy bites his lip and looks around. Rocío is coding away on her laptop with AirPods in her ears. "I heard Kaylee say that it's an authorization problem."

"Authorization?"

"For the funds to be disbursed and new equipment to be brought in, several people need to sign off."

I frown. "Who needs to sign off?"

"Well, Boris. His superiors. Levi, of course. Whatever the holdup is, I'm sure he'll fix it soon."

Levi is as likely to be the holdup as I am to make a mistake while filing my taxes (i.e., very), but I don't point that out. "Have you known him long? Levi, I mean."

"Years. He was very close to Peter. I think that's why Levi threw his name in the hat for BLINK." I want to ask who Peter is, but Guy seems to assume I already know. Is he someone I met yesterday? I'm so bad with names. "He's a fantastic engineer and a great team leader. He was at the Jet Propulsion Lab when I was on my first space mission. I know they were sad to see him transfer."

I frown. This morning I walked past him chatting with the engineers, and they were all laughing at something sportsball he'd just said. I choose to believe that they were just sucking up to him. Okay, he's good at his job, but he can't possibly be a beloved boss, can he? Not Dr. Wardness of the intractable disposition and wintery personality. And since we're talking, why the hell did they decide to transfer someone from the JPL instead of having Guy lead?

Must be divine punishment. I guess I kicked lots of puppies in a past life. Maybe I used to be Dracula.

"Levi's a good guy," Guy continues. "A good bro, too. He owns a truck, helped me move out after my ex kicked me out." *Of course* he does. *Of course* he drives a vehicle with a huge environmental footprint that's probably responsible for the death of twenty seagulls a day. While chomping on *my* vegan donut. "Also, we sometimes baby-sit playdates together. Having beers and talking about *Battlestar Galactica* vastly improves the experience of watching two six-year-olds arguing over who gets to be Moana."

My jaw drops. *What?* Levi has a *child*? A small, *human* child?

"I wouldn't worry about the equipment, Bee. Levi will take care of it. He's great at getting stuff done." Guy winks at me as he stands. "I can't wait to see what you two geniuses come up with."

Levi will take care of it.

I watch Guy step out and wonder if more ominous words were ever uttered.

FUN FACT ABOUT me: I am a fairly mellow person, but I happen to have a very violent fantasy life.

Maybe it's an overactive amygdala. Maybe it's too much estrogen. Maybe it's the lack of parental role models in my formative years. I honestly don't know what the cause is, but the fact remains: I sometimes daydream about murdering people.

By "sometimes," I mean often.

And by "people," I mean Levi Ward.

I have my first vivid reverie on my third day at NASA, when I imagine offing him with poison. I'd be satisfied with a quick and painless end, as long as I got to proudly stand over his lifeless body, kick it in the ribs, and proclaim, "This is for not answering even one of my seven emails." Then I'd casually stomp on one of his humongous hands and add, "And this is for never being in your office when I tried to corner you there." It's a nice fantasy. It sustains me in my free time, which is . . . plentiful. Because my ability to do my work hinges on my ability to magnetically stimulate brains, which in turn hinges on the arrival of my damn equipment.

By the fourth day, I'm convinced that Levi needs some miracle-blade stabbing. I ambush him in the shared kitchen on the second floor, where he's pouring coffee into a Star Wars mug with a Baby Yoda picture. It says *Yoda Best Engineer* and it's so adorably cute, he doesn't deserve it. I briefly wonder if he bought it himself, or if it's a present from his child. If that's the case, he doesn't deserve the child, either.

"Hey." I smile up at him, leaning my hip against the sink. God, he's so tall. And broad. He's a thousand-year oak. Someone with a body like this has no business owning a nerdy mug. "How are you?"

His head jerks down to look at me, and for a split moment his eyes look panicked. Trapped. It quickly melts into his usual non-expression, but not before his hand slips. Some coffee sloshes over the rim, and he almost gives himself third degree burns.

I'm a cave troll. I'm so unpleasant to be around, I make him clumsy. The sheer power I hold.

"Hi," he says, drying himself with kitchen paper. No *Fine*. No *And you?* No *Boy howdy, the weather's humid today.*

I sigh internally. "Any news about the equipment?"

"We're working on it."

It's amazing how good he is at looking *to* me without actually looking *at* me. If it were an Olympic discipline, he'd have a gold medal and his picture on a Wheaties box.

"Why exactly is it not here yet? Any issues with the NIH funds?"

"Authorizations. But we're—"

"Working on it, yes." I'm still smiling. Murderously polite. The neuroscience on positive reinforcement is solid—it's all about the do-pamine. "Whose authorizations are we waiting for?"

His muscles, many and enormous, stiffen. "A couple." His eyes fall on me and then on my thumb, which is twisting around my grandmother's ring. They immediately bounce away.

"Who are we missing? Maybe I can talk to them. See if I can speed up things."

"No."

Right. Of course. "Can I see the blueprints for the prototype? Make a few notes?"

"They're on the server. You have access."

"Do I? I sent you an email about that, and about——"

A phone rings in his pocket. He checks the caller ID and answers with a soft "Hey" before I can continue. I hear a female voice on the other side. Levi doesn't look at me as he mouths, "Excuse me," and slips out of the kitchen. I'm left alone.

Alone with my stabbing dreams.

On the fifth day, my fantasies evolve yet again. I'm walking to my office, schlepping a refill bottle for the water cooler and half-heartedly considering using it to drown Levi (his hair seems long enough to hold on to while I push his head underwater, but I could also tie an anvil to his neck). Then I hear voices inside and stop to listen.

Okay, fine: to eavesdrop.

"——in Houston?" Rocío is asking.

"Five or six years," a deep voice answers. Levi's.

"And how many times have you seen La Llorona?"

A pause. "Is that the woman from the legend?"

"Not a *woman*," she scoffs. "A tall lady ghost with dark hair. Wronged by a man, she drowned her own children in revenge. Now she dresses in white, like a bride, and weeps on the banks of rivers and streams throughout the south."

"Because she regrets it?"

"No. She's trying to lure more children to bodies of water and drown them. She's amazing. I want to be her."

Levi's soft laugh surprises me. And so does his tone, gently teasing. Warm. What the hell? "I've never had the, um, pleasure, but I can recommend nearby hiking trails with water. I'll send you an email."

What is *happening*? Why is he *conversing*? Like a *normal person*? Not with grunts, or nods, or clipped fragments of words, but in actual sentences? And why is he promising to send *emails*? Does he know how to? And why, why, *why* am I thinking about the way he pinned me against that stupid wall? *Again?*

"That would be great. I normally avoid nature, but I am ready to brave clean air and sunlight for my favorite celebrity."

"I don't think she qualifies as a—"

I step into the office and immediately halt, dumbstruck by the most extraordinary sight I have ever laid my eyes upon.

Dr. Levi Ward. Is. Smiling.

Apparently, The Wardass can smile. At people. He possesses the necessary facial muscles. Though the second I step inside, his dimpled, boyish grin fades, and his eyes darken. Maybe he can only smile at *some* people? Maybe I'm just not considered "people"?

"Morning, boss." Rocío waves at me from her desk. "Levi let me in. Our badges still aren't working."

"Thanks, Levi. Any idea when they will?"

Icy green. Can green be icy? The one in his eyes sure manages to. "We're working on it." He makes for the door, and I think he's going to leave, but instead he picks up the refill bottle I dragged here, lifts it with one hand—*one! (1)! hand!*—and lodges it on top of the cooler.

"You don't have to—"

"It's no problem," he says. He should be sent to jail for the way his

biceps look. At least for a little bit. Also, please lock him up for being gone before I can ask if our equipment will ever arrive, if he'll
ever answer my emails, if I'll ever be worthy of a compound sentence
made of multiple clauses.

"Boss?"

I slowly turn to Rocío. She's looking at me, inquisitive. "Yep?"

"I don't think Levi likes you very much."

I sigh. I shouldn't be involving Rocío in this weird feud of ours—
partly because it seems unprofessional, partly because I'm not sure
what she'll blurt out at the most inappropriate moment. On the other
hand, there's no point in denying the obvious. "We know each other
from before. Levi and I."

"Before you publicly announced that he's shit at neuroscience, you
mean?"

"Yeah."

"I see."

"You do?"

"Of course. You two had a passionate love story that slowly soured,
culminating when you caught Levi in an intimate embrace with your
butler, stabbed his abdomen sixty-nine times, and left him for dead—
only to be astonished to find him still alive when you arrived in Houston."

I cock my head. "Do you really think two scientists could afford
a butler?"

She mulls it over. "Okay, that part's unrealistic."

"Levi and I were in grad school together. And we . . ." I honestly
have no idea how to put it diplomatically. I want to say "didn't get
along," but there was never an along to be gotten. We never inter-
acted, because he discouraged it or avoided it. "He was never a fan."

She nods like she finds the idea relatable. That little scorpion. I
love her. "Did he hate you at first sight, or did he grow into it?"

"Oh, he—" I stop short.

I actually have no idea. I try to think back to my first meeting with him, but I can't remember it. It must have been on my first day of grad school, when Tim and I joined Sam's lab, but I have no memories. He was vaguely hostile to me well before the incident in Sam's office, when he declined to collaborate, but I can't place the start of it. Interesting. I guess Tim or Annie might know. Except that I'd rather slowly perish from cobalt poisoning than ever speak to either of them again.

"I'm not sure." I shrug. "A combination?"

"Is Levi's dislike related to the fact that I just spent a week on TikTok because I don't have a decent computer to work on?"

I plop down in my chair. I suspect the two things are very related, but it's not as if I can prove it, or know what to do about it. It's an isolating situation. I've considered talking to other people here at NASA, or even at NIH, but they'd just point out that Levi needs me to make the project succeed, and that the idea of him *self*-sabotaging just to sabotage *me* is preposterous. They might even think that I'm the one who's in the wrong, since I haven't proven myself as a project leader yet.

And there's something else to consider. Something that I don't want to say out loud, or even think in my head, but here goes: if my career is a sapling, Levi's is a baobab. It can withstand a lot more. He has a history of completed grants and successful collaborations. BLINK's failure would be a bump in the road for him, and a car-totaling crash for me.

Am I being paranoid? Probably. I need to lay off the coffee and stop spending my nights plotting Levi's demise. He's living rent free in my head. Meanwhile, he doesn't even know my last name.

"I don't know, Ro." I sigh. "They might be related? Or not?"

"Hmm." She rocks back in her chair. "I wonder if pointing out that his revenge plan is harming not just *your* career prospects but an innocent bystander's, too, would help. The innocent bystander is me, by the way."

I bite back a smile. "Thank you for clarifying."

"You know what you should do?"

"Please don't say 'stab his abdomen sixty-nine times.'"

"I wasn't going to. That's too good advice to waste on you. No, you should ask @WhatWouldMarieDo. On Twitter. You know her?"

I freeze. My cheeks warm. I study Rocío's expression, but it looks as sullenly bored as usual. I briefly consider saying "Never heard of her," but it seems like overcompensating. "Yeah."

"I figured, since you're a Marie Curie stan. You own, like, three pairs of Marie Curie socks." I own seven but I just hum, noncommittal. "You can tweet at Marie with your problem. She'll retweet and you'll get advice. I ask all the time."

Does she? "Really? From your professional Twitter?"

"Nah, I make burner accounts. I don't want other people knowing my private business."

"Why?"

"I complain a lot. About you, for instance."

I try not to smile. It's very hard. "What did I do?"

"The vegan Lean Cuisine you always eat at your desk?"

"Yeah?"

"It smells like farts."

That night I drag a chair out on the balcony and stare at my depressingly deserted hummingbird feeder, trying to formulate a question as vaguely as possible.

> @WhatWouldMarieDo . . . if she suspected that a
> collaborator has a vendetta against her and is
> sabotaging their shared project?

When put into words it feels so stupid, I can't even hit send. Instead, I google whether I'm within the age of onset for paranoid ideation—shit, I am—and call Reike to update her on current events.

"What do you mean, you almost *died*? Did you see your life replay before your eyes? Did you think of me? Of the cats you never adopted? Of the love you never allow yourself to give? Did you un-fence the Bee-fence?"

I'm not sure why I persevere with telling my sister every little humiliating thing that happens to me. My life is mortifying enough without her ruthless commentary. "I didn't think about anything."

"You thought of Marie Curie, didn't you?" Reike laughs. "Weirdo. How did The Wardass manage to save you? Where did he come from?"

That's actually a good question. I have no idea how he was able to intervene so quickly. "Right place, right time kind of thing, probably."

"And now you *owe* him. Your archnemesis. This is delightful."

"You're enjoying this way too much."

"Beetch, I spent the day teaching the German dative for thirty euros. I deserve this."

I sigh. My hummingbird feeder is still despondently empty, and my heart squeezes. I miss Finneas. I miss the tchotchkes I accumulated in my Bethesda apartment that made it feel like home. I miss Reike—seeing her in person, hugging her, being in the same time zone. I miss knowing where the olives are at the supermarket. I miss doing science. I miss the elation I felt during my three days of celebration when I thought BLINK would be the opportunity of a lifetime. I miss not having to google whether I'm having a psychotic episode.

"Am I crazy? Is Levi really sabotaging me?"

"You're not crazy. If you were, I'd be, too. Genes and stuff." Knowing Reike, I don't find this reassuring. At all. "But as much as he dislikes you, it's hard to believe that he's sabotaging you. That level of hatred requires so much effort and motivation and commitment, it's basically love. I doubt he cares that much. My guess is that he's just being a testicle and not actively helping you. Which is why you should have a calm but firm conversation with him."

I sigh again. "You're probably right."

"Probably?"

I smile. "Likely."

"Hmm. Tell me about Astronaut Guy. Is Astronaut Guy cute?"

"He's nice."

"Aw. Not cute, then?"

When I go to bed, I'm convinced that Reike is right. I need to be firmer in my demands. I have a plan for next week: if there is no ETA for my equipment by Monday morning, I'm going to civilly confront Levi and tell him to cut the crap. If things get ugly, I'll threaten him with wearing the dress again. It was clearly his kryptonite. I'd be open to doing laundry every night and subjecting him to it for the rest of my stay in Houston.

I smile at the ceiling, thinking that being revolting sometimes has its own advantages. I turn around, and when the sheets rustle, I'm almost in a good mood. Cautiously optimistic. BLINK will work out; I'll make sure of it.

And then Monday happens.

5

AMYGDALA: ANGER

IT STARTS WITH Trevor, my NIH boss, wanting to talk "as soon as you can, Bee," which has me groaning into my oatmeal.

Neuroscience is a relatively new field, and Trevor is a mediocre scientist who was lucky enough to be at the right place when tons of neuro positions and funding opportunities were created. Fast forward twenty years, and he has made just enough connections to avoid being fired—even though I strongly suspect that if given a human brain, he wouldn't be able to point to the occipital lobe.

I call him while walking to work, the humid morning air instantly pasting a sticky layer on my skin. His first words are: "Bee, where are you with BLINK?"

Oh, I'm just peachy, thank you. What about you? "About to start week two."

"But where's the project at?" He bristles. "Are the suits ready?"

"Helmets. They're helmets." Seems like that would be an easy detail to remember, since we study the brain.

"Whatever," he says impatiently. "Are they ready?"

I miss him *so* little. I can't wait till BLINK makes my CV awesome and I can move to a position that doesn't require acknowledging his existence. "They're not. The projected timeline is three months. We haven't even started."

A pause. "What do you mean, you haven't started?"

"I currently have no equipment. No EEG. No TMS. No *computers*, not even access to my office. Everything I asked for in my application, *weeks* ago, has yet to be delivered."

"What?"

"There are mysterious authorizations that need to be collected. But it's impossible to figure out *whose* authorizations."

"Are you *serious*?"

My heart beats faster at the indignation in his voice. Trevor sounds mad—do I have an ally? A horrible ally, but a useful one. If he exerts some pressure at higher levels, they'll intervene and Levi won't be able to drag his feet anymore.

Oh my God. Why didn't I just call Trevor on day one? "I *know*—it's stupid, a waste of time, and unprofessional. I'm not sure who can help us fix this situation, but—"

"Then you better figure it the hell out. What have *you* been doing there for a week, visiting the space museum? Bee, you're not on vacation."

"I—"

"It's *your* responsibility to get BLINK going. What do you think you were hired for?"

Right. *This* is why I didn't call Trevor. "I have no power or connections here. My liaison is Levi, and whatever I do is—"

"Clearly, whatever you do is not enough." He takes a deep breath. "Listen carefully, Bee. George Kramer called me last night." Kramer is the head of our NIH institute—so far removed from my lowly postdoc position that it takes me a moment to place the name. "On Friday, he talked with the director of NIH and with two members of Congress. The general consensus is that BLINK is the kind of project that taxpayers eat up. It mixes astronauts and brains, which market-test well among average Americans. They're sexy topics." I recoil. I can never hear Trevor and his smelly breath use the word "sexy" again. "Plus, it's the joint collaboration of two already beloved government agencies. It'll make the current administration look good, and they *need* to look good."

I frown. He has been talking for over a minute and hasn't mentioned science once. "I don't see what this means?"

"It means that as of right now there's a lot of scrutiny over BLINK. Over *your* performance. Kramer wants weekly updates, starting today."

"He wants an update *today*?"

"And every week from today."

Well, this is going to be a problem. What the hell am I supposed to tell him? That I have no progress to report—but will he accept an R-rated list of elaborately intricate murder fantasies I have spun regarding Dr. Levi Ward? I am toying with the idea of turning them into a graphic novel.

"And, Bee," Trevor is saying, "Kramer doesn't care about attempts. He wants *results*."

"Wait a minute. I can give Kramer however many updates he wants. But this is science, not PR. I want results as much as he does, but we're talking about building a piece of equipment that will alter astronauts' brain activity. I'm not going to rush through experiments and make a possibly fatal mistake—"

"Then you're off this project."

My jaw drops. I stop in the middle of the crosswalk—until a Nissan honks and startles me into running to the sidewalk. "What—what did you just say?"

"If you don't get your act together, I'm going to pull you and send someone else."

"Why? *Who?*"

"Hank. Or Jan. Or someone else—you know how long the list is? How many people applied for this position?"

"But that's the point! I got BLINK because I'm the most qualified, you can't just send someone else!"

"I can if you've been there for an entire week and got nothing done. Bee, I don't care if you're the best I have at neurostimulation—if you don't get it together soon, you're out."

By the time I get to the office, my heart is pounding and my head's in chaos. Can Trevor take me off of BLINK? No. He can't. Or maybe he can. I have no clue.

Shit, of course he can. He can do whatever he wants, especially if he can prove that I'm not doing enough. Which he will be able to do, thanks to Levi Wardass. God, I hate him. My murder fantasies reach their final form: longitudinal impalement. Vlad-style. I'll plant the stake right outside my bedroom window. His suffering can be the last thing I see before I sleep and the first when I wake up. I'll sprinkle nectar all over him, so the hummingbirds can feast on his blood. Solid plan.

Rocío asked for the morning off. I'm alone in the office and free to do what my heart desires: head-desk. What are my options here? I need to get a straight answer on when the equipment will be delivered, but I don't know who to ask. Guy will direct me to Levi, Levi won't talk to me, and . . .

I sit up as an idea starts forming in my head. Two minutes later I'm on the phone with StimCase, the company that produces the system I use. "This is Dr. Bee Königswasser, calling from the Sullivan Discovery Institute, NASA. I wanted to check on the status of our order—it's a TMS system."

"Of course." The customer service lady's voice is low and soothing. "Do you have an order number?"

"Um, not at hand. My, um, assistant is out. But the listed principal investigator should be either me or Dr. Levi Ward."

"Just a moment, then. Oh, yes. Under Dr. Ward's name. But it looks like the order was canceled."

My stomach twists in knots. I tighten my fingers around the phone to avoid dropping it. "Could you . . ." I clear my throat. "Could you check again?"

"It was supposed to be shipped last Monday, but Dr. Ward canceled it the previous Friday." The day Levi first saw me in Houston. The day he saved my life. The day he decided that he had no intention of working with me, ever.

"I . . . Okay." I nod, even though she can't possibly see me. "Thank you." The hang-up noise is deafeningly loud, echoing through my head for long moments.

I don't know what to do. What do I do? Shit. *Shit.* You know who would know what to do? Dr. Curie, of course. But also: Annie. When she was a third year, some guy stole her optic fibers, so she installed a subroutine on his computer that made lobster porn pop-up every time he typed the letter *x*. He almost dropped out of grad school. That night we celebrated by making watermelon sangria and reinventing the Macarena on the roof of her apartment building.

Of course, what Annie knows or *doesn't* know is irrelevant. She's not in my life anymore. She's made her choices. For reasons that I'll never understand. And I—

"Bee?"

I set my phone on the table, wipe my sweaty palms over my jeans, and look to the door. "Hey, Kaylee." She's wearing a bright pink lace dress that looks the opposite of what I'm feeling.

"Is Rocío here?"

"She's out. Taking a test." I swallow, my mind still reeling from the phone call. Phone *calls*. "Can I help you with anything?"

"No. I just wanted to ask her if . . ." She shrugs uncomfortably, flushes a little, but then quickly adds, "I was surprised you weren't at the meeting this morning."

I tilt my head. "What meeting?"

"The one with the astronauts."

The knots in my stomach tighten. I don't like where this is going. "The astronauts."

"Yeah, the one Levi and Guy organized. For feedback. To brainstorm options for the helmets. It was really useful."

"When . . . when was it scheduled for?"

"This morning. Eight a.m. It was set up last week, and . . ." Kaylee's eyes widen. "You knew about it, right?"

I look away and shake my head. This is humiliating. And infuriating. And other things, too.

"Oh my God." She sounds genuinely distraught. "I am *so* sorry— I have no idea how that could happen."

I exhale a silent, bitter laugh. "I do."

"Is there anything I can do to fix this? As project manager, I want to apologize!"

"No, I . . ." I paste a smile on my face. "It's not your fault, Kaylee. You've been great." I'm tempted to explain to her that her boss has also been great—a great pain in my ass. But I don't want to put her in an uncomfortable position, and I'm not sure I trust myself not to blurt out a string of insults.

I sit for a long time after she leaves, staring at the empty desks, the empty chairs, the empty white walls of my supposed office, where I am supposed to do the science that will supposedly launch my career and make a happy, fulfilled woman out of me. I sit until my hands are not shaking and my chest doesn't feel like it's being squeezed by a large hand anymore.

Then I stand, take a deep breath, and march straight to Levi's office.

I KNOCK, BUT I don't bother waiting for a response. I open the door, close it behind me, and start speaking as soon as I'm in, my arms folded on my chest. For reasons I cannot discern, I'm smiling.

"Why?" Levi's gaze lifts from his computer screen to me, and his double take is small, but noticeable. He always has the same look in his eyes when he first sees me: a flash of panic. Then he collects himself and his entire face shutters. He should really work on expanding his emotional range. What does he think I'm going to do, anyway? Convert him to Scientology? Sell him Avon products? Give him full-blown typhoid? "Really, I just want to know why. I'm not even asking you to stop, I just need to know . . . *why*? Do I smell like cilantro? Did I steal your parking spot in grad school? Do I remind you of the kid who poured Snapple on your Game Boy when you were about to finish *The Legend of Zelda*?"

He blinks at me from his chair and has the audacity to look confused. I have to give it to him, he has giant balls. Likely to compensate for his micro-dick. "What are you talking about?"

My smile turns bitter. "Levi. Please."

"I have no idea what you're referring to. But I'm really busy, so—"

"See, I'm not. I'm not busy *at all*. I haven't been this *un*busy since

I was on summer break in middle school—but you know that already, so . . . why?"

He sits back in his chair. Even half-hidden by his desk, his presence is overwhelming. Winter-frosty. Snow-covered spruces, his eyes. "There are things I need to be doing right this moment. Can we schedule a meeting for another time?"

I laugh softly. "Sure. Should I send you an email?"

"That works."

"I bet. Will it get the same number of answers as the other emails I sent you?"

He frowns. "Of course."

"Zero, then."

He frowns harder. "I've answered all your emails."

"Is that so?" I don't believe it for a second. "Then maybe it's an email problem. If I were to check my spam folder I'd find a message from you inviting me to this morning's meeting?"

That's the moment something shifts. The moment Levi realizes that he's going to have to deal with me. He stands, walks around his desk, leans against it. He folds his arms on his chest and regards me calmly for a minute.

Look at us. Just two archnemeses, casually standing in front of each other in fake-relaxed poses while tumbleweeds roll their merry way around us. A modern spaghetti western.

I shoot first. "So, it's all a big email misunderstanding?"

He doesn't answer. Just stares somewhere above my right shoulder.

"It checks out. Emails that *should* be delivered, aren't. Emails that *shouldn't*, are. It would explain the one that canceled the order for my TMS equipment. It probably just sent itself. Vigilante emails going rogue. Uh-oh, Outlook's in trouble." His fake-calm is getting less convincing. "If you think about it, it's the only possible explanation.

Because last week, when I asked you if you had an ETA, you said that we were *close*. And you would never lie to me, would you?"

His annoyingly handsome face hardens. Yes, even more than usual. "I would *not* lie to you." He says it in an earnest, pissed-off tone, as though it's important to him that I believe him. Ha.

"I'm sure you wouldn't." I push away from the door and amble around the office. "And you would *not* single me out to point out a dress code that is obviously never enforced, nor would you make it impossible for me to get into my office without having to beg to be let in." I stop in front of a library shelf. Scattered between the engineering tomes I notice a handful of personal items. They humanize Levi in a way I'm not ready for: a child's drawing of a black cat; a few bobbleheads from sci-fi movies; two framed pictures. One is Levi and another tall, dark-haired man free-climbing a rock formation. The other, a woman. Very beautiful. Long, dark blond hair. Young, probably Levi's age. She smiles at the camera, holding a toddler with a full head of dark curls. The frame is clearly homemade, buttons and shells and sticks glued together.

My heart lurches, heavy.

I knew he had a child. I've even turned this piece of information around in my head several times since finding out. And I'm not surprised that he's married. He doesn't wear a ring, but that doesn't mean anything—I often *do* wear a ring, and I'm most definitely *not* married. Honestly, I'm not sure why this hits me so hard. I certainly have no personal stake in Levi's romantic life, and I don't usually go about feeling jealous when people find themselves happily paired. But the domesticity that the picture conjures, just like the soft, intimate tone his voice took last week when he answered the call . . . very clearly, Levi has a *home*. A place in the world, just for himself. Someone to go back to every night. And on top of that, his career is more stable than mine.

Levi Ward, lord of a thousand glares and a million rude nods, *belongs*. And I don't. The universe is truly not fair.

I sigh, defeated, and turn around to face him. "Just tell me why, Levi."

"It's a complicated situation."

"Is it? Seems pretty simple."

He shakes his head, carefully considers what to say, and then somehow lands on the most ridiculous five words I've ever heard. "Give me a few days."

"A few days? Levi, Rocío and I moved here to work. We left our friends, families, partners in Maryland, and now we're twiddling our thumbs—"

"Then go home for a few days." His tone is harsh. "Visit your partner, come back later—"

"That's *not* the damn point!" I aggressively run a hand through my bangs. Reike said that I should confront him calmly, but that horse is out of the stable and galloping around the moors. I'm pretty sure Levi's neighbors can hear me raise my voice, and I'm fully okay with it. "I have the head of NIH wanting progress reports from me, and my boss threatening to send in someone else if I don't get him results soon. I *need* my equipment. I'm not asking you to do this for me—do it for the project!" I must have moved closer, or maybe he to me, because all of a sudden I can smell him. Pine and soap and clean male skin. "Do you even care about BLINK?"

His eyes blaze. "I *care*. Do not *ever* imply otherwise," he grits out, leaning forward. I've never hated someone this intensely. I never will again. I believe it as deeply as I do cell theory.

"You sure don't *act* like you do."

"You don't know what you're talking about."

73

"And *you*"—I step closer, stabbing my finger into his chest—"don't know how to run a project."

"I am asking you to *trust* me."

"Trust you?" I laugh in his face. "Why the hell should I trust *you*?" I stab my finger at him again, and this time he closes his palm around it to stop me.

Something odd happens. His grip slides down to my palm, and for a moment he's almost holding my hand in his. It makes my skin tingle and my breath catch—his, too. It must be his cue to realize that he's touching me—me, the most abhorrent creature of the seven seas. He lets go immediately, as if burned.

"I am doing what I can," he begins.

"Which is *nothing*."

"—with the resources I have—"

"Oh, come *on*."

"—and there are things you don't know—"

"Then *tell* me! Explain!"

The ensuing silence clinches it for me. The way his jaw tightens, the fact that he straightens and turns abruptly, pacing three steps away as though he is finished with this. With me. *You never even started, asshole.*

"Right. Well." I shrug. "I'm going to your superior, Levi."

He gives me a shocked look. "What?"

Oh, *now* he is worried. How the worm has turned. How the cookie crumbles. "I need to get BLINK started. You're leaving me no choice but to go over your head."

"Over my head?" He briefly closes his eyes. "There is no such thing."

"I— Do you—" I sputter. God, this man's ego must have its own gravitational field. He's a human pit stuffed full of dark matter and hubris. "Do you even *hear* yourself?"

"Don't do it, Bee."

"Why *shouldn't* I? Are you going to call StimCase and get me my equipment? Are you going to get us an office that isn't away from everyone? Are you going to start inviting us to essential meetings?"

"It's not that simple—"

What an asswipe. "But it is. It's pretty damn simple, and if you don't commit to fixing this, you don't get to tell me not to go to your superior."

"You don't want to do that."

Is he *threatening* me? "See, I thought so, too. But now I'm pretty sure I do. Watch me."

I spin on my heels and head for the door, ready to walk straight to Boris's office, but when my hand is on the knob something occurs to me and I turn around.

"And one more thing," I snarl into his stony face. "Vegan donuts are for *vegans*, you absolute walnut."

LEVI CAN'T BE too distressed by our conversation, because he doesn't even attempt to come after me. I'm pumped full of rage and want to march to Boris, but I run into Rocío down the hallway. She's dragging her feet, staring vacantly at the floor like an inmate on death row. Even more than usual.

I stop. As impatient as I am to get my equipment and ruin a career, I think I love Rocío more than I hate Levi. Though it's a close call.

"How did the GRE go?" The Graduate Record Examination is like the SATs: a stupid standardized test on which students need to get an absurdly high score to be accepted into grad school—even though it tests nothing that has to do with academic success. I remember agonizing over my scores in my last year of college, terrified that they wouldn't be high enough to get me into the same programs as Tim. As it turned out, mine were higher than his, and I ended up with several more acceptances than he had. In hindsight, I should have gone to UCLA and left him behind. It would have saved me a lot of heartache *and* minimized my Wardass exposure.

"Bee." Rocío shakes her head gloomily. "Which way is the ocean?"

I point to my left. She immediately begins shuffling her feet in that direction.

"Ro, you first have to get out of the building and . . . what are you doing?"

"I shall walk into the sea. Farewell."

"Wait." I circle around her. "How did it go?"

She shakes her head again. Her eyes are red-rimmed. "Low."

"How low?"

"*Too* low."

"Well, you don't need ninety-ninth percentile to get into Johns Hopkins—"

"Fortieth for quantitative. Fifty-second for verbal."

Okay. That *is* low. "—and you can always retake."

"For two hundred bucks. And it's my third time—I don't get any better, no matter how much I practice. It's like I'm jinxed." She stares into the distance. "Is it La Llorona? Does she want me to quit academia and haunt creeks with her? Perhaps I should depart my scientific pursuits."

"No. I'll help you get your scores up, okay?"

"How? Will you cast a counterspell? Will you promise her your firstborn and the blood of one hundred virgin ravens?"

"What? No. I'll tutor you."

"Tutor me?" She scowls. "Can you even do math?"

I don't point out that my entire body of work consists of high-level statistics applied to the study of the brain, and instead pull her in for a hug. "It'll be okay, I promise."

"What's happening? Why are you squeezing me with your body?"

The entire conversation lasts less than ten minutes, but it proves to be a fatal mistake. Because by the time I'm on the mostly deserted third floor of the building, standing outside Boris's office and ready to rat Levi out within an inch of his life, the door is closed, and I can hear voices inside.

And one of those voices is Levi Ward's.

6

HESCHL'S GYRUS: HEAR, HEAR

I CANNOT BELIEVE he got to Boris before I could. I cannot believe he sneaked past me while I was talking with Rocío. Though I absolutely should, since it's the exact kind of dick move I've come to expect from him. I actually stomp my foot like a surly six-year-old. That's what I've been reduced to. What do I do? Do I barge in and stop Levi from poisoning Boris's mind with lies? Do I wait for Levi to get out and focus on damage control? Do I curl into a ball and cry?

Dr. Curie would know what to do. Dr. Königswasser, on the other hand, is looking around like a lost calf, grateful that there's no one around to see her sulking outside the director of research's office. When I decided to become a scientist, I figured I'd grapple with theoretical framework issues, research protocols, statistical modeling. Instead here I am, living my best high school life.

And then I realize I can make out some words.

"—unprofessional," Levi is saying.

"I agree," Boris replies.

"And not conducive to scientific progress." He sounds calmly exasperated, which should be technically impossible, but Levi does have a knack for bringing oxymorons to life. "The situation is unsustainable."

"I *fully* agree."

"You've said that every time we've talked before, but I doubt you understand how catastrophic the long-term repercussions can be for BLINK, for NIH, and for NASA. And this is unpleasant on an interpersonal level, too." I lean closer to the door, white-knuckled. I cannot believe he's feeding Boris this crap. *I* am unpleasant to him? *How?* By being offensive to look at? I'm about to slam the door open to defend myself when he continues, "She cannot continue like this. Something must be done." Oh my God. Am I trapped in a bizarro dimension?

"Okay. What would you have me do with her?"

I'm going to screech. Whatever Levi says, it's going to make me yell with rage. I'm already vibrating with an un-screamed howl. It's rising up my throat.

"I want you to let her do her job."

Up and up and up my larynx, through my vocal box, and—wait. *What?* What did Levi say?

"I've done as much as I can." Boris is faintly apologetic. Levi, on the other hand, is hard and uncompromising.

"It's not enough. I need her to have authorized access to every BLINK-related area in the building, to have a NASA.gov email address, to attend project meetings. I need every single piece of equipment she asked for to be here *now*—it should have arrived ages ago."

"You're the one who canceled the order that was placed."

"Because it wasn't the system she asked for. Why would I blow a chunk of our budget on an inferior product?"

"Levi, just like I told you every single day you've come to me with this last week, sometimes it's not about science—it's about politics."

I am fully leaning my ear and palms against the door now. My fingers shake against the wood, but I don't *feel* them. I'm numb.

"Politics is above my pay grade, Boris."

"Not above mine. We've been over this—things have changed a lot, and very quickly. The director was on board with an NIH-NASA collaboration as long as NASA got credit and autonomy on the project. Then NIH insisted on having a larger role. NASA can't have it."

"NASA *must* have it."

"The director is under lots of pressure. The possible ramifications are huge—if we patent the technology, there's no telling how widely it can be applied and what the revenue might be. He doesn't want NIH to own half of the patent."

A pause, brimming with frustration. I can almost picture Levi running a hand through his hair. "NASA doesn't have the budget to do the project alone—that's why NIH was brought in to begin with. Are you telling me that they'd rather have BLINK not happen at all than share the credit? And who will be in charge of the neuroscience portion?"

"Dr. Königswasser is not the only neuroscientist in the world. We have several at NASA who are—"

"Not *nearly* as good as her, not when it comes to neurostimulation."

This *is* a bizarro world. More bizarre than I could ever imagine. I'm in the Upside Down, my heart's thudding in my ears, and Levi Ward just said something *nice* about me. A cold, slimy feeling coils in the pit of my stomach. I might throw up, except that I'm completely hollow. I was full of rage when I came here, but that's draining.

"We'll make do. Levi, BLINK will be moved to the next budget review, and by then NASA will approve full funding. That way we won't need NIH. You'll still be in charge."

"That's a *year* from now, and you can't guarantee that. Just like you can't guarantee that the Sullivan prototype will be used."

A pause. "Son, I understand this is important to you. I feel the same, but—"

"I doubt it."

"Excuse me?"

Levi's voice could cut titanium. "I seriously doubt you feel the same."

"Levi—"

"If you do, authorize the equipment purchase."

A sigh. "Levi, I like you. I really do. You're a smart guy. One of the best engineers I know—maybe the best. But you're young and have no idea about the pressure everyone's under. BLINK's unlikely to happen this year. Better make peace with it."

Seconds pass. I can't hear Levi's reply, so I lean in even farther—which turns out to be a terrible idea, because the door swings open. I jump back quickly enough that Boris doesn't see me, but when Levi steps outside I'm still standing right there, by the office. He slams the door and begins stalking away angrily. Then he notices me and freezes.

He looks furious. And big. Furiously big.

I should say something. Play it cool. Make it seem like I only just wandered here, looking for the office supply closet. *Oh, Levi, do you know where they keep the pencil sharpeners?* Problem is, that ship has long sailed, and while we study each other with equally raw expressions, I experience an odd, transient feeling. Like this is the first time Levi sees me. No, not quite: like this is the first time *I* see him. Like the elaborate maze of mirrors through which we've been looking at each other has been shattered, the shards swept away.

I can't bear it. I lower my gaze to my feet. Thankfully, the feeling dissolves as I stare at the pretty daisies on my faux-leather sandals.

My fingers need to quit shaking or I'll chop them off. If my tear ducts dare to let even a single drop slip through, I'll tie them shut forever. I'm almost ready to look up again without making a fool of myself, when a large hand closes firmly around my elbow. Shouldn't have worn a sleeveless top today. "What are you—?"

Levi lifts one finger to his lips to signal me to be quiet and leads me away from the office.

"Where—" I start, but he interrupts me with a low whisper.

"Hush." His grip is gentle but tight around my flesh. I'm dismayed to find that it seems to help with my nausea.

Without having a clue of what to do, I close my eyes and follow his lead.

I'M A SLOW processor. Always have been.

When my nonna died, everyone around me had been sobbing for several minutes by the time I finally parsed what the white-haired doctor was saying. When Reike decided to take a gap decade to go travel the world, I didn't realize how lonely I'd be until she was on a plane to Indonesia. When Tim moved out of our apartment, the implications only hit me several days later, the moment I found two of his mismatched socks still in the dryer.

Probably why the enormity of what I heard outside Boris's office doesn't fully dawn on me until I'm on one of the benches in the little picnic area behind the Discovery Building, elbows on my knees and forehead in my hands.

It's such a lovely spot. The shades of two cedar elms and a live oak cross right where I'm sitting. *I need to eat lunch out here from now on,* I think. *Then my Lean Cuisine won't stink up the office.* My stomach twists. There might not be an *on* from this *now.*

"Are you okay?"

I glance up, and up, and up. Levi is standing in front me, still icily furious but more in control. Like he counted to ten to calm down a bit, but would gladly go back to one and flip a desk or three. There's a hint of concern in his eyes, and for some reason I'm thinking *again* of him pinning me to the wall, of the smell of his skin, the feeling of his hard muscles under my fingers.

There's something *very* wrong with my brain.

"I double-checked," he murmurs. "I received seven emails from you, and all my replies were sent. I'm not sure why they didn't deliver. I'm assuming the same happened to the one Guy sent to invite you to today's meeting, and I take responsibility for it. You should have a NASA email address by now."

The weather outside is perfectly nice, but I'm cold and sweaty at the same time. What a complex organism, my body.

"Why?" I ask. I'm not even sure what I'm referring to.

He exhales slowly. "How much did you hear?"

"I don't know. A lot."

He nods. "NASA wants exclusive control of whatever patent comes out of BLINK. But it currently doesn't have the budget to pull off the project, and there was some arm-twisting to include NIH. But NIH is insisting on co-owning the patent, and NASA decided that letting BLINK die a natural death is better than picking a fight with NIH."

"And this is it? The natural death?"

He doesn't answer, simply continuing to study me with worry and something else, something I can't quite put my finger on. It's unsettling, and I nearly laugh when I realize why: this is the first time Levi has sustained eye contact with me for more than a second. The first time his eyes don't flit away to some point above my head right after meeting mine.

I turn away. I'm not in the mood for ice green. "What if I told NIH?"

A brief hesitation. "You could."

"But?"

"No buts. It'd be fully within your rights. I'll support you, if you need me to."

"... *But?*"

I look at him. There are small scratches on his hand; hairs dust his forearm; his shirt stretches across his shoulder. He's so imposing from this angle, even more than usual. What did they feed him growing up, fertilizer? "If you told NIH, the only outcome I can imagine is NIH pulling out and the relationship between NIH and the human research branch of NASA souring. BLINK would be shelved until—"

"—until next year. And it would still be a NASA-only project." Either way, I'm screwed. Catch-22. Never liked that novel.

"I'm not saying you shouldn't do it," he says carefully, "but if the endgame is to make BLINK happen as a collaborative project, it might not be the best move."

Not to mention that I'd need to get Trevor to believe that this isn't my fault. Seems like I'd have better luck just telling him that NASA has been taken over by shape-shifting aliens. Yeah, I'll try that. Might as well.

"What's the alternative?" I ask. I see none.

"I've been working on it."

"How?"

"I think having Boris on our side would help immensely. And there are . . . things that I might be able to leverage to persuade him."

"And how are those *things* working out for you?"

He gives me a dirty look, but there's no real heat behind it. "Not great. *Yet*," he grumbles.

No shit, Sherlock. "Basically, I'm the only person in the world who wants BLINK to happen now."

He frowns. "I want it, too." I remember his earlier anger, when I accused him of not caring. God, that was probably less than an hour ago. Feels like nine decades. "And so do other people. The engineers, the astronauts, contractors who'd be out of a job if it were postponed." His broad shoulders seem to deflate a bit. "Though you and I seem to be the highest-ranking people on board. Which is why we need Boris."

"It sounds like if you sit tight for a few months the project will fall in your lap and—"

"No." He shakes his head. "BLINK has to happen now. If it's delayed there's a chance that I won't be in charge, or that the original prototype will be modified." He sounds so uncompromising, I wonder if this is his pick-up-your-toys-and-go-to-bed dad voice. It sure seems effective. If I end up having kids, I hope I can pull off something this authoritative.

"Still, you'll be fine no matter what." I can't keep the bitterness out of my tone. "While NIH is making personnel cuts, and the main criterion is successfully completed grants. Which I don't have because of . . . reasons, reasons that have little to do with me not trying or not being a good scientist—which I am, I promise I *am* good at this, and—"

"I know you are," he interrupts. He sounds sincere. "And this project is not just another assignment for me. I transferred teams to be here. I pulled strings."

I run a hand down my face. What a dumpster fire. "You could have told me that NASA was roadblocking. Instead of letting me believe that you were . . ."

He looks at me blankly. "That I was?"

"You know. Trying to oust me for the usual reasons."

"The usual reasons?"

"Yeah." I shrug. "From grad school."

"What reasons from grad school?"

"Just the fact that you . . . you know."

"I'm not sure I do."

I scratch my forehead, exhausted. "That you despise me."

He gives me an astonished look, like I just coughed up a hair ball. Like the person who avoided me like I was a flesh-eating porcupine was his evil twin. He's speechless for a moment, and then says, somehow managing to sound honest, "Bee. I don't despise you."

Wow. *Wow*, for so many reasons. The blatant lie, for instance, like he doesn't consider me the human equivalent of gas station sushi, but also . . . this is the first time Levi has used my name. I haven't kept track or anything, but there's something so uniquely *him* in the way he says the word, I could never forget.

"Right." He keeps staring at me with the same disoriented, earnest expression. I snort and smile. "I guess I must have misread every single one of our grad school interactions, then." He did tell Boris I'm a good neuroscientist, so maybe he doesn't think I'm incompetent like I always suspected. Maybe he just hates . . . literally everything else about me. Lovely.

"You *know* I don't despise you," he insists with a hint of accusation.

"Sure I do."

"Bee."

He says my name again, with that *voice*, and all I see is red.

"But *of course* I know. How could I *not* know when you've been so relentlessly cold, arrogant, and unapproachable." I stand, anger bubbling up my throat. "For years you have avoided me, refused to collaborate with me without valid reasons, denied me even minimally polite conversation, treated me as though I was repulsive and inferior—you even told my fiancé that he should marry someone else, but *of course you don't despise me, Levi*."

His Adam's apple bobs. He stares at me like that, stricken, disconcerted, like I just hit him with a polo mallet—when all I've done is tell the truth. My eyes sting. I bite my lip to keep the tears at bay, but my stupid body betrays me once again and I'm crying, I'm crying in front of him, and I *hate* him.

I'm not mad at him—I *hate* him.

For the way he's treated me. For having the solid career I don't. For concealing the politics of this damn septic tank of a project. I hate him, hate him, *hate him*, with a passion I thought I could only reserve for defective airbags, or Tim, or the third move of the year. I hate him for reducing me to this, and for sticking around to see his handiwork.

I hate him. And I don't want to feel so much.

"Bee—"

"This is not worth it." I wipe my cheek with the back of my hand and walk past without looking at him. Of course he has to be massive and make *that* hard, too.

"Wait."

"I'll tell NIH about what's happening," I say without stopping or turning back. "I can't risk my superiors thinking that the project failed because of me. I'm sorry if that puts you in a bad position, and I'm sorry if that means delaying BLINK."

"That's okay. But please, wait—"

No. I don't want to wait, or to listen to even one more word. I keep on walking in my pretty daisy sandals until I can't hear him anymore, until I can't see through the blur of my tears. I walk out of the Space Center and fantasize that I'm leaving Houston, Texas, the United States. I fantasize about getting on a plane and flying to Portugal to get a hug from Reike.

I fantasize all the way home, and it doesn't make me feel any better.

I'M STARING AT my phone—just that: brooding and staring at my phone—when a Twitter notification pops up on my screen.

> @SabriRocks95 Second year geology
> Ph.D. student going through a rough patch,
> here. @WhatWouldMarieDo if she felt like the
> universe is trying to tell her to give up?

Ouch. This one hits a little too close. My sense of helplessness reached critical mass earlier today, halfway through Alanis Morissette's discography and well past my second tub of orange sherbet. I feel like I was run through a paper shredder. Like a used Q-tip. A flushable wipe. Not fit to give advice to the moth that's been fluttering against my window, let alone an intelligent young woman with career trouble. I retweet, hoping that the WWMD community will take care of @SabriRocks95.

"Maybe I should quit academia," I muse, leaning back in my chair, staring across the open-plan kitchen to Dr. Curie's magnet. "Should I quit my job?"

Marie doesn't reply. Silent approval? There are things I could do. Brush up on the German accusative and meet Reike in Greece, where olive oil tycoons would hire us to instruct their teenaged heirs. Shop that sitcom idea I once had: a Bayesian statistician and a frequentist become reluctant roommates. Write my mermaid YA series. Move under a bridge and ask riddles in exchange for safe passage.

Maybe I shouldn't quit. At least one Königswasser twin needs a stable job, to post bail when the other gets arrested for indecent exposure. Knowing Reike, that's any day now.

Then again, I'm fairly sure that without BLINK, Trevor won't renew my contract anyway.

My career is the ultimate unrequited love story, littered with well-reviewed grants that never got funded for political reasons, a shitty boss instead of the rock star I was promised, and now NIH and NASA petty-fighting like cousins at Thanksgiving. When your supposed big break turns into a losing game, that's when you cut your losses, right?

But what would be left of me without neuroscience? Who would I even be without my burning need to correct people who say that humans use only 10 percent of their brain? (They even made *a movie* about this. For fuck's sake, does no one fact-check Hollywood scripts?) Did you know that conservatives tend to have larger amygdalae than liberals? That taxi drivers' hippocampi grow bigger as they memorize how to navigate London? That brain differences predict variations in personality? We are our nervous systems, the complex combination of billions of neurons firing in distinctive patterns. What's more exciting than spending my life figuring out what a little chunk of these neurons can accomplish?

I avoid my reflection as I brush my teeth. Maybe I love what I do too much. I should go back to school for something boring. Auctioneering. Naval architecture. Sports broadcasting. I should also stop crying. Or maybe not. Maybe I should feel all my feelings now, so I can be solution-oriented later. All wept-out for tomorrow, when I explain this mess to Trevor. When I tell Rocío to pack her bags.

The second my head touches my pillow I know I'll explode if I don't do something. *Anything*. On impulse, I message Shmac.

> **MARIE:** Do you ever think of leaving research?

His reply is immediate.

> **SHMAC:** Sure am today
>
> **MARIE:** You hate your life, too? What are the chances.
>
> **SHMAC:** Maybe we're the same astrological sign.
>
> **MARIE:** lol
>
> **SHMAC:** What's going on?
>
> **MARIE:** My project's a shitshow. And I'm working with this total camel dick who's the worst. I bet he's one of those assholes who doesn't switch to airplane mode during takeoff, Shmac. He probably bites into popsicles. I'm positive he sneezes in his palm and then shakes people's hands.
>
> **SHMAC:** Eerily specific.
>
> **MARIE:** But true!
>
> **SHMAC:** I don't doubt it.

MARIE: How's the girl?

SHMAC: Still married. Plus, she probably thinks I'm a camel dick.

MARIE: She could never. You two having a torrid affair yet?

SHMAC: The opposite.

MARIE: Did she at least get ugly while she was gone?

SHMAC: She's still the most beautiful thing I've ever seen.

My heart skips a beat. Oh, Shmac.

SHMAC: That aside, I've been thinking about how much easier my life would be if I quit and became a cat trainer. Except, I can't even convince my cat not to piss under my living room carpet.

MARIE: I can see how that would be an issue.

MARIE: Do you ever feel like we put too much of ourselves into this?

SHMAC: On the bad days, for sure.

MARIE: Are there good days? Ever?

SHMAC: My last one was in middle school. Second place at the science fair.

MARIE: Did you win a Toys R Us gift certificate?

SHMAC: Nope. A Marie Curie bobblehead, holding two beakers that glow in the dark.

MARIE: Omg. I would MURDER for that.

SHMAC: If we ever meet in person, it's yours.

We chat for a long time, and it's nice to commiserate while it lasts, but once I set my phone on the nightstand I feel hopeless again. The last thing I see before falling asleep is Levi's stricken expression when I threw at him all the things he did to me, painted on the back of my eyelids like the poster of a movie I never want to watch again.

7

ORBITOFRONTAL CORTEX: HOPE

MY ALARM RINGS, but I let it snooze.

Once. Twice. Three times, five, eight, twelve, why the hell is it still ringing, why did I even set it—

"Bee?"

I open my eyes. Barely. They're bleary, sticky with sleep.

"Bee?"

Crap. I inadvertently answered a call from an unknown number. "Shisshishee," I slur. Then I spit out my retainer. "Sorry, this is she."

"I need you to come in right now."

I instantly recognize the baritone. "Levi?" I blink at my alarm. It's 6:43 a.m. I can't keep my lids up. "What? Come where?"

"Can you be in Boris's office by seven?"

That makes me sit up in bed. Or as close as I can manage at this hour. "What are you talking about?"

"Do you want to stay and work on BLINK?" His voice is firm. Decisive. I can hear background noise. He must be outside, walking somewhere.

"What?"

"Have you told NIH about what NASA is doing yet?"

"Not yet, but—"

"Then do you want to stay and work on BLINK?"

I press my palm into my eye. This is a nightmare, right? "I thought we agreed that's not an option."

"It might be now. I have . . . something." A pause. "A bit of a gamble, though."

"What is it?"

"Something that'll get Boris to support us." He cuts off for a second. "—can't explain on the phone."

It sounds sketchy. Like he's trying to lure me to a secondary location to traffic me to people who'll harvest my femurs to make handles for badminton racquets.

"Can't we just meet later?"

"No. Boris is having a call with the NASA director in one hour, we need to catch him before then."

I run a hand over my face. I'm way too pooped for this. "Levi, this sounds very weird and I just woke up. If you're trying to get me alone to assassinate me, could we just go ahead, pretend you did it, and go our separate ways—"

"Listen. What you said yesterday . . ." He must have stepped inside, because the background noise is gone. His voice is rich and deep in my ear. I think I can actually hear him swallow. "There is no other neuroscientist I'd want to do this project with. Not a single one."

It's a blow to the sternum. The words knock the air out of my lungs, and a weird, nonsensical, untimely thought crosses my mind:

it's not *that* surprising that this broody, reserved man snagged himself a beautiful bride. Not if he's capable of saying things like this.

At least I'm awake now. "What's happening?"

"Bee, do you *want* to stay in Houston and work on BLINK?" he asks again, but this time after a pause he adds, "With me?"

That's when I know that I'm a lunatic. Insane. An utterly insane lunatic. Because my alarm says six forty-five a.m., and a shiver runs down my spine—or where my spine would be if I had one. I screw my eyes shut, and the word that comes out of my mouth is:

"Yeah."

I STUMBLE OUT of the elevator two minutes past seven, energized by a night of restful sleep and dressed for success.

Just kidding. I'm wearing leggings and a flannel shirt, I forgot to put on a bra, and having to choose between brushing my teeth and washing my face I went for the former, which means that when Levi spots me I'm frantically trying to scrape sleep boogers from my eyes. I feel jittery *and* drowsy—the worst possible combination. Levi is waiting by Boris's office, put together like it's not the middle of the night, and knocks on the door the moment he sees me. I break into a light jog, and by the time I get there I'm also sweaty and out of breath.

My life is so lovely. As lovely as a spinal tap.

"What is going on?"

"No time to explain. But like I said, it's a gamble. Pretend you already know when we're in there."

I frown. "Know *what*?"

Boris yells at us to come in.

"Just follow my lead," Levi says, gesturing me inside.

"We're supposed to be co-leads," I mutter.

The corner of his lip twitches up. "Follow my co-lead, then."

"Please, tell me this mess doesn't end in a murder-suicide."

He opens the door and shrugs, ushering me in with a hand between my shoulder blades. "Guess we'll see."

Boris had no idea we'd show up. His eyes roll and narrow, a mix of *I'm tired* and *Not you two* and *I don't have time for this*, and he stands from behind his desk with his hands on his hips.

I take a step back. What is this car crash of a meeting? What did I get myself into? And why, oh *why* did I ever think that trusting Levi Ward would be a good idea?

"No," Boris says, "Levi, I'm not going to go over this again, and not in front of an NIH employee. I have a meeting that I need to prep for, so . . ." The annoyance in his voice fades as Levi, unruffled, sets his phone on the desk. There's a picture on the screen, but I can't make out what it is. I push up on my toes and lean forward to see, but Levi pulls on the back of my flannel and lifts one eyebrow—which I believe means *You're supposed to follow my lead.* I frown in my best *Sure would be nice to know what's going on, but whatever.*

When I glance at Boris, there's a deep horizontal line in the middle of his forehead. "Did you make some changes to the helmet prototype? I don't remember authorizing—"

"I did not."

"This doesn't look like what I approved."

"It's not." Levi holds out his hand, and when Boris returns the phone, he pulls up another picture. A person, wearing something on their head. The line on Boris's brow deepens even more.

"When was the picture taken?"

"That, I'd rather not say."

Boris's gaze sharpens. "Levi, if you're making this up because of yesterday's conversation—"

"The name of the company is MagTech. They are very well-established, based in Rotterdam, and do science tech. They've been open about the fact that they're working on wireless neurostimulation helmets." A pause. "They have a fairly long history of supplying armed forces and militias with combat gadgets."

"Which armed forces?"

"Whoever can pay."

"How far ahead are they?"

"Based on those blueprints and on my . . . contact's information, pretty much where BLINK's at." He holds Boris's eyes a little too intensely. "At least, where BLINK *was* at. Before it was shelved."

Boris risks a quick glance at me. "Technically, the project was never shelved," he says defensively.

"Technically." There is something commanding about the way Levi talks, even to his boss. Boris flushes and returns the phone. I pluck it from Levi's hand before he can pocket it and study the pictures.

It's a neurostimulation helmet—the blueprints and the prototype. Not quite ours, but similar. *Scarily* similar. *Oh shit we have competition* similar.

"Do they know about BLINK?" Boris is asking.

"Unclear. But they wouldn't have seen our prototype."

"They don't have a neuroscientist on their team. Not a good one," I add distractedly.

"How do you know that?" Boris asks.

I shrug. "Well, it's pretty obvious. They're making the same mistake Levi is—the output locations. Honestly, why can't engineers ever be bothered to consult with experts outside of their discipline? Is it part of vector calculus? First rule of engineering: do not display weakness. Never ask questions. Better to finish a wrong, unusable prototype on your own than to collaborate with—" I look up, notice the way Boris and Levi are staring at me, and slap my mouth shut. I really shouldn't be allowed in public before coffee. "Point is," I say after clearing my throat, "they're not doing so hot, and as soon as they start trying out the helmet in action they'll realize it." I give Levi's phone back, and his fingers brush mine, rough and warm. Our eyes meet for a split second, then flit away.

"The blueprint," Boris says. "And the picture. Where did you get them?"

"That's not important."

Boris's eyes go dinner-plate wide. "Please, tell me my lead engineer didn't just jeopardize his career by engaging in some light industrial espionage—"

"Boris," Levi interrupts him, "this changes things. We need to be working on BLINK. Now. Those helmets are conceptually similar to ours. If MagTech gets to a working prototype and patents the tech before we do, we'll have flushed millions of dollars down the toilet. And there's no telling what they'll do with their design. Who they'll sell it to." Boris closes his eyes and scratches his forehead. It must be the sign of weariness Levi was waiting for, because he adds, "Bee and I are here. Ready. We can finish this project in three months—*if* we have the necessary equipment. We can see this through."

Boris doesn't open his eyes. The opposite: he scrunches them shut, as though he hates every second of this. "Can you really? Get this done in three months?"

Levi turns to me.

I honestly have no idea. Science doesn't work like that. It doesn't do deadlines or consolation trophies. You can design the perfect study, sleep one hour a night, feed on nothing but despair and Lean Cuisine for months on end, and your results can still be the opposite of what you were hoping to find. Science doesn't give a shit. Science is reliable in its variability. Science does whatever the fuck it wants. God, I love science.

But I smile brilliantly. "Of course we can. And much better than those Dutch guys."

"Okay. Okay." Boris runs a hand through his hair, harried. "I have a meeting with the director in—damn, ten minutes. I'll push for this. I'll be in touch later today, but . . . yeah. Things are different, with this." He gives Levi a part-irritated, part-exhausted, part-admiring look. "I suppose I owe you my congratulations on bringing BLINK back from the dead." My stomach somersaults. Holy shit. *Holy shit.* This is happening after all. "If I convince the director, there's *no* margin of error. You'll have to make the best neurostimulation helmets in the damn world." Levi and I exchange a long glance and nod at the same time. When we step out of the office, Boris is swearing softly.

I'm mildly terrified by this turn of events. If we do get the go-ahead, everyone and their mother will be breathing down our necks. The honchos at NASA and NIH will vulture-circle on top of us. I'm going to have to explain to some creationist white guy on his twelfth senate term that brain stimulation is *not* the same thing as acupressure.

Oh, who am I kidding? I wouldn't even mind it for a chance to actually work on BLINK and fix all those stubborn engineers' mistakes. A chance that seemed long gone less than an hour ago, but now . . .

I press a hand against my lips, exhaling a laugh. It's going to happen. Well, it's *probably* going to happen. But NASA's supposed to be chock-full of geniuses who'll get us to Mars, no? They won't be so stupid to block the project, not if it's a now-or-never situation. I have no idea how Levi did it, but—

Levi.

I look up and there he is, staring at me with a soft smile as I grin into the ether like an idiot. I should snap at him to look away, but when our eyes meet I only want to grin more. We stand like that for several seconds, smiling moronically outside Boris's office, until his expression goes serious.

"Bee." What *is* it about the way he says my name? The pitch? His deep voice? Something else altogether? "About yesterday—"

I shake my head. "No. I . . ." God, this apology is going to be painful. Humiliating, too. The colonoscopy of apologies. Better get it over with. "Listen, you should have been more forthcoming about what was going on, but I probably shouldn't have called you a . . . boob. Or a walnut. I'm not sure what was in my head and what I actually said out loud but . . . I'm sorry about coming to your office and insulting you." There. Done. Colonoscopy's over. My intestines are sparkling clean.

Except that Levi doesn't even acknowledge my apology. "What you said, about me despising you. About things that I have done, I—"

"No, I was out of line. I mean, it's all true, but—" I take a deep breath. "Listen, you have every right not to like me as long as you deal with it professionally. Even though, let's be real, what's wrong with you? I'm an absolute delight." I give him an impish grin, but he doesn't get that I'm teasing, because he stares at me with a toned-down version of yesterday's stricken expression. Oops. I rock on my heels and clear my throat. "Sorry. Just kidding. I know there's plenty to dislike about me and you are . . . you, while I am . . . yeah. Me. Very different. I know we're nemesis of sorts—nemeses? Nemesi? Anyway, I got upset because I thought you were letting that dictate your behavior on BLINK. But clearly that's not the case, so I apologize for assuming, and—feel free to carry on." I manage a mostly sincere smile. "As long as you're civil and fair at work, you can dislike away. Loathe me up. Abhor me to the moon. Detest me into the unknown." I really mean it. Not that I relish the idea of him hating me, but it's such a great improvement over yesterday, when I thought that his dislike would ruin my career, that I'm coming to peace with this. Sort of. "Did you *actually* engage in industrial espionage?"

"No. Maybe. A friend knows someone who works for—" Levi closes his eyes. "Bee. You don't understand."

I cock my head. "What don't I understand?"

"I don't dislike you."

"Right." Uh-huh. "So you've been acting like an ass to me for seven years because . . . ?"

He sighs, his broad chest moving up and down. There's a tuft of fur on the sleeve of his shirt. Does he have a pet? He looks like a dog person. Maybe it's his daughter's dog.

"Because I *am* an ass. An idiot, too."

"Levi, it's fine. I understand, really. When we lived in France, my sister loved this classmate of ours, Ines, and I could *not* stand her. I wanted to pull her braid for no reason. I actually did, once, which was . . . unfortunate, because my French aunt believed in sending kids to bed without dinner." I shrug. Levi is pinching the bridge of his nose, probably shocked by how much I ramble when I'm still half-asleep. One more thing for him to hate about me, I guess. "The point is, sometimes dislike is a gut reaction. Like falling in love at first sight, you know? Just . . . the opposite."

His eyes spring open. "Bee." He swallows. "I—"

"Levi! Here you are." Kaylee is walking toward us, an iPad in her hand. I wave at her, but Levi doesn't stop staring. At me. "I need your approval on two items, and you and Guy have a meeting with Jonas in . . . Levi?"

He is, for unknown reasons, *still* staring at me. And the stricken expression is back. Do I have a sleep booger on my nose?

"Levi?"

Third time must be the charm, because he finally looks away. "Hey, Kaylee."

They start talking and I walk away with another wave, daydreaming about coffee and a bra. I don't know why I turn around one last time, right before stepping into the elevator. I really don't know why, but Levi is looking at me again.

Even though Kaylee is still talking.

IT'S TWO P.M., I'm wearing a bra (yes, a sports bra is a real bra; no, I do not accept constructive criticism) and sipping my eleventh coffee of the day when I get a text from Levi.

Bee, I'm using texts since emails are unreliable. Your equipment and computers will be here tomorrow. Let's schedule a meeting to go over BLINK at your earliest convenience. Kaylee will be there shortly to set you up with NASA.gov email, so that you can access our servers. Let me know what else you need.

I can't help myself. I must have learned nothing in the past weeks, because I do it again: I shoot off my chair and jump up and down, screeching loudly and joyously in the middle of the office. *It's happening. It's happening. It's happening, it's happening, it's—*

"Um . . . Bee?"

I whirl around. Rocío is blinking at me from her desk, alarmed.

"Sorry." I flush and quickly sit back down. "Sorry. Just . . . good news."

"The dictator of veganism released you from his tyrannical clutches and you can finally eat real food?"

"What? No."

"Have you been able to reserve a cemetery plot close to Marie Curie's?"

"That would be impossible, as her ashes are enshrined in the Paris Panthéon and—" I shake my head. "Our equipment is coming! Tomorrow!"

She actually smiles. Where's a digital camera when you need it? "For real?"

"Yes! And Kaylee's on her way to set us up with NASA.gov addresses— Where are you going?" I notice her panicky expression as she stuffs her laptop in her bag.

"Home."

"But—"

"Since the computers will be here tomorrow, there's no point in staying."

"But we can still—"

She's gone before I can remind her that I'm her boss—I *will* learn to exert authority, but today's not the day. I don't mind too much anyway. Because when the door closes behind her, I spring out of my chair again and jump up and down a little bit more.

8

PRECENTRAL GYRUS: MOVEMENT

FUN FACT: DR. Curie's BFF was an engineer.

Seems unlikely, huh? I sit across from the best and brightest of Levi's team—total Cockcluster™, naturally—and think: Who would voluntarily spend time with the engineering ilk? And yet it's true, like turkey-flavored candy corn, pimple-popping videos, and many other unlikely things.

It's painful even to think about it, but here goes my least favorite Marie fact: after Pierre died, she started seeing a strapping young physicist named Paul Langevin. Honestly, it's what she deserved. My girl was a young widow who spent most of her time stomping on uranium ore like it was wine grapes. We can all agree that if she wanted to get laid, the only adequate response should have been: "Where would you like your mattress placed, Madame Curie?" Right?

Wrong.

The press got ahold of the gossip and crucified her for it. They treated her like she'd boarded a train to Sarajevo and assassinated Franz Ferdinand herself. They whined about the lamest things: Madame Curie is a home-wrecker (Paul had separated from his wife *ages* before); Madame Curie is tarnishing Pierre's good name (Pierre was probably high-fiving her from physics heaven, which is full of atheist scientists and apple trees for Newton and his buddies to sit under); Madame Curie is five years older than almost-forty-year-old Paul (gasp!) and therefore a cradle-robber (double-gasp!!). If there is one thing men hate more than a smart woman, it's a smart woman who makes her own choices when it comes to her own sex life. It was a whole thing: lots of sexist, anti-Semitic crap was written, pistol duels were held, the words "Polish scum" were used, and Dr. Curie plunged into a deep depression.

But that's where the engineer BFF comes in.

Her name was Hertha Ayrton and she was a bit of a polymath. Think of your high school friend who always got straight A's but was also the captain of the soccer team, did lights for the drama club, and moonlighted as a suffragette leader. Hertha's famous for studying electric arcs—lightning, but way cooler. I like to fantasize about her using her scientific knowledge to burn Marie's enemies to a crisp, Zeus-style, but the truth is that their mutual love and support mostly translated into vacationing together to escape the French press.

Sometimes friendship is made of quiet little moments and doesn't involve lethal lightning bolts. Disappointing, I know. Then again, other times friendship is made of betrayal, and heartache, and spending two years trying to forget that you blocked the number of someone whose take-out orders you used to have memorized.

Anyway. The moral of this particular story is, I believe, that engineers are not *all* bad. But the ones I'm attempting to collaborate with are often stabable. Like now, for example. I have Mark, the materials guy on BLINK, looking me in the eye and telling me for the third time in two minutes: "Impossible."

Okay. Let's try again. "If we don't move the output channels farther apart—"

"Impossible."

Four. Four times in . . . Welp. *Still* two minutes.

I take a deep breath, remembering a technique my old therapist used. I saw her for a short time after Tim and I broke up, when my self-confidence was six feet under, partying it up with disgruntled grubs and Mesozoic fossils. She taught me the importance of letting go of what I cannot control (others) and focusing on what I can (my reactions). She'd often do this crafty little thing: reframe my own statements to help me achieve self-realization.

Time to therapize Mark the Material Engineer.

"I understand that I'm asking you to do something that is *currently* impossible, given the inner shell of the helmet." I smile encouragingly. "But maybe, if I explain what needs to be done from a neuroscience perspective, we can find a way to achieve a middle ground—"

"Impossible."

I don't head-desk, but only because Levi happens to enter the room right at that moment, nodding his good morning in our general direction and rolling up the sleeves of his Henley. His forearms are strong and insanely attractive—and *why the hell am I even noticing them?* Aargh. Kaylee let us know he'd be late because of something at Penny's school. Which, I guess, is the name of his daughter. Because Levi has a daughter. I promise I'll stop repeating this fact as soon as it becomes less shocking to me (i.e., never).

Everyone greets him, and I feel a jolt to my stomach. We've been emailing, but we haven't talked in person since yesterday, when I gave him official permission to abhor me—as long as he's professional about it. I'm curious to see how he'll play. In deference to his tender sensibilities I'm wearing my tiniest septum ring and the single Ann Taylor dress I own. It's an olive branch; he damn better appreciate it.

"I see what you're saying," I tell Mark. "There are physical impossibilities inherent to the materials, but we might be able to—"

He repeats the only word he knows. "Impossible."

"—find a solution that—"

"No."

I'm about to praise the sudden variety in his vocabulary when Levi interjects. "Let her finish, Mark." He takes a seat next to me. "What were you saying, Bee?"

Huh? What's happening? "The . . . um, the issue is the outputs placement. They need to be positioned differently if we want to stimulate the intended region."

Levi nods. "Like the angular gyrus?"

I flush. Come on, I apologized for that! I glare at him for shading me in front of his team, but I notice an odd gleam in his eyes, as though he . . . Wait. It's not possible. He's not teasing me, is he?

"Y-yes," I stammer, lost. "Like the angular gyrus. And other brain regions, too."

"And what I told her," Mark says with all the petulance of a six-year-old who's too short for the roller coaster, "is that given the property of the Kevlar blend we're using for the inner shell, the distance between outputs needs to stay the way it is."

Actually, what he told me was "Impossible." I'm about to point that out when Levi says, "Then we change the Kevlar blend." It seems to me like a perfectly reasonable avenue to explore, but the other five people at the table seem to think it's as controversial as the concept of gluten in the twenty-first century. Murmurs rise. Tongues cluck. A guy whose name might be Fred gasps.

"That would be a significant change," Mark whines.

"It's unavoidable. We need to do proper neurostimulation with the helmets."

"But that's not what the Sullivan prototype calls for."

This is the second time I've heard the Sullivan prototype mentioned, and the second time a dense silence ensues when it's brought up. The difference today is that I'm in the room, and I can see how everyone looks to Levi uneasily. Is he the main author of the prototype? Can't be, since he's new to BLINK. Sullivan is the name of the Discovery Institute, so maybe that's where it's from? I want to ask Guy, but he's off setting up equipment with Rocío and Kaylee this morning.

"We'll be as faithful as possible to the Sullivan prototype, but it was always meant to be a vehicle for the neuroscience," Levi says, firm and final as usual, with that competent, big-dick calm of his, and everyone nods somberly, more so than one would expect from a bunch of dudes who throttle one another over donuts and come into work in their pajamas. There's clearly something I don't know. What is this place, Twin Peaks? Why's everyone so full of secrets?

We hammer out details for a couple more hours, deciding that for the next weeks I'll focus on mapping the individual brains of the first batch of astronauts while engineering refines the shell. With Levi present, his team tends to agree to my suggestions more quickly—a phenomenon known as Sausage Referencing™. Well, to Annie and me, at least. In Cockcluster™ or WurstFest™ situations, having a man vouch for you will help you be taken seriously—the better-regarded the man, the higher his Sausage Referencing™ power.

Notable example: Dr. Curie was not originally included in the Nobel Prize nomination for the radioactivity theory *she had come up with*, until Gösta Mittag-Leffler, a Swedish mathematician dude, interceded for her with the all-male award committee. Less notable example: halfway through my meeting with the engineers, when I point out that we won't be able to stimulate deep into the temporal lobe, Maybe Fred tells me, "*Actually*, we can. I took a neuroscience class in undergrad." Oh, boy. That was probably two weeks ago. "I'm *pretty* sure they stimulated the medial temporal lobe."

I sigh. On the inside. "Who?"

"Something . . . Welch? In Chicago?"

"Jack Walsh? Northwestern?"

"Yeah."

I nod and smile. Though maybe I shouldn't smile. Maybe the reason I have to deal with this crap is that I smile too much. "Jack did not stimulate the hippocampus directly—he stimulated occipital areas connected to it."

"But in the paper—"

"Fred," Levi says. He's sitting back in his chair, dwarfing it, holding a half-eaten apple in his right hand. "I think we can take the word of a Ph.D.-trained neuroscientist with dozens of publications on this," he adds, calm but authoritative. Then he takes another bite of his apple, and that's the end of the conversation.

See? Sausage Referencing™. Works every time. And every time it makes me want to flip a table, but I just move on to the next topic. What can I say? I'm tired.

And now I crave an apple.

My stomach growls when I slip out to fill my water bottle. I'm thinking wistfully of the Lean Cuisine currently unthawing at my desk when I hear it.

"Meow."

I recognize the chirpy quality of it immediately. It's my calico—well, *the* calico—peeking at me from behind the water fountain.

"Hey, sweetie." I go down on my knees to pet her. "Where did you go the other day?"

Chirp, meow. Some purrs.

"What are you doing all alone?"

A headbutt.

"Are you hunting mice? Do you work as *c*-law enforcement?" I laugh at my own pun. The cat gives me a scathing look and wanders away. "Oh, come on, it was a good joke. It was *hiss*-terical!"

One last indignant glare, and she turns the corner. I giggle, then hear steps coming up behind me. I don't look back. I don't need to, since I already know who it is. "There was a cat," I say weakly.

Levi walks past me to fill his water bottle. He's so tall, he needs to hunch over the fountain. His biceps shift under the cotton of his shirt. Was he this big in grad school? Or did I get even shorter? Maybe it's the stress. Maybe early onset osteoporosis is kicking in. Gotta buy some calcium-set tofu. "Right," he says, noncommittal. His eyes are on the water.

"No, for real."

"Uh-huh."

"I'm serious. She went that way." I point to my right. Levi looks in that direction with a polite nod and then walks back inside the room, sipping his water.

I stay on my knees in the dead middle of the hallway and sigh. I don't care if Levi Wardass believes me.

He probably hates cats anyway.

"EQUIPMENT'S READY. AND Guy set up our computers," Rocío says as we walk back to our apartments.

I smile into the soupy afternoon air. "Awesome. How was working with Guy and Kaylee?"

"How was working with your lifelong sworn archfoe?"

I give her the stink eye. "Ro." My time with her is perfect practice for the adolescent daughter I might never have.

"It was fine," she mutters. I frown at her tone.

"You sure?"

"Yeah."

"It doesn't sound fine. Is there a problem?"

"Yes. Several. Global warming, systemic racism, the overpopulation of ecological niches, the unnecessary American remake of Swedish romantic horror masterpiece *Let the Right One In*—"

"Rocío." I stop on the sidewalk. "If there's something off in the way you're being treated, if Guy's making you uncomfortable, please feel free to—"

"Have you *seen* Guy?" she scoffs. "He looks like the harmless love child of a meerkat and an altar boy."

"That is very rude and"—I blink—"disturbingly accurate, but it sounds like you had an unpleasant day, so if there's anything that bothers you, I—" She mutters something I can't hear. I lean closer. "What did you say?"

Another mumbled reply.

"What? I can't—"

"I said, *I hate Kaylee*." She screams it so loud, a man pushing a stroller on the other side of the street turns to look at us.

"You hate . . . Kaylee?"

She whirls around and starts walking. "I said what I said." I hurry after her.

"Wait—are you serious?"

"I'm always serious."

She's not. "Did she do something to you?"

"Yes."

"Then tell me, please." I put my hand on her shoulder, trying to be reassuring. "I'm here for you, whatever it is—"

"Her stupid *curls*," Rocío spits out. "They look like a damn Fibonacci spiral. They're logarithmic, and their growth factor is the golden ratio—not to mention that they even *look* like spun gold. Is she Cinderella? Is this Disneyland Paris?"

I blink. "Ro, are you—"

"And what self-respecting person wears that much glitter? Unironically?"

"I like glitter—"

"*No, you don't*," she growls. I can only nod. Okay. Don't like glitter anymore. "And earlier she dropped something and you know what she said?"

"Oops?"

"'Lordy.' She said, 'Oh, Lordy!'—do you understand *why* I cannot work with her?"

I nod to buy time. This is . . . interesting. At the very least. "I, um, understand that you two are very different and might never be friends, but I need you to overcome your . . . revulsion for sequins—"

"*Pink* sequins."

"—for *pink* sequins, and to get along with her."

"Impossible. I quit."

"Listen, none of these things are grounds for a formal complaint. We can't police our coworkers' sense of fashion."

Rocío frowns. "What if I told you that she had a lollipop? The kind with gum inside?"

"Still no." I smile. "Wanna know something? Everything you feel about Kaylee, Levi feels about me."

"What do you mean?"

"He hates my hair. My piercings. My clothes. I'm pretty sure he thinks my face is on par with a splatterpunk movie."

"Splatterpunk movies are the best."

"Somehow I don't think he'd agree. But he ignores the fact that I'm a total swamp hag so we can collaborate. And you should do the same."

Rocío resumes walking, morose. "Does he really hate the way you look?"

"Yep. Always did."

"It's strange, then."

"What's strange?"

"He stares at you. Plenty."

"Oh, no." I laugh. "He puts a lot of effort into *not* staring at me. It's his CrossFit."

"It's the opposite. At least when you're not looking." I'm about to ask her if she's high, but she shrugs. "Whatever. If you won't support me in my hatred for Kaylee I have no choice but to call Alex and rage at him while I listen to Norwegian death metal."

I pat her back. "Sounds like the loveliest of evenings."

At home, I just want to stuff my face with peanut butter cups and send twelve @WhatWouldMarieDo tweets about the injustice of Sausage Referencing™, but I limit myself to checking my DMs. I smile when I find one from Shmac:

SHMAC: How are things?

MARIE: Weirdly, much better.

SHMAC: Did camel dick burst into flames?

MARIE: Lol, no. I do think he might be less of a camel dick than I thought. Still a dick, don't get me

wrong. But maybe not camel. Maybe he's like, idk, a
duck dick?

SHMAC: Have you ever seen a duck dick?

MARIE: No? But they're small and cute, right?

I watch the wheel spin as the picture he sends me loads. I initially
think it's a corkscrew. Then I realize that it's attached to a little feath-
ered body and—

MARIE: OMG WHAT IS THAT ABOMINATION

SHMAC: Your colleague.

MARIE: I take it back! I un-demote him! He's a camel
dick again!

MARIE: How's your girlfriend?

SHMAC: Yet again: I wish.

MARIE: How are things with her?

There's a long pause after, in which I decide to act like the motivated adult that I'm not and put on running shorts and my *Marie
Curie & The Isotopes—European Tour 1911* T-shirt.

SHMAC: A mess.

MARIE: How come?

SHMAC: I fucked things up.

MARIE: Beyond repair?

SHMAC: I think so. There's a lot of history here.

MARIE: Want to tell me?

The three dots at the base of the screen bounce for a while, so I check my Couch-to-5K app. Looks like today I need to run five minutes, walk one minute, and then run five more minutes. Sounds feasible.

Oh, who am I kidding? It sounds *harrowing*.

SHMAC: It's complicated. Part of it is that I first met her when I was younger.

MARIE: Please don't tell me you have a secret stemlord past.

SHMAC: I have an asshole past.

MARIE: How many ladies have you harassed on the internet?

SHMAC: Zero. But I did grow up in a hostile, uncommunicative environment. I was an uncommunicative person before I realized that I couldn't spend the rest of my life like that. I got therapy, which helped me figure out how to deal with feelings that are . . . overwhelming. Except every time I talk to her my brain blanks and I become the person I used to be.

MARIE: Ouch.

SHMAC: I never suspected how some of my actions came across, but in hindsight they make complete sense. Still, something she said makes me wonder if her husband told her some lies that aggravated the situation.

MARIE: You should tell her. If it were me, I'd want to know.

SHMAC: In the end it doesn't matter. She's happy with him.

I take a deep breath.

MARIE: Okay, listen. For years I thought that I was happy in a relationship with someone who turned out to be a chronic liar. And in my experience relationships that are based on lies can't last. Not in the long term. You'd be doing her a favor, if you came clean.

I don't mention to him that *all* relationships can't last. People tend to get defensive when I do. They have to figure it out on their own.

SHMAC: I'm sorry that happened to you.

MARIE: I'm sorry this is happening to you.

SHMAC: Look at us. Two sorry scientists.

MARIE: Is there any other kind?

SHMAC: Not that I know of.

My heart hurts for Shmac as I put on my sneakers. I can't even imagine how awful it must be, to be in love with a married person.

Heartbreaking situations like this vindicate the corporate mission of Bee, Inc.: keep up the Bee-fence. Never, *ever* fall for someone. If my heart gets broken again, neuroscience will be the one. It's sure to do a much cleaner job than stupid Tim, anyway. Doctor Curie would support me in this decision, I'm positive.

I spring up from the couch and venture out into the soup-like Houston air for my run.

IF I RUN at the Space Center, someone I know might see me crawl my way about, and I wouldn't wish that sight upon an innocent bystander. Google comes to my aid: there's a little cemetery about five minutes away. Reading baby names like Alford or Brockholst on gravestones might be a nice distraction from the gut-wrenching torment of exercising. I slip in my AirPods, start an Alanis Morissette album, and head that way. It's 6:43, which means that I can be home and showered in time to watch *Love Island*.

Don't judge. It's an underrated show.

Disappointingly, sitting on the couch thinking about working out has *not* improved my aerobic fitness. I realize it on minute three of my run, when I collapse in front of the tombstone of Noah F. Moore (surprisingly fitting), 1834–1902. I lie in the grass drenched in sweat, listening to my heart pound in my ears. Or maybe it's just Alanis screaming.

I'm not meant for this. And by "this" I mean using my body for anything more strenuous than reaching for my treat cupboard. Which, incidentally, is *all* my cupboards. Yes, okay: Dr. Curie bonded with her husband over their shared love of cycling and nature walks, but we can't all be like her: gentlewoman, scholar, *and* athlete.

When I notice that the sun is setting, I scrape myself off the ground, bid farewell to Noah, and start hobbling home. I'm almost back at the entrance when I notice something: there is *no* entrance. The tall gates I ran through on my way here are now closed. I try to shake them open, but no dice. I look around. The walls are too high for me to climb—because I'm five feet tall and *everything* is too high for me to climb.

I take a deep breath. This is okay. It's fine. I'm not stuck in here. If I follow the walls I'll find a shorter segment I can easily climb over.

Or not. I definitely haven't found one fifteen minutes later, when Houston's firmly in dusk territory and I have to turn on my flashlight app to see a few feet away from me. I sum up the situation in my head: I'm alone (sorry, Noah, you don't count), stuck in a cemetery after sundown, and my phone is at 20 percent. Oops.

I feel a wave of panic swell and immediately leash it. No. Down. *Bad* panic. No treats for you. I need to engage in some goal-oriented problem-solving before I can wallow in despair. What can I do?

I could yell and hope someone hears me, but what could they do? Build a makeshift rope with their belts? Hmm. Seems like a traumatic brain injury waiting to happen. Pass.

I could call 911, then. Though 911 is probably busy saving people who actually deserve to be saved. People who didn't moronically get themselves locked inside a cemetery at night. Calling someone I know would be better. I could *ask* someone to bring me a ladder. Yes, that sounds good.

I have the phone numbers of two people who currently live in Houston. The second doesn't count, because I'll sleep cradled by the slimy arms of Noah's skeleton before calling it. But that's okay, because the first is Rocío, who could ask the super for a ladder and drive here in our rental. Let's be real: cemeteries at night are her natural habitat. She'll love this immensely.

If only she bothered to answer her phone. I call her once, twice. Seven times. Then I remember that Gen Zs would rather roll around in nettles than talk on the phone, and I text her. No answer. My stupid battery is at 18 percent, mosquitos are sucking blood out of my shins, and Rocío is probably having Skype sex to a band called Thorr's Hammer.

Who else can I call? How long would it take Reike to fly here? Is it too late to ask her for the number of nose-tongue guy? What are the chances that Shmac secretly lives in Houston? Should I email Guy? But he has a kid. He might not check his email at night.

My phone is at 12 percent, and my eyes fall on the 832 number in my incoming call log. I haven't even bothered saving it. Because I thought I'd never use it.

I can't. I can't. I can't call Levi. He's probably at home, having a Stepford dinner with his wife, playing with his dog, helping his daughter with math homework. Penny of the black curls. No. I can't. He'd hate me even more. And the humiliation. He's already saved me once.

Nine percent, the world is pitch black, and I hate myself. There's no alternative. I have successfully defended a Ph.D. dissertation, overcome a depressive episode, gotten my chuncha fully waxed every month for years, and yet tapping once on Levi's number feels like the hardest thing I've ever done. Maybe I should just settle in for the night. Maybe a pack of bobcats will let me snuggle in their pile. Maybe—

"Yes?"

Oh, shit. He answered. Why did he answer? He's a millennial; we also hate talking on the—

"Hello?"

"Um, sorry. This is Bee. Königswasser. We, um, work together? At NASA?"

A pause. "I know who you are, Bee."

"Right. Yes. So . . ." I close my eyes. "I am having a bit of a problem and I was wondering if you could—"

He doesn't hesitate. "Where are you?"

"See, I'm in this little cemetery by the Space Center. Greenwood?"

"Greenforest. Are you locked in?"

"I— How do you know?"

"You're calling me from a cemetery after sundown. Cemeteries close at sundown."

That would have been a useful piece of information forty-five minutes ago. "Yeah, so . . . the walls are sort of tall, and my phone is sort of dying, and I'm sort of—"

"Go stand by the gates. Turn off the flashlight if you have it on. Don't talk to anyone you don't know. I'll be there in ten minutes." A beat. "I've got you. Don't worry, okay?"

He hangs up before I can tell him to bring a ladder. And, come to think of it, before I can ask him to come rescue me.

9

MEDIAL FRONTAL CORTEX:
MAYBE I WAS WRONG?

THE SECOND LEVI appears I want to kiss him for rescuing me
from the mosquitos, and the ghosts, and the ghosts of the mosquitos.
I also want to kill him for witnessing the extent of the humiliation of
Bee Königswasser, human disaster. What can I say? I contain multitudes.

He steps out of an oil-guzzling truck that I sadly have no right to
complain about anymore, surveys the wall, and comes to stand on the
other side of the gate. To his credit, if he's smirking he's doing it on
the inside. His expression is neutral when he asks, "You okay?"

Does thoroughly mortified count as okay? Let's say: "Yeah."

"Good. This is what we're going to do: I'll slide in the ladder
through the gates, and you'll use it to get on top of the wall. I'll be
on the other side to catch you."

I frown. He sounds very . . . in charge. Self-assured. Not that he usually doesn't, but it's having a new . . . effect on me. Oh my God. Am I a damsel in distress?

"How will we retrieve the ladder?"

"I'll drive by tomorrow morning and pick it up."

"What if someone steals it?"

"I'll have lost a precious heirloom passed down my family for generations."

"Really?"

"No. Ready?"

I'm not, but it doesn't matter. He lifts the ladder like it's a feather and slides it through the gate. It feels a little less-than-cool when I find that it's so heavy, I can barely hold it upright. I tell myself that I have other talents as he has to patiently guide me through the process of releasing the catches and setting the safety mechanism. He must notice how annoying I find being coached, because he says, "At least you know about the angular gyrus."

I turn to hiss at him, but stop when I see his expression. Is he teasing me *again*? For the *second* time? In *a day*?

Whatever. I climb up, which proves to be a nice distraction. Because you know how I mentioned that my body likes to faint? Well. Heights make it like to faint *even more*. I'm halfway to the top, and my head starts spinning. I clutch the sidebars and take a deep breath. I can do this. I can maintain normal blood pressure without passing out. I'm not even that high up. Here, if I look down I can—

"Don't," Levi orders.

I turn to him. I'm a few inches taller, and he looks even more handsome from this angle. God, I hate him. And myself. "Don't what?"

"Don't look down. It'll be worse."

How does he even know that—

"Look up. Take one step after the other, slowly. Yes, good." I don't know if his advice works, or if my blood pressure naturally spikes when I'm told what to do, but I make it to the top without crumpling like a sack of potatoes. At which point I realize that the worst is yet ahead. "Just lower yourself from the edge," Levi says. He's standing right below me, arms raised to catch me, his head a few inches from my dangling feet.

"Jesus." Forget fainting. I'm about to barf. "What if you don't catch me? What if I'm too heavy? What if we both fall? What if I break your neck?"

"I will, you're obviously not, we won't, and you won't. Come on, Bee," he says patiently. "Just close your eyes."

See? This is what you get yourself into when you work out. Stay in the safe harbor of your couch, kids.

"You ready?" he asks encouragingly. Trust falls. With Levi Ward-ass. God, when did this become my life? Dr. Curie, please watch out for me.

I let myself go. For a second I'm suspended in air, sure that I'll splatter Humpty-Dumpty style. Then strong fingers close around my waist, and I'm in Levi's arms for the second time in ten days. I must have pushed from the wall a little too forcefully, because we end up closer than I intended. My front rubs against him as he lowers me to the ground, and I feel everything. *Everything.* The hard muscles of his shoulders under my hands. The heat of his flesh through the shirt. The way his belt bites into my abdomen. The dangerous tingling in my lower belly as he— What? *No.*

I step back. This is Levi Ward. A married man. A father. A camel dick. What am I even thinking?

"Are you okay?"

I nod, flustered. "Thank you for getting here so quickly."

He looks away. He may be flushing. "You're welcome."

"I'm so sorry to disrupt your evening. I tried to call Rocío, but she was . . . I'm not sure where."

"I'm glad you called me."

Is he? I seriously doubt it. "Anyway, thank you so much. How can I return the favor? Can I pay for gas?"

He shakes his head. "I'll drive you home."

"Oh, there's no need. I'm just five minutes away."

"It's pitch black and there are no sidewalks." He holds the passenger door open, and I have no choice but to get in. Whatever. I can survive one more minute in close proximity with him.

The inside of his truck is pristine *and* smells good—not something I believed possible—with a handful of Lärabars in the back that make my stomach cramp with hunger, and a half-full Camel-Bak that I'd risk his germs for. He also drives a stick shift. Hmph. Show-off.

"You're staying at the lodging facilities, right?"

I nod, pulling at the hem of my shorts. I don't like how high they ride when I sit. Not that Levi would ever voluntarily look at my thighs, but I'm a bit self-conscious, since Tim used to make fun of me for being bowlegged. And Annie would defend me, growl at him that my legs were perfect and his opinion was unnecessary, and I would—

The truck starts. A familiar voice fills the cabin, but Levi quickly switches to NPR. I blink. The anchor is talking about mail-in ballots. "Was that . . . Pearl Jam?"

"Yeah."

"*Vitalogy?*"

"Yep."

Humph. Pearl Jam's not my favorite, but it's good, and I hate that

Levi likes good music. I need him to love Dave Matthews Band. To stan the Insane Clown Posse. To have a Nickelback tramp stamp. It's what I deserve.

"What were you doing in a cemetery?" he asks.

"Just . . . running."

"You run?" He sounds surprised. Offensively so.

"Hey, I know I look like a wimp, but—"

"You don't," he interjects. "Look like a wimp, I mean. Just, in grad school you . . ."

I turn to him. The corner of his mouth is curving upward. "I what?"

"Once you said that time spent working out is time one never gets back."

I have no memories of saying that. Especially to Levi, since we exchanged approximately twelve words at Pitt. Though it *does* sound like something I'd say. "As it turns out, the higher your aerobic fitness, the healthier your hippocampus. Not to mention the over-all connectivity of your Default Mode Network and multiple axon bundles, so . . ." I shrug. "I find myself resentfully acknowledging that according to science, exercise is a good thing." He chuckles. Crow's-feet crinkle the corners of his eyes, and it makes me want to continue. Not that I care about making him laugh. Why would I? "I'm doing this Couch-to-5K program, but . . . ew."

"Ew?"

"Ew."

His smile widens a millimeter. "How long's the program?"

"Four weeks."

"How long have you been on it?"

"Couple weeks."

"What distance are you up to?"

". . . Point two miles. I hit the wall. On, um, minute three." He gives me a skeptical glance. "To be fair, this is only my second time running since I was in middle school."

"The heat here is terrible. You might want to run in the morning. But you're not a morning person, right?" He bites his lip pensively. I wonder how he could possibly know that, and realize that sadly, one needs only to take a look at me before eleven a.m. "There's a gym in the Space Center you should have access to."

"I checked. It's not free for contractors, and I'm not sure the health of my nervous system is worth seventy bucks a month." Ari Shapiro is asking a correspondent about some Facebook lawsuit. "You run 5Ks?" I ask.

"No."

My eyes narrow. "Is it because you only run marathons and above?"

"I . . ." He hesitates, looking sheepish. "I run half marathons, sometimes."

"Well, then," I say conversationally as he pulls into the parking lot, "thank you very much for the rescue and the ride, but I need to be alone so I can hate you in peace now."

He laughs again. Why does it sound so nice? "Hey, I struggle with running, too."

I'm sure he does. Around mile thirty-four or so. "Well, thanks. It's the second time you saved me." *Despite the fact that we're nemeses.* Outstanding, huh?

"The second?"

"Yeah." I release the seat belt. "The other time was at work. When I was almost . . . pancaked?"

"Ah." Something jumps in his jaw at the mention. "Yeah."

"Well, have a great night." I pat my pockets. "Apologies for—" I pat some more. Then I twist around in the seat, inspect it for something that might have slipped out, and find nothing. It's as pristine as when I got in. "Uh . . ."

"What's going on?"

"I—" I close my eyes, trying to remember my day. I put on shorts. Put my keys into the pocket. Felt them bounce against my leg while I was running, up until . . . Shit. I think they fell out when I collapsed on the grave. "Damn you, Noah Moore," I mutter.

"What?"

"I think I left my keys in the cemetery." I groan. "Shit, the super leaves at seven." Jesus, what's wrong with this day? I bite my lower lip, rifling through options. I could sleep on Rocío's couch and go pick up my keys first thing in the morning. Of course, I'm not sure where Rocío is, or whether she'll come to the door. The fact that my phone is at 4 percent does not—

I startle when Levi starts the truck again. "Oh, thanks, but there's no need to go back to the cemetery. I wouldn't know how to get in, and—"

"I'm not taking you to the cemetery." He's not looking at me. "Fasten your seat belt."

"What?"

"Fasten your seat belt," he repeats.

I do, confused. "Where are we going?"

"Home."

"Whose home?"

"My home."

My jaw drops. I must have misheard. "What?"

"You need a place to stay, no?"

"Yeah, but—Rocío's couch. Or I'll call a locksmith. I can't come to your house."

"Why?"

"Because," I say, sounding like a shrill twelve-year-old. Why is he being so nice all of a sudden? Does he feel guilty for not telling me about the NASA mess? Well, he should. But I'd rather sleep under a bridge and eat plankton than go to his place and see his perfect family life. Nothing personal, but the envy would gut me. And I can't meet his wife smelling like dirty socks and graveyard. Who knows what Levi already told her about me? "You probably have plans for the evening."

"I don't."

"And I'd put you out."

"You wouldn't."

"Plus, you hate me."

He briefly closes his eyes in exasperation, which worries me. He's driving, after all. "Is there any nonimaginary reason you don't want to stay at my place, Bee?" he asks with a sigh.

"I . . . It's very nice of you to offer, but I don't feel comfortable."

That gets through to him. His hands tighten on the wheel and he says calmly, "If you don't feel safe around me, I absolutely respect that. I'll drive you back to your place. But I'm not going to leave until I'm sure that you have a secure place to—"

"What? No. I feel safe around you." As I say it, I realize how true it is, and how rare for me. There's often a constant undercurrent of threat when I'm alone with men I don't know very well. The other night Guy came by my office to chat, and even though he's never been anything but nice, I couldn't stop glancing at the door. But Levi's different, which is odd, especially considering that our interactions have always been antagonistic. And especially considering that he's built like a Victorian mansion. "It's not that."

"Then . . . ?"

I close my eyes and let my head fall back against the headrest. There's no way I'm going to be able to avoid this, is there? Might as well lean in to the clusterfuck.

"Then, thank you," I say, trying not to sound as dejected as I feel. "I'd love to stay with you tonight, if it's not too much trouble."

THE SECOND I see Levi's house I want to burn it down with a flamethrower. Because it's perfect.

To be fair, it's a totally normal house. But it perfectly matches my ideal, which, to be fair again, is not particularly lofty. My lifelong dream is a pretty brick home in the suburbs, a family with two point five children, and a yard to grow butterfly-friendly plants. I'm pretty sure a psychoanalyst would say that it has to do with the nomadic lifestyle of my formative years. I'm a stability slut, what can I say?

Of course, when I say "lifelong dream" I mean until a couple of years ago. Once I realized how life-alteringly cruel humans can be, I scrapped the family part from the dream. The house lingers, though, at least according to the pang in my heart when Levi pulls up the driveway. First thing I notice: he grows hummingbird mint in his garden—nature's hummingbird feeder, and my favorite plant. Grrr. Second: there are no cars in the driveway. Weird. But some lights inside are on, so maybe his wife's is just in the garage. Yeah, that's probably it.

I jump out of the truck—which is unjustly tall—with already-sore muscles and already-itchy legs. "Are you sure this is okay?"

He gives me a silent look that seems to mean *Haven't we been over this seven times already?* and leads me up his driveway, where we're surrounded by a delightful amount of fireflies. I'm *explosively* jealous of this place. And I'm about to meet Levi's significant other, who probably has a nickname for me, her husband's ugly former lab mate. Something like FrankenBee. Or Beezilla. Wait, those nicknames are actually pretty cute. I hope for their sake that they came up with something meaner.

The inside of the house is silent, and I wonder if the family is already asleep. "Should I be quiet?" I whisper.

He gives me a puzzled look. "If you want," he says at regular volume. Maybe the walls are soundproof?

Either Levi is a very strict dad, or he and his wife are pros at picking up after their kid. The house is immaculate and sparsely furnished, no toys or clutter in sight. There are some engineering journals, a handful of sci-fi posters on the walls, and an open Asimov book on the coffee table—one of my favorite authors. How is this man I hate surrounded by everything I love? It's the ultimate mindfuck.

"There are three unused bedrooms upstairs. You can pick the one you like best." *Three* unused bedrooms? How big is this house? "One's technically my office, but the couch pulls out. Do you want to shower?"

"Shower?"

"I didn't mean to—" He looks flustered. "If you want to. Because you ran. You don't have to. I don't mean to imply that—"

"That I smell like the sweaty crotch of a trout?"

"Uh . . ."

"That I'm as dirty as a gas station restroom?"

He's *definitely* flustered, and I laugh. The blush makes him almost endearing. "Don't worry. I smell gross and I'd love a shower."

He swallows and nods. "You'll have to use my en suite. Soap and towels are in there."

But isn't his wife—?

"I can wash and dry your clothes if you want. Give you something of mine in the meantime. Though I don't have anything that will fit. You're very . . ." He clears his throat. "Small."

Wait a minute—is he divorced? Is that why he doesn't wear a ring? But then he wouldn't have pics of his wife in his office, would he? Oh my God, is she dead? No, Guy would have told me. Or would he?

"You have an iPhone, right?" He exits the living room and comes back holding out a charger. "Here you go."

I don't take it. I just stare up at his irritatingly handsome face, and—God, this is driving me *nuts*. "Listen," I say, perhaps more aggressively than I should, "I know it's rude, but I'm too weirded out not to, so I'm just going to ask you right out." I take a deep breath. "*Where* is your family?"

He shrugs, still holding out the charger. "It's not rude. My parents are in Dallas. My eldest brother lives on the Air Force base in Vegas, and the other recently deployed to Belgium—"

"Not *that* family. Your *other* family."

His head tilts. "Does my father have a secret family you want to tell me about, or . . . ?"

"No. Your kid, where is she?"

"My what?" He squints at me.

"There's a picture of her in your office," I say weakly. "And Guy told me you two babysit together."

"Ah." He shakes his head with a smile. "Penny's not my kid. But she gave me that picture. She made the frame in school."

She's not his— *Oh*. "You're with her mother, then?"

"No. Lily and I dated briefly ages ago, but now we're friends. She's a teacher, and a single mother for the past year. Sometimes I'll watch Penny for her, or drop her off at school if she's running late. Stuff like that."

Oh. "Oh." Boy, do I love feeling like an idiot. "So you live . . . alone?"

He nods. And then his eyes widen and he takes a step back. "Oh. I see."

"See what?"

"Why you asked. I'm sorry, I didn't even think that you might feel unsafe sleeping here if it's just the two of us. I will—"

"Oh, no." I take a step forward to reassure him. "I asked because I was curious. Honestly, it seemed incredibly weird to me that you—" I realize what I'm about to say and snap my jaw shut before I continue. Levi's not fooled.

"Were you shocked that someone would marry me?" he asks, biting back a smile.

Yup. "Not at all! You're smart. And, um, tall. Still have all your hair. And I'm sure that with women you don't hate you're nicer than you have historically been with me!"

"Bee, I don't—" He exhales hard. "Get in the truck."

"Why?"

"I'm driving you back to the cemetery and feeding you to the coyotes."

"*Historically*," I hurry to say. "You've been nice to me today! You saved me from a zombie attack, for sure. And from Fred and Mark!"

He frowns. "I'm not sure what's wrong with them."

"Lots of misogyny's my guess." I debate whether continuing. Then I think: fuck it. "Also, it doesn't help that your team is exclusively male and almost exclusively white."

I expect him to contradict me. Instead he says, "You're right. It's appalling."

"You chose the members."

He shakes his head. "I inherited the team from my predecessor."

"Oh?"

"The only new hire I made was Kaylee." He sighs. "I officially reprimanded Mark. His behavior today is in his file. And I called a team meeting this afternoon, in which I reiterated that you are co-leader and that what you say goes. If anything like today ever happens again, let me know. I'll deal with it. Come, I'll find you something to wear."

I'm a little shell-shocked that he called a meeting to officially Sausage Reference™ me, so I follow him without questions. The upstairs area is just as pretty as the first floor, but with more personality. I spot a vinyl player and CDs, pictures on the walls, even some Pitt swag I recognize from my own apartment. His bedroom, though . . . his bedroom is magic. Something out of a catalog. It's a corner room with two large windows, wooden furniture, ceiling-high bookshelves, and, in the middle of the king-sized bed, sleeping softly on top of the comforter . . .

"Are you allergic to cats?" he asks, rummaging through a drawer.

I shake my head, then remember that he's not looking at me. "No."

"Schrödinger's probably going to leave you alone, anyway. He's old and grumpy."

Schrödinger! "I thought you hated cats."

He turns with a confused look. "Why?"

"I don't know. You seemed a bit hostile toward *my* cat today."

"You mean, your cat that doesn't exist?"

"Félicette exists! I have literally wiped boogers from her eyes, so—"

"Félicette?"

I press my lips together. "It's the name of the first cat in space."

He lifts one eyebrow. "And you named your imaginary cat after her. I see."

I roll my eyes and drop the topic. There's nothing I want more than to pet the black ball of fur curled on the bed, but Levi's holding out a white V-neck T-shirt and . . .

"How offended would you be if I offered you boxers a friend gave me as a joke? They're very small, I don't think I've ever worn them."

"Is that . . . flamingoes?"

His cheeks redden. "The size isn't the only reason I never wear them. Also, you might want this." It's a tube of itch-relief cream.

"Thanks. How did you know?"

He shrugs, still a little flushed. "You've been scratching your legs a lot."

"Yeah, bugs love me." I roll my eyes. "My ex used to say that he only kept me around as a decoy for mosquitos." Looking back to Tim's behaviors, it probably wasn't even a joke.

Ten minutes later I make my way downstairs, hair wet and pine scented, reflecting that out of all the implausible roller coasters of events that have befallen me in the past weeks, the weirdest is knowing that Levi and I use the same deodorant. What can I say? Men's products are cheaper, smell better, and block my BO more effectively. Not sure how I feel about the fact that Levi's armpits and mine have similar needs, but I'm going to let that slide.

The kitchen, which is cozy and surprisingly well-equipped, smells like the most delicious meal I've never had. Levi works at the stove, his back to me, and I'm reasonably sure that he's wearing the same shirt I have on in a different color. Except that it fits him perfectly. On me it looks like a circus tent.

"Food will be . . ." he starts, and then stops when he turns around and sees me in the room.

I grab two fistfuls of my shirt and pretend to curtsy. "Thank you for this gown, my good sir."

"You're . . ." He sounds hoarse. "You're welcome. Food will be ready in five minutes."

I wince as he turns back to the pans and pots. There's no way he cooked without meat and dairy. God, why is he being so damn nice? "Thank you, but . . ." I pad to the stove. He's making tacos. Ugh. I love tacos. "You didn't have to."

"I was going to make myself dinner anyway."

"It's really kind of you to offer, but I doubt I can eat . . ." I stop when my eyes fall to the filling. It's not meat, but portobello mushrooms. Beside a jar of dairy-free sour cream, and a bag of shredded plant-based cheddar.

My eyes narrow. On impulse, I push on my toes and open the cabinet closest to me. I find quinoa, agar powder, and maple syrup. In the next one there are nuts, seeds, a package of dates. I scowl harder and move to the fridge, which looks like a richer, better version of mine. Almond milk, tofu, fruits and vegetables, coconut-based yogurts, miso paste. Oh my God.

Oh. My. God.

"He's a vegan," I mutter to myself.

"He is."

I look up. Levi is staring at me with a puzzled, patient expression, and I have no idea how to tell him that this is, like, the *tenth* thing we have in common. Sci-fi and cats and science and obviously men's deodorants and who knows what else. It's so incredibly upsetting to *me*, I can't even imagine how much *he'd* hate it if he knew. I toy with the idea of telling him, but he doesn't deserve it. He's been very nice today. Instead I just clear my throat. "Um, me too."

"I figured. When you . . . scolded me. About the donut."

"Oh, *God*. I'd forgotten about that." I bury my face in my hands. "I'm sorry. So sorry. Believe it or not, I'm usually not a deranged asshole who scares her colleagues away from plant-based products."

"It's fine."

I massage my temple. "In my defense, you drive the least environmentally friendly vehicle."

"It's a Ford F-150. Pretty friendly, actually."

"Is it?" I wince. "Well, in *another* defense of mine, weren't you a hunter back in grad school?"

His shoulders stiffen imperceptibly. "My entire family hunts, and I've gone on more hunting trips than I'd have liked as a teen. Before I could say no."

"That sounds awful." He shrugs, but it looks a little forced. "Okay. I guess I have no defense at all. I'm just an asshole."

He smiles. "I didn't know you were a vegan, either. I remember Tim bringing you meat lunches back at Pitt."

"Yeah." I roll my eyes. "Tim was of the school of thought that I was being stubborn and that a taste of meat would convert me back to a regular diet." I laugh at Levi's appalled expression. "Yeah. He'd sneak non-vegan stuff into my food all the time. He was *the worst* back then. Anyway, how long have you been a vegan?"

"Twenty years, give or take."

"Ooh. Which animal was it for you?"

He knows exactly what I mean. "A goat. In a cheese commercial. She looked so . . . cogent."

I nod somberly. "It must have been very emotional."

"Sure was for my parents. We fought over whether white meat is really meat for the better part of a decade." He hands me a plate, gesturing for me to fill it. "What about you?"

"A chicken. Really cute. He'd sometimes sit next to me and lean against my side. Until . . . yeah."

He sighs. "Yeah."

Five minutes later, sitting in a breakfast nook I'd literally give my pinkie to own, plates full of delicious food and imported beer in front of us, something occurs to me: I've been here for one hour and I haven't felt uneasy—not once. I was fully ready to spend the night pretending to be in my happy place (with Dr. Curie under a blooming cherry tree in Nara, Japan), but Levi has made things weirdly . . . easy for me.

"Hey," I say before he can take a bite of his tacos, "thank you for today. It can't be easy, to be so welcoming to someone you don't particularly get along with or like, or to have them stay in your house."

He closes his eyes, like every other time I mention the obvious fact that there's no love lost between us (he is surprisingly truth-averse). But when he opens them, he holds my gaze. "You're right. It's not easy. But not for any reason you think."

I frown, meaning to ask him what exactly he means by that, but he beats me to it.

"Eat up, Bee," he orders gently.

I'm starving, so I do just that.

10

DORSOLATERAL PREFRONTAL CORTEX: UNTRUTHS

"I'M GOING TO switch off your speech center, now."

Guy looks up from under his eyelashes with a defeated sigh. "Man, I hate it when people do that."

I laugh. Guy's the third astronaut I've tested this morning. He works on BLINK, so we weren't originally planning to map his brain, but someone pulled out of the pilot group last minute. Brain stimulation is tricky business: it's complicated to predict how neurons will respond, and even harder in people who have a history of epilepsy or electric misfiring. Just drinking a cup of strong coffee can mess up brain chemistry enough to make a well-consolidated stimulation protocol dangerous. When we found out that one of the astronauts we selected had a history of seizures, we decided to give his spot to Guy. Guy was *ecstatic*.

"I'm going to target your Broca's area," I tell him.

"Ah, yes. The famed Broca's area." He nods knowingly.

I smile. "That would be your left posterior-inferior frontal gyrus. I'll stimulate it with trains up to twenty-five hertz."

"Without even buying me dinner first?" He clucks his tongue.

"To see whether it's working, I'll need you to talk. You can recite a poem, free-style it, doesn't matter." The other astronauts I tested today chose a Shakespeare sonnet and the Pledge of Allegiance.

"Whatever I want?"

I position the stimulation coil one inch from his ear. "Yep."

"Very well, then." He clears his throat. *"My loneliness is killing me and I, I must confess I still believe—"*

I laugh, like everyone else in the room. Including Levi, who appears to be fairly close to Guy. It speaks highly of him (Guy, not Levi; I refuse to speak highly of Levi), considering he probably should have been BLINK's leader. Guy doesn't seem to mind, at least judging by the chummy chat they had over some sportsball game's lineup while I was setting up my equipment.

". . . *my loneliness is killing me and I, I must c—"* Guy frowns. "Sorry, *I must c—"* He frowns harder. *"Must c—"* he sputters one last time, blinking fast. I turn to Rocío, who's taking notes. "Speech arrest at MNI coordinates minus thirty-eight, sixteen, fifty."

The ensuing applause is unnecessary, but a tiny bit welcome. Earlier this morning, when the entire engineering team dragged their feet to the neurostimulation lab to observe my first brain mapping session, it was obvious that they'd rather be pretty much anywhere else. It was equally obvious that Levi had instructed them not to say so much as a peep about their total lack of interest.

They're good guys. They *tried* to fake it. Sadly, there's a reason that in high school, engineers tend to gravitate toward the robotics shop instead of drama club.

Thankfully, neuroscience has a way of defending her own honor. I just had to pick up my coil and show a few tricks. With stimulation at the right spot and frequency, decorated astronauts with IQs well into the triple digits and drawers full of graduate diplomas can temporarily forget how to count ("Woah! Is that for real?"), or move their fingers ("Freaky!"), or recognize the faces of people they work with every day ("Bee, how are you even doing that?"), and, of course, how to speak ("This is the coolest thing I've ever seen in my entire damn life."). Brain stimulation kicks ass, and anyone who says otherwise shall know her wrath. Which is why the lab is still crammed. The engineers were supposed to leave after the first demonstration but decided to stick around . . . indefinitely, it seems.

It's nice to convert a bunch of skeptics to the wonders of neuroscience. I wonder if Dr. Curie felt the same when she shared her love for ionizing radiation. Of course in her case, long-term unshielded exposure to unstable isotopes eventually led to chronic aplastic anemia and death in a sanatorium, but . . . you get my point. Which is that when I say, "I think I got all I need from Guy. We're done for today," the room erupts into a disappointed groan. Levi and I exchange an amused look.

To be clear: we're not friends or anything. One dinner together, one night sleeping in a room that happens to contain three-quarters of my favorite books, and one yawny car ride to Noah Moore's grave, during which he politely respected that I'm not a morning person and remained blissfully quiet, did *not* make Levi and me friends. We still dislike each other, rue the day we met, wish the pox on the other's house, etc., etc. But it's like last week, over vegan tacos, we managed to form an uneasy, rudimentary alliance. I help him do his thing, and he helps me do mine.

It almost feels like we're actually collaborating. Crazy, huh?

For lunch, I heat up my ever-so-sad Lean Cuisine, grab a stack of academic articles I've been meaning to read, and make my way to the picnic tables behind the building. I've been nibbling on chickpeas for about five minutes when I hear a familiar voice.

"Bee!" Guy and Levi are walking toward me, holding paper cups and sandwich bags. "Mind if we join you?" Guy asks.

I do a little, since this paper on electrotherapy isn't going to read itself, but I shake my head. I shoot Levi an apologetic look (*Sorry you're stuck eating with me because Guy doesn't know that we're arch-enemies*), but he doesn't seem to get it and takes a seat across from me, smiling faintly as though he doesn't mind. I watch the play of muscles under his shirt, and a frisson of warmth licks down my spine.

Hmm. Weird.

Guy sits next to me with a grin, and I think to myself, not for the first time, that he's wholesome, charming, and truly a Cute Guy™.

This is incredibly objectifying and reductive, and if you tell anyone I'll flatly deny it, but back in grad school Annie told me that there are three types of attractive men. I don't know if she came up with this taxonomy herself, if Aphrodite announced it to her in a dream, or if she stole it from *Teen Vogue*, but here they are:

There is the cute type, which consists of guys who are attractive in a nonthreatening, accessible way, as a combination of their nice looks and captivating personalities. Tim falls into this group, just like Guy and most male scientists—including, I suspect, Pierre Curie. Come to think of it, all the guys who ever hit on me do, perhaps because I'm small, and dress quirky, and try to be friendly. If I were a dude, I'd be a Cute Guy™; Cute Guys™ recognize that at some elemental level, and they make passes at me.

Then there's the handsome type. According to Annie, this category is a bit of a waste. The Handsome Guy™ has the kind of face you see in movie trailers and perfume ads, geometrically perfect and objectively amazing, but there's something inaccessible about him. Those guys are so dreamy, they're almost abstract. They need something to anchor them to reality—a personality quirk, a flaw, a circumscribed interest—otherwise they'll float away in a bubble of boredom. Of course, society doesn't exactly encourage Handsome Guys™ to develop brilliant personalities, so I tend to concur with Annie: they're useless.

Last but not least, the Sexy Guys™. Annie would go on and on about how Levi is the epitome of the Sexy Guy™, but I'd like to formally object. In fact, I don't even acknowledge the existence of this category. It's preposterous, the idea that there are men you can't help yourself from being attracted to. Men who give you the tingles, men you can't stop thinking about, men who pop up in your brain like flashes of light after stimulation of the occipital cortex. Men who are physical, elemental, primordial. Masculine. Present. Solid. Sounds fake, right?

"Hit me," Guy tells me with a Cute Guy™ smile. "What's wrong with my brain?"

"Nothing, as far as I can tell."

"Amazing news. Could you help me convince my ex-wife that I'm certifiably sane?"

"I'll write you a note."

"Nice." He winks at me. He winks at me a lot, I'm noticing. "So, how are you liking Houston?"

"I haven't really seen much yet. Besides the Space Center."

"And a cemetery," Levi interjects. I give him a dirty look and steal a cluster of his grapes in revenge. He lets me with a small smile.

"I could help you out," Guy offers.

"Sure," I say distractedly, busy glaring at Levi and making a show of chewing on his grapes.

"Really?"

"Uh-huh."

Levi lifts one eyebrow and bites into his sandwich. It feels a lot like a challenge, so I steal a strawberry, too.

"Maybe we could go to dinner," Guy says. "Are you free tomorrow night?"

Levi and I instantly turn toward him. I mentally rewind the conversation, trying to recall what I agreed to. A date? Exploring Houston? *Marriage?*

No. No, no, *no.* I have zero interest in dating, zero interest in Guy, and subzero interest in dating Guy. You know what I *do* have? Weird, intrusive thoughts. For instance, I'm currently remembering the way Levi's hands felt around my waist as he slid me down his body. "Um, I . . ."

"Or this weekend?"

"Oh." I give Levi a panicked glance. *Help. Please help.* "Thanks, um, but actually I . . ."

"Just name the night. I'm flexible and—"

"Guy," Levi says, voice deep and low. "You might want to take a look at her left hand."

I glance down, confused. My fingers are still clutching the strawberry. What does he— Oh. My grandmother's wedding ring. I put it on this morning. Some good luck for the brain mapping sessions.

"Shit, I'm sorry," Guy immediately apologizes. "I had no idea that you—"

"Oh, it's fine. I'm not . . ." *Married*, I want to say, but it would be a waste of the amazing out Levi gave me. I cough. "I'm not bothered."

"Okay. My apologies, again." He leans toward Levi, asking with a conspiratorial tone, "Out of curiosity, how big's her husband? And how prone to violent rage?"

"Oh, no." I shake my head. "He doesn't really . . ." *exist.*

"Don't worry," Levi tells Guy. "Tim's mild mannered."

I face-palm internally. I can't believe Levi told Guy that I'm married to Tim. It's the worst, most easily disprovable lie ever. Couldn't he make up a random dude?

"Should I still get a groin protection cup?" Guy asks.

Levi shrugs. "Might be safest."

I look down at my chickpeas, wishing they were Levi's lunch. Fruit's so much better. *Believable lies* are so much better.

"You sure you're not mad, Bee?" Guy asks, a touch concerned. "I didn't mean to make you uncomfortable."

This is what I get for asking The Wardass for help. I give Levi the stink eye, snatch another strawberry, and sigh. "Nope. Not mad at all."

REIKE: What do you mean, Levi lied and said you're married to Tim???

BEE: He saw how flustered I was and tried to help me out.

REIKE: First: Guy Fieri has no business putting you in that position.

BEE: NOT his name!

BEE: But valid point.

REIKE: Second: this is a terrible lie, easily refutable if Guy Fieri talks with literally anyone else who knows you. It's going to bite you in the ass.

BEE: I am aware.

REIKE: Third: Levi does know you're not married to Tim, right?

BEE: Yeah. He and Tim are buds, they collaborate. Levi was the one who told Tim to find someone better back in grad school.

REIKE: Honestly, you should have just told Guy Fieri no. You screwed up.

BEE: I know but you're my sister and I'm human I NEED LOVE AND COMPASSION NOT JUDGMENT

REIKE: You need a full psychiatric evaluation.

REIKE: But 🖤🖤🖤

I sip on a blueberry smoothie and look around the busy coffee shop, waiting for Rocío to show up for our first GRE tutoring session.

It's probably going to be fine. My marital life (or lack thereof) is unlikely to come up with Guy. And I have other things to think about. Like the stimulation protocols I'm creating. Or income inequality. Or the fact that I haven't seen Félicette in a while, but I think she's been eating the little treats I left for her in my office. Important stuff.

"Did you know," Rocío greets me, sliding into the chair across from me, "that blood is the perfect substitute for eggs?" I blink. She takes it as an invitation to continue. "Sixty-five grams per egg. Exceedingly similar protein composition."

". . . Interesting." Not.

"You could have blood cake. Blood ice cream. Blood meringues. Blood pappardelle. Blood pound cake. Blood omelet or, if you prefer, scrambled blood. Blood tiramisu. Blood quiche—"

"I think I got the gist."

"Good." She smiles. "I wanted to let you know. Just in case blood is vegan."

I open my mouth to point out several things, but settle on, "Thank you, Ro. Very thoughtful of you. Why's your hair wet? Please don't say 'blood.'"

"I went to the gym. I like to channel Ophelia in the lazy river, pretend I'm drowning in a Danish brook after a flimsy willow branch collapsed under my weight."

"What was she doing on a willow?"

"She was *mad*. For *love*." Rocío glares at me. "And they say a woman's heart is fickle."

Right. "Sounds like a nice pool."

"It's like a Sir John Everett Millais painting. Except that swim caps are mandatory and medieval dresses forbidden. Fascists."

"Hmm. Maybe I should buy the membership after all."

"You don't need to, it's free for NASA employees."

"But not for contractors, right?"

"They didn't make me pay." She shrugs and pulls a GRE prep book out of her backpack. "Can we start with quantitative reasoning? Though parallelograms make me want to drown myself in a Danish brook. Again."

Half an hour later, the reason my intelligent, math-savvy, articulate RA has been scoring so poorly on the GRE becomes unmistakably clear: this test is too dumb for her. In related news: we're about to murder each other.

"The correct answer is B," I repeat, seriously considering ripping a page off the book and stuffing it into her mouth. "You don't need to solve for other options. X is a factor of y squared—"

"You're assuming that X is an integer. What if it's a rational number? A real number? Or, even worse, an irrational number?"

"I guarantee you that X is not an irrational number," I hiss.

"How do you know?" she growls.

"Common sense!"

"Common sense is for people who are not smart enough to solve for pi."

"Are you implying that—"

"Hey, girls!"

"*What?*" we bark in unison. Kaylee blinks at us from above a very pink drink.

"I didn't mean to interrupt—"

"No, no." I smile reassuringly. "Sorry, we got carried away. We're having some . . . issues." She's wearing a purple jumpsuit and heart-shaped sunglasses, and her hair is pulled over her shoulder into a fishtail braid that reaches her rib cage. Her purse is shaped like a watermelon, and her necklace is a pink flower with the letter *K* in its middle.

I want to be her.

"Aw." She tilts her head. "Can I help?" There is something earnest about the way she asks, like she actually cares.

I ignore Rocío's kicks under the table and ask Kaylee, "Would you like to join us in fighting the hegemony of the Graduate Record Examination?"

I'm not sure what reaction I expected, but Kaylee huffing, eye-rolling, and pulling a chair up to our table was *not* it. "It's an indignity. GRE, SATs, all these tests are institutionalized gatekeepers, and the extent to which graduate programs over-rely on them for student admission is obscene. We are two decades into the twenty-first century, but we're still using a test based on a conceptualization of intelligence that's about as outdated as the Triassic. Graduate school success depends on qualities that are not measured by the GRE—we all know it. Why aren't we moving toward a holistic approach to graduate admission? Also, the GRE costs *hundreds* of dollars! Who has the financial solubility for that? Or for the prep courses, the materials, the tutors? Let me tell you who doesn't: *not-rich people.*" She wags her finger at me, precise and wildly graceful. I am mesmerized. "You know who traditionally does poorly on standardized tests?

Women and marginalized individuals. It's a self-fulfilling prophecy: groups that are constantly told by society that they're less smart walk into a testing situation anxious as hell and end up underperforming. It's called Stereotype Threat, and there's tons of literature on that. Just like there's tons of literature showing that the GRE does a terrible job at predicting who'll finish grad school. But the heads of graduate admission all over the country don't care and persist in using an instrument made to elevate rich white men." She shakes out her hair. "Burn it down, I say."

"Burn . . . what down?"

"*All of it*," Kaylee says fiercely with her high-pitched voice. Then she sucks a delicate sip from her straw. I *really* want to be her.

I glance at Rocío and do a double take. She's staring at Kaylee, breathing quickly, lips parted and cheeks flushed. Her right hand clutches the prep book like it's the edge of a ravine. "You okay, Ro?" I ask her. She nods without breaking her stare.

"Anyway," Kaylee continues with a shrug, "why are we talking about the GRE?"

"Rocío is taking it, and I was helping her out. With"—I clear my throat—"mixed results. I believe we were about to shank each other over irrational numbers?"

"Sounds about right," Rocío mumbles.

"Oh"—Kaylee waves her hand airily—"you shouldn't be talking about irrational numbers. The thing about the GRE is, the less you know the better off you are." I give Rocío my best *told you so* look. She kicks me again. "If you take a prep class, they teach you little tricks useful to pass the test—more so than actually knowing math."

"You've taken the GRE?" Rocío asks.

"Yep. This manager thing is a temporary gig—I'm starting my Ph.D. in education in the fall. At Johns Hopkins."

Rocío frowns. "You're . . . going to Johns Hopkins?"

"Yes!" Kaylee nods happily. "My parents paid for a prep course, and I have tons of notes. Plus I remember most of it. Why don't I help you?"

Rocío turns to me with an aghast look that almost makes me laugh. *Almost*. Instead, I grab my smoothie and stand. "It's so lovely of you to offer." Rocío tries to kick me again, but I slither away. "I'm going to check out the gym at the Space Center. Rocío said that it might be free."

"It is. Levi had me change your status the other day."

"Whose status?"

"Yours. And Rocío's." She winks. "I switched you to team members in the system, so you can get some of the perks."

"Oh, thank you. That was very—" *Unexpected? Out of character? Something you must have made up on the spot because why would he do that?* "—generous."

"Levi's awesome. Best boss I ever had. He harassed NASA into giving me health insurance!" She smiles and turns to Rocío, who looks ready to drown herself in a Danish brook. Again. "Where did you want to start?"

Rocío incinerates me with her eyes as I wave goodbye. Honestly, she's in excellent hands. Doesn't even deserve it. On the sidewalk, I take out my phone and quickly type up a tweet.

@WhatWouldMarieDo . . . if one of the major obstacles preventing access to higher education were the GRE, a test that is 1) expensive 2) poorly predictive of overall graduate school success, and 3) biased against individuals who are lower-income, BIPOC, and non-cis-males?

I slip my phone into my pocket, and my thoughts go back to the gym. Levi probably just wants me to be able to use it so he doesn't have to retrieve me from a different cemetery every week. Can't blame him, honestly.

Yeah. That must be it.

11

NUCLEUS ACCUMBENS: GAMBLING

"LEVI? COULD YOU send me the newest—"

"Blueprints are on the server," he mumbles around the miniature screwdriver he's holding between his teeth. He doesn't look up from the mound of wires and plates he's working on.

It's past nine on a Friday. Everyone else has left. We're alone in the engineering lab, like most nights this week, in what I've come to think of as our Hostile Companionable Silence™. It's very similar to other types of silence, except that I know that Levi doesn't like me, and Levi knows that I know he doesn't like me and that I don't like him in return. But he doesn't bring it up, and I don't really think about it. Because we have no reason to.

So, yeah. Our Hostile Companionable Silence™ is basically a regular companionable silence. We sit facing each other at different workbenches. We dim the lights to see the shapes of the outside trees.

We focus on our respective tasks. Every once in a while, we exchange comments, thoughts, doubts regarding BLINK. We could do the same from our respective offices, but looking up from my laptop and verbally asking a question beats writing it out in an email. Typing out, *Hey, Levi* and *Best, Bee* is such a pain.

Plus, Levi packs snacks. He brings them to work for himself, but he's lousy at gauging portions and always makes too much. So far I've had homemade trail mix, guac and saltines, rice cakes, popcorn, pita chips and bean dip, and about four kinds of energy balls.

Yes, he's a better cook than I'll ever be.

No, I'm not too proud to accept his food. I'm not too proud to accept *anyone's* food.

Plus, I've been in Houston for a month, and we're already close to a working version of the prototype. I deserve some celebratory face-stuffing.

"The *old* blueprint is on the server, not the new one."

He takes the screwdriver out of his mouth. "It is. I put it there."

"That's not the correct file."

He looks up. "Could you check again, please?"

I roll my eyes and sigh heavily, but I comply. Because today he made dark chocolate and peanut butter energy balls, and they were life-shatteringly good. "Done. Still not here."

"Are you sure?"

"Yes."

"It has to be there." He gives me an impatient look, like I'm pulling him away from the crucial task of securing the country's nuclear codes.

"It's not. Do you want to bet something on it?"

"What would you like to bet?"

"Let's see." His face when he finds that I'm right is going to be better than sex. Better than sex with Tim, for sure. "A million dollars."

"I don't have a million dollars. Do you?"

"Of course I do, I'm a junior scientist." He chuckles. Something flutters inside me, and I ignore it. "Let's bet Schrödinger."

"I'm not betting my cat."

"Because you know you're going to lose."

"No, because my cat is seventeen and needs regular manual expression of his anal glands. But if you still want him . . ."

I make a face. "No, I'm good." I drum my fingers on my biceps, wondering what else Levi has that I want. I could make him cook for me every day for a month, but he's sort of already doing that without realizing. Why change something that works? "If I win, you get a tattoo."

"Of what?"

"A goat. Alive," I add magnanimously.

"Can't."

"Why?"

"Already have one."

I laugh. "Oh, I've got it! Your mug? The one that says *Yoda Best Engineer*?"

"Yeah?"

"I want one. But it needs to say 'neuroscientist,' of course."

He lifts one eyebrow. "This is the equivalent to someone buying their own *World's Best Boss* mug. Congratulations, you're officially NASA's Michael Scott."

"And proud of it. Okay," I say, turning my computer around for him to see. "Deal. Come marvel at the lack of blueprints on the server."

"Wait. What about me?"

153

"What about you?"

"What will *you* do if *I* win?"

"Oh." I shrug. "Whatever you want. I'm right anyway. Would you like my hard-earned million dollars?"

"Nope." He shakes his head, pensive.

"Should I come over and express poor Schrödinger's anal glands for the duration of my stay in Houston?"

"Tempting, but Schrödinger's intensely private about his anus." He taps his masculine, chiseled chin. Huh? Why am I even noticing? "If I win, you're going to sign up for a 5K here in Houston."

I shrug. "Sure. I'll sign up for a—"

"And you're going to run it."

I burst into laughter. "There is no way."

"Why?"

"Because I'm currently on step four of my program, and still unable to run more than half a mile without collapsing. Running a 5K sounds about as pleasant as bloodletting. By leeches."

"I'll run with you."

"You mean, you'll walk next to me with your seventy-mile-long legs?"

"I'll train you."

"Oh, Levi. Levi. You sweet summer child." I point at myself. Tonight I'm wearing a nose stud, galaxy leggings, and a white tank top. My purple hair is loose on my shoulders. I'm pretty sure one of my back tattoos is visible. Everything about me screams *Levi's kryptonite*. "You see this scrawny, stunted, unmuscled body? It's built to live in parasitic symbiosis with a couch. It resists training with the force of many million ohms."

Levi does stare at my body for a considerable amount of time, but then he looks away, flushed. Poor guy. Must be a tough sight for him. "It doesn't matter, does it? Since you're sure that you'll win?"

"True." I shrug. "Deal. Come taste the bitterness of defeat."

He does come, stalking to my bench in a few strides with those ridiculous seventy-mile-long legs. However, he doesn't stop in front of the laptop I conveniently turned for him. Instead he circles around the bench, comes to stand behind me, and then slides the computer in our direction. For me to better witness his impending massacre, I assume. "I can't wait to sip your tears out of my new mug," I murmur.

"We'll see." He leans his left hand against the bench and grabs the mouse with the other. Even on my high stool, he's still many inches taller than me, effectively caging me at my seat. It should feel uneasy, suffocating, but he leaves me enough room that I don't mind. Plus, I know it doesn't mean anything. Because he's Levi. And I'm Bee. It's actually almost pleasant, the heat he radiates in the blasting AC. He could have a successful second career as a weighted blanket.

"This is weird." I hear the frown in his voice. "The file's missing."

"Can the mug be twenty ounces?"

"It should be here." He leans forward, and his chin brushes the crown of my hair. It's not terrible. Sort of the opposite. "I saved it."

"Maybe you dreamt it? Sometimes in the mornings I think that I got up and brushed my teeth even though I'm still in bed. Though with my new mug I'll be extra motivated to wake up early and have my coffee."

"Weird." Pity he's not paying attention to my gloating. I'm doing a pretty good bit, if I say so myself. "Look." He types quickly, the inside of his elbows brushing against my upper arms, pulling up a log interface. "See? Someone—me—saved the file at 1:16 p.m. Then at 4:23 someone else removed it . . ."

I know immediately where he's going with this. I tilt my neck back to look up at him, and he's already staring down from two inches above. God, *his eyes*. He invented a new color green. "It wasn't me!" I blurt out.

"How much do you want my cat?"

"Considerably less now that I know about his colorectal issues."

"And my mug?"

"A lot, but I swear it wasn't me!"

He hums skeptically. I can feel his breath against my face. Mint, with a hint of peanut butter. "I'm inclined to believe you, but only because this is not the first time."

"What do you mean?"

"The frequencies list for the parietal electrodes you sent me yesterday? The one you emailed *and* put on the server? It wasn't there."

I scowl. "But I put it there."

"I know. The engineers complained about missing and misplaced files, too, corrupted stuff. Lots of little things."

"Probably a server error."

"Or people screwing up."

"Can you tell who moved the file?"

He types a few more strokes. "Not from the logs. The system isn't coded that way. You know what it *can* do?" I shake my head, bumping against some spot on his chest. "It can tell me where the file was moved, and if it's still on the server but in a different folder. Which in the case of the blueprints is"—he presses the space bar and pulls up an image—"right here."

"Oh, perfect. That's exactly what I was—" My teeth click as I shut my mouth. "Wait a minute."

"What 5K should we sign up for?" He's roaming the inside of his cheek with his tongue. "There's usually a space-themed one in June—"

"No way." I twist around. "The file was *not* where it was supposed to be."

"The terms of the bet were that the file should be on the server." He gives me a satisfied smile. "Bet you're glad I didn't agree to the anal expression."

"You know I meant *in a specific folder.*"

"How unfortunate that you didn't specify, then." He puts a hand on my shoulder in mock reassurance—I seriously consider biting it off—and it's ridiculous, how much every part of him dwarfs every part of me. Also ridiculous? The way those stupid intrusive thoughts of his body pressed against mine can't seem to let up. And that having him so close reminds me of his thigh pushing up between my legs, solid and insistent against the seam of my—

"What are you two doing?"

Boris is standing in the entrance of the lab, and my first instinct is to push away from Levi and scream that *nothing happened, nothing happened, we were just working.* But the distance between us is perfectly appropriate. It just *feels* like it isn't, because Levi is so large. And warm. Because he's Levi.

"We were just about to sign up for a 5K," he says. "How are you, Boris?"

"A 5K, huh?" He stays under the doorframe, studying us with his customary tired expression. "Actually, I come bearing news."

"Bad news?"

"Not good."

"Bad, then."

Boris comes closer, holding a printout. "You guys planning to go to Human Brain Imaging?"

HBI is one of many academic conferences in neuroscience. It's not particularly prestigious, but over the years it has cultivated a "party" reputation: it takes place in fun cities, with lots of satellite events and industry sponsorships. It's where young, hip neuroscientists network and get drunk together.

But I'm not hip. And Levi is not a neuroscientist. "No," I tell Boris. "Where is it this year?"

"New Orleans. This coming weekend."

"Fun. You planning on going?"

He shakes his head and holds out the printout. "No. But someone is."

"MagTech?" Levi says, reading from above my shoulder.

"We've been keeping tabs on them. The company will present a version of their helmets at HBI."

"Have they filed for a patent?"

"Not yet."

"Then going public seems like . . ."

"A less-than-intelligent move? I think they're trying to get visibility to pull in new investors. Which is a great opportunity for us to find out where they're at."

"You're suggesting we send someone to New Orleans, have them attend HBI, and report back on what MagTech's progress is compared to ours?"

"No." Boris smiles for the first time since stepping inside the room. "I'm *ordering* the two of you to do that."

"I JUST DON'T think that driving to New Orleans to play Inspector Gadget is the best use of our time," I tell Levi as he walks me home like he insisted on (*"Houston is dangerous at night," "You never know who's lurking around," "Either you let me walk you home, or I follow ten feet behind you. Your choice"*). He's pushing his bike, which he apparently rides to work most days. Hmph. Overachiever. His helmet, strapped to his belt, bounces against his thigh every few steps. The soothing rhythm provides a solid backdrop to my bitching.

"We're at least Inspector Columbo."

"Gadget outranks Columbo," I point out. "Don't get me wrong, I see the value of keeping tabs on the competition, but wouldn't it be better to send someone else?"

"No one else is as familiar with BLINK as we are, and you're the only person who knows the neuroscience."

"Fred *did* take that class in undergrad."

Levi smiles. "At least it's over the weekend. We won't miss workdays."

I lift one eyebrow. We've both worked every single weekend. "Why are you taking this so well?"

He shrugs. "I pick my battles with Boris carefully."

"Isn't this worth fighting for? We're talking about two days in close quarters with the person you most despise in history."

"Elon Musk is coming, too?"

"No—*me*."

He sighs heavily, rubbing his forehead. "We've been over this, Bee. Besides, the team keeps screwing up basic stuff like file backup," he adds wryly. "I wouldn't trust them with . . . espionage." He smiles when he says the last word, and my heart jumps. I'm inexplicably getting Cute Guy™ vibes from him—maybe because when he's amused he looks damn cute.

"I still think it's not human error," I say, trying not to think about things like cuteness.

"Either way, I'll call a meeting with the engineers and scare them into being more careful."

"Wait." I stop under my building. "You can't do that if you're not sure that it's someone on the team."

"*I'm* sure."

"But you have no proof." He looks at me with a puzzled expression. "You don't want to accuse them of something they might not have even done, do you?"

"They did."

I huff, frustrated. "What if it's a weird fluke?"

"It's not."

"But you—" I press my lips together. "Listen, we're co-leaders. We should make disciplinary decisions together, which means that you can't accuse anyone of anything until I'm on board, too. And that's not going to happen until I see actual proof that someone on the team is doing this." He's looking down at me with a soft, amused expression, as if he finds my irritation particularly endearing. *What a sadist.* "Okay?" I prompt him.

He nods. "Okay." He unlocks his helmet and ties it under his chin. I most definitely do *not* notice the flex of his biceps. "And, Bee?"

"Yeah?"

He mounts the bike and starts riding away. "I'll let you know which 5K I settle on."

He's giving me his back, but I flip him off anyway.

12

VENTRAL STRIATUM: YEARNING

SHMAC: That GRE tweet is becoming a bit of a thing, huh?

It sure is.

If by "bit" he means "a lot." And if by "thing" he means "shit-storm."

I have no idea how it even happened. The day I sent the tweet I went to bed after reading comments of people talking about their negative experiences with the test. When I woke up, there was a hashtag (#FairGraduateAdmissions), and dozens of associations of women and minorities in STEM had announced a GRE strike, encouraging students to turn in their grad school applications without the GRE.

@OliviaWeiBio If everyone does it, grad programs
will have no choice but to evaluate us based on our
experiences, CV, previous efforts, and skills.
Basically, what they should already be doing.

Have I mentioned how much I love women in STEM? Because I *loooove* women in STEM.

Two hours later, a journalist from *The Atlantic* messaged me, asking for an interview. Then CNN. Then *Chronicle of Higher Ed.* Then Fox News (as if!). I paired up with Shmac to reach an even wider audience, and together we issued a thousand-word essay summarizing the lack of scientific evidence supporting the use of the GRE as an admission tool. I encouraged news outlets to interview the women who started the hashtag (except for Fox News, which I left on read). Several people came forward and talked to the media about the number of minimum-wage hours necessary to afford the test, about their frustration when wealthier classmates with access to private tutoring performed better, about the crushing disappointment of being rejected by dream institutions despite perfect GPAs and research experience because their scores didn't meet some arbitrary cutoff by a few percentage points. They're still doing the rounds, with more people opening up.

#FairGraduateAdmissions is a movement, and it has a real chance at getting rid of this stupid, unfair test. I've been all aflutter.

You know who else has been aflutter? Rocío. Who barged into the office declaring: "I won't be preparing for the GRE anymore, in solidarity with my brethren. Johns Hopkins will have to acknowledge how badass I am from my other application materials."

I looked up from my laptop and nodded. "I support that."

"You know why this is happening, right?" She leaned conspiratorially over my desk. "The other day we talked about how shitty the

GRE is, and now people are rallying against it because Marie started the conversation. It can't be a coincidence."

"Oh," I stammered, "well, it probably *is* just a coincidence—"

"There are no coincidences," she said, beautiful dark eyes staring into mine. "Bee, we both know who I owe this to."

"Oh—I'm sure—"

"La Llorona." She took her phone out of her pocket and showed me pictures of beautiful creeks. Her eyes shone. "I've been visiting nearby places where she was sighted, leaving little tokens of appreciation."

"Tokens?"

"Yes. Tarots, poems I wrote extolling the beauty of the macabre, pentagrams made of twigs. The usual."

"The . . . usual."

"I think it's her way of saying, 'Rocío, I recognize a kindred spirit, perhaps even a successor in you.'" She smiled at me, setting her bag on her desk. "I am so happy, Bee."

I smiled back and went back to work, relieved that Rocío doesn't suspect who's behind WWMD. Sometimes I wonder if Dr. Curie, too, had a secret identity she couldn't reveal. Period-wise, she could have been Jack the Ripper. Never say never, right?

> **MARIE:** Do you think we're actually going to get rid of the GRE?
>
> **SHMAC:** We're closer than ever, for sure.
>
> **MARIE:** Agreed. Thank you for helping out, by the way.

Shmac and I have the same number of followers but completely different reaches. I hate thanking dudes for Sausage Referencing™, but truth is, there are plenty of male academics who'd rather guzzle curdled milk than engage with WWMD. Which is fine, because I'd love nothing more than pouring gallons of curdled milk down their throats. Still, #FairGraduateAdmissions can use all the support it can get.

> **MARIE:** How's The Girl?
>
> **SHMAC:** How's Camel Dick?
>
> **MARIE:** Astonishingly, we're almost getting along. If we haven't come to blows yet, are we even collaborating? Also, nice deflection. Tell me about The Girl.
>
> **SHMAC:** Everything's fine.
>
> **MARIE:** Fine has variable definitions. Narrow it down.
>
> **SHMAC:** How narrow?
>
> **MARIE:** Very.
>
> **SHMAC:** Okay. Narrowingly: things are great, in the worst possible way. We've been working together a lot because that's what the project demands. Which might be why I'm on my fourth beer on a Thursday night.
>
> **MARIE:** Why is working together bad?
>
> **SHMAC:** It's just . . . I know things about her.
>
> **MARIE:** Things?

SHMAC: I know what she loves to eat, what shows she watches, what makes her laugh, her opinions on pets. I know her dislikes (aside from me). I've been cataloging a million little quirks of hers in my head, and they are enchanting. She is enchanting. Smart, funny, an incredible scientist. And . . . there are things. Things I think about. But I'm drunk, and this is inappropriate.

MARIE: I love inappropriate.

SHMAC: Do you?

MARIE: Sometimes. Hit me.

SHMAC: I need you to know that I'd never do anything to make her uncomfortable.

MARIE: Shmac, I know that. And if you ever did, I'd cut your dick off with a rusty scalpel.

SHMAC: Fair.

MARIE: Tell me.

The clock in the kitchen ticks on. Late-night cars make soft noises past the window, and the screen of my phone goes black. I don't think Shmac will continue. I don't think he'll open up, and it makes me sad. Even though I don't know anything about his life, I get the impression that if he doesn't do it with me, he won't with anyone else. My eyes drift closed, accustomed to the dark, and that's when my screen lights up again.

The air rushes out of my lungs.

SHMAC: I know what she smells like. This little
freckle on her neck when she pulls up her hair.
Her upper lip is a little plumper than the lower. The
curve of her wrist, when she holds a pen. It's wrong,
really wrong, but I know the shape of her. I go to
sleep thinking about it, and then I wake up, go to
work, and she is there, and it's impossible. I tell her
stuff I know she'll agree to, just to hear her hum back
at me. It's like hot water down my fucking spine.
She's married. She's brilliant. She trusts me, and all I
think about is taking her to my office, stripping her,
doing unspeakable things to her. And I want to tell
her. I want to tell her that she's luminous, she's so
bright in my mind, sometimes I can't focus.
Sometimes I forget why I came into the room. I'm
distracted. I want to push her against a wall, and I
want her to push back. I want to go back in time and
punch her stupid husband on the day I met him and
then travel back to the future and punch him
again. I want to buy her flowers, food, books. I want
to hold her hand, and I want to lock her in my
bedroom. She's everything I ever wanted and I want
to inject her into my veins and also to never see her
again. There's nothing like her and these
feelings, they are fucking intolerable. They were half-
asleep while she was gone, but now she's
here and my body thinks it's a fucking
teenager and I don't know what to do. I don't
know what to do. There is nothing I can do, so I'll
just . . . not.

I can't breathe. I can't move. I can't even swallow the knot in my throat. I might actually cry. For him. For this girl, who'll never know that someone holds these mountains of want inside. And maybe for me, because I've made the choice to never feel this, never again. Never ever, and I realize now, now for the first time, what a terrible price I will pay. What a loss it will be.

MARIE: Oh, Shmac.

What else is there to say? He's in love with someone who doesn't love him back. Who is married. This story has no happy ending. And I think he knows, because he only replies with,

SHMAC: Yeah.

"HEY, BEE."

I set aside my article and smile at Lamar. "What's up?"

"Not much. Just wanted to tell you that I've updated the log system on the server."

"Oh?"

"Yeah. Nothing is changing on your end, but now users removing, replacing, or modifying files are automatically tracked. If something's iffy, we'll know who's responsible."

"Great." I frown. "Why did you do that?"

"Because of the issues."

"The issues?"

"Yeah. Missing files and all that. Levi called an engineering meeting to tear us a new one and asked me to change the server code." He shrugs sheepishly. "Sorry about the mess." He slips out of my office, leaving me to stare at my article. I am still staring three minutes later when someone else knocks on the doorframe.

"What's with your return air vent?" Levi's in the entrance, filling it like Lamar couldn't quite manage. "It's missing the grille. I'll call maintenance—"

"No!" I swivel around. "It's how Félicette gets inside at night. To eat the treats I leave for her!"

He lifts one eyebrow. "You want an uncovered vent because your imaginary cat—"

"She's not imaginary. I found a paw print next to my computer the other day. I texted it to you." And he replied, Looks like a splotch of Lean Cuisine. I hate him.

"Right. About tomorrow, we should head out early since New Orleans is over five hours away. I don't mind picking up the rental and driving. You can sleep in the car, but I'd like to leave around six—"

"You called the meeting."

He cocks his head. A wisp of black hair falls on his brow. "Excuse me?"

"You told the engineers about the missing files."

"Ah." He presses his lips together. "I did."

I stand without knowing why. Put my hands on my hips, still not knowing why. "I asked you not to."

"Bee. It needed to be done."

"We agreed that we wouldn't until we had proof."

He folds his arms on his chest, a stubborn line to his shoulders. "We didn't agree. You told me you didn't want to call a full meeting about it, and I didn't. But I'm head of the engineering division, and I decided to tell *my* team about the issue."

I snort. "Your team is everyone but me and Rocío. Nice loophole."

"Why does it bother you so much?"

"Because."

"You're going to have to be a little more articulate than that."

"*Because* you did it behind my back." I bristle. "Just like a month ago, when you didn't tell me about NASA trying to get BLINK canceled."

"It's not the same at all."

"It is in theory. And it's a matter of principle." I bite the inside of my cheek. "If we're co-leaders, we need to agree before taking disciplinary measures."

"No disciplinary measure was taken. It was a five-minute meeting in which I asked my team to stop messing around with important files. I run a tight ship, and my team knows it—no one made a big deal about this except for you."

"Then why didn't you tell me you were going to do it?"

His eyes harden, hot and dark and frustrated. He scans my face, silent, and I feel the tension rise in the room. This is about to escalate. To a full-blown fight. He'll yell at me to mind my business. I'll throw my Lean Cuisine at him. We'll pummel each other, people will rush to separate us, we will cause a spectacle.

But he just says, "I'll pick you up at six." His tone is steely. Inflexible. Cold. So different from the one he's used with me for the past five weeks.

I wonder why that is. I wonder if he hates me. I wonder if *I* hate him. I wonder so much that I forget to answer him, but it doesn't matter. Because he's already gone.

13

SUPERIOR COLLICULI: WILL YOU LOOK AT THAT?

ONE HOUR, TWENTY-FOUR minutes, and seventeen seconds.

Eighteen.

Nineteen.

Twenty.

That's how long I've been in this Nissan Altima that smells faintly like lemon and faux leather and Levi's delicious, masculine scent. And that's how long we've been silent. Thoroughly, *wholeheartedly* silent.

It's going to be a craptastic weekend. We're going to play 007 while barely talking to each other. I see no flaw in this plan.

Is this my fault? Perhaps. Perhaps I initiated this—remarkably immature, I must admit—standoff, when I didn't say "Hi" back to him this morning. Perhaps I'm the culprit. But I don't give a flying squirrel because I'm mad. So I'm leaning in to it. I'm hoarding all of my grievances against Levi and bulking them up into a big, withering, incandescent supernova of silent treatment that . . .

Honestly, I'm not sure he's noticed.

He *did* lift his eyebrow after I refused to say "Hi," in my best impression of an eleven-year-old just done rereading *The Baby-Sitters Club*. But he shrugged it off pretty quickly. He put on a CD (*Mer de Noms* by A Perfect Circle, and God, his amazing musical taste is like a knife to my ovaries) and started driving. Impassible. Relaxed.

I bet he's not even thinking about it. I bet he doesn't care. I bet I'm here, playing nervously with my grandmother's ring, sulking to the rhythm of "Judith," while he's probably pondering the laws of thermodynamics or whether to join the No-Poo movement. What do dudes even think about all the time? The Dow Jones. MILF porn. Their next date.

Does Levi date? I'm sure he does, given the number of people who seem to think of him as a Sexy Guy™. He might not be married, but maybe he's in a long-term relationship. Maybe he's deeply in love, like Shmac. Poor Shmac. My chest hurts in a messy, confusing way when I think about what he said. About Levi feeling similarly intense, scary, powerful things for a woman. About Levi *doing* the things Shmac talked about doing to her.

I shiver, wondering why stray memories of Levi pressing me against a wall are *still* popping up in my head. Wondering whether the girlfriend he might not even have would be extraordinarily lucky or the very opposite. Wondering *why* I'm even wondering—

"I'm sorry."

I turn so fast I pull a muscle. "What?"

"I'm sorry."

"For what?" I massage my neck.

He stares at the road and lifts one eyebrow. "Is this some educational technique? 'Apologizing for dummies'?"

"No. I'm honestly befuddled."

"Then, I'm sorry for calling the meeting without asking for your approval."

I squint. ". . . Really?"

"Really, what?"

"Are you . . . actually apologizing?"

"Yep."

"Oh." I nod. "To be precise, then, you *did* ask for my approval. And I explicitly did *not* give it."

"Correct." I think he's biting the inside of his cheek to avoid smiling. "I didn't heed your *explicit* advice. I wasn't trying to undermine your authority, or to act like your opinion is irrelevant. I think . . ." He presses his lips together. "Actually, I *know* I'm overly invested in BLINK. Which makes me overly controlling and bossy. You're right, it was the second time I didn't discuss important issues with you." He finally looks at me. "I'm sorry, Bee."

I blink. Several times. "Wow."

"Wow?"

"That was an excellent apology." I shake my head, disappointed. "How am I supposed to keep up my very adult silent treatment for the next three and a half hours?"

"You were planning to stop once we got to New Orleans?"

"I wasn't, but realistically: well-executed cold shoulders require an enormous amount of upkeep, and I'm first and foremost lazy."

He laughs softly. "Should we switch albums, then?"

"Why?"

"I thought late-nineties grunge might fit your mood, but if you're outgrowing your wrath, maybe we can listen to something a little less . . ."

"Angry?"

"Yeah."

"What are our options?"

There's something exquisitely weird about Levi Ward telling me his phone's passcode (338338) and letting me poke around his music folder. His collection doesn't include a single embarrassing Nickelback song (I hate him). It's a mix of nineties bands—my decade of choice—except that they're all . . .

I opt for shuffle, settle back into my seat to gaze at the beautiful landscape, and give him the only criticism I can think of. "You do know women make music, too, right?"

"What does that mean?"

"Nothing." I shrug. "Just that the entirety of your music library is angry white boys."

He frowns. "Not true."

"Right. That's why you have exactly . . ." I scroll down for a few seconds. More seconds. A minute. ". . . a grand total of zero female-performed songs on your phone."

"That's not possible."

"And yet."

His scowl deepens. "It's just a coincidence."

"Mmm."

"Okay—I'm not proud of it, but it's possible that my musical taste was influenced by the fact that in my formative years I, too, was an angry white boy."

I snort. "I bet you were. Well, if you ever want to work through that rage productively I could recommend some singer-songwriters—" There's something on the side of the road. I crane my neck to see better. "Oh my *God*."

He gives me a worried look. "What's going on?"

"Nothing. I just—" I wipe my eyes. "Nothing."

"Bee? Are you . . . crying?"

"No," I lie. Poorly.

"Is it about female singer-songwriters?" he says, panicky. "I'll buy an album. Just let me know which one is best. Honestly, I don't know enough about them to—"

"No. No, I— There was a dead possum. On the side of the road."

"Oh."

"I . . . have issues. With roadkill."

"Issues?"

"It's just . . . animals are so cute. Except for spiders. But spiders are not *really* animals."

"They . . . are."

"And who knows where the possum was going? Maybe she had a family? Maybe she was bringing home food to kids who now wonder where Mommy is?" I'm making myself cry harder. I wipe my cheek and sniffle.

"I'm not sure wildlife abides by the rules of traditional nuclear family structure—" Levi notices my glare and instantly shuts up. He scratches his nape and adds, "It's sad."

"It's okay. I'm fine. I'm emotionally stable."

His lips curl up. "Are you?"

"This is nothing. Tim used to make me play this stupid 'Guess the Roadkill' game to toughen me up, and once I *literally* ran out of tears." Levi's jaw hardens visibly. "And when I was twelve we saw a family of splattered hedgehogs on a Belgian highway and I cried so hard that when we stopped to get gas, a *Federale Politie* agent questioned my uncle on suspicion of child maltreatment."

"Got it. No stops until New Orleans."

"No, I promise I'm done crying. I'm an adult with a shriveled, hardened heart now."

He gives me a skeptical glance, but then says, "Belgium, huh?" and his voice is curious.

"Yeah. But don't get too excited, it was the Flemish part."

"I thought you said you were from France."

"I'm from all over the place." I take off my sandals and push my legs against the dashboard, hoping Levi won't take offense at my bright yellow nail polish and my incredibly ugly pinkies. I call them the Quasimotoes. "We were born in Germany. My father was German and Polish, and my mother half-Italian, half-American. They were very . . . nomadic? My dad was a technical writer, so he could work anywhere. They'd settle in one place, stay for a few months, then move to a new one. And our extended family was very scattered. So when they died, we—"

"They died?" Levi turns to me, wide-eyed.

"Yeah. Freak car accident. Airbags didn't work. They'd been recalled, but . . ." I shrug. "We'd just turned four."

"We?" He's more invested in my life story than I expected. I thought he just wanted to fill the silence.

"Me and my twin sister. We don't really have memories of our parents. Anyway, after their death we were sent from relative to relative. There was Italy, Germany, Germany again, Switzerland, the US, Poland, Spain, France, Belgium, the UK, Germany again, a brief stint in Japan, the US again. And so on."

"And you'd learn the language?"

"More or less. We were enrolled in local schools—which, *total* pain, having to make new friends every few months. There were times I thought in so many languages I didn't even speak, I couldn't understand the inside of my own head. Not to mention, we'd always be the kids with an accent, the kids who didn't really get the culture, so we never properly fit in, and— Shouldn't you be monitoring the road instead of staring at me?"

He blinks repeatedly, as if shaking off the shock, and then looks straight ahead. "Sorry," he mumbles.

"Anyway. There were lots of countries, lots of relatives. Eventually we landed in the US with my maternal aunt for the last two years of high school." I shrug. "I've been here ever since."

"And your sister?"

"Reike's like my parents used to be. All wanderlustful. She left as soon as she legally could, and for the past decade she's been going from place to place, doing odd jobs, living day by day. She likes to . . . just be, you know?" I laugh. "I'm positive that if my parents were alive they'd gang up with Reike against me for not loving to travel like they do. But I don't. Reike's all about seeing new places and making new memories, but to me, if you constantly go after new things, there's never *enough* of anything." I run a hand through my hair, playing with the purple tips. "I don't know. Maybe I'm just lazy."

"It's not that," Levi says. I glance up. "You want stability. Permanency." He nods, as if he just found the missing piece of a puzzle and the resulting picture suddenly makes sense. "To be somewhere long enough to build a sense of belonging."

"Hey, Freud," I say mildly, "you done with the unsolicited therapy?"

He flushes. "That will be three hundred dollars."

"Seems like the going rate."

"Are you and your sister identical?"

"Yes. Though she insists that she's prettier. That dumbass." I roll my eyes fondly.

"Do you see her often?"

I shake my head. "I haven't seen her in person in almost two years." And even then, it was two days, a layover in New York on her way to Alaska from . . . I have no clue. I've long lost track. "But we talk on the phone a lot." I grin. "For example, I bitch to her about you."

"Flattering." He smiles. "Must be nice to be close with your sibling."

"You're not? Did you drive a rift between you and your brothers with your bad habit of doing stuff without clearing it with them first?"

He shakes his head, still smiling. "There is no rift. Just . . . what's the opposite of a rift?"

"A closing?"

"Yeah. That."

Whatever the state of his relationship with his brothers is, he doesn't seem happy about it, and I feel a pang of guilt. "Sorry. I didn't mean to imply that your family hates you because you're a control freak."

He smiles. "You're just as much a control freak as I am, Bee. And I think it has more to do with the fact that I'm the only member of my extended family who's not in some military career."

"Really?"

"Yup."

I bend my legs and angle myself to face him. "Is it an unspoken rule in your family? You must be in the armed forces, or you shall be a failure?"

"It's absolutely spoken. I'm the official disappointment. Only cousin who's a civilian—out of seven. The peer pressure is intense."

"Whoa."

"Last year, at Thanksgiving, my uncle publicly asked me to change my name to stop bringing shame to the family. This was *before* he guzzled a case of Blue Moon."

I scowl. "You are a NASA engineer with *Nature* publications."

"You kept track of my pubs?"

I eye-roll. "I don't. Sam just likes to blabber about how amazing you are."

"Maybe I should bring her to Thanksgiving next year."

"Hey." I poke his bicep with my index finger. It's hard and warm through the sleeve of his shirt. "I know we're . . . nemesi?"

"Nemeses."

"—nemeses, but your family doesn't. And I usually spend Thanksgiving trying to see how many vegan marshmallows I can stuff into my mouth. So if next year you need someone to explain exactly how amazing you are at your job—or even just to bitch-slap them—I'm available." I smile, and after a few seconds he smiles back, a little soft.

There is something relaxing about this. About *here*. About the moment we're having. Maybe it's that Levi and I know exactly where we stand when it comes to each other. Or that for both of us, the most important thing in the world right now is BLINK. Maybe there is a connection between us. A very odd, very complicated one.

I lean back in my seat. "That," I muse, "is the one pro of being an orphan."

"What is?"

"Having no parents to disappoint."

He mulls it over. "Can't argue with that logic."

After that we go back to our Hostile Companionable Silence™. And after a little longer I fall asleep, Thom Yorke's voice low and soothing in my ears.

I HAVE BEEN at HBI for three and a half minutes when I meet the first person I know, a former RA in Sam's lab who's now a Ph.D. student at—I glance at his badge—Stony Brook. We hug, catch up a bit, promise to get together for drinks over the weekend (we won't). By the time I turn around, Levi has met someone *he* knows (an elderly guy with a fanny pack and an eyeglass chain that scream "engineer" from the top of the Grand Canyon). The cycle lasts about twenty minutes.

"Jesus," I mutter once we're alone. It's not as though we're famous, or anything like that, but the world of neuroimaging is very insular. Incestuous. Inescapable. And lots of other *I* adjectives.

"I had more social interactions in the past twenty minutes than in the last ten months," he mumbles.

"I saw you smile at least four times." I pat his arm comfortingly. "That can't have been easy."

"I might have to lie down."

"I'll get an ice pack for your cheeks." I look around the crowded hall, suddenly reminded of why I hate academic conferences. "Why did we come today, anyway? MagTech's presentation's not until tomorrow."

"Boris's order. A feeble attempt to look like we're not *just* here to snoop, I believe."

I grin. "Do you ever feel like we're super-spies and he's our handler?"

He gives me a half-amused, half-withering look. "No."

"Come on. Boris's totally the M to my James Bond."

"If you're James Bond, who am I?"

"You're the Bond girl. I'm going to seduce you in exchange for blueprints and stab you while I sip on my martini." I wink at Levi, then realize that he's flushing. Did I go too far? "I didn't mean to—"

"There are a couple of engineering talks I want to go to," he says abruptly, pointing at the conference program and sounding remarkably normal. I must have imagined it. "You?"

"There's a panel at four that sounds interesting. Also, it's my sacred duty to go out for a drink. Big Easy and all that."

"Oh. Did you want to . . ."

I cock my head. "Want to?"

He clears his throat. "Did you want company? Were you already planning to go with your friend, or—"

"My friend?"

"That friend of yours."

"Who?"

"I forgot her name. That girl who was in Sam's lab? Dark hair, did fNIRS research, and . . ." He squints. "Nah, that's all I remember."

"Are you talking about Annie Johansson?"

He glances back at the program. "Maybe? That sounds right."

I can't believe Levi forgot Annie's name after she pursued him mercilessly for ages. She knew his damn blood type, for cake's sake. Probably his social security number, too. "Why would I go for drinks with her?"

"I just assumed," he says absentmindedly. "You two were inseparable."

My heartbeat picks up. Probably for no reason. "But she's not here."

Levi's still reading the program, not really paying attention to me. "I thought I saw her a minute ago."

I whirl around. Yes, my palms are starting to sweat, but just because sometimes they do. All palms sweat sometimes, right? I look about frantically, but I'm sure that Annie's not here. She can't be. Levi didn't even remember her name—he can't be right about this. He probably thinks that all women with dark hair look the same and—

Annie.

With a shorter haircut. And a pretty lilac dress. And a big smile on her pretty lips. Standing in line at the badge reclamation station, chatting with someone, someone who just walked up and is handing her a cup of coffee, someone who—

Tim.

Tim. I see Tim, but only for a second. Then my vision blurs, large black dots swallowing the world. I'm hot. I'm cold. I'm sweaty. I'm shaking like a leaf and my heart is pounding and I'm flying away.

"Bee." Levi's voice grounds me for a second, warm and deep and worried and solid and thank God he's here, or I'd be scattered all over, debris in the wind. "Bee, are you okay?"

I'm not. I'm dying. I'm fainting. I'm having a panic attack. My heart and my head are exploding.

"Bee?"

Levi is holding me now. Holding me again and I'm in his arms and it feels like I'm safe, how is it possible that when he's around, only when he's around, I really feel sa—

14

PERIAQUEDUCTAL GRAY & THE
HIPPOCAMPUS: PAINFUL MEMORIES

THIS IS NOT my hotel room.

First of all, it has a *way* better view. A busy, picturesque New Orleans street, instead of that cluttered courtyard with stacked patio furniture. Second, it smells faintly like pine and soap. Third, and perhaps most important: it's not messy, and if I have one talent in the world, it's turning a hotel room into complete non-vandalic chaos within the first three minutes of my stay.

Your girl has some serious splinter skills.

I sit up in the bed, which I assume is also not mine. The first thing I see is green. A particular brand of green: Levi Green™.

"Yo," I tell him, a little stupidly, and immediately slump back on the pillow. I feel drained. Exhausted. Nauseous. Out of it. How did I get here, anyway?

Levi comes to sit next to me, on the side of the bed. "How are you?" The rich rumble of his voice is a hint of sorts. The last time I heard it was very recently. And I couldn't breathe. I couldn't breathe because . . . ?

"Did I lose consciousness?"

He nods. "Not immediately. You walked with me to the elevator. Then I carried you here."

It comes back to me at once. Tim. Annie. Tim *and* Annie. They're here at the conference. Talking. To each other. I must be in Levi's bed and the inside of my head is rotten and I'm losing it again and—

"Deep breaths," he orders. "In and out. Don't think about it, okay? Just breathe. Steady." His voice is just in-charge enough. The perfect amount of commanding. When I'm like this, a hairbreadth from exploding, I need structure. External frontal lobes. I need someone to think for me until I've calmed down. I don't know what's more upsetting: that Levi is doing this for me, or that I'm not even surprised about it.

"Thank you," I say when I'm more in control. I turn to my side, and my right cheek brushes against the pillow. "This was . . . Thank you."

He scans my face, unconvinced. "Are you feeling better?"

"A little. Thank you for not freaking out."

He shakes his head, holding my eyes, and I take more deep breaths. Seems like a good idea. "Want to talk about it?"

"Not really."

He nods and does what he did weeks ago, after saving me from the almost-pancaking: he puts his warm hand on my brow and pushes my hair back. It might be the best thing I've felt in months. Years. "Is there anything I can do?"

"No."

He nods again and makes to stand. The dread in the pit of my stomach is back with a vengeance. "Can you—" I realize that I slid my finger through one of the belt loops in his jeans and immediately flush and let go. Still, all the embarrassment in the world isn't enough to keep me from continuing. "Can you stay? Please? I know you'd probably rather be—"

"Nowhere else," he says, without skipping a beat. "There's nowhere else I'd rather be." We stay like that, in the Hostile Companionable Silence™ that's as much a part of our relationship as BLINK, and peanut-butter energy balls, and arguing about Félicette's existence. After a minute, or maybe thirty, he asks, "What happened, Bee?" and if he sounded pushy, or accusing, or embarrassed, it would be so easy to shut him down. But there's only pure, naked concern in his eyes, and I don't just *want* to tell him. I *need* to.

"Annie and I had a falling out in our last year of grad school. We haven't talked since."

He closes his eyes. "I'm a fucking asshole."

"No." I close my fingers around his wrist. "Levi, you—"

"I fucking pointed her out to you—"

"You couldn't have known." I sniffle. "I mean, you *are* an asshole, but for other reasons." I smile. I must look ridiculous, my cheeks glistening with sweat and tears and smudged mascara. He doesn't seem to mind, at least judging from the way he cups my face, his thumb warm on my skin. It's a lot of touching for two nemeses, but I'll allow it. I might even welcome it.

"Annie's at Vanderbilt," he says with the tone of someone who's talking to himself. "With Schreiber."

"You do remember her, then."

"Seeing you like this definitely jostled my memory. Other things, too." He doesn't move his hand, which is totally fine by me. "Is that why you're not working with Schreiber? Why you're with that idiot, Trevor Slate?"

"Trevor is *not* an idiot," I correct him. "He's a sexist, imbecile dickhead. But, yeah. We were supposed to do our postdocs together. We even timed our graduations so we'd move to Nashville at the same time. And then . . ." I shrug as best as I can. "Then that mess happened, and I couldn't go anymore. I couldn't be with her and Tim."

He frowns. "Tim?"

"All three of us were supposed to work with Schreiber."

"But what does Tim have to do with this?"

This is the hard bit. The part I've only said out loud twice. Once to Reike, and later to my therapist. I tell myself to breathe. Deeply. In and out. "It was over Tim, the falling out Annie and I had."

Levi tenses. His hand moves lower, to cup the back of my neck. Somehow it's exactly what I need. "Bee."

"I think you know how Tim was. Because everyone knew how Tim was." I smile. The tears are flowing again, quietly unstoppable. "Well, except for me. I just . . . I met him in my freshman year of college, you know? And he liked me. And that winter I had nowhere to go, and he asked if I wanted to spend it with his family. Which, of course, I did. It was amazing. God, I miss his family. His mother would knit me socks—isn't it the loveliest thing, knitting something warm for someone? I still wear them when it's cold." I wipe my cheeks with my wrists. "My therapist said that I didn't *want* to see. To admit how Tim truly was, because I overinvested in our relationship. Because if I acknowledged that he was a jerk, then I'd have to give up on the rest of his family, too. Maybe she's right, but I think I just wanted to trust him, you know? We were together for years. He asked me to marry him. He invited me into his life when no one else ever had. You trust a person like that, don't you?"

"Bee." Levi's looking at me in a way that I cannot comprehend. Because no one has ever looked at me like that.

"So, there were all these other girls. Women. I never blamed them—it wasn't their job to look after my relationship. I only ever blamed Tim." My lips taste like salt and too much water. "We'd been engaged for three years when I found out. I confronted him and took off my engagement ring and told him that we were done, that he'd betrayed me, that I hoped he got gonorrhea and his dick fell off—I don't even know what I told him. I was so mad I wasn't even crying. But he said that it didn't mean anything. That he didn't think I'd be so upset about it, and that he'd stop. That if I'd been . . ." I can't even bring myself to repeat it, the way he twisted everything to make it my fault. *If you fucked me a little more frequently*, he'd said. *If you were better. If you knew how to enjoy it and make it enjoyable. You could at least put in some effort.* "We'd been together for seven years. No one else had been in my life that long before, so I took him back. And I tried harder. I put more effort in . . . in our relationship. In making him happy. I'm not a victim—I made an informed choice. Figured that if getting married, if *stability* was what I wanted, then I shouldn't give up on Tim too quickly. You reap what you sow." I let out a shuddering sigh. "And then he and Annie—" My voice breaks, but Levi can imagine the rest. He knows enough already, probably more than he ever cared to. He doesn't need it spelled out, that I was such a needy, pitiful doormat that not only did I take back my cheater of a fiancé, but I also never realized that he *kept* cheating on me. With my closest friend. In the lab where I was working every day. I don't think about Annie too often, because the pain of losing *her*, I never quite learned how to manage. "I don't know why she did it. But I couldn't go with them to Vanderbilt. It was career suicide, but I just couldn't."

"You . . ." Levi's hand tightens on my nape. "You *didn't* marry him. You never married him."

I smile, rueful. "The worst thing is, I *tried* to forgive him for a long time. But then I couldn't, and . . ." I shake my head.

Levi is blinking, a dumbfounded expression on his face. "You're *not* married," he repeats, and I sit up as his shock finally penetrates my brain.

"You—you thought I was?" He nods, and I let out a wet laugh. "I was sure you knew, since you and Tim collaborate. And I let Guy believe it, because I thought you were trying to give me an out, but"— I lift my left hand—"this is my grandmother's ring. I'm not married. Tim and I haven't spoken in years."

Levi mouths something I cannot make out and pulls his hand back, as though all of a sudden my skin is scorching him. He stands and walks to the window, staring outside as he runs a hand through his hair. Is he angry?

"Levi?"

No reply. He rubs his mouth with his fingers, as if deep in thought, as if coming to terms with some seismic event.

"Levi, I know you and Tim collaborate. If this puts you in a weird position, you can—"

"We don't." He finally turns around. Whatever just happened, he seems to have collected himself. The green of his eyes, though, is brighter than before. Brighter than ever. "Collaborate, that is."

I sit up, legs dangling over the mattress. "You and Tim don't collaborate anymore?"

"Nope."

"Since when?"

"Now."

"What? But—"

"I don't feel like going to the conference," he interrupts. "Do you need to rest?"

"Rest?"

"Because of the"—he gestures vaguely at me and the bed—"fainting."

"Oh, I'm fine. If I needed rest every time I fainted, I'd need . . . a *lot* of rest."

"In that case, there's something I'd like to do."

"What is it?"

He doesn't answer. "Want to join me?"

I have no idea what he's referring to, but it's not as though I have a busy schedule. "Sure?"

He smiles, a little smug, and a terrible thought occurs to me: I'm going to regret whatever's about to happen.

"I *HATE* THIS."

"I know."

"What gave it away?" I push a sweaty purple strand from my forehead. My hands are shaking. My legs are twigs, but made of slime. There's a distinctive taste of iron in my throat. A sign that I'm dying? Possibly. I want to stop but I can't, because the treadmill is still going. If I collapse, the walking belt is going to swallow me in a vortex of clammy darkness. "Is it the wheezing? The near-puking?"

"Mostly the way you've said it eight times since starting to run—which, by the way, was exactly sixty seconds ago." He leans forward from his own treadmill and hits the speed button, slowing it. "You did great. Now walk a bit." He straightens and keeps on running at a pace I wouldn't achieve even hunted by a swarm of maggots. "In three minutes, you're going to run sixty more seconds." He's not even short of breath. Does he have bionic lungs? "Then you'll walk three more minutes, and then you'll cool down."

"Wait." I tuck my hair behind my ear. I need to invest in a headband. "That's it?"

"Yup."

"I only run for two minutes? That's my training?"

"Yep."

"How do you know? Have you ever done a Couch-to-5K? Have you ever even *been* on a couch?" I give him a skeptical once-over. He looks upsettingly good in his mid-thigh shorts and Pitt T-shirt. A patch of sweat is spreading on his back, making the cotton stick to his skin. I can't believe there are people who manage to look hot while running. Screw them.

"I did some research."

I laugh. "You did research?"

"Of course." He gives me an affronted look. "I said I'd train you for the 5K, and I will."

"Or you could just release me from our bet."

"Nice try."

I shake my head, laughing some more. "I can't believe you did research. It's either incredibly nice, or the most sadistic thing I've ever heard." I contemplate it. "I'm leaning toward the latter."

"Hush, or I'll sign you up for the Meat Lovers 5K."

I shut up and keep on walking.

Three hours later, we end up in a bar in the French Quarter. Together.

As in, me and Levi Ward. Getting drinks. Sipping Sazerac at the same table. Giggling because the waitress served mine with a heart-shaped straw.

I'm not sure how it happened. I think some googling was involved, and intense skimming of a website called Drinking NOLA, and then a five-minute walk in which I determined that one of Levi's steps equals exactly two of mine. But I'm blanking on how we came to the decision that venturing out together would be a good idea.

Oh well. Might as well focus on the Sazerac.

"So," I ask after a long sip, whiskey burning sweetly down my throat, "who's engaging with Schrödinger's anus this weekend?"

Levi smiles, swirling the amber liquid in his tumbler. After his shower he didn't dry his hair, and some damp wisps are still sticking to his ears. "Guy."

"Poor Guy." I lean forward. The corners of the world are starting to get fuzzy in a soft, pleasant way. Mmm, alcohol. "Is it difficult? Who taught you? Does it require tools? Does Schrödinger like it? What does it smell like?"

"No, the vet, just gloves and some treats, if he does he hides it well, and *awful.*"

I take another sip, fully entertained. "How did you end up with a cat who needs . . . expression, anyway?"

"He didn't when I first got him, seventeen years ago. He spent fifteen years long-conning me into loving him, and now here I am." He shrugs. "Expressing once a week."

I burst into more laughter than is probably warranted. Mmm, alcohol. "You got him as a kitten? From the shelter?"

"From under the garden shed. He was chomping on a sad-looking pigeon wing. I figured he needed me."

"How old were you?"

"Fifteen."

"You guys have been together most of your lives."

He nods. "My parents aren't exactly pet people, so it was either bringing him wherever I went or leaving him to fend for himself. He came to college with me. And grad school. He'd jump on my desk and stare at me all accusing and squinty-eyed when I slacked off. That little asshole."

"He's the real secret of your academic success!"

"I wouldn't go *that* far—"

"The source of your intelligence!"

"Seems excessive—"

"The only reason you have a job!" He lifts one eyebrow and I laugh some more. I'm hilarious. Mmm, alcohol. "It's so nice of Guy to do this for you."

"To be clear, Guy's just feeding Schrödinger. I did the expressing before leaving. But yeah, he's great."

"I have an inappropriate question for you. Did you steal Guy's job?"

He nods pensively. "Yes and no. He'd probably be BLINK's lead if I hadn't transferred. But I have more team-leading and neuro experience."

"He's awfully graceful about it."

"Yup."

"If it were me, I'd stab you with my nail filer."

He smiles. "I don't doubt it."

"I guess deep down Guy knows he's cooler." I take in Levi's confused expression. "I mean, he's an *astronaut*."

". . . And?"

"Well, here's the deal: if NASA were a high school, and its different divisions were cliques, the astronauts would be the football players."

"Is football *still* a thing in high school? Despite the brain damage?"

"Yes! Crazy, right? Anyway, the engineers would be more like the nerds."

"So I'm a nerd?"

I sit back and study him carefully. He's built like a linebacker.

"I actually played tight end," he points out.

Shit. Did I say it out loud? "Yes. You're a nerd."

"Fair. What about the neuroscientists?"

"Hmm. Neuroscientists are the artsy kids. Or maybe the exchange students. Intrinsically cool, but forever misunderstood. My point is: Guy's been to space, therefore he's part of a better clique."

"I see your reasoning, but counterpoint: Guy has never been to space, never will."

I frown. "He said he worked with you on his first space mission."

"As ground crew. He was supposed to go to the ISS, but he failed the psychological screening last minute—not that it means anything. Those tests are ridiculously selective. Anyway, most of the astronauts I've met are very down to earth—"

"*Down to Earth!*" I laugh so hard, people turn to stare. Levi shakes his head fondly.

"And to become an astronaut, you're required to have a STEM degree. Which means that they're nerds, too—nerds who decided to take on additional training."

"Wait a minute." I lean forward again. "You want to eventually be an astronaut, too?"

He presses his lips together, pensive. "I could tell you a story."

"Oooh. A story!"

"But you'd have to keep it secret."

"Because it's embarrassing?"

"A little."

I pout. "Then I can't do that. You're my archenemy—I *have* to slander you. It's in the contract."

"No story, then."

"Oh, come on!" I roll my eyes. "Fine, I won't tell anyone. But FYI, it will probably kill me."

He nods. "I'm willing to risk it. You know how my family isn't happy with me?"

"Still looking forward to kicking their collective ass at Thanksgiving."

"Appreciated. Once I started working for NASA, my mother took me aside and told me that I might be able to redeem myself in my father's eyes if I applied for the Astronaut Corps."

My eyes widen. "Did you do it?"

"Yep."

"And?" I'm leaning closer and closer. This is *engrossing*. "Did you get in?"

"Nope. Didn't even make it through the elimination round."

"No! Why?"

"Too tall. They recently tightened the height restriction—can't be taller than six two, or shorter than five one."

I briefly contemplate the notion that neither Levi nor I fall within astronaut height requirements, but for dramatically different reasons. Wild. "Were you heartbroken?"

"My family was, yeah." He looks me straight in the eye. "I was so relieved, my friend and I got passed-out drunk that night."

"What?"

He tips back his head and downs the rest of his drink. I'm *not* staring at his Adam's apple, I'm *not*. "Outer space is fucking *terrifying*. I'm thankful for the ozone layer and the gravitational pull of the moon and whatnot, but they'd have to tie me like a spit-roasted pig to send me out there. The universe keeps expanding and getting colder, chunks of our galaxy are sucked away, black holes hurl through space at millions of miles per hour, and solar superstorms flare up at the drop of a hat. Meanwhile NASA astronauts are out there in their frankly inadequate suits, drinking liters of their own recycled urine, getting alligator skin on the top of their feet, and shitting rubber balls that float around at eye level. Their cerebrospinal fluid expands and presses on their eyeballs to the point that their eyesight deteriorates, their gut bacteria are a shitshow—no pun intended—and gamma rays that could *literally* pulverize them in less than a second wander around. But you know what's even worse? The smell. Space smells like a toilet full of rotten eggs, and there's no escape. You're just stuck there until Houston allows you to come back home. So believe me when I say: I'm grateful every damn day for those two extra inches."

I stare at him. And stare at him. And stare a little more, open-mouthed. I stare at this man who is six four and two hundred pounds of muscle and just vented to me for five minutes about the fact that space is a scary place.

God. Oh, *God*. I think I like him.

"There's one single format in which space is tolerable," he says.

"Which is?"

"Star Wars movies."

Oh, *God*.

I jump out of my seat, grab his hand, and pull him out of the bar. He follows without resisting. "Bee? Where are we—?"

I don't bother looking back. "To my hotel room. To watch *The Empire Strikes Back*."

• • • •

"YODA'S A BIT of a dick." I lean over to steal a handful of popcorn from Levi's lap. My own bag, sadly, is long gone. Should have paced myself.

"All Jedi are dicks." Levi shrugs. "It's the forced celibacy."

I can't believe I'm on a bed. With Levi Ward. Watching a movie. With Levi Ward. And it doesn't even feel weird. I steal more popcorn, and inadvertently grab his thumb. "Sorry!"

"That's not vegan," he says, a hint of something in his voice, and I am mesmerized by the shadows the TV light casts on his face. His elegant nose, the unexpected fullness of his lips, his black hair, blue-tinted in the dark.

"What?" he asks, without taking his eyes off the screen.

"What, what?"

"You're staring."

"Oh." I should avert my gaze, but I'm a bit drunk. And I like looking at him. "Nothing. Just . . ."

He finally turns. "Just?"

"Just . . . look at us." I smile. "It doesn't even feel like we hate each other."

"That's because we don't."

"Aw." I tilt my head. "You stopped hating me?"

"New rule." He turns more fully toward me, and his ridiculously long legs brush against mine. In the swampy forests of Dagobah, Yoda's torturing poor Luke under the guise of training him. "Every time you say that I hate you, you have to come over and express Schrödinger's glands."

"You say it like it wouldn't be enjoyable."

"Since you clearly have a fetish: every time you mention this non-existent enmity I supposedly feel, I'll add a mile to the race you owe me."

"That's *crazy*."

"You know what to do to make it stop." He pops a kernel into his mouth.

"Hmm. Can I say that *I* hate *you*?"

He looks away. "I don't know. Do you hate me?"

Do I hate him? No. Yes. No. I haven't forgotten how much of a dipshit he was in grad school, or that he reprimanded me about *my clothes* on my first day of work, or any of the dickish things he's done to me. But after a big day like today, when he saved me from total, catastrophic implosion, it all seems so distant.

No, then. I don't hate him. In fact, I kind of like him. But I don't want to admit it, so while Han and Leia bicker about how much they love each other on the screen, I punt.

"What are you wearing tomorrow?"

He gives me a puzzled look. "I don't know. Is it relevant?"

"Of course! We're spying."

He nods in a way that clearly showcases how full of shit he thinks I am. "Something inconspicuous, then. A trench coat. Sunglasses. You brought your fake mustache, right?"

I smack his arm. "Not all of us have a long history of espionage—by the way, what's the story behind the MagTech pics?"

"That's a secret."

"Did you really risk your career, like Boris said?"

"No comment."

I roll my eyes. "Well, if you did . . . thank you." I settle back into my pillow, focusing on the movie.

"Hey, Bee?"

I love Wookiees so much. Best aliens ever. "Yeah?"

"If tomorrow you see Annie and Tim and feel . . . like you felt today. Just take my hand, okay?"

I should ask what that would even accomplish. I should point out that his hand is not a powerful brand of instant-release benzodiazepines. But I think he might be right. I think it might just do the trick. So I nod, and steal the entire bag of popcorn from his lap.

He does have a point. Space *is* kind of scary.

15

FUSIFORM AREA: FAMILIAR FACES

"THEY HIRED A neuroscientist," Levi says, gaze locked on the podium where engineers with heavy Dutch accents are discussing their stimulation headgear.

I'd nod, but I feel queasy. MagTech's helmets are at the same stage as ours. Maybe a bit further. A *tiny* bit further, but still. The banana I had for breakfast is lurching in my stomach. "Yup."

"They solved the output location problems in a different way," he murmurs. He's talking to himself, one hand clenched on the armrest, white-knuckled.

Yep. This sucks.

Hey, Dr. Curie. I know you're busy frolicking naked with Pierre, and I know that it's unfair of me to ask, but if you or Hertha could do me a solid and zap MagTech's stimulation headgear with radioactive lightning, that'd be lovely. If they patent the technology before we do, they'll just sell

it to whatever militia pays the most, and as you know, humans don't need
cognitive enhancement when it comes to killing each other. Kthxbye.

"They're stuck on merging hardware and software," Levi says.

"Yep. Just like us." I squirm in my chair. This trip was pointless.
Absolutely pointless. I want to go back to Houston and put in five,
ten, twenty hours of work. Go through every single piece of data
we've collected and see if I missed anything that will help us move
forward.

This is a race. It always was, from the very start, but after the
uncertainty of my first week on BLINK, I was so grateful for the opportunity to have a shot at it, it almost slipped my mind. Doing our
best, making progress—that seemed enough. Spoiler: it wasn't. For
the first time in weeks I think, *really* think, about my job at NIH. I've
been sending weekly reports to Trevor and the Institute director. There
hasn't been much of a reaction on their end except for "Nice job" and
"Keep up the good work." I wonder whether they read or just skim
for buzzwords. *Neural networks. Magnetic pulses. Neuroplasticity*'s always a hit, too.

What would they say if I told them that MagTech might reach the
finish line first? Would they blame *me*? Would my job be safe? And
what would happen to the promotion I want? I'll either be fired or
work for Trevor in perpetuity—is this what my career ambitions have
come to, an eternal quest for the lesser evil?

Become a scientist, they said. *It will be fun*, they said.

"Let's go." Levi springs up from his chair the second the presentation ends. "If we leave now, we can be home by mid-afternoon."

I've never been more eager to get out of an air-conditioned room.
"You want to hole up in the lab and work until you pass out?"

"Yup." He pops the *P*.

At least we're on the same page. "You know what?" I muse, weaving my way through the crowd. "I might have an idea on how to tackle the gradient fields issue—"

"*As I live and breathe*. Levi and Bee!"

We stop dead. But we don't turn around, because we don't need to. Voices are like faces, after all: one never forgets them, not if they belong to people who are important. Your parents. Siblings. Best friends, partners, crushes.

Ph.D. advisors.

"I cannot believe you're *here* and I didn't *know it*."

Levi's eyes lock with mine. *Fuck*, I read in the way his pupils dilate. I telepathically answer, *Indeed*. His expression darkens.

I love Sam. We both love Sam. I've never talked about her with Levi, but I know they had a special relationship, just like she and I did. She was an outstanding advisor: intelligent, supportive, and she cared, really *cared*, about us. After my falling out with Tim and Annie, I didn't have the heart to tell her what really happened. So I made up some lies about a friendly breakup and about needing to be in Baltimore with nonexistent relatives. Sam was the one who helped me find my job with Trevor, and she never criticized me for turning down a better position at Vanderbilt. I always love hearing from her, catching up on her work, getting coffee together. Always.

Except for right now.

I smile as she engulfs me in a bear hug, and—okay, this feels amazing. She's tall and sturdily built. A truly committed hugger. I find myself laughing, squeezing her back. "It's so nice to see you, Sam."

"That's my line. And you, Levi, look at you. Are you even taller?" Their hug is significantly more subdued. I'm nonetheless shocked that Levi does hugs, and by the affectionate smile on his lips.

"Not that I know. It's nice to see you, Sam."

"Why didn't I know you two were here?"

"Because we're not on the program. We just drove up for a specific presentation."

"We?" Sam's eyes widen. She looks between us a few times before settling on Levi with a huge pleased grin that I cannot interpret. Then she takes one of his hands. "I didn't know there was a 'we,' Levi. I'm so happy for you. I've been hoping for so long, and finally, such an incredible—"

"Bee and I are working together on a NASA project. *Temporarily.*" He says it quickly, like a teenager stopping his mother from revealing that he still sleeps with a stuffed triceratops.

Sam gasps, covering her mouth. "Of course. Of course, the NASA project. I can't believe it slipped my mind. Still, you two should come to my brunch. In"—she glances at her phone—"ten minutes. All my grads are coming. Food's on me, of course."

Uh-oh.

Uh-*shitshitshitshit*-oh.

I glance up at Levi, ready to beg him not to make me watch Tim and Annie eat huevos rancheros for thirty minutes, but he's already shaking his head. "Thank you, but we can't. We need to get on the road."

"Oh, nonsense. It'll be less than an hour. Just make an appearance, say hi to everyone, have breakfast on me. You're both so skinny."

I wonder how one could possibly look at Levi's chest, or biceps, or legs, or . . . anything, really, and think the word "skinny," but he doesn't skip a beat. "We need to get going."

"You can't," she insists. Have I mentioned that Sam's bossy? I guess it's a professional hazard when you've been running a lab for decades. "You were my favorite grads. What's the point of having a lab brunch if you two aren't there? Might as well cancel!"

"You didn't even know we were here until three minutes ago," Levi points out patiently.

"But now I do. And . . ." She leans forward and puts a hand on both our shoulders. "I'll be making an important announcement today. I'm retiring at the end of the semester. And once I'm out, I'm not planning to do the conference circuit anymore. So there might not be a next time."

Levi nods. "I get it, Sam. But we really—"

"We'll come," I interrupt. "Just tell us where." I chuckle at the excited way Sam claps her hands.

"Are you sure you want to do this?" Levi asks me calmly once Sam is out of earshot.

"I'm sure I do *not* want to do this." If I had to type a comprehensive list of the things I'd rather do, I'd need several gigabytes of cloud space. "But if she's announcing her retirement and it's important for her, we can't *not* go, not after everything she's done for us." I massage my temple, thinking longingly of ibuprofen. "Plus, my old therapist would be proud of me."

He studies me for a long beat. Then he nods, once. I can tell he doesn't like this. "Fine. But if you're not feeling well, you tell me immediately and I'll take you away." He speaks in an authoritative way that should make me want to tell him to shove it, but . . . it doesn't. The opposite, actually. What a mystery. "And remember my hand."

"Okay, Daddy." I realize the blunder only once the words are out of my mouth. Since I can't take it back, I turn around and walk out of the conference center, blushing. Oops.

What a cluster of a day. And it's only seven minutes past ten.

VISUALIZE THIS: YOU step into a restaurant, and the hostess guides you to your party's table. It's round and full, but when you and your companion arrive two chairs will be pulled up, guaranteeing lots of cozy elbowing. Yay. You're welcomed by many pairs of wide eyes, and gasps, and a few "My gosh, how long has it been?" Some are for you, some for your companion. Some for both. You realize that aside from the person who invited you, no one was expecting you. Double yay.

You want to focus on catching up, ask old friends about their lives, but there's something that nags at you. A tiny worm slithering in the back of your skull. It has to do, you initially think, with the two people who've yet to stand to greet you, and with the fact that you used to be engaged to one of them, and to love the other like a sister. Fair. That would nag at anyone, right?

But then there's an extra *something* cranking up the tension: almost everyone at the table knows *exactly* what happened between you, your former fiancé, and your not-so-sister. They know how poorly you left off, how you ended up having to find another job, how miserable it made you, and even though they're not mean people, there's a sense swarming around, a sense that a show is about to happen. A show that involves you.

You following this? Good. Because there's one more layer to this onion. It elevates this brunch above your run-of-the-mill trash-fire, and it has to do with your companion. He wasn't exactly a fan of yours the last time you two hung out with these people, and seeing you arrive with him is making their heads *explode*. They cannot compute. The show was always gonna be good, but now? Now it's fucking *Hamilton*, baby.

Are you visualizing this? Are you feeling the deep unpleasantness of the situation smack inside your bones? Are you considering crawling under the table and rocking yourself to sleep? Okay. Good. Because it's *exactly* where I'm at when Timothy William Carson comes to stand in front of me and says, "Hi, Bee."

I want to kick him in the nuts. But I'm sad to report that there are lots of pairs of eyes on me, and while I haven't passed the Louisiana bar, I fear nut-kicking might be considered assault in this great state. So I smile my best fake smile, ignore the crawling feeling in the pit of my stomach, and reply, "Hey, Tim. You look great."

He doesn't. He looks okay. He looks fine. He looks like a Cute Guy™ who needs a Dorian Gray portrait, because his rotten personality is starting to show. He looks acceptable, but nothing compared to the guy standing next to me. Who, by the way, is saying, "Tim."

"Levi! What's up?"

"Not much."

"We gotta start working on those collabs again." Tim puckers his lips like the asshole he is. "I've been *swamped*."

Levi's smile stays on, and when Tim leans in for a bro hug, he accepts it.

Which has me scowling. What the hell? I thought Levi was on *my* side. Which sounds stupid when said out loud, and unfair of me to expect, because Levi and I are barely friends and my battles are not his and he has every right to man-hug whoever. . . .

My train of thought fades as I notice Levi is not just *hugging* Tim. He's also gripping his shoulders tightly, fingers digging painfully into Tim's flesh as he murmurs something in his ear. I can't make out the words, but by the time Levi straightens back up, Tim's mouth is pulled in a thin, straight line, his face is milk white in a way I don't remember ever seeing before, and his expression looks almost . . . scared.

Is Tim *scared*?

"I— You— I didn't mean to," he stammers, but Levi interrupts him.

"Nice to see you again," he says in a commanding, dismissive tone. Tim must take it as what it is: an order to scurry away.

"What just happened?" I whisper while Levi pulls out my chair. Apparently, we're in 1963.

"Look." He points at Sam's food. "They have quinoa bowls."

"Why does Tim look *terrified*?"

He gives me an innocent look. "He does?"

"Levi. What did you say to him?"

Levi ignores me. "Sam, does that bowl have eggs in it?"

The first twenty minutes aren't that bad. The problem with round tables is that you can't fully ignore anyone's existence, but Tim and Annie are distant enough that I can chat with others without it being too awkward. Aspects of this are genuinely nice—having Sam around, hearing that old acquaintances got married, had kids, found academic jobs, bought houses. Once in a while Levi's elbow brushes against mine, reminding me that I'm not wholly alone. There's someone in my corner. A guy who loves Star Wars, and is too tall for space, and will take care of a kitten for half his life.

Then there's a lull in conversation, and someone asks from across the table, "How did you two end up working together, anyway?"

Everyone tunes in after that. All eyes are on Levi and me. Sadly, Levi is chewing on a potato wedge. So I say, "It's an NIH-NASA collab, Mike."

"Oh yeah, right." Mike looks a bit buzzed, but he takes another sip of his punch. He was a third year when I joined the lab. Also: he was a shithead. "But, like, how are *you two* managing it? Levi, do you bleach your brain after every meeting, or . . . ?"

My cheeks burn. Some people chuckle, a couple laugh outright, and others look away, clearly embarrassed. Sam frowns, and from the corner of my eye I see Tim smirk. I wish I had a witty comeback, but I'm too mortified by the fact that Levi finding me disgusting is still the lab's funniest inside joke. I open my mouth without knowing what to say, and—

"We're doing great," Levi tells Mike, his tone a mix of big-dick calm and *I could kill a man with a beach ball.* He leisurely puts his arm on the back of my chair, and plucks a grape from my plate. A deafening silence falls at the table. Everyone is looking at us. *Everyone.* "What about you, Mike?" Levi asks without bothering to look up from my food. "I heard there were problems with your tenure packet. How's that coming along?"

"Oh, um . . ."

"Yeah. I thought so."

Holy shit. Holy shit. *Holy shit.* I guess Levi's done eating his potatoes?

"Out of curiosity," he whispers in my ear once the conversation has moved along and Mike is looking down at his own plate, chastised. "Did *everyone* think that I hated you, back in grad school? It wasn't just *your* delusion?"

"It was a widely known truth."

His arm tenses around my shoulders, as tight as his jaw.

A few minutes later I excuse myself to go to the restroom. I have eye makeup on, but I say "Screw it" and wash my face with cold water anyway. Who's going to be looking at my runny eyeliner anyway? Levi? Weepy Mess Bee is nothing he hasn't already seen.

Then I notice her. Annie, in the mirror. She's standing right behind me, waiting for me to finish using the sink. Except there are three more sinks, and zero other people in the bathroom. So maybe it's just me she's waiting for.

My head hurts. And so does my heart, around the edges Annie cracked in it two years ago. I can't talk to her. Can't. *Can't.* I take my time drying my face with my sleeves. Then I buck up, turn around, and face her.

She's stunningly beautiful. Always has been. There's something indescribable about her, something magic that made me happy to be in her presence. Oddly enough, the feeling is still there, a mix of familiarity and love and awe that knifes deep as I stare at her face. Seeing Tim again was painful, but it's nothing, *nothing* compared to having Annie right here.

For a moment I'm terrified. She can hurt me very, *very* deeply with just a few choice words. But then she says, "Bee," and I realize that she's crying. Judging by the burning in my eyes, so am I.

"Hey, Annie." I attempt a smile. "Long time no see."

"Yeah, I . . . yeah." She nods. Her lips are trembling. "I love your hair. Purple might be my favorite."

"Thank you." A beat. "I tried orange last year. I looked like a traffic cone." Silence stretches, wistful. It reminds me of when we'd fill every second together with chatter. "Well, I need to . . ." I move for the door, but she stops me with a hand on my forearm.

"No—*please*. Please, Bee, can we just . . ." She smiles. "I missed you."

I missed her, too. I miss her all the time, but I won't tell her. Because I hate her. Me and my multitudes.

"I've been listening to that album you gave me a lot. Even though I'm still not sure I like it. And last year I went to Disneyland and there was this new Star Wars park and I thought of you. And I haven't been able to make friends in Schreiber's lab because they're all dudes. Total WurstFest™. Except for two girls, but they're best friends already, and I don't think they like me much, and . . ." She's crying harder now, but also laughing in that self-deprecating way that is *so* Annie. "So, you and Levi, huh? He's even hotter than back at Pitt."

I shake my head. "It's not like that."

"You probably made all his dreams come true. He looks happier than I've ever seen him. Not that I'd seen him happy, like *ever*, before today."

A cold shiver runs down my spine. I have no idea what she's talking about. "Actually, Levi hated me," I say stubbornly.

"I doubt it. Not by any definition of that term. He just really—" She shakes her head firmly. "This isn't what I came to talk about, I don't know why I'm going on about stuff that . . ." She takes a deep breath. "I'm sorry."

I could pretend not to know what she's apologizing for. I could pretend that I didn't think about her every day for the last two years. I could pretend that I don't miss the way we'd make each other laugh until our abs ached, but it would be exhausting, and even though it's eleven fifteen in the morning, I am already so very tired.

"Why?" I ask. A question I rarely allow myself when it comes to Annie. "Why did you do it?"

"I don't know." Her eyes close. "I don't know, Bee. I've been trying to figure it out for years. I just . . . don't know."

I nod, because I believe her. I never doubted Annie's love for me.

"Maybe I was jealous?"

"Jealous?"

She shrugs. "You were beautiful. The best in the lab. With the glamorous globe-trotting past. You were always good at everything, always so . . . so happy and cool and fun. You made it seem effortless."

I was never any of those things. Not by a long shot. But I think of Levi—impenetrable, cold, arrogant Levi, who turned out not to be impenetrable, cold, arrogant at all. Being so dramatically misunderstood doesn't seem that unlikely.

"And you and Tim . . . You and I were always together, but in the

end, you'd go home to Tim and I'd be alone, and there was this . . .
thing that I was never part of."

"Were you trying to . . . to punish me?"

"No! No, I was just trying to feel . . . more like you." She rolls her
eyes. "And because I'm a dumbass, I picked the worst part of you to
do that. Fucking Tim." She lets out a bubbly, moist laugh. "We
never . . . It lasted a week between us. And I—I *never* liked him, you
know it. I *despised* him. You were so much better than him, and everyone knew it. I knew it. He knew it, too. The moment I did it, *while* I
was doing it—I thought of you the whole time. And not just because
he was a lousy lay. I kept wondering if doing such an unspeakably
bad thing would . . . elevate me, somehow. Make me more like you.
God, I was messed up. I still am." She wipes her tears with two fingers. There's already more, flowing down. "I wanted to apologize.
But you blocked my number, and I told myself I'd give you space and
see you at Vanderbilt. Then the summer passed, and you weren't
there . . ." She shakes her head. "I'm so sorry. I'm *so* sorry, and I think
about it every day, and—"

"I'm sorry, too."

She gives me an incredulous look. "You have nothing to be sorry
about."

"I may not have fucked your fiancé, but I'm sorry I wasn't there
for you when you felt like you weren't good enough. You were my best
friend, but I always thought you were . . . invincible."

We are quiet until she says, "This is in no way meant as self-
congratulatory, but I'm glad you didn't marry Tim. I'm glad you're
with Levi. He's the kind of person you deserve."

I don't see the point in contradicting her. Not when I agree with
everything she's said, including things that aren't quite true. So I nod
and make to leave.

"Bee?" she calls.

I turn.

"Would you mind it if I texted you, once in a while?"

I should probably be thinking big thoughts about forgiveness, and punishment, and self-preservation. I should throw the question back at her and ask if *she*'d let me text her if our situations were reversed. I should reflect on this when my brain is not a mushy mess. But I forget all the "shoulds," and tell her the first thing to cross my heart. "We could try."

She nods, relieved.

Levi is outside the bathroom, a hulking mountain leaning against the wall. I don't have to ask to know that he saw Annie come after me, and decided to follow in case I needed him. I don't have to lie or reassure him that I'm fine even as I wipe my cheeks. I don't have to explain anything.

I can just nod when he asks if I'm ready to go, and take his hand when he offers it.

16

SUBTHALAMIC NUCLEUS: INTERRUPTIONS

I WAKE UP from a four-hour stress-nap as Levi merges onto the interstate for the last stretch of the trip, and BLINK is instantly on my mind. "About the frequency trains, I wonder if we could take advantage of the magnetothermal—" Something splattered on the side of the road catches my eye. "What's *that?*"

"Wow." Levi's tone is forcefully cheerful. "Check out that farm on the right!"

"But what's that on the— Oh *no.*"

"I didn't see anything."

"Is it a dead raccoon?"

"No."

"Yes, it was!" I start crying. Again. For the seventh time in forty-eight hours. You'd think my lacrimal ducts would have runneth over, but nope. "Poor baby."

"You know what? It *was* a raccoon, but it had clearly died of old age."

"What?"

"In that very spot. He died peacefully in his sleep, then someone ran him over. Nothing to be sad about." I glare at him. At least I'm not crying anymore. "What were you saying about leveraging magnetothermal properties?"

"You're full of shit." I lift my legs, kick his forearm, and then lay my foot on the glove compartment. His eyes follow my every movement, linger briefly on my bare knees. "But thank you. For babysitting my feelings this weekend. For not letting me free-fall into a pit of despair. I promise I'm going to revert to adult status. Starting now."

"Finally," he deadpans.

I laugh. "For real—what did you tell Tim?"

"I said hi. Asked how he was."

"Come on. You were speaking into his ear."

"Just whispering sweet nothings."

I snort. "Wouldn't be surprising. You might be the only person in the lab he didn't cheat on me with." His long fingers grip the steering wheel and I instantly regret my words. "Hey, I was joking. I actually don't care much anymore. Would I mind seeing Tim bent in two with a severe hemorrhoid attack? Nope. But neither would I go out of my way to stab him. Which I didn't know before this weekend, and that's . . . freeing." Liberating, this almost-indifference. It makes me much happier than the resentment I harbored for years. And the conversation with Annie . . . I haven't processed it yet, but maybe this weekend was less of a waste than I thought. Except that I'm low-key panicking about my job again. "Whatever you told Tim . . . thank you. It was nice to see him almost shit his pants."

He shakes his head. "You shouldn't thank me. It was selfish."

"What did he do to you? Did he sneak bacon into your sandwich? Because that's totally his signature move——"

"No." He presses his lips together, staring at the road. "He lied to me."

"Oh, yeah." I nod knowingly. "His *other* signature move."

The local NPR fills the silence. Something about Rachmaninoff. Until Levi says, "Bee, I . . . I'm not sure I should be telling you this. But hiding things from you hasn't worked out in our favor. And you asked me to be honest."

"I did." I study him, unsure where he's heading.

"When you and I first met," he says slowly, carefully weighing his words, "I had issues talking to people. About certain things."

"Like . . . aphasia?"

He smiles, shaking his head. "Not quite."

I try to think back to fifth-year Levi—he seemed larger than life, indomitable, whip-smart. Then again, Annie seemed invincible, and I apparently seemed effortless. Grad school really screwed us up, didn't it? "I never noticed it. You were capable, self-assured, and got along with most people." I mull it over. "Except for me, of course."

"I'm not explaining myself well. I had no issues talking to normal people. My issues were . . . with you."

I scowl. "Are you saying that I'm not *normal*?"

He laughs silently. "You're not normal. Not to me."

"What does that mean?" I turn in the seat to face him, not sure why he's insulting me again, after two days of being incredibly lovely. Is he having a relapse? "Just because you thought I was ugly or unlikable, it doesn't mean that I wasn't *normal*——"

"I never thought of you as ugly." His hands tighten even more around the wheel. "Never."

"Come on. The way you always acted was——"

"The opposite, in fact."

I frown. "What do you even—" Oh.

Oh.

Oh.

Does he mean that—? No. Impossible. He wouldn't. Would he? Even if we . . . He can't possibly be implying *that.* Can he?

"I—" My mind goes blank for a split second—complete, utter white-out void. I'm suddenly frozen numb, so I lean forward to turn off the AC. I have no clue how to answer him. How to stop my heart from beating out of my throat. "Do you mean that you . . . ?"

He nods.

"You didn't . . . you didn't even let me finish the sentence."

"Whatever you're imagining, from the tamest to the most . . . in-appropriate thoughts, that's probably where my mind was at." He swallows visibly. I watch his throat move. "You were always in my head. And I could never get you out."

I turn to the window, scarlet. There's no universe in which I'm parsing his words correctly. This is a misunderstanding. I'm having some neurological event. And all I want to ask is, *What about now? Am I still in your head?* "You always stared at me like I was some ob-scene monstrosity."

"I tried not to stare, but . . . it wasn't easy."

"No. No, you—the dress. You hated me in that dress. My blue dress, the one with—"

"I know what dress, Bee."

"You know because you *hated* it," I say in a panic.

"I didn't hate it." His words are quiet. "It just took me by sur-prise."

"My *Target dress* took you by surprise?"

"No, Bee. My . . . reaction to *you* wearing it did."

214

I shake my head. This cannot be true. "You wouldn't even *sit* next to me."

"It was hard to think when you were close." His voice is husky.

"No. No! You refused to collaborate with me. You told Tim he should marry someone better, you avoided me like the bubonic plague—"

"Tim warned me off."

I turn to him. "What?"

"He asked me to back off and leave you alone."

"He . . ." I cover my mouth and imagine Tim, *very* average-sized Tim, confronting Levi, a not-so-gentle bison. "How did he . . . ?"

"He told me you knew that I was . . . interested. That I was making you uncomfortable. That you found me unpleasant." Levi's throat works. "He asked me to avoid you as much as I could. And I did. In a way, it was easier."

"Easier?"

He shrugs with a self-deprecating smile. "Just . . . wanting and not having, it can get unbearable. Quickly so." He wets his lips. "I didn't know what to say anyway. You have to understand, people don't talk about the things they feel where I come from. I got really tongue-tied around you—leading you and everyone else to believe that I despised you, apparently. I . . . I had no idea. I owe you an apology for that."

I can't believe what he's saying. I can't believe what I'm hearing. I can't believe Tim knew and successfully manipulated Levi into staying away while he screwed his way through Pitt's student body.

"Why are you telling this to me? Why now?"

He looks at me, serious and earnest like only Levi Ward could ever be, and something surges into me. Something painful and delightful and confusing. Something breathtaking and spellbinding, rich and frightening. Not a fully formed feeling, but an early draft of it. It's on the back of my throat and on the tip of my tongue. I want to get a grasp of its taste before it's gone. I am reaching out, almost there when Levi says, "Bee, I—"

My phone rings. I groan in frustration and relief and scramble to pick up. "Hello?"

"Bee, this is Boris Covington." *Huh?* "Are you and Levi back?"

I glance at Google Maps. "We're about ten minutes out."

"Could you both come to the Discovery Building as soon as you get in?"

"Sure." I frown, switching to speakerphone. "Does this have to do with BLINK?"

"No. Well, yes. But only indirectly." Boris sounds tired and almost . . . embarrassed? Levi and I exchange a long glance.

"What's this about?"

Boris sighs. "It's about Ms. Jackson and Ms. Cortoreal. Please, come in as soon as you can."

Levi presses on the gas pedal.

I LOOK AROUND Boris's office and blink at least four times before asking, "What do you mean, 'sexual intercourse is forbidden in work areas'?"

Boris's skin's even redder than usual, and he retreats farther into his desk. "Exactly what I said. It's—"

"Bee's not my mother and I'm not a minor," Rocío proclaims from one of the guest chairs. "This conversation is a HIPAA violation."

Boris pinches the bridge of his nose. He's clearly been at this for a while. "HIPAA rules apply to medical records, not to you being caught having sex in your office. Which, just like *every other space in the building*, is video-surveilled twenty-four-seven because of the high-security projects it houses. Now, no need to worry about that, Guy is a security admin and has agreed to delete all footage. But Bee is your direct supervisor, just like Levi is Ms. Jackson's, and because of the disciplinary actions required when NASA employees engage in activities such as . . . intercourse in work spaces, they need to be informed."

I glance at Levi. His face is a blank void. I'm positive that inside he's rolling with laughter like a pork in mud. *Positive.*

"Sorry." I scratch the back of my neck. "Just to be clear, you two were having intercourse with . . ."

"With each other," Rocío tells me proudly.

I nod. Next to Rocío, Kaylee appears enraptured by her own pink nail polish. She hasn't looked up since we came in.

"Um . . ." I have no idea what to say. Zero. Nada. Maybe Dr. Curie left behind helpful tips to handle similar situations? If only her notes weren't too radioactive to be touched before the year 3500. Maybe I can go to the Bibliothèque Nationale with a hazmat suit and—

"I won't write up a complaint," Boris says, "and I trust Bee and Levi will take care of . . ." He gestures vaguely at two of the smartest women I've ever met, who must be going through a spell of nymphomania. "But I beg you on my knees. Don't do anything similar *ever again.*"

"Thank you, Boris," I say, hoping I sound as grateful as I feel.

The walk to the outside of the building is deadly silent—until we form a circle and stare at one another with varying levels of hostility (Rocío), mortification (Kaylee), and poorly hidden amusement (Levi). I hope I look neutral. I probably don't.

"So . . . that happened," I start.

Rocío nods. "Sure did."

"How did Boris even . . . find you?"

"Guy came into our office looking for something, found us on your desk, ratted us out."

"On *my*—why did you have to do it on *my*—" I stop. Take a deep breath. "To be clear." I look between them. "This was . . . consensual?"

"Very," they answer in unison, locking eyes and smiling like idiots.

I clear my throat. "Is there anything you'd like to add?" I ask Levi, meaning *please help*, but he shakes his head, biting his lip to avoid smiling. He fails.

"Okay. Well. It's none of our business what you guys do."

"For the first time in my life I agree with you," Rocío says.

"Really? For the *first time*?" She nods. Ungrateful little gremlin. "If you're happy about this, so are we. But please, don't, um, have intercourse in front of cameras. Unless you're making a sex tape," I rush to add, "in which case just . . . don't do it in public places?"

Kaylee nods silently, looking a smidge less mortified. Rocío rolls her eyes. "Whatever." She takes Kaylee's hand and drags her away. *"You're not my real mother, Bee!"* she yells without turning around.

Levi and I watch them walk away in the late afternoon sunlight. When they're just little dots on the street, he tells me, "That was excellent practice for when we'll have teenage daughters."

My heart skips. *He doesn't mean together, idiot.* "They're young. Their frontal lobes are not fully developed yet."

He takes the car keys out of his pocket and dangles them in front of my face. "Want to process the trauma of our twenty-three-year-olds role-playing on top of your Marie Curie mouse pad while I take you home?"

"They better be going to Kaylee's place."

"Why?"

"The walls between my apartment and Rocío's are very thin."

"You should invest in noise-canceling headphones." He tugs me toward the car. "Order online while I drive."

"IT JUST SEEMS far-fetched," I say in the passenger seat. "First of all, Rocío's in a relationship. Oh—I wonder if they're poly?"

"Should we be discussing our RAs' love lives?"

"I'd normally say no, but them bumping uglies on my desk automatically grants us a waiver."

He contemplates it. "Fair."

"And—those two are so different from each other."

"You think that's a problem?"

It might not be. They might produce well-rounded children who know how to apply raccoon-style eyeliner *and* glitter. "Okay, it's not. But Rocío *disliked* Kaylee. She kept clamming up whenever Kaylee was around. She made an entire list of things she hated about her."

Levi half smiles. "You sure about that?"

"Yeah. She told me that—" I recall what Levi told me less than one hour ago and shut my mouth. I forgot when Boris's call sent me into emergency mode, but now it's all back, swirling around the forefront of my brain, and with that my heart is heavy in my throat, a liquid warmth in the pit of my stomach, the sense of being on a precipice. I could be falling. I *will* be falling, fast and hard, if only I take one step forward and let myself—

A thought hits me. Smack in the head. Like a freight train.

I gasp. "I've got it."

Levi pulls into my driveway. "What did you say?"

"I got it!"

"Got . . . what?"

"The helmet. BLINK. I know how to fix the compatibility issue—do you have paper? Why don't you have paper in your stupid car?"

"It's a rental—"

"My apartment! I have paper up there!" The car hasn't fully stopped, but I jump out and run upstairs anyway. I unlock the door, hunt down a pen and notebook, and start scribbling as fast as my fingers will go, pitifully out of breath. A minute later I hear steps behind me and Levi closing the door I left open. Oops.

"I'm assuming you wanted me to follow you in, but if not—"

"Look." I push the notebook under his nose. "We're going to do this. Look at this."

He blinks a few times. "Bee, I don't think this is . . . English."

I turn the notebook around. Shit, I wrote in German. "Okay— *don't* look at this. Just listen to me. And don't be scared. We've been having issues with the switchboard, right? We've been trying to fix it, but . . . what if we just bypass it?"

"But the different frequencies—"

"Right. That's where I'm going to scare you."

"Scare me?"

"Yes." I make room on the table, and start sketching a diagram. "But don't be scared."

"I'm not scared."

"Good. Stay unscared."

"I— Why would I be scared?"

"Because of what I'm about to show you. Which you might find scary." I tap the back of the pen on the top of my diagram. "Okay. We remove the switchboard." I draw a cross on it. "We build separate circuits. And then we leverage the magnetothermal properties of each one—"

"—for speed." Levi's eyes are wide. "And if we have separate circuits—"

"—we can rely on the wireless remote." I grin at him. "Will it work?"

He bites into his lower lip, staring at the diagram. "The wiring will be tricky. And isolating each circuit. But if we work around that . . ." He turns to me with a wide, breathless grin. "This could work. It could really work."

"And it will be so much better than what MagTech is doing."

"We'd have a final prototype in . . . weeks. Days." He rubs his mouth. "This is a fantastic idea."

I jump up and down excitedly. It's obnoxious, but I can't stop myself. Where does all this energy go when I try to run? "Am I a genius, or what?"

He shakes his head even as he says, "You *are*."

"Should we go to the lab? Start working on it?"

"Before the cleaning crew has a chance to disinfect your desk?"

"Good point. But I need to *do* something."

He smiles fondly. "Maybe you can keep jumping up and down?"

"I'm starting to get tired, actually."

"Okay, then . . ." He shrugs, and before I know what's going on I'm in his arms and he's spinning me around, my legs wrapped around his waist and his hands on my thighs.

I laugh. I laugh like I'm happy. What a *weekend*. I'm a feather. I'm invincible. I'm doing science. I'm having *fun*. I'm building things, useful, important things. I'm facing demons from my past. I'm being whirled around when I'm too tired to do it myself. I'm bubbling, exhilarated, brave. I'm the most myself and not myself at all. I'm tightening my hands around Levi's neck, and when he slows down I'm asking him, "Are you going to kiss me?"

No idea where *that* came from. But I'm not sorry it's out there.

His smile doesn't falter, but he shakes his head. "I don't think so," he says quietly. Strands of purple hair brush against his forehead. His cheeks. We are close, *so* close. He smells *so* good.

"Why?"

"Because I'm not sure you want me to kiss you."

"Oh." I nod. My hair tickles his nose. He scrunches it, and I laugh. "What if I told you that I do? Would you kiss me then?"

"I still don't think so," he says calmly. Seriously.

My smile fades. Oh, shit. *Shit*, I made a mess. "You don't want to?" My voice is small, insecure. He shakes his head.

"That's not it."

It must be. What else? "Right." I've been in his arms for a while, but suddenly I feel self-conscious. He's *not* okay with this. He *used* to be attracted to me, but not anymore. I'm overstepping. "I'm sorry. I didn't mean to go too far."

"You don't understand, Bee." A small smile. Our foreheads touch, his skin warm against mine. I really, *really* want a kiss from this man. I want it bad enough to burn. "You can't go too far."

"Then why . . . ?"

His eyes flutter closed. His lips move closer. "I'm terrified that you won't go far enough."

When Tim kissed her for the first time—after a screening of *2001: A Space Odyssey*, which I later found out he slept through—eighteen-year-old Bee called her sister to say she'd had the loveliest of kisses. But eighteen-year-old Bee was a fool. Eighteen-year-old Bee had no idea. Eighteen-year-old Bee overrated that Tim wasn't overly clumsy and brushed his teeth. And twenty-eight-year-old Bee would consider going back in time to slap her upside the head, but she's busy having a real, true, actual, honest-to-God good kiss.

The best kiss.

It has to do with how slow it starts. With the way Levi and I breathe against each other for a moment, just breathe and taste the air between us. It should feel ridiculous, but there's something unique about how he looks at my mouth from lowered eyelashes. Wrapped around him like I am, I can feel his pounding heartbeat, the heat of his skin, and suddenly I'm not scared anymore. He wants this—he wants *me*. I know it in the liquid, messy warmth of my abdomen, in the red spreading over his cheekbones, in his breathing, even faster and louder than mine.

"Bee."

The tension stretches so unbearably tight, we might as well be on different sides of the world. So I close the distance, and then it's not slow anymore. It's hard and fast and open-mouthed. Wet and pressing and half bites. It's messy, the least smooth kiss of my life—but maybe it's not a kiss at all. Just two people trying to be as close as possible. His hands are sliding up my ass. My nails are in his scalp. He grunts choppy, surprised praise into my throat—"Yeah. *Yeah*."—licks the dip of my collarbone, and I'm on fire, half a minute of this and I'm already aflame, *pulsating* with want and need. I have no brakes: I grind myself helplessly against him, my nipples hard against his chest, his hard abs the perfect slate for my core to rub on.

"You are so—" He groans deep, like he's halfway to insane. I'm too busy desperately seeking friction to even try to keep up with my end of the kiss, but it's okay. He's got me. His large palm comes up, wraps around my neck, angles my head sharply, just so. His tongue is inside my mouth, pressing against mine, and . . .

Dirty. This is not a kiss—this is *dirty*. Obscene. He pushes me against the wall, and I push back, and back, and back, like there can be no air between us. His hand under my shirt is possessive, confident, so large that it completely spans my rib cage, and I arch up, swallowing a whimper in the back of my throat. My head is spinning, my body is melting, I can hear bells, and—

Not bells. A phone. Ringing. It slowly penetrates the thick haze of Levi mouthing my breasts, leaving a wet trail over my T-shirt— God *oh God.* "Your phone," I whisper, forcing myself to still my hips. It's the loudest my voice will go. Then one of his hands slips inside the back of my panties, and he starts grinding me up and down on his abs, and I forget what I meant to say. It's the *exact* spot, the *exact* rhythm I'd been trying to reach. He learned it, and he's helping me keep it up, fingers digging into the flesh of my ass. A perfect thrust. He growls, and I whimper at the spear of pleasure. My eyes roll in the back of my head, and . . . Yes. Right against— *Yes.*

There.

"Levi," I gasp. "Your phone—do you maybe want to—*oh*—pick up?" Or we can just continue until the ache disappears. Yes, that would be lovely. And stopping would be *unbearable.* Is that his cock rubbing against my ass? No. Impossible. No one's that big, right?

The phone is still ringing. I'm all about ignoring it, but Levi— I realize that Levi is not ignoring it. Levi is making his way under my shorts, sucking on the spot under my ear, and not even *hearing* it.

"Levi." He doesn't quite snap out of it. He doesn't pull back, doesn't move his mouth from my skin, but he stops. His grip tightens around me. A child, reluctant to let go of a favorite toy. "Your phone. Do you want to . . . ?"

His eyes are glassy. His hands not fully steady as he lets go of me, gingerly, with difficulty. I watch him try to collect himself for long seconds before he picks up. "Ward."

He is winded, chest moving up and down. He palms his erection like it hurts, all the while staring at me, *me*, only me. Then he looks away and his demeanor abruptly changes. "Say that again?" The speaker on the other end is female. I can't make out the words, but I recognize the voice from before. From the picture in his office. "Yeah, of course," Levi says reassuringly. His voice is still husky, but soft. Caring. Intimate. He turns around and gives me his back, like I'm not here anymore. *They used to date*, a nagging voice provides. *What you just did with Levi? He used to do it with her. And much more.*

"I'll be right there."

Reality's catching up fast. I just—I did *that*. I haven't been this close to another human being in years, and now—with *Levi*. I liked it, too. I forgot myself and probably all decency, but maybe he didn't? He's leaving in the middle of it. Because of a phone call. From a friend. Whom he used to date. Shit. *Shit*—

"Bee?" I look up. His eyes are ablaze. His jeans tented. Okay—he *is* that big. "I need to go." His throat bobs before and after he says it. He doesn't seem fully in control. Could I convince him to stay, if I tried?

Probably not. I won't, anyway. "Of course."

"I would . . ."

"It's okay."

"I will . . ."

"Yeah, you can . . ."

"Yes."

I've no clue what he's trying to say, and I seriously doubt he knows what *I* mean, since I have no idea myself. We're talking over each other. Just like we *were* all over each other. *Ba Dum Tss.*

One last glance and he leaves. He's halfway down the stairs when I notice the car keys on the table, on top of the diagram I drew. I grab them and run after him. "Hey, you forgot your keys!"

He stops on the landing and holds out his hand, so I go to him and drop them into his palm. I expect him to leave right after, but he surprises me by stepping closer. Then closer still.

For long moments he just looks at me, eyes full of beautiful, undecipherable green things. My throat constricts, my stomach twists, and I want to tell him that I'm sorry, that it's okay, that I know he made a mistake, that we never need to talk about this, never again. But before I can say anything, he cups my cheek and leans down to kiss me once more.

This time it's sweet, slow, savoring. Patient. This time it's lingering and gentle—everything our other kiss wasn't.

I want to try them all. All the kisses Levi Ward is capable of, I want to sample them like fine wine.

I touch my lips, feel his residual warmth, and don't take my eyes off his back as he disappears.

17

PULVINAR: REACHING & GRASPING

From: Levi-ward@nasa.gov
To: BLINK-CORE-ENGINEERING@MAILSERV, Bee-Koenigswasser@nasa.gov
Re: BLINK—Monday

I'll be taking personal time and I won't be in at all today (Monday). I uploaded three designs for you to work on. Bee came up with a great solution to the hardware/software incompatibility issues, and I want to finalize its implementation ASAP. Reach me via text if you have questions.

LW

I read the email for the seventh time, and for the seventh time I marvel that I was given credit for my idea. Goes to show how low the bar is for cis dudes in STEM, doesn't it? Thank you, Oh Penised Overlords, for the recognition I deserve.

Not that I'm not grateful he introduced the idea, since I'm not sure his underlings would have taken it seriously if it came from me. Remember June 1903, when the Royal Institution invited Dr. Curie to give a lecture and then didn't allow her to lecture because of her inferior lady brain? Pierre ended up speaking for her, even though she was sitting in the audience.

Anyway: the more things change, the more they stay the same. Sausage Referencing™ is still a thing, and sometimes I get angry at myself for the way I accept it.

Sometimes I get angry at myself for other things. Like the fact that I should be working, instead of checking my phone to see if Levi texted. Or the fact that I'm upset he hasn't. Or the fact that suddenly I care to be updated about what he's doing every second of every minute of every day.

It's not my business, anyway. He has stuff to do. With his ex. Maybe if Tim hadn't cheated on me for a number of years that cannot be counted on the fingers of one hand I wouldn't think twice about this. But Levi's lack of an explanation has me wondering whether he's hiding something. Don't get me wrong—I'm aware that our kiss meant nothing to him. So he had a crush on me in grad school? Big deal. It's been six years. Lots of things changed dramatically in the past six years. The writing on *Game of Thrones*. The importance of hand sanitizer. My opinions on duck penises. But it was still a *kiss*. If Levi's in a relationship with someone else . . . yikes. Is he Tim 2.0? No, he's not that verminous. He wouldn't. But aren't all men the same?

Is my head exploding?

"Are you picturing me and Kay doing it?"

I startle. Rocío is sitting at her desk, black Dr. Martens propped next to her keyboard and a pink lollipop in her mouth. "How long have you been here?"

"Like, five minutes. You were staring into the distance with a weird deer-in-the-headlights expression, so . . ." She stops sucking with a loud pop. "So, was it me and Kay? On your desk?"

"I'm pretty sure this is sexual harassment."

"I don't mind."

"No, *you* are harassing *me*—" I sigh and shake my head. She's impossible. I want to adopt her and keep her in my life forever. "Is everything okay?"

She nods, sticking the lollipop back into her mouth.

"Is that . . . strawberry?"

"Bubblegum. Kay gave it to me."

"Kay, huh?"

"Yup."

I clear my throat. "I was thinking about a recent conversation we had, in which you told me you weren't exactly a fan of . . . *Kay*, and—"

Rocío's boots hit the floor. Hard. "I love her," she declares. "She's perfect. I want her to be my beautiful California Bride with pink ribbons in her hair. I want to give her bubble baths that smell like cotton candy. I want to buy her fruity cocktails with little umbrellas in them." She leans forward, pinning me with her gaze. "I will wear glitter for her, Bee. Black glitter."

I'm a little out of breath at the intensity. "Does Alex know?"

"I broke up with him. Told him he wasn't pink enough." She shrugs. "He barely cares."

I grin. "I'm *so* happy for you."

She sobers up. "Don't be. Life is pain and then you die."

"Ah, yes. I forgot."

"Anyway. It's more important than ever that I get into Johns Hopkins's neuro program, since that's where Kay's going. So we decided to redirect the time and efforts we spent on GRE prep to GRE destruction."

"Destruction?"

"We're joining #FairGraduateAdmissions. It's a whole movement now. People are fundraising, building awareness, pressuring grad programs to drop the test. We're going to help organize." There's a savage gleam in her eyes. "I've spent hundreds of dollars and hours on that test, Bee. *Hundreds*. I will get my revenge—especially after that stupid *Chronicle of Higher Ed* article."

I have no idea what article she's talking about, but I find it easily. It's an op-ed by a Benjamin Green—who, a quick Google search informs me, is a VP at STC. The company that sells the GRE.

CHALLENGING THE CHALLENGERS:
What #FairGraduateAdmissions gets wrong

The new trend is to do away with the GRE, which has been widely used by graduate admission committees for decades. @WhatWouldMarieDo was the first to use her platform to bring attention to the "injustice" it perpetuates, and @Shmacademics helped her amplify the signal by posting reviews of the literature debunking it. Together, the two have almost two million followers. But who are these influencers? What vast monetary operations are behind them? Do they have financial ties with STC competitors? Moreover, these influencers do not provide useful alternatives to the GRE. They talk of holistic admission protocols, but fully reading thousands of applications is too time consuming for admission committees . . .

My eyes roll to the back of my skull. Committees need to do right by applicants and should make the time. And who's this dude? This one-man homeowners' association? What's a "vast monetary operation"? I want to break into his house and show him that my salary is probably what he tips his pool boy—and none of it comes from Twitter. But I don't know where Mr. Green lives, so I just DM Shmac the link.

> **MARIE:** Did you see this stupid article? Benjamin Green is officially Camel Dick 2.0.

My eyes fall on the messages he sent the last time we talked, when he told me about the girl. My chest clenches, and for some reason I think of Levi. Of him being gone. Of what his opinion on the GRE might be. Maybe I'm going insane.

I don't wait for Shmac's response. I log out of the app and force myself to go back to work.

"WHAT?"

"Listen—"

"What?!"

"It's—"

"What?"

"I—"

"What?!"

I sigh. "Okay, Reike. Let me know when you're done."

My sister yells "What?!" eight more times. "Okay, it's out of my system. Let us resume. So, you and The Wardass smooched—"

"Feels like there should be a better word for that."

"You sucked faces. Exchanged germs. Swapped saliva. Canoodled. Snogged."

"The other day you told me in great detail about that Ukrainian guy you pegged, and I didn't make half the fuss."

"It's different."

"Why?"

"Because I'm a seasoned pegger, but you *never* do this. You were all like, 'Neuro's my wife now, zip up my chastity belt, dig a moat around the Bee-fence,' and now you're making out with your nemesis who is apparently into you—"

"Was. *Was* into me. And it's just a kiss." If I say it enough, maybe it'll erase how close I got to being naked with Levi on my kitchen floor. How I've been obsessing over his whereabouts all day long.

"FYI, I'll return to the States for your wedding, but I recently discovered the bridezilla subreddit, and I'm *not* going to dye my hair blond to fit the ceremony's color scheme—"

"Not happening."

"Right, you'd probably ask for teal green—still a resounding no."

"Reike, it was just . . . a kiss. He doesn't care. And *I* have no intention of caring ever again. One round of returning wedding gifts was enough."

"I never got mine back!"

"You never sent one. Anyway, it was just a kiss. Purely . . ." Physical. Burning. Good. Electric. Obscene. Heavy. Dangerous. Good. Wild. Good, good, *good*. The most erotic moment of my life. But my head has cooled off, I'm not a horny black hole of sexual tension anymore, and I can see how dumb it was. A stupid idea. Three out of ten, would *not* do again. Plus, I have other concerns. BLINK. My job. Who'll feed Félicette once I'm gone. "Nothing. Purely nothing."

"Right. Emotions are still scary. Boundary maintenance is a priority. The Bee-fence is up in arms. So when you see him at work tomorrow—"

"I'll be too busy building the best damn helmet this world has ever seen and securing myself a lifetime of professional stability. Away from Trevor."

"Of course. And I assume The Wardass is perfectly okay pretending that—"

A knock at my door and I glance at the time—10:28 p.m. "Gotta go. It's probably Rocío coming to reiterate that I'm not her real mother. Or that after you die the enzymes in your digestive tract devour your body from the inside."

"Of all your colleagues, this girl is my absolute favorite."

"She was caught *porking*. On *my desk*."

"How does she constantly top herself?"

I roll my eyes. "Bye, Reike."

"Warmest regards, Beetch."

It's not Rocío. Instead, there's a large chest where her head should be. And several inches above that, Levi's face. "You forgot this in the rental." He lifts his left hand, my backpack dangling from his fingers.

"Oh. Thank you." I hug it to the front of my body. I'm wearing a sleeveless top I've owned since middle school and pajama pants that could moonlight as underwear. I really thought it'd be Rocío at the door. I may be blushing all over. "Did you, um, want to come in?"

He shakes his head. "I just wanted to return the backpack."

I nod. He nods. There's a stretch of silent, more awkward nodding, and then he says, "I'll get going."

"Yeah. Sure. Have a good night."

He's wearing a light blue Henley that does marvelous things for his back. Which I have now touched. Extensively. That's why I stare as he walks away: I'm mesmerized by how broad, firm, solid he looks. And that's why when he reaches the stairs and turns around he finds me still there. Still looking.

He smiles. And I smile. The smiles linger, warm, honest, and I hear myself ask, "You sure you don't want to come in?"

"It's not that I . . ." His throat works. "I didn't come here for that."

"I didn't think you did." I make room for him, and with a few tentative, lumbering steps he's inside. In all his hulking, massive grace. He looks around, running a hand through his hair. Is he thinking about what happened here twenty-four hours ago? Well, more like twenty-eight point five, but which maniac is counting?

"Is that a hummingbird feeder?" he asks.

"Yep."

"Any hummingbirds?"

"Not yet."

"Me neither. In my garden, I mean."

"I noticed the mint you're growing." We exchange another smile. "Want to sit on the balcony? I have fancy German beer."

The chairs I comfortably sprawl on look like kid's furniture under Levi. His hand dwarfs the beer bottle. His profile, as he stares pensively at the Houston skyline, is unbearably handsome. He looks almost aggressively out of place. I want to know what he's thinking about. I want to ask if he regrets our kiss. I want to touch him again.

"I'm sorry about the other night. And about missing work when we're at a critical point. It was an emergency."

Oh. "Was it . . . was it something about your non-wife? From the photo?"

He chuckles. "I can't believe the conversation material that picture's giving us."

"Amazing, huh?"

His smile fades. "Penny's ill. Epilepsy. It's under control, but she's growing up fast and her meds need to be adjusted often. It's tricky, finding the right dosage."

"I'm sorry."

"It's okay. Weirdly enough, Penny takes it in stride. She's a remarkably resourceful kid." He takes a swig and makes a face at the beer. What a heathen. "Lily, though—her mom—she struggles. Understandably. I try to be around when things get bad."

I stare into the distance. Of course he does. He's that kind of person. "I'm glad they have you."

"I'm pretty useless. I mostly play UNO with Penny, or buy her slime that has some toxic ingredient—"

"Borax."

"—that drives Lily crazy. Yes, Borax. How did you know?"

"I have mom friends. They complain about it." I shrug. "Where's her dad?"

"He died a little over a year ago." He hesitates before adding, "Rock-climbing accident." For a moment I don't think much of it. Then I remember the picture in his office. Levi and the tall, dark-haired man.

"Were you related?"

"No." His expression darkens. "But I'd known him forever. Since kindergarten. We'd line up in pairs till the end of elementary school. Peter Sullivan and Levi Ward. Not many T, U, or V names, apparently."

I set my bottle on the table and study his face. Sullivan. That name again. It's common, that's why it crops up so often. And yet . . .

"Like the prototype?" I murmur. "Like the Discovery Institute?"

I wish he'd look at me. But he keeps staring at the city and says, "I didn't even want to be an engineer. I wanted to major in veterinary science. Had even declared it, but Peter convinced me to take an engineering class as an elective. We did this project together—we built an olfactory cortex. A piece of hardware that could correctly identify smells. He did most of the work and had to teach me everything, but it was a blast. Thinking that something like that could maybe be used for patients, you know? Somewhere down the line?"

"That's impressive."

"It wasn't *always* correct." He bites the inside of his cheek. "On our final presentation, while the instructor was examining it, the cortex announced that it was smelling feces." I burst into laughter. "It maybe needed a few tweaks. But I fell in love with brain-computer interface because of Peter. He was the most brilliant engineer I've ever met." He presses his lips together. "I saw his skull crack in two when he fell. I was ten feet away, halfway through my climb. The noise—it was unlike anything. I didn't know how to tell Lily. And Penny wouldn't leave the room . . ."

His voice is so deceptively level, so painfully neutral, I'm shocked when I realize that my cheeks are wet. I want to reach out to Levi. I *need* to reach out. But I'm locked inside my head, paralyzed, finally making connections and understanding things.

"They renamed the Institute after him. And he came up with the prototype." Before dying. That's why Levi needed to be on BLINK. Why it needed to happen with him in charge. Why he fought so hard for it.

Levi. *Oh, Levi.*

"I'm going to build those helmets." He's still staring into the distance. His grip on the bottle is a vise. "Like he envisioned them. And they'll have his name. And Penny will know it was her dad, and she—" He stops. Like his voice will break if he continues.

Suddenly, I'm not scared anymore. I know what to do—or at least what I *want* to do. I stand, slide the beer out of Levi's hand, and set it on the metal railing with a clink. Then I lower myself into his lap, legs on each side of his waist, my arms around his neck. I wait until his hands are around my waist. Until his eyes shine up at me in the darkness. Then I say, "We're going to build those helmets. Together." I smile fiercely against his lips. "Peter will know. Penny will know. Lily will know. And you will know."

The kiss is a punch-out drug, but a familiar one. After all, I've thought about nothing else for the past day. Pleasure hums through me with every stroke of his tongue against mine, every brush of his fingers against my lower back, every reverent breath against my jaw. He pulls me closer and groans into my skin, half sentences that drive me crazy an inch at a time.

"You're so— *Fuck*, Bee," as I run my teeth down his throat. "I used to dream of you," when my fingertips brush against the fine hair underneath his belly button. "I'm going to—we have to slow down, or I'm going to—" after I start rocking on top of him, and the friction of his erection against my clit is already the best sex I've ever had. I'm shuddering, pulsating, about to explode with pleasure. My underwear is soaked and I want to get closer. *Closer.*

But our clothes stay on. Frustratingly, maddeningly on, even when he brings me to bed, the kitchen light trickling inside the room. Levi's grip on my hip is near-bruising, every breath a sharp intake. My body feels warm, buoyant, filled with cutting heat. He looks down at me and says, "I want to fuck you." He nips at my collarbone, and—he likes teeth. To bite, to clutch, to suck. There's something devouring about him, something clumsy and overeager, but it's not a turnoff.

He's usually so patient, meticulous, but now he can't wait. Can't have enough. "Can I fuck you?"

I nod up at him, let him take my top, my pants, *everything* off, and the way he looks at me like he has found answers all of a sudden, like my body is a religious experience, has me squirming up for contact.

"This," he says breathlessly, his thumb tracing reverently the piercing on my nipple.

"If you don't like it, I—"

He shushes me, and it's okay. I'm okay. I'm totally okay with him staring at my small breasts as though they're something wondrous, with him kissing them until his lips are plump, until I have to pull at his hair, until I'm so wet, I feel it trickle down my thigh. I'm okay with being told ridiculous things: I'm a good girl, I'm perfect, I've been driving him insane, when he first saw me I changed the chemistry of his brain.

He makes me laugh when I roll us around, push him underneath me, his elbows smacking against the hard wall. He mumbles a few obscenities, but when I bend down to kiss him again he forgets all about it. "You're too big for the bed," I tell him between giggles, peeling his shirt from his skin. He has abs. Defined ones. And pecs. He has muscle groups I thought were myths.

"Your bed's too small for me. Next time we'll do this in mine," he says, lifting his hips and letting me undo his zipper. The sound of each catch fills the room, and it shouldn't be so erotic, but I'm naked on top of him, his length rubbing against my core, and there's no mistaking how deliciously, furiously, eagerly big he is.

"It's been a while," he says.

I blink at him, breathless, hazy. "Yeah. Me too." I can't help myself. I touch the damp head of his erection, just a brush of my fingertips. He grunts, bites his lip. His hips jerk. It's a little like riding a horse. A bull.

"Do we need a condom?" he asks. I shake my head and mouth "birth control," eager to continue. "This might be over very quickly," he husks, hands gripping my thighs as I position him at my entrance. "But I'll make it up to you. With my mouth. Or my fingers. If— Bee. *Bee.*"

I don't know what I expected from having Levi inside of me. Probably the same as with Tim: something vaguely pleasant. At best, sex made me feel close to him. At worst, I was bored for a few minutes and remembered that taxes were due soon. With Levi it's nothing like that. I'm in control. I'm easing his cock into my body. I struggle inch by inch to adjust, to accommodate, but it's my decision. I close my eyes and feel my face twist, half pleasure and half pain. I need more. He needs more. We both need more, and I push down to take him farther inside, thighs and hands trembling as I strain to fill myself with him, and . . .

I can't do it.

There is no room. I try again, grinding down to take more of him. My skin beads with sweat. The sense of fullness grows, turns into a sting of pain, but I push through it, force myself to—

"Slow down," Levi orders, a little more than a growl. His hands clasp my hips to still me.

I open my eyes. Shake my head. "I need to—"

"You need a minute," he says firmly, and his voice brooks no argument. We're both shaking, gasping, sweaty against each other, but I pause for a moment, and he nods, choppy, pleased. "Good girl."

He stares at me like he doesn't know where to settle his eyes. Then he finds the place where we're joined and starts touching me there, slow, wet strokes of his thumb on my clit that soften me and help me take him all the way. His hip bones press into the undersides of my thighs when he bottoms out. I feel my channel clench and grip him, and his groan tells me that he does, too. He's in me to the hilt, and I collapse on top of him.

"Levi," I stutter into his mouth. "You are *really* big."

Something vibrates between us. Not physical—a feeling. It resonates in my body and in my brain.

"You'll get used to me," he gasps against my temple, pushing my hair back from my forehead with trembling hands, and then I am so full, I cannot be still anymore. I roll my hips to test the waters, see what hurts (very little) and what's good (a whole lot). I learn what I want. Which angle. Which rhythm. In exchange, I let Levi's hands roam my body wherever he likes—and it's *everywhere*. There are wet, filthy, shameful sounds, but I don't care, too busy gripping the headboard and grinding myself against that spot inside me which— Yes. *Yes.* He's immense, stretching me to my limit and a bit past. I balance myself on his chest. His heart beats a drum against my palm, and I move up and down. Delicious pressure. Pleasure pulses deep in my belly. "Like this?" I ask.

He doesn't answer. Or he does, but in murmurs, incoherent little things, like *Please, Be still, Don't move, You're so tight, I'm going to— Oh, shit.* It gets worse when I clench around him on purpose, just to see where I can go. There's no extra room inside me. Nothing at all, and my vision dots. My pulse spikes. My head snaps blank, my lungs void of air, and I come like an avalanche, a wash of blinding pleasure as my body contracts rhythmically. I whimper my orgasm into the skin of his collarbone.

When I can think again, I find Levi on top of me, panting against my throat, fingers tight around my hips. He babbles, groans, desperately grinds his cock against my stomach, but he has pulled out. I am painfully empty, clenching against nothing.

"Did you—?" My voice is hoarse.

"I'm trying to make it last," he pants. "I don't want this to end." I try to guide him into me once again, but he pins my wrists above my head and kisses me, endless, deep, without restraint, swallowing my soft whimpers in his mouth. Then he slides back inside. In this position he gets deeper. Harder. Different angles. He covers me, all of me, and I let him do what *he* let me do: find his pleasure in my body. His thrusts are shallow, then slow, then deep. Then his control snaps in two, long movements that drag delicious friction against all of my nerve endings. I love his weight on me. I love his guttural groans. I love the absent, awestruck green of his eyes. I'm so close. So close again.

This is good. He is good. We are good. Together. Like this.

"Bee," he slurs against my cheek. "Bee. You are everything I—"

My hands slide against his sweat-slick back, and I hold him together as he shatters into a million pieces.

18

RAPHE NUCLEI: HAPPINESS

"AMAZING." GUY'S VOICE trembles slightly, a tinge of fear to his admiration. Awe, I guess it's called? All that matters is that it opens the floodgates for everyone else to speak up.

"Incredible."

"—we have a working prototype—"

"—can't believe there was such a simple solution—"

"—BLINK is basically done—"

"—such an elegant way of—"

"*Fucking* awesome," Rocío declares, the loudest voice. Everyone looks at her, and that's when the impressed whispers become more like a frat party. High fives, hugs, the occasional chant. I'm surprised a keg isn't suddenly produced out of thin air.

Levi leans against a bench on the opposite side of the room, wearing last night's Henley. This morning I offered him my stretchy tie-dye camisole, but he just glared at me. Ingrate. He notices I'm staring and we both look away, bashful to have been caught. Then our eyes lock again. This time, we share a smile.

"We should celebrate!" someone's yelling. We ignore him and keep on smiling.

The first time Tim and I had sex, I was terrified he hadn't enjoyed it. He didn't call me for two days, which I spent wondering if I was shit in bed—instead of focusing on how shitty *he* was. In the fight that ended our engagement, he accused me of pushing him to sleep with other women because I was "a total starfish" during sex (I had to google what that even meant after he left). On reflection, our relationship was bookended by Tim making me feel terrible about myself. How poetic.

Maybe in the past years I've learned to give considerably fewer fucks about what dudes think of me, and that's why I've spent zero seconds of the last twenty-four hours wondering whether Levi thinks I'm a shit lay. But maybe that's not the only reason. Maybe it has to do with the way he looked at me this morning, when I woke up on top of him in my twin bed that he accused of being "an instrument of torture repurposed as a piece of furniture." Maybe it was the quiet, sweetly bashful conversation we had about me being on birth control, and about the fact that we've both been living like ascetic monks for long enough that we're sure to be clean. Maybe it's the appalled face he made when he saw me guzzle unsweetened soy milk directly from the carton. Maybe it's the swift, covert glances he's been giving me all day long.

We haven't talked much. Or—we've talked a lot. About circuits and high-frequency stimulation trains and Brodmann areas. The usual.

Today's not usual, though.

"Looks like you got it." Boris comes to stand beside me. He glances at his engineers—currently giving one another celebratory wedgies—with mild disapproval.

"We still need to tweak the neuro software. Then we'll test the model on the first astronaut. Guy has volunteered." A euphemism: Guy *begged* to be test subject number one. It's nice knowing that someone else is so invested in BLINK.

"When's that?"

"Next week."

He nods. "I'm going to set up a demonstration for the end of next week, then."

"A demonstration?"

"I'll invite my bosses, your bosses. They'll invite someone higher up still."

I stare at him, alarmed. "That's way too soon. We have weeks before the project deadline, and there's lots to troubleshoot. Human subjects are involved—plenty of things could go wrong."

"Yes." He gives me a level look. "But you know what the stakes are, especially with MagTech so close to catching up. And you know the pushback against the project. We've got lots of eyes on us. Lots of people who know very little about science, and yet are very invested in BLINK."

I hesitate. Ten days is much fewer than I'm comfortable with. On the other hand, I understand the pressure Boris is under. After all, he's the one who got us approval to start. "Okay. We'll do our best." I push away from the bench. "I'll tell Levi."

"Wait." I stop. "Bee, what are your plans when this is over?"

"My plans?"

"You want to keep working for Trevor?" I press my lips together to temporize, but Boris is no fool. "I've chatted with him a few times. He seems to be under the impression that we're making suits?"

"Trevor is . . ." I sigh. "Yeah."

He gives me a commiserating look. "If the prototype's a success, NIH will likely promote you, maybe give you your own lab. You'll have options. But if you don't like those options . . . come see me, please."

I stare at him wide-eyed. "What?"

"I've been wanting to start a dedicated neuroscience team. This"—he points at the helmet—"is one of *many* things we can do. Our neuro unit is scattered and underutilized. I need someone who can actually lead it." He smiles tiredly. "Anyway, I'll go tell Levi about the demonstration. I'm partial to the way he scowls when I give him bad news."

I stand there like an idiot, blinking into the distance. Was I just offered a job? At NASA? *Leading* a lab? Did I hallucinate? Is there a carbon monoxide leak in the building?

"You coming out to celebrate?" Guy asks, startling me.

I shake my head. Celebration seems premature. "But you guys have fun."

"Sure will." His eyes lift to a spot above my head. "And you?"

I turn around. Levi is right behind me. "Another time."

"You have plans?" I ask once Guy has left. I look around to make sure we're alone, like I'm asking Levi for his secret apple pie recipe. I'm ridiculous.

"I *was* going to spend some quality time with my cat."

"Expression night?"

"Schrödinger and I do sometimes have interactions that don't involve his rectum," he points out. "But no. There's a restaurant.

Vegan." His eyes wander away, as though he's embarrassed to ask. "I've been wanting to try it. We could . . ."

I laugh. "You don't have to."

He gives me a curious look. "Do what?"

"Take me out. On a date."

He scowls. "I know I don't have to."

"I'm aware this isn't . . ." I start to tell him that I know it's not like that between us. That he doesn't need to take me out. That the sex was excellent, and even though I'm sore and sleepy and possibly all orgasmed out, I'd be happy to have more. With him. If he's interested. I'm familiar with the concept of friends with benefits. Bed buddies. Frenefits. Fuckfriends. But then I remember the weekend. Watching Star Wars together, drinking Sazerac. This friendship of ours is older than the benefits, even if just by a few hours, and I'd be happy to spend time *talking* with him. Plus, he probably has no one to try vegan restaurants with. I'm the same in Bethesda. Yeah, that's why he's asking me out. "Actually, that sounds amazing. Do we need a reservation?"

He lifts one eyebrow. "It's a vegan restaurant in Texas. We'll be fine."

I know how this is going to be: *Levi* will get to work out of his system whatever's left of his years-old attraction toward me; *I* will finally get to have some decent sex; we'll *both* get to do so without the pressure of being in a relationship and the disastrous stickiness that always happens when you let yourself care too much about someone. Tonight's dinner is not going to be a date—just a meal between two horny friends who happen to share dietary preferences. Still, I find myself putting more care than usual into my appearance. I choose a thin rose-gold septum ring, my favorite piercings, and classic red lipstick. I curl my hair to fall in waves down my shoulders. I'm ready well before Levi's supposed to pick me up, so I go wait on the balcony.

Shmac has finally gotten back to me, apologetic for having been offline for *the best, then worst, then best weekend of my life.*

> **SHMAC:** STC is grasping. Everyone knows you have no financial interests and are supporting #FairGraduateAdmissions because you believe in it.

> **MARIE:** I hate what they said about fair admissions being impractical. Who cares? We can and must do better.

> **SHMAC:** Orally.

> **MARIE:** ???

> **SHMAC:** *Totally.

> **SHMAC:** Sorry, speech to text. I'm driving.

> **MARIE:** LOL!

> **MARIE:** Where are you going? And, does it have to do with your best-then-worst-then-best weekend? And does that have to do with The Girl?

> **SHMAC:** I'm taking her out for dinner.

> **MARIE:** djhsgasgarguyfgquergqe

> **MARIE:** (That was a keyboard smash, in case text-to-speech is failing you)

> **SHMAC:** It was, thank you.

MARIE: I'm soooo happy for you, Shmac!

SHMAC: I am, too. Though she's still a bit skittish.

MARIE: Skittish?

SHMAC: For valid reasons. But I don't think she's quite ready to admit it to herself.

MARIE: Admit what?

SHMAC: That I'm serious about this. That I'm in it for the long haul. Or at least for as long as she'll have me.

I frown. Wait—isn't the girl in a relationship? There's no long haul unless she divorces, is there? I want to ask, but I wouldn't want Shmac to think that I'm judging him for taking up with a married woman—I really don't, especially since her husband sounds like someone I wouldn't mind pushing down the Eiffel Tower stairs. I consider telling him that I, too, am going out for dinner—with Camel Dick, no less—but I hear a soft noise.

A little ball of red and gray is hovering in midair around the feeder, pretty wings beating happily at a fluttering rhythm. The first hummingbird of the year. "Hey, beauty." He sticks his thin beak into one hole and leaves before I can take a picture. I watch him fly over the parking lot and notice Levi's truck pulling up.

I run downstairs like I'm eleven and heading to the splash pad. "I got my first hummingbird!" I say excitedly, climbing into the truck. Levi has barely finished parking. "Red throat! I didn't get a picture but they're territorial, so he'll be back. And I'll have the coconut-ginger chickpea soup! My sister says that it's uncool to read restaurant menus online, but I fully embrace my obsession with food. . . ." I stop. Levi is staring at me open-mouthed. "I have hummingbird shit on my face, don't I?"

He keeps staring.

"Do you have a tissue?" I look around the cabin. "Or even a piece of paper—"

"No. No, you don't . . ." He shakes his head, lost for words.

"What's wrong?"

"You . . ." He swallows.

". . . I?"

"The dress. You wore . . . the dress."

I glance at myself. Oh. Yes. I did wear my Target dress. "I thought you said you didn't really hate it?"

"And I don't." He swallows. "I *really* don't."

I take a better look at him and realize the *way* he's staring. Which is . . . "Oh." My heartbeat picks up.

"Can I kiss you?" he asks, and I could fall in love with this hesitant, shy version of Levi Ward—the same man who nibbled my throat awake at three a.m. to say that he'd die if he couldn't fuck me again. I let him, enthusiastically. Just like I let him kiss me now, until we're making out like teenagers, deep, fingers holding my neck, tongues stroking, his weight pressing me into the seat and he's really, really good at this, charmingly assertive, deliciously insistent. That's his hand on my knee, under my dress and up my smooth leg, up and up until it's wrapped around my inner thigh. A light brush against the front of my panties, and I whimper in his mouth just as he groans. I think I'm already wet. And he *knows* I'm already wet, because his fingertips slip under the elastic and hook it to the side. I gasp against his mouth and his thumb slides against my—

Someone honks one street over, and we both pull back. Oops.

"We should probably . . ."

"Yeah. We should."

We're both in agreement. And both reluctant. We're slow to let go of each other, and when he turns the key in the ignition, the same hand that uses precision screwdrivers on a daily basis is trembling slightly.

I glance out the window. "Levi?"

"Yeah?"

"I just wanted to say that . . ." I smile. "Red lipstick looks great on you."

IT'S NOT A date.

But if it were—which it isn't—it would be the best date of my life.

Of course, because it's *not* a date, the point is moot.

But. *If* it were.

Though it's not.

Even when, I must admit, it almost feels like one. Maybe it's that he paid while I was in the bathroom (I briefly protested, but honestly, I'll let any dude buy me dinner until the gender pay gap is ungapped). Maybe it's that we never stopped talking, never, not even for a minute—just polite nods for Archie the Overzealous Waiter when he kept coming by to inquire about our meals. But maybe it's the hour we spent reframing some of our most traumatic grad school memories.

"I presented my data during lab meeting. Halfway through my first year. And you looked out the window for *the entire time*."

He smiles and takes his time chewing. "You were wearing this"—he gestures in the middle of his forehead—"thing. On your hair."

"A headband, probably. I was smack in my boho-chic phase." I shudder. "Okay, you've got a doctor's note for this one. But it was *excellent* data."

"I know—I was listening. Your salience network research—very compelling. I just . . ." He shrugs. His hand closes around his glass, but he doesn't drink. "It was cute. I didn't want to stare."

I burst into laughter. "Cute?"

His eyebrow lifts, challenging. "Some of us haven't outgrown their boho-chic phase."

"Uh-huh. What does boho-chic mean, Levi?"

"It's a . . . city? In France?"

I laugh harder. "Okay. Another one. That time that friend of yours from microbiology came into lab. That guy you played baseball with?"

"Dan. Basketball. I've never played baseball in my life—I'm not even sure how it works."

"A bunch of guys stand around in their jammies and chat amiably. Anyway, Dan came into lab to pick you up for a game of *a sport*, and you introduced him to everyone except for me."

He nods. Tears off a piece of bread. Doesn't eat it. "I remember."

"We can agree it was a dick move."

"Or." He drops the bread, leaning back. "Or, we could agree that a few nights before, after a few drinks, I blurted out to Dan that I was . . . *interested* in a girl named Bee, that Bee's not a common name, and that Dan was totally the kind of person to look you in the eye and ask, 'Aren't you that chick my bro blubbers about when he's sloshed?'"

My heart skips a beat, but I power through. "You can't have an excuse for every single time you acted like a dick."

He shrugs. "Try me."

"The dress code. A few weeks ago."

He covers his eyes. "You mean, when I asked you to dress professionally while I was wearing a T-shirt with a hole in the right armpit?"

"Were you really?"

"Most of my T-shirts have armpit holes. Statistically speaking, yes."

"What's the excuse?"

He sighs. "That morning, Boris said something to me about how he thought NASA might use whatever they could to get NIH off their backs. He said, 'I wouldn't be surprised if they got rid of her because of the hair.' It was probably a throwaway line, but I panicked." He lifts his hands. "Then you called me out for promoting gender bias in the workplace, and I felt like a Bond villain bragging about his doomsday device."

"I can't believe you didn't just *tell* me." In retaliation, I pluck a broccoli rabe from his plate.

"I'm an excellent communicator with outstanding interpersonal skills, according to my résumé."

"Mine says that I'm fluent in Portuguese, but the last time I tried to order food in Coimbra I accidentally told the waiter that there was a bomb in the bathroom. Okay, last one: What about when you refused to collaborate? I overheard you through the door. You told Sam you didn't want to be on the project because of me."

"You overheard me?" He sounds skeptical. "Through Sam's solid wood slab of a door?"

I bat my eyes angelically. "Yes."

"Were you eavesdropping in the ficus?"

"Perhaps. Anything to say in your defense?"

"Did you leave right after I mentioned that I didn't want the project because of you?"

"Yup. I stomped my way to my office with the rage of a murder of dragons."

"Is that their collective noun?"

"It should be."

He nods. "If you left right after you heard your name, then you didn't hear everything I told Sam. And that misunderstanding is on you."

I scowl. "Is it?"

"Yup. There's a lesson for all of us here." He picks up the piece of bread he dropped earlier.

"Which would be? Don't eavesdrop in the ficus?"

"Nope. If you eavesdrop, you shouldn't half-ass it." He pops the bread into his mouth, and has the audacity to grin at me.

SCHRÖDINGER REMEMBERS ME. Possibly from the other night, when he slept on my windpipe, gave me suffocation nightmares, and left black tufts of hair in my mouth. He slinks from his spot on the couch the moment we come in and twines himself around my bare ankles while Levi stores our leftovers in his fridge.

"I love you," I coo at him. "You're a perfect, magnificent beast, and I'll protect you with my life. I will slay a murder of dragons for you."

"I looked it up," Levi says from the doorjamb. "It's a thunder of dragons."

"Fascinating." I rub the underside of Schrödinger's chin. He squints in feline bliss. "But we like 'murder' better, don't we? Yes, we do." I glance up. "I believe I was promised some anal expression?"

He shakes his head. "It was to lure you here. Don't believe everything you're told."

"You heard that, Schrödinger? Your daddy uses your malfunctioning glands as bait."

Levi smiles. "He's not like that, usually."

"Hmm?"

"Schrödinger's shy with most people. Hides under the couch a lot. He used to be very aggressive with my . . ." The way he trails off has me dying to know.

"Your?"

He shrugs and looks away. "I lived with a girlfriend. For a few months."

"Oh." The cat flops on his side into a waterfall of purrs. "Lily?"

"Before her."

I think I can stop lying to myself and the tiny porcelain frog that passes as my brain and just admit that Levi is the perfect combination of Sexy Guy™, Handsome Guy™, and Cute Guy™. You know when you've been in love with someone for years, and then they do something horrible, like forgetting to water your Chia Pet unicorn or screwing your best friend, and you stop seeing them through rose-colored lenses? All their shortcomings are thrown in sharp relief, like you just put on 3D glasses for inside ugliness? Well, now that I've gotten rid of my asshole goggles, I can acknowledge that Levi's been eligible-bacheloring it up just fine. He'll make some lucky girl an even luckier girl someday. And I have no idea why the idea of him having a live-in girlfriend sends that cold tingle in my belly—we've been fuckbuddies for less than twenty-four hours, for cake's sake. It's not my business, and the last thing I want is another relationship doomed to a messy, painful ending (i.e., *any* romantic relationship).

"Schrödinger didn't like her?" He gnaws lovingly on my thumb.

"To be fair, she was a dog person."

"When was this?" I ask, as nosy as a curtain-twitcher.

"In grad school. Before . . ." He doesn't finish the sentence, but his gaze lingers on me for a moment, and I wonder if he meant "Before *you*."

Annie used to have a funny theory: we all have a Year Zero around which the calendars of our lives pivot. At some point you meet someone, and they become so important, so metamorphic, that ten, twenty, sixty-five years down the line you look back and realize that you could split your existence in two. Before they showed (BCE), and your Common Era. Your very own Gregorian calendar.

I used to think Tim was my Common Era, but I don't anymore. In fact, I don't *want* another flaky, fickle human being to become my Common Era. You know what would work great as a pivotal lifetime point? Me, getting my own NIH lab—which, I'm thrilled to say, is closer than ever. I almost want to text Annie to ask if new jobs can be Year Zeros, but I'm not quite there yet. Still, it's nice to know that I could. That the door between us is ajar.

Levi wasn't going to say "Before you," because I'm *not* his Common Era. I don't care to be. But I'm positive he'll meet her soon. Probably a girl who's five eleven, knows how to build a microwave from scratch, and has the astounding grace of Simone Biles. They'll produce fierce, athletic kids with scarily smart brains and have sex every night, even when there are grant deadlines, even when the in-laws are in the guest room. Hummingbirds will flock to their yard during the spring months, and Levi will study them from his screened-in porch and be implacably happy—just like I'll be happy with my lab, my research, my students, my RAs (Yes, they'll all be women. No, I don't care if you think it's unfair).

But I'm glad I found out that Levi used to like me. I'm glad I get to have excellent sex for the first time in my life. I'm glad we're doing this sleeping-together thing without all the ugly that comes from actually investing in a relationship. I'm glad we can be part of each other's BCE for a while. I'm glad to be here. With him. I might even be *happy*.

"I think you're the best," I say, ruffling the fur around Schröding-er's ears. "He's very small."

"Runt of the litter."

I smile at the perfect beany underside of his paws. "I've always loved an underdog. Undercat?"

"I'm surprised someone who likes cats as much as you doesn't . . ."

"Have one?"

"I was going to say five."

I chuckle. "There *is* Félicette . . ."

"I was thinking more of *existing* cats."

I glare at him. "I'd love to dedicate my life to embodying the cultural archetype of the crazy cat lady. But it's a bad idea."

"Why?"

"Because." I hesitate, and Schrödinger purrs against my fingers. My love for him knows no bounds. "I couldn't take it."

"Couldn't take what?"

"When they die."

Levi gives me a curious look. "Not for years. Decades, sometimes. And a lot happens between the beginning and the end."

"But the end *does* happen. Unavoidably. All relationships between living beings end somewhere, somehow. That's just the way it is. One party dies, or is called away by other biological needs. Emotions are transient by nature. They're temporary states brought on by neuro-physiological changes that aren't meant to be long-lasting. The nervous system must revert back to homeostasis. All relationships associated with affective events are destined to end."

He seems unconvinced. "*All* relationships?"

"Yup. It's science."

He nods, but then says, "What about prairie voles?"

"What about them?"

"They pair-bond for life, don't they?"

His eyes glint appraisingly, like he's observing a fascinating biological phenomenon. We might not be talking about the misery of having to flush a goldfish down the toilet anymore. "Then prairie voles are the exception, because their oxytocin and vasopressin receptors are scattered across their reward systems."

"Isn't that biological proof that emotions and relationships *can* be long lasting?"

"Not at all. So you have two cute rodents and they stick together. Amazing. But one night husband vole crosses the highway to catch *Ratatouille* at the local theater and ends up pancaked by a Ford Mustang owned by a dipshit who's driving to cheat on his wife with an unknowing college girl. Cue: grieving widow vole. It sucks, but it's like I told you: one way or another."

"And what happens in between doesn't make it worth it?"

Have you ever been left behind? I want to ask him. *Have you ever lost it all? Do you know how it feels? Because it doesn't sound like you do.* But I don't want to be cruel. I'm not cruel. I just want to protect myself, and if Levi doesn't want to do the same . . . he's stronger than I am.

"Maybe," I say, noncommital, and watch Schrödinger gracefully steal to where Levi is standing. "So, what's the plan for tonight?"

"What do you want to do?"

I shrug. "I don't know. What do *you* want to do?"

He smiles at me mischievously. "I thought maybe we could go for a jog."

I'D EXPECTED HIM to be reserved about sex.

Not that I'd thought about it very much, but if someone had held a gun to my head and forced me to guess, I'd have probably told them,

"I bet Levi Ward is quiet in bed. Boring. Because he's such a guarded person *out* of bed. A few low grunts, maybe. A handful of words, all directives. Faster. Slower. *Actually*, this other angle is better." I'd have been wrong. Because there's nothing reserved in the way he takes his pleasure out of my body. Nothing at all.

I'm not sure how I find myself spread out on my stomach in the middle of his bed, trying to breathe steadily as he traces the line of small tattoos down my spine.

"The UK," he says, hoarse and a little shaky. "And—I don't know this one. Or the next. But Italy. Japan."

"Italy's—*ah*—a boot. Easy." I push my forehead into the pillow, biting my lower lip. This would be easier if he weren't inside me. If he hadn't pushed to the side the green panties I'd bought to celebrate BLINK—the ones that I regretted the second Levi was announced as my co-lead, the ones I didn't think I'd use anytime soon, the ones Levi stared at speechless for a whole minute—and slowly, inexorably slid in to the hilt.

"They're pretty. The outlines." He lowers himself to kiss the skin of my neck. It makes his cock shift inside me, and we both groan. It's just embarrassing, the way my back arches, the way my ass bucks back into his abdomen like my body isn't mine anymore. "You might be too tight this way. It might be too good."

Sex isn't like this. *I'm* not like this. I'm not the type to come quickly, or uncontrollably, or loudly. I'm not the type to come very often. But there's a place inside me that he hits. He found it last night, too, but now, in this position, or maybe just because it's slower . . . I don't know what it is, but it's even better.

He thrusts inside me a couple times, shallow, experimental, and I have to fist my hands into his sheets. They are shaking.

"They're—" I have to stop. Collect myself. Clear my throat. Tense. Release. "They're my homes. All the places I've lived."

"Beautiful." He presses a soft kiss to the ball of my shoulder. "So damn beautiful," he repeats, almost to himself, like it's not about my tattoos anymore. Then the mattress shifts, I hear a frustrated groan, and all of a sudden I feel cold. He's not touching me anymore. He has pulled back. Pulled out.

"What are you . . . ?" I try to turn around, but his hand splays between my shoulder blades to hold me down gently.

"Just trying to pace myself." His voice is all strained, self-effacing amusement. I can't see his smile, but I picture it in my head, faint, warm, beautiful. I take a deep, shuddering breath, trying to relax into the sheets, feeling his eyes roam my body. His fingers trail down my back and then he begins to arrange me ever so slightly, tilting my hips at a different angle.

Levi exhales. "All those years ago. And then later. There were lots of things that I imagined doing to you, but I always went back to . . ." He trails off. For a few seconds I hear very little, but it's okay. I'm unwinding from the trembling, needy, overheated mess he makes of me, and it's good to have a moment to calm down. It'll be nice to keep some dignity in this bed—

The palms of his hands move between my legs and spread them apart. My panties are yanked all the way to the side. I gasp, feeling cold air on my core, feeling so open, exposed, it's almost obscene. "You look . . ." His voice is quiet, and then he half explodes in a low, "Fuck." I'm a fraction of a second from asking him what's wrong with me when I feel him pull my hips higher.

"Levi?"

His tongue, his lips, his nose press into me from behind, and I inhale sharply. First it's careful, delicate licks, flicking my clit and nudging my opening; then it's deep kisses, mapping me thoroughly.

"Oh my *God*," I moan.

His only response is a low, satisfied growl against my folds, and I don't know if it's the vibrations, or the enthusiastic way he's working on me, or the fact that he's holding me wide open like I am a feast made for him to consume, but my belly tenses, and my limbs are shaking, and keeping my pleading noises in is a losing game. It can't last, not like this. It takes him less than a minute to push me tumbling over the edge.

This is not my body. Or maybe it is, but Levi's in charge, and I don't mind. The pleasure takes over, crashes over me like a tidal wave, and before it even dries out I feel him rearranging me once more, pressing my stomach into the mattress again until I'm at his mercy.

His fingers are on me, parting me open. Then there is a stretch, a split-second burn, and he's pushing deep inside. He was there before and it was heaven, but I'm wetter now, and the friction is even more delicious. I feel myself tighten, quick, fluttering contractions around his length.

This is. So. Unbelievably. Good.

"*Jesus*," Levi grunts. Tests a deep, shaky thrust. "You're still coming, aren't you?"

Yes. No. I don't know. I twist my neck and turn back. He's looking down at me. At my flushed skin and my trembling flesh. He's not going to stop anytime soon, I know it. I'm going to come disastrously quickly, again, or maybe I'll never stop, and he's going to stare at me for every last second of it. Caging me, propped up on his huge, shaking arms, with that hungry, spellbound gleam in his eyes. "You're some kind of fantasy. Built to do this. Built for me. Fuck, Bee." His rhythm picks up. Uneven and choppy, but it picks up.

And I can't bear it.

"You can't," I moan.

He immediately pauses.

"No," I whine. "Don't stop."

"You said—?"

"Just . . . Please, don't look at me."

He seems to finally get it. "Hush." He lowers himself and presses a kiss to my cheekbones. It's getting—it's impossible, but it's getting even better. He's figured it out, the inside of me. How to angle his thrusts. They're more shallow, more purposeful, and I'm . . .

Babbling. Things like *Oh my god* and *More* and *Please* and *Please harder* and he somehow knows what I mean. He makes sense of me, and bends down to run his tongue down the skin of my throat, to bite my shoulder, to grunt his pleasure against my nape.

"I'm not sure," he murmurs gutturally, breath harsh against my ear, "how I haven't come yet."

Me neither, I think. I say his name, muffled in the pillow, and just let go.

19

BASOLATERAL AMYGDALA: ARACHNOPHOBIA

I'D LIKE TO take back everything I've said so far.

Well, not *everything*. Just the whole *I'm going to dedicate my life to the pursuit of neuroscience and forsake all bodily pleasure with the sole exception of vegan Nutella* bit I've been going on about. I'd like to take that part back: having a friend-slash-coworker-slash-whatever with benefits suits me. Deliciously, fantastically, magically so. I am unbothered. Moisturized. Happy. In my lane. Focused. Flourishing. I suspect I'm having the best weeks of my adult life—including the one spent as a Donuts & Art Camp counselor, where the extent of my duties was to stuff my face with frosting and keep an eye on ten-year-olds as they proclaimed that Cézanne's paintings were "cute, but very orange." Maybe it's the mind-altering sex. I'm sure it's the mind-altering sex. Undoubtedly it's the mind-altering sex, but there's more than that.

Take BLINK, for example: the demonstration is set for next Friday. Would I feel a tad more relaxed if I had four more weeks before Boris drags half of Congress in front of me? Of course. I'm obsessive and like to be overprepared. But every single test we ran since our breakthrough gave us excellent results. We're moving to a stage that feels less "thankless grueling groundwork" and more "groundbreaking scientific advance," and most of the balls are in my court. Each helmet has to be customized for the astronaut who'll wear it based on the mapping of their brain. It's a lot of fine-tuning, and I love every second of it. Everyone does: seeing something we've been working on tirelessly yield results is a big morale boost, and the engineers have been arriving early and staying late, buzzing around Levi and me with constant questions, and . . .

We've been keeping it secret. This thing Levi and I are doing. Obviously. There's no point in telling the engineers. Or Rocío. Or Guy—who mostly alternates between questions about my nonexistent husband and inviting Levi out. On Wednesday it's: "Basketball tonight?" On Thursday: "Beers?" Friday: "What's going on this weekend?" I'd feel guilty at Levi's standard response ("Sorry, man, I'm swamped."), but it's only temporary. Just one of those things: girl with no interest in relationships meets dude who was into her years ago and they take up the horizontal mambo—no strings attached. In a few weeks I'll be home, and Guy will have Levi all to himself. In the meantime, we're stocking up on time together like camels. Time and sex. Have I mentioned the sex? I must be twenty hours behind on sleep, but somehow I'm not tired. My body might be evolving into a sophisticated bioweapon capable of converting orgasms into rest.

"You should just move in," Levi tells me on Friday morning. I blink bleary-eyed over coffee he poured me, my brain struggling to decipher the words.

"What do you mean?"

"Bring your stuff here." He just got home from his run and looks sweaty, disheveled, and disturbingly good. "Pack a bag. Then you won't have to go back and forth to get a change of clothes. It's not your real apartment anyway."

I study him over my mug. Maybe he's suffering from heatstroke. "I can't move in with you." I'm pretty sure there's language about that in the fuckbuddying contract.

"Why?"

"Because. What if you need to . . ." *Watch pornography?* He probably wouldn't—I'd be his live-in pornography. *Bring home other girls?* I don't see him doing that, either. *Man cave it up?* It's a big house. *Walk around naked?* He already does it. I can't believe I'm having sex with someone with a six-pack.

"I'm serious," he continues. "I have a better bed. Better cat. Better hummingbirds."

"Lies. There are no hummingbirds in your garden."

"They show up when you're not around. You'll have to move in to see them."

"Rocío might notice."

He is quiet, waiting for me to elaborate. "And?"

"Then Kaylee would. And she might tell others. If I'd found out that Sam was screwing Dr. Mosley on the side, I'd have hollered it to the winds." I frown. "I'm a monster. Poor Sam."

"If Kaylee tells others, then she tells others. That's not a problem."

I rub my eyes. "I'm not sure I want your entire team to know that I'm having a thing with a colleague. It sounds like the type of thing . . ."

". . . for which women in STEM get unfair shit all the time?"

"Yup."

"Fair. But even if Rocío noticed, she wouldn't know that you are at my place. Plus she might have other stuff on her mind, given the number of times I've heard her and Kaylee call each other 'babe' in the last week."

"True." I bite my lower lip, actually considering moving in. Am I insane? I don't think so. I just like him—like *this*, *being* with him. Fuckbuddyship with Levi Ward suits me, and I just want . . . a little more of it. "FYI, I wear a retainer at night."

"Sexy."

"And your bathroom will be stained purple forever. Seriously. Five showers and your bathtub will be a giant eggplant emoji."

He gives me a solemn nod and pulls me closer. "It's everything I ever wanted."

IT'S SATURDAY MORNING and we're cooking together—by which I mean Levi's making pancakes and I'm standing next to him, stealing blueberries and telling him about *The Mermaid's Tale*, the Young Adult book idea I've been nursing since grad school (nothing like a nanoscopic office and perennially skirting the poverty line to stimulate a gal's imagination for escapist fiction).

"Wait." He frowns. "Ondine doesn't know she's half mermaid before joining the swim team?"

"Nope, she doesn't know she was adopted. She finds out on the first practice, when they throw her in the water and she swims one lap in . . . I'll have to research how long it takes to swim one lap, but she's as fast as . . ."

"Michael Phelps?" Levi flips a pancake.

"Sure, whoever that is. And Joe Waters, cutest senior in school, sees her and becomes her faithful sidekick in her journey of self-discovery."

"Do they end up together?"

"Nope. He goes to college, she sprouts a tail."

"Can't they do long distance?"

"No. I won't lie to impressionable youths about the durability of human relationships."

He scowls. "That's a bad ending—"

"It's not—it's mer-mazing!"

"—and long-distance relationships are not a lie."

"Happy-ending long-distance relationships sure are. Just like all other happy-ending relationships."

He pins me with a look. The corners of the pancake are darkening dangerously. "And ours will end poorly, too?"

"Nah." I wave my hand. "We'll be fine, because we're casual."

He stiffens, lips thinning. "I see." He relaxes with visible effort, and . . . there's something odd about his expression.

"What's that face?" I ask.

"What face?"

"That one. The one you put on when you're about to try to convince me that Nirvana is better than Ani DiFranco."

"I'm not going to try to convince you."

"Ah. So you admit that I'm right."

"You're *not* right. You're stubborn, and misguided, and often wrong—about music and other things. But there's no use in trying to reason with you." He leans closer and kisses me—lingering, soft, deep. I lose myself a little. "I'll just have to show you."

"Show me wh—?"

Levi's phone rings. He takes a moment to turn off the stove before picking up. "Yes?"

The voice on the other end is almost familiar—Lily Sullivan.

"Hey. I'm with Bee." I give him a curious look. Why would Lily know who I am? "Sure. Of course . . . I'll ask." He presses his phone against his shoulder, looking at me. "Any interest in spending a few hours hanging out with a six-year-old who wants to be a spider vet and has strong opinions on Pokémons?"

I'm briefly confused. Then I realize what he's asking and my face splits into a grin. "*Lots* of interest. But, Levi?" I whisper as he puts the phone back to his ear. "Pokémon is uncountable."

LILY SULLIVAN IS warm, personable, and sweet in a delicious Southern way that has me instantly liking her and feeling welcome in her beautiful Early American home. Penny Sullivan, though . . . I fall in love with Penny the second I lay my eyes on her.

Not true. I fall for her when she looks up from lying facedown on the living room rug and moans with wide, pleading eyes, "My kingdom. My entire kingdom for a Twinkie."

"She's on her fourth day of Keto," Lily whispers. "For her epilepsy." She gives me the doleful look of a mother who's been feeding her kid eggs and avocados for too many meals. "I don't think she ever asked for a Twinkie before today."

I remember the cravings of nine-year-old Bee, who was brutally informed by her cousin Magdalena that gummy bears are made with animal bones and didn't find out about vegan alternatives for years. "Yeah, diets are funny like that."

Though Penny seems fine now that Levi's here, laughing uncontrollably when he picks her up, throws her over his shoulder, and starts making his way across the house. "Penny Lane and I will be in the backyard, if you want to join us." It's clear that they have a routine, which consists of Levi pushing a long swing that dangles from the branch of a tall tree, and Penny yelling, "More! *More!*" as

Lily sits on the patio and smiles fondly at them. I take the chair next to hers, and thank her when she pours me a glass of lemonade.

"I'm so glad you came over. Penny was supposed to have a sleepover tonight, but we postponed after the seizure earlier this week. She didn't take it well."

"I'd be grumpy, too. And it's no problem at all—your home is so lovely, thank you for having me."

She smiles, covering my hand with her palm. "Thank *you* for not thinking that"—she gestures vaguely to herself, the house, Levi, and even me—"*all of this* is weird. Having this woman who's always calling the man you're dating—"

"Oh, it's not like that. We're just—" My eyes dart to the swing. Can I talk about sex within one hundred feet of a child? Is there a law against it?

"It must be uncomfortable, considering that Levi and I once . . ." She gives me an apologetic look. I want her to stop talking about this for many reasons, including the fact that while I have no right to be jealous, judging by the little pang in my stomach I . . . apparently am? A little bit? Yikes, me. "It's long over," Lily continues. "And it was just a few weeks. We met here in Houston when he came to spend the summer with Peter, before the last year of his Ph.D. Then he went back to Pittsburgh. We were supposed to try long distance, but he said he met someone else. . . ."

The pang turns into a thud. Who did Levi meet in his fifth year? Well, me. Duh. But he can't have *broken up* with someone like Lily for—

"When he told Peter that we'd split, Peter admitted that he liked me and asked me out." She spreads her hands, as though she cannot believe her own story. "We got married two months later, and I got pregnant right after. Can you believe it?"

I smile. "It's so romantic. I'm so sorry about what happened to Peter."

"Yeah. It was . . . It's not easy." She looks away. "Thank you for what you're doing for BLINK. I know it's high security and you can't talk about it, but when you came on board, Levi mentioned what an asset you'd be. It means a lot, having someone like you carry out Peter's legacy. And thank you for sharing Levi with us."

There's a lump in my throat. "He's not mine to share."

"I think he might be, actually. Oh, that *little*— Penny, you need a hat! You can't be in the sun like that!"

"Levi said I could!"

Levi lifts one eyebrow, clearly having said no such thing. Penny sullenly stalks to her mother, only to stop in front of me with a shy, hesitant look.

"Does that hurt?" she asks, shifting her weight from one foot to the other.

"What— Oh, my nose piercing. Just a tiny bit when I first got it, many years ago."

She nods skeptically. "Is your name really Bee?"

"It is."

"Like the bug?"

"Yup."

"Why?"

Levi and I laugh. Lily covers her eyes with a hand.

"My mom was a poet, and she *really* liked a set of poems about bees."

Penny nods. Apparently, it makes as much sense to her as it did to Maria DeLuca-Königswasser. "Where's your mom?"

"Gone, now."

"Oh. My daddy's gone, too." I can feel the tension in the adults, but there's something matter-of-fact about the way Penny talks. "What's your favorite animal?"

"Will you be disappointed if I don't say bees?"

She mulls it over. "Depends. Not if it's a good one."

"Okay. Are cats good?"

"Yes! They're Levi's favorite, too. He has a black kitty!"

"That's right," Levi interjects. "And Bee has a kitty, too. A see-through one."

I glare at him.

"*My* favorite animals are spiders," Penny informs me.

"Oh, spiders are, um"—I suppress a shudder—"cool, too. My sister's favorite animals are blobfish. Have you ever seen one?"

Her eyes widen, and she climbs on my lap to look at the picture I'm pulling up on my phone. God, I love children. I love *this* child. I look up and notice the way Levi's staring at me with an odd light in his eyes.

"Is your sister a child?" Penny asks after making a face at the blobfish.

"She's my twin."

"Really? Does she look like you?"

"Yep." I scroll to my favorites and tap on a picture of the two of us at fifteen, before I started what Reike calls my "journey of soft-core body modification." "Wow! Which one is you?"

"On the right."

"Do you get along?"

"Yeah. Well, we insult each other a lot, too. But yeah."

"Do you live together?"

I shake my head. "I actually don't see her in person much. She travels a lot."

"Are you mad that she's gone?"

270

Ah, children. And their loaded questions. "I used to be. But now I'm just a bit . . . sad. But it's okay. She needs to travel just as much as I need to stay put."

"My friend said that if you're a twin, your children will be twins, too."

"You have a higher probability, yes."

"Do you want twins?"

"Penny," Lily reprimands her gently, "no grilling guests on family planning before lunch."

"Oh, that's fine. I would *love* to have twins." I used to dream of it, actually. Even though at this point I probably won't. For obvious reasons. That I won't bother Penny with.

She smiles. "That's good, because so does Levi."

"Oh. Oh, I—" I feel myself go crimson and look at Levi, expecting to find him just as embarrassed, but he's staring at me with the same expression from before, only about twenty times more intense, and—

"Does anyone want sherbet?" Lily asks, clearly picking up on the weirdness.

"Mother," Penny says darkly, "must you *torture* me?"

"I got special ice cream at the store for you." Penny's eyes widen and she runs inside the house. "Poor girl," Lily mutters as we follow her inside. "Keto ice cream's probably disgusting."

"You underestimate how desperate she might be," I tell her. "There are things I used to find appalling after going vegan that I started loving out of—"

"Bee! Bee! Look, I want to show you something!"

"What's that?" I smile and crouch to her height.

"This is Shaggy, my—"

My eyes fall on the stuffed tarantula plush toy in her hands, and sound recedes. My vision fogs. I'm hot and cold at the same time, and all of a sudden, everything goes dark.

"THAT WAS SO cool! Levi, I love your girlfriend soooo much!"

"I know the feeling."

"Goodness. Should I call 911?"

"Nah, she's fine." Everything's foggy, but I think I'm in Levi's arms. He's patiently holding my head up, no concern in his tone. In fact, he sounds weirdly charmed. "This happens to her every other day."

"Slander," I mumble, fighting to open my eyes. "Lies."

He smiles down at me and—he's *so* handsome. I love his face. "Look who's gracing us with her presence."

"Is it low blood sugar?" Lily asks apprehensively. "Can I get you anything to—?"

"Bee is like me!" Penny is saying, clapping her hands excitedly. "She has the same bursts of electricity in her brain! She has seizures!"

"It's a bit like seizures," I say, straightening up.

"Bee has a useless parasympathetic nervous system, which is an endless source of entertainment," Levi explains to Penny.

"Excuse me." I scowl. "Some of us don't have the luxury of stable blood pressure."

"I didn't say it wasn't cute," he murmurs inaudibly against my temple. The scratch of his stubble against my skin is rough. His lips, soft.

Penny seems to be a fan, too. "Does your twin faint, too?"

"Nope. She got all the best things." Like the ability to burp the French national anthem.

"It's so cool!"

"It's actually a very maladaptive autonomic response."

"Can you do it again?"

"Not really, sweetie. Not on command."

"When do you do it, then?"

"It depends. Sometimes it's highly stressful, surprising situations. Other times it's just seeing things that I'm afraid of, like snakes or spiders."

Penny's eyes widen. "So if I show you Shaggy again—"

Levi and Lily yell, "No!" at the same time, but it's too late. Penny whips the toy back out from behind her back, and everything goes dark again.

WE STAY WITH the Sullivans all day, and after Shaggy gets locked in an out-of-reach cupboard, we have a blast. By the time we're ready to leave, I know more about Pokémon than I ever cared to, and Penny has tried to make me faint again approximately twenty times by drawing spiders on every available piece of paper.

That little monster. I love her to death.

But when we say goodbye in the entrance, agreeing that we should do it again soon, it's a bit like a pianoforte crashing on my head.

"How long will you be in Houston?" Lily asks.

All I can do is burrow farther into Levi's side. "Unclear. The project was originally supposed to last around three months, but things are going very well, so . . ." I shrug. Levi's arm tightens around me. I'm fully aware that Levi and I are the Merriam-Webster definition of transitory. But I'm enjoying this so much. His company. His friends. His food. I'll be sad when this is over in a couple of weeks.

"Are your parents still going to be in town next week?" Lily asks.

Levi's arm tightens again, this time in a completely different fashion. Before it was possessive, comforting. Now it's just tense. "Yeah."

"Ugh. Sorry about that. Let me know if you need anything."

Curious, I bring it up as soon as we're alone in the truck. "Your family will be here?"

He starts the truck, looking straight ahead. I'm beginning to recognize his moods, but this one I'm not familiar with. Yet. "My parents. There's some event on the Air Force base here."

"And you're going to see them?"

"We'll probably have dinner."

"When?"

"Not sure. My father will let me know when he's free."

I nod. And then I hear a voice that sounds a lot like mine ask, "Can I come?"

He puffs out a laugh. "Are you a fan of strained silences interrupted by the occasional 'Pass the garlic salt'?"

"It can't be that bad. Otherwise you wouldn't even get together."

"You'd be surprised by the lengths my father will go to let me know the depth of his disappointment."

"What about your mom?"

He just shrugs.

"Listen—I can drop hints on how amazingly BLINK is going. I can say that you're the go-to engineer for most neuroscientists. I can print out your *Nature* publication and use it to gently dab my mouth after the first course."

"There better only be one course. And, Bee—" He shakes his head. "It's not that I don't want you to meet them, or that I'm embarrassed. It's just that it's going to be *truly* bad."

At least you have a shitty family to hold on to, I think, but I don't say it. I'm almost positive that Levi's parents are not as horrible as he says. I'm equally positive that he experiences them like that, and that's all that matters. "I don't want to be pushy, but I also really want to be there. I could come, and we could pretend that I'm your girlfriend."

He gives me a puzzled look. "There wouldn't be much to pretend."

"No—we can pretend that we're an inch from marriage. I can put on my lotus septum ring and leave my tattoos out. I'll wear my AOC top and ripped jeans. Think how much they'll hate me!"

I can see how little he wants to smile, and how little he can help it. "No one could hate you. Not even my father."

I wink at him. "Game on, then."

20

VENTRAL TEGMENTAL AREA: ROMANTIC LOVE

LEVI'S FATHER, AS it turns out, is perfectly capable of hating me. And so are Levi's mother and his eldest brother, who join us for dinner in a less-than-pleasantly-surprising plot twist.

But first things first. Before The Dinner there are days of intense prep for the upcoming BLINK demonstration. Bolts are tightened; stimulating frequencies are adjusted; Guy is prodded, poked, and shocked on his scalp. He's a trooper: the demonstration is about the helmet, but as test subject number one he'll be front and center, and it's clear that he's nervous about it. In the past couple of days he's been moody, anxious, and more tired than ever. I think he's been keeping his fears to himself to avoid disrupting morale, which makes me want to hug him. The other night I stopped by his office to check on him: he startled like a coil spring and quickly closed all his tabs. I guess even astronauts de-stress on YouPorn?

Rocío and Kaylee are getting chummier and chummier. I overhear them in the break room while heating up the stir fry I made yesterday in an attempt to impress Levi with the one dish I can cook—which resulted in the painful realization that I can cook zero dishes.

"If she's willing to say a few words about how the movement started, that would be amazing," Rocío is saying.

"She seems pretty private."

"We could blur her face. Auto-tune her. Use a helium voice app."

"Baby, that would undercut the seriousness of the message."

"What about a Guy Fawkes mask?"

"I do love *V for Vendetta*—but no."

"What are you guys talking about?" I ask, spearing a piece of carrot that manages to be at once burnt *and* undercooked. Amazing. This has to be a transferable skill set.

"You know #FairGraduateAdmissions, right?" Kaylee asks.

I drop my carrot back into the Tupperware. "Ah . . . vaguely."

"It's about guaranteeing inclusivity in the admission process. Student organizations are really active in the movement, but Ro and I are technically not students, so . . ." She turns her laptop. "We're making the #FairGraduateAdmissions website! Not ready yet, but we'll launch it soon. There will be information, resources, mentorship opportunities. And we'll ask Marie Curie for an interview."

I finish chewing and swallow. Even though I never put the carrot in my mouth. I must be eating my tongue. "Marie Curie?"

"Not the *real* Marie Curie! That would be *hilarious*, though!" Kaylee giggles at the misunderstanding for about half a minute. Rocío stares at her for the entire duration, heart-eyed. Ah, young love. "It's the person who started the conversation. We want to launch the website with her interview, but she's pretty anon." She spreads her hands. Her nails are an iridescent baby blue.

I clear my throat. "She might agree to do it via email."

"This is actually a great idea!" Ro and Kaylee exchange an offensively impressed look. Then Kaylee licks her thumb and wipes something from the corner of Rocío's eye. "Hang on, baby. You have a smudge."

I walk out of the room holding Rocío's gaze and mouthing, "Goodbye, baby." I cannot overstate how much I love this relationship development.

With so much at stake for Friday, everyone's too frantic to notice that Levi has taken to bringing coffee to my workstation; to making sure that I don't go too long without a break; to smiling faintly and asking if I'm going to pass out whenever a bug flies into the lab; to teasing me about the little mounds of treats I leave for Félicette.

I have noticed. And I know he's just being a friend, a kind person, an awesome collaborator, but it hurts a little. Not hurt *hurt*. But those pangs? Those little twinges I experience when Levi stares at me? When we're running together and he effortlessly matches his pace to mine? When he leaves me the yellow vegan M&Ms because he knows they're my favorites? (Yes, they taste better than the red.) Well, those little twinges are starting to get a bit painful. Knifing at my general chest area.

Weird. Odd. Strange. Peculiar. I make a note in my Reminders app: *Visit primary care doc in Bethesda*. I'm overdue for a checkup.

Anywho. Work's fantastic, sex is even better, and #FairGraduateAdmissions is about to shake things up in academia, the last bastion of the medieval guild apprenticeship model. Things are going great, right?

Wrong. Let's loop back to The Dinner.

The first hint that it might possibly not go *super* well (or, as I think of it, my first Uh-Oh™) comes when I find out that Levi's family suggested having dinner at an upscale steakhouse. And when I say "suggested," I mean decided. I've no problem with people eating meat, but the complete disregard for Levi's dietary preferences seems less than fatherly.

The smell of grilled steak envelops us the second we step inside. I glance up at Levi and he says, apologetic, "I'll make you dinner afterward." Which causes a bit of a . . . tsunami inside me. Seriously. The pangs? Those are *nothing*. I'm being swept over by a ridiculous surge of affection for this vegan man whose probably annoying parents invited him to a steakhouse, and whose first concern is that *I* don't go hungry tonight. It's a warm feeling that threatens to explode inside my chest, which is why I stop him in the entrance with a hand on his gray button-down and pull him to me for a kiss.

We don't exactly kiss in public. And even in private, I'm not usually the one who initiates contact. His eyes widen, but he instantly bends to meet me halfway.

"I'll also, um," I murmur against his lips, "do stuff for you. Afterward." *Whoa. Very sexy, Bee. Very smooth, you temptress.*

He flushes with heat. "You . . . will?"

I nod, suddenly shy. But we kiss, and that's my second Uh-Oh™. Because a throat clears behind us, and I immediately know whose it is.

Oops.

Levi's father is a shorter, slightly less handsome, slightly less built version of him. His mother is where he gets his wavy hair and green eyes from. And the third person . . . There's another man with them, and it's clear that Levi's surprised. Given the resemblance, it's also clear that he's Levi's brother.

Oh my God. This is Levi's family. Levi's *life*. I find myself incredibly curious. I want to know everything about him. Which is probably why I'm staring a little too hard and missing the introductions. Possibly, a third Uh-Oh™.

". . . my eldest brother, Isaac. And this is Dr. Bee Königswasser."

I smile, ready for my brightest *Nice to meet you*, but Levi's father interrupts me. "A girlfriend, huh?"

I try not to stiffen. "Yup. Coworker, too."

He nods indifferently and heads for the table, tossing an indifferent "I told you he probably wasn't gay" to his wife, who follows him with a healthy dose of indifference. Isaac goes next after a brief smile to the two of us, a touch less indifferent. The kicker is, when I glance up at Levi, he seems indifferent, too. He just takes my hand and leads me to the table.

"You can leave anytime, okay?" I wonder who he's telling that to.

Levi and I need about half a second with the menu before settling on our order (house salad, no cheese, olive oil dressing). We're silent as his parents continue a conversation with Isaac that clearly began in the car. No one has asked Levi so much as "How are you?" and he seems . . . disturbingly fine with it. If anything, he looks elsewhere. Staring in the mid-distance, playing with the fingers of my left hand under the table, like I'm a miraculous anti-stress toy. I'm no expert in family dinners—or in families—but this is fucked up. So when there's a moment of quiet I try to remind the Wards of our existence.

"Mr. Ward, do you—"

"Colonel," he says. "Please, call me Colonel." Then immediately turns to say something to Isaac. How's that for a fourth Uh-Oh™?

The first interaction is after the food arrives. "How's your salad, Levi?" his mother asks. He finishes chewing before saying, "Great." He manages to sound sincere, as though he's not a six four, two-hundred-pound brickhouse who needs four thousand calories a day. I study him in disbelief and realize something: He's not calm, or indifferent, or relaxed. He's *closed off*. Shuttered. Inscrutable.

"All good at work?" Isaac asks.

"Yup. Couple of new projects."

"We recently had a breakthrough on something that has the potential to be great," I say excitedly. "Something Levi's leading—"

"Any way NASA will reconsider your application for the Astronaut Corps?" the Colonel asks, ignoring me. Uh-Oh™ five. Should this have been a drinking game?

"I doubt it. Unless I cut off my feet."

"I don't like your tone, son."

"They won't reconsider." Levi's voice is mild. Unbothered.

"The Air Force has no height restrictions," Isaac says with his mouth full. "And they like people with fancy degrees."

"Yes, Levi." His mother now. "And the Air Force will only take you until you're thirty-nine. The Navy is . . ."

"Forty-two," Isaac supplies.

"Yes, forty-two. You don't have a lot of time to make the decision."

I thought Levi's parents were probably not as terrible as he made them out to be, but they're ten times worse.

"And the Army's thirty-five—how old are you, Levi?"

"Thirty-two, mom."

"Well, the Army probably wouldn't be your first choice—"

"What about the French Foreign Legion?" I ask, twirling a lock of purple hair. Forks stop clinking. Three pairs of eyes study me with distrust. Levi's just . . . alert, as though curious at what might happen. God, what have these people *done* to him? "What are the age requirements for the French Foreign Legion?"

"Why would he want to join another country's army?" the Colonel asks icily.

"Why would he want to join the US Army?" I quip back. I cannot believe that rotten Tim Carson spawned from a loving, perfect family, and someone who's as perfect and loving as Levi comes from such rotten relatives. "Or the Air Force, or the Navy, or the Boy Scouts? It's obviously not his calling. It's not as though he works as an accountant who money-launders for a drug cartel. He's a NASA engineer cited by thousands of people. He has a high-paying position." I actually have no idea how much Levi makes, but I lift one eyebrow and carry on. "He's not wasting his life in a dead-end job."

Uh-Oh™ number six. The drinking game was *totally* a missed opportunity. It sure would make the silence more bearable as it stretches. And stretches. And stretches.

Until the Colonel breaks it. "Miss Königswasser, you are very rude—"

"She's not," Levi interrupts firmly. Calmly. But forcefully. "And she's a doctor." Levi holds his father's gaze for a moment, and then moves on to his brother. "What about you, Isaac? How's work been?"

I lean back in my chair, noticing the suspicious, hateful way the Colonel is looking at me. I give him a fake, bright smile and tune in to what Levi is saying.

THE SECOND WE'RE in the truck I take off my Converse, push the soles of my feet against the dashboard, and—Quasimotoes in full sight—I explode. "I cannot believe it!"

"Mm?"

"It's *unfathomable*. We should make a damn case study out of this. *Science* would publish it. *Nature*. The *New England Journal of* damn *Medicine*. It would get me a Nobel Prize. Marie Curie. Malala Yousafzai. Bee Königswasser."

"Sounds lovely. What's 'it' again?"

"At the very least we'd get short-listed! We could take a trip to Stockholm. See the fjords. Meet up with my wayward sister."

He turns up the AC. "I'll take you to Stockholm whenever you like, but you'll have to give me a topic if you want me to follow this conversation."

"I just cannot believe how—how *well-adjusted* you are! I mean, okay, you and I have had our . . . issues when it comes to social interactions, but I'm befuddled that you haven't turned out a titanic psychopath despite the family you came from. There has to be a miracle in there, no?"

"Ah." He half smiles. "Do you want to get ice cream?"

"You had neither nature *nor* nurture on your side!"

"So, no ice cream?"

"*Of course* yes ice cream!"

He nods and takes a right. "There was some therapy involved."

"How much therapy are we talking about here?"

"Couple years."

"Did it entail a brain transplant?"

"Just lots of talking through how my inability to functionally communicate my needs stemmed from a family that never allowed me to. Same old."

"They *still* don't allow you! They're trying to—to *erase* you and turn you into something else!" I am incensed. Enraged. Incensedly enraged. I want to mutate into Beezilla and pillage the extended Ward family at the next Thanksgiving. Levi better invite me.

"I've tried to reason with them. I've yelled. I've explained myself calmly. I've tried . . . a lot of things, believe me." He sighs. "Eventually I had to accept what my therapist always said: all you can change is your own reaction to events."

"Your therapist sounds great."

"He was."

"But I still want to commit patricide."

"It's not patricide if it's not your own father."

An angry scream bubbles out of me. "You should never talk to them again."

He smiles. "That will send a strong message."

"No, seriously. They don't deserve you."

"They're not . . . good. For sure. I've considered the possibility of cutting them off many times, but my brothers and my mom are much better when my father isn't around. And anyway . . ." He hesitates. "Today wasn't that bad. It might have been the best dinner I've had with them in a long time. Which I'll chalk up to you telling my father to can it and shocking him into temporary speechlessness."

If that dinner was "not bad," then I'm a K-pop idol. I gaze at the dusky Houston lights, thinking that the way his family treats him should diminish him in my eyes, realizing the truth is just the opposite. There's something patient about the way he quietly stands up for himself. About the way he *sees* others.

Another pang near my heart. I don't know what they're about. I just really . . . "Levi?"

"Mm?"

"I want to tell you something."

"I told you: your lungs are not shrinking because you're training for a 5K—"

"My lungs are *totally* shrinking, but that's not it."

"What, then?"

I take a deep breath, still staring out the window. "I really, really, *really* like you."

He doesn't reply for a long moment. Then: "I'm pretty sure I like you more."

"I doubt it. I just want you to know, not everyone is like your family. You can be . . . you can be *you* with me. You can talk, say, do however you want. And I'll never hurt you like they did." I make myself smile at him. It's easy now. "I promise I don't bite."

He reaches over to take my hand, his skin warm and rough against mine. He smiles back. Just a little.

"You could rip me to shreds, Bee."

We are silent for the rest of the drive.

SCHRÖDINGER BURROWED INTO my backpack, tore a package of kale chips, decided they were not to his liking, and went for a nap with his head pillowed on the half-empty bag. I burst into laughter and forbid Levi to wake him up before I can take a million pictures to send Reike. It's the best thing to happen all day—a reminder that while Levi's actual family might suck balls, his chosen one is the best.

"I'm very impressed," I coo to Schrödinger while petting his fur.

"Don't cuddle him, or he'll feel rewarded," Levi warns me.

"Are you feeling rewarded, kitty?"

Schrödinger purrs. Levi sighs.

"Whatever Bee's doing, do not experience it as cuddles. Those are punishment pets," he says in what he probably means as a firm tone but is instead adorably helpless, and I get another pang, to my heart *and* my ovaries. I do hope he'll have kids. He'd be an amazing dad.

"Those chips were on my desk for days and Félicette never managed to open them."

"And that's not at all because Félicette doesn't exist," Levi yells from the kitchen.

"You should teach Félicette your ways," I whisper to Schrödinger, and then join Levi in the kitchen just in time to see him throw away what's left of my unjustifiably overpriced Whole Foods chips.

"Are you still hungry? Should I make you food?"

I shake my head.

"You sure? I don't mind making—"

He falls silent as I fall to my knees. His eyes widen as my smile does.

"Bee," he says. Though he doesn't quite *say* it. He mouths it breathlessly, like he often does when I touch him. And now my fingers are on his belt, which qualifies as touching. Right? "Bee," he repeats, a little guttural this time.

"I said I'd do stuff," I tell him with a smile. The clink of his belt buckle bounces off the kitchen appliances. His fingers weave into my hair.

"I figured you meant . . . watching sports with me. Or another of your burnt—*ah*—stir-fries."

I take him out of his boxers and wrap my small hand around him. He's completely hard already. Huge. Shockingly warm against my flesh. He smells like soap and himself, and I want to bottle his delicious scent and bring it with me always. "I'm not very good at stir-fries." My breath is on his skin, making his cock twitch. "This, I hope I can do well."

I'm not exactly confident, and maybe I'm a little clumsy, too, but when I softly lick the head there is a quiet, surprised groan coming from above me, and I think that maybe I'll be fine. I close my lips around him, feel Levi's hands tighten on my scalp, and my insecurities melt.

I don't know why we haven't done this before. It has to do, perhaps, with how impatient he usually is, impatient to be in me, on me, with me. There is often an undercurrent of haste with us, like we both want, need, deserve to be as close as physically possible, as quickly as physically possible, and . . . It doesn't leave much time for delays, I guess.

Levi wants it, though. It might not be something he'd ever ask for, but I can see the shape of pleasure on his face, hear his intakes of breath. I suckle right beneath the head and he lets out a sound of shocked, overwhelming pleasure. Then he threads his fingers through my hair and starts guiding me. He's too thick for me to do much, but I try to relax, to let myself enjoy this, lose myself to the taste, the fullness, his soft, deep groans as he tells me how good it feels, how much he loves my mouth, how much he loves *this*, how much he loves . . .

"Fuck." Softly, with his thumb, he traces the bulge of his cock through the skin of my cheek. My lips, stretched obscenely around him. "You really *are* everything I've ever wanted," he mutters, gentle, reverent, hoarse, and then he's angling me again, this time a rhythm that's deeper, purposeful, working my jaw for his pleasure. When he holds me close and says, "I'm going to come in your mouth," like it's inevitable, like we both need this too badly to stop, I whimper around his flesh from how much I want this for him.

He loses control a little when he comes, his grunts deep and unusually rough, his grip viselike, and I feel his orgasm course through me as if it were my own. I suck him gently through the end of it, and when I look up at him I'm wet and swollen and I feel empty, trembling, a messy lump on the floor.

"Open your mouth," he rasps.

I blink at him, confused. He cups my cheek.

"I want you to open your mouth and show me."

I comply, and the sound he makes, possessive and hungry and pleased at last, travels through me like a wave. He massages the back of my neck while I swallow, his thumb caresses my jaw, and when I smile up at him, he stares at me like I've just gifted him with something divine.

It's a long night, this one. Somehow different from all the others.

Levi takes his time undressing me, stopping often, lingering, losing track of his progress as if distracted by my flesh, my curves, the sounds I make. I moan, I squirm, I beg, and he still won't slide inside, too busy tracing the swell of my breast, pressing his tongue against the bump of my clit, nuzzling against the skin of my throat. I teeter on the edge for too long, and so does Levi, immobile within me, then thick and delicious and slow, slow inside and then slow out, long, drugging kisses stretching the pleasure between us, making my body twitch for his own. And then he looks down at me, hands twined with my hands, eyes twined with my eyes, breath twined with my breath.

"Bee," he says. Just my name, half gasp, all heated plea. He stares down at me as though I own him. As though his future hangs from my hands. As though everything he's ever wanted, I hold it within me. It makes my chest hurt and leap with a dangerous, thunderous kind of joy.

I close my eyes not to see and let the liquid heat swell inside me like the tide, high and low all night long.

21

RIGHT INFERIOR FRONTAL GYRUS: SUPERSTITION

THEY SAY DISASTERS come in threes, but it's not true. It's just a quirk of the human mind, always on the lookout for patterns in random statistical observations to make sense of chaos.

For instance, say you're Dr. Marie Skłodowska-Curie, circa 1911. Your health has been declining after decades spent frolicking in kiddie pools of polonium. Everything's painful and you can barely see, walk, sleep, frolic in more polonium. Sucks, right?

Well, things could suck more. You decide to do that thing you've been putting off: applying for membership at the French Academy of Sciences. You have two Nobel Prizes, so you should be a shoo-in, yes? *Non.* The Academy rejects you, and instead admits this Édouard Branly guy, who I'm sure has many great qualities—such as a penis. (If you're wondering "Who's Édouard? Never heard of this guy!"

that's *exactly* my point. Excellent job, FA of S! Take your seat on the Loser Side of History, next to the University of Krakow.)

Our tally is two major bummers, and you're probably thinking: the shit-cake has been frosted. No other catastrophe will happen for a while. But you forgot the cherry on top: someone breaks into your young stud muffin's apartment, steals your love letters, and sells them to the Fox News equivalent of early nineteenth-century France. Jean Hannity has a field day.

Imagine being Dr. Curie. Imagine sitting in your minuscule Paris apartment, trying to eat a Camembert baguette while the mob rages outside your window because you dared (gasp!) to be an *immigrant*! To be a *woman in STEM*! To *fuck*! Wouldn't you tell yourself that there's a reason this cluster of shit came about? Saturn ascending to the house of Sagittarius. Not enough lambs sacrificed to the Spaghetti Monster. Bad things come in threes. We're only humans. We're full of "whys," drowning in "whys." Every once in a while, we need a bit of "because," and if it's not readily available, we make it up.

Long story long: despite popular belief, a saying is just a saying, and disasters do *not* come in threes.

Except when they do.

The first is on Thursday night, right after the successful dress rehearsal for Friday's presentation. I'm almost looking forward to seeing Trevor tomorrow—well, not *him*, but his face when he realizes what my simpering womanly brain has accomplished. I distractedly exchange a high five with Lamar while checking my phone, and I'm so shocked by my Twitter notifications that I forget my hand in midair.

They're blowing up. In a bad way. As they often do. Except that this time the chaotic mess of insults isn't coming from the incels, or the stemlords, or the men's rights activists—but from other women in STEM.

"You gonna leave it there?" Lamar asks, pointing at my arm. I smile weakly and walk away.

> @SabineMarch I cannot believe how you have betrayed us.
>
> @AstroLena I hope STC presses charges, you bitch. #WhatWouldMarieDoIsOverParty
>
> @Sarah_08980 Hundreds of women in STEM have been working tirelessly for #FairGraduateAdmissions, and all along you have been pretending to be an ally while only looking out for your gain. Shame.

The last tweet is from someone I've chatted with as recently as yesterday. We talked about the events she was organizing, she asked me for advice, told me she loved my account. I blink at my screen and begin scouring for the source of whatever the hell this is.

I find it soon enough. On the account of one Benjamin Green—a name that's familiar but not easy to place until I read the Twitter bio. VP at STC. I frown, and then I see the tweet.

It's a screenshot. Many screenshots. Of a conversation that happened in a private Twitter chat between Mr. Green and someone else. Someone whose icon looks a lot like Marie Curie wearing sunglasses. I read the name: @WhatWouldMarieDo. Me.

Impossible. I've never chatted with this guy. I rapidly scan the handle again, one, two, three times, looking for typos or missing letters that would signal an imposter. There are none. I frown and start reading the conversation. The time stamp is from last night.

@WHATWOULDMARIEDO Hi, Jonathan. I'm aware this is a bit unorthodox, but I hope that what I have to say will be beneficial to the both of us. I know STC has been struggling with the negative publicity #FairGraduateAdmissions has brought upon you, and that you are concerned about the movement gaining even further momentum. As you know, I'm one of its most prominent activists, and played a significant role in its inception. You probably see me as an enemy, but it doesn't have to be like that.

@WHATWOULDMARIEDO I'd like to offer you a deal. I'm open to help shift the narrative toward STC, and to tell my followers and collaborators that the demands of #FairGraduateAdmissions are excessive. That while there might be a need for reform, we do need standardized testing, and therefore it would be in our best interest to work with companies that already exist to improve on instruments that are already widely utilized. Of course, I would not be doing this for free. My real name is ███████████████, in case you need to look up my credentials. I am open to hearing your offers.

I blink at my screen, floored. Then I scroll up to read the public comment Green made on top of the screenshots.

@JgreenSTC #FairGraduateAdmissions activists and the universities and institutions who take them seriously should read what @WhatWouldMarieDo, one of their leaders, asked of me. This is the real agenda of this movement: extortion.

@JgreenSTC At STC we've decided not to make this individual's identity public (for now.) We're consulting with our lawyers and keeping our options open. In the meantime, time to reconsider where you stand #FairGraduateAdmissions.

I feel light-headed. Because I haven't been breathing. I force myself to inhale some air, in and out and in again. This has to be photoshopped. Yes. There's no other explanation. Very well done, but . . . in grad school Annie photoshopped a tentacle coming out of her butt. Anything's possible, right?

I sit at my desk, noticing that lots of people I've talked with recently have blocked me—do they believe this rubbish? They can't possibly. They *know* me. Right?

MARIE: Shmac, I just saw the STC shitshow. Have you?

I bounce my foot and wait for his answer. Minutes later Rocío comes in and starts sliding stuff into her backpack. When I say "sliding," what I mean is "aggressively throwing as though she's practicing her pitch for an upcoming stoning."

"You okay?" I ask, regretting it even before the words are out. I'm probably too anxious to help her with whatever she's going to tell me.

"No."

Shit. "Is Kaylee okay?"

"No. She feels like *crap*." She zips up her backpack, forcefully sliding her arm through one of the straps. "All the work we've been doing for #FairGraduateAdmissions, flushed down the toilet because one of the leaders outed herself as a damn crook."

I freeze. Of all the conversations, I cannot imagine one more uncomfortable, untimely, unpleasant—lots of *Un*s.

"I—I saw," I stammer. My mouth is dry. "But . . . is that even true? It's probably something made up—"

"I bet it's not. People kept saying that STC's screenshots were fake, so he gave proof to some #FairGraduateAdmissions leaders. Marie really did slide into this guy's DMs and asked for money. She fucked us over—she was the one who started #FairGraduateAdmissions, so we won't be taken seriously any longer. That means lots of horrible things for lots of good people—and even for some evil ones. Like me. I'll have to spend thousands of dollars I don't have to retake a test that's less valid a predictor of my ability to succeed in grad school than the number of mummified scorpions I own. Which is seven, by the way." Her voice breaks a little on the last word, which in turn breaks my heart. She looks away, but not before I can see the lone tear sliding down her face. "I won't get into Johns Hopkins. I'll be a jobless failure while Kaylee goes to grad school and forgets all about me."

I stand. "No. No, it won't happen—"

"I'm just so disappointed." She takes a deep breath, shuddering and despondent. "You can't trust anyone. The world really is a vampire." She shrugs, backpack bouncing on her slim shoulder. "You should stop doing that, by the way."

"What?" I follow her gaze. She's staring at my hand, where I'm furiously twisting my grandmother's ring.

"Yesterday I spent fifteen minutes arguing with Guy about

whether you're married. That's what happens when you wear other people's wedding rings, Bee."

Shit. Shit, shit, *shit.* Did Guy find out? He did seem a little distant today, but I thought he was just nervous about tomorrow's demonstration. Should I go find him to explain?

"You going home?" Rocío asks.

"No, I . . ." I was supposed to leave with Levi, as usual. But I don't think I can pretend nothing happened, and telling him about this mess seems . . . well, I could, I guess. If there's someone I could trust with WWMD, it's Levi. But my shitty mood as I try to wrangle my online identity is probably more than he's bargained for. "Yeah, sure. I'll walk with you."

I shoot Levi a quick text about the change of plans and fall in step with Rocío. He doesn't answer until I'm home, asking me if everything's okay, if I want him to pick me up, if he should stop by. A few seconds later, Shmac finally replies:

> **SHMAC:** Yeah. I saw.

> **MARIE:** I have no idea what's happening. I never messaged Green, of course.

> **SHMAC:** Problem is, people on #FairGraduateAdmissions side say they have proof it was you.

> **MARIE:** Please, tell me you don't believe them.

> **SHMAC:** I don't.

I close my eyes. *Thank God.*

SHMAC: Let me think about this, okay? Talk to some people. There must be a way to fix this. Also, check your logs. In case you've been hacked.

I have not. There's nothing out of place—every access to my account has been from Houston. I'm jittery, nervous, scared. I pace around my apartment, long and aggressively enough that it's probably a workout. I should log it into the stupid exercise app Levi made me download ("You'll keep track of your progress. It'll be rewarding." "You know what else is rewarding?" "Don't say 'Not working out,' Bee." ". . . Fine."). I'm actually considering going for a run to clear my head (Have I been body-snatched? By aliens?) when I get an email notification.

It's from a fancy legal firm, one that probably has eight names on the wall and toilet seats covered in gold leaf. The message is innocent enough, but there's a PDF attached to it. I start skimming the content, and that's when my stomach and the world around me turn.

Dr. Königswasser,

This letter is served as notice of your recent acts of unwarranted harassment. You are required to cease and desist all acts of harassment including but not limited to:

- Producing tweets under the alias "@WhatWouldMarieDo"

- Posting public content aimed at damaging the image of STC and its products

- Attempting to extort financial or other benefits from STC in exchange for unsolicited PR (or other) services

Sincerely,

J. F. Timberworth, Attorney-at-Law, on behalf of STC

22

ANTERIOR CINGULATE CORTEX: OH, SHIT

I'M NOT SURE how I spend the night after reading the letter. It's all a blur. The hours go by, and I cry. I breathe. I try to figure out what this mess is. I feel angry, shocked, beaten, lonely, sad.

Levi calls me, twice, but I remember Rocío's lone tear glistening down her cheek and feel too dirty and tainted to make myself pick up. What would Levi say if he knew? Would he believe me? How could he, if STC has my real name? I'm not sure I'd believe myself anymore.

The following day it takes all of my compartmentalizing skills to focus on work—and they're not very many. Pushing things out of my mind is not one of my talents, but I give a moderately good performance. Levi calls again in the morning, and again I don't answer, but I text him that I've been swamped with BLINK (terrible excuse, since we work together) and that I'm busy picking up Trevor at the airport (not an excuse, but equally terrible).

"Kramer couldn't come—something about a WHO symposium—but he's *very* happy," Trevor says instead of *Hi* or *How are you?* or other things normal, decent people start a conversation with. "And you know what happens when Kramer's happy?"

He gives me a lab far away from you. At least down the hallway, possibly on a different floor, ideally in another building. If I even have a future in academia. If I don't get outed as a grossly hypocritical racketeer. "Nope."

"He funnels funds to our lab, that's what. When will the suits be ready?"

I roll my eyes, driving out of Arrivals. "They're helmets. And theoretically the prototype is ready. Some adjustments will have to be made for each individual astronaut."

"Right, you mentioned as much in one of the reports." I talk about this in *all* the reports, but reading comprehension was never Trevor's forte. "The Ward guy, the one who's leading on NASA's side? Must be a damn genius for getting this done so quickly."

I exhale slowly. I'm having a shitty enough day that I probably shouldn't complicate it by telling my boss that he's a urinal cake. Then again, *because* I'm having such a shitty day, I might not be able to help myself from telling him that he's a urinal cake. What a quandary. "Dr. Ward and I are co-leads," I say, my tone harsher than it's ever been with Trevor. He must realize, because he gives me an irritated glance.

"Yeah, but—"

"But?"

He looks out the window, chastised. "Nothing."

Better be.

Trevor the Urinal Cake is the smallest of the big shots in attendance. There are two Texas congressmen, at least three of Boris's bosses, and lots of Space Center employees who aren't directly involved in BLINK. I'm introduced to everyone, but don't retain anyone's name. There's a lot of *Impressive*, and *Can't wait to see the helmets in action*, and *This is history in the making* being thrown around, which makes me nervous and apprehensive, but I tell myself that it'll be fine. Right now, my job is the one thing I have under control—thank Dr. Curie for that.

The goal of the demonstration is to show that the helmet improves Guy's attention during a flight simulation. Guests will observe on a large screen from the conference room next door while Levi, the core engineering team, and I will be in the control room to make sure everything proceeds smoothly. I toy with the idea of taking five minutes alone with Guy to come clean about the marriage thing, but the throng and chaos make it impossible.

I'm double-checking my protocols when Levi comes in, making a beeline to me. "Hey." His eyes are serious. Dark green. Beautiful, like the underbrush of a forest. He drags a chair next to mine, the distance between us blurring the line between colleagues and something more. I should pull back, but no one's looking at us, and the sight of him overwhelms me anyway: it's like all those mysterious pangs elevated to the tenth. I realize that last night was the first we spent apart since . . . since whatever *us* is happened, and that being with him again feels like . . .

No. It does *not* feel like home. Home is something else. Home is the new lab this gig is going to get me. Home is the publications I'll write about today. Home is the community of women in STEM I made for myself that I'll somehow have to fight for. *That's* home, not Levi.

"Hey," I say, averting my eyes.

"You okay?"

"Nervous. You?"

"Fine." He doesn't seem fine. I must be communicating it because he adds, "There's a mess. Not work related—I'll explain later."

I nod, and for a wild, reckless second, I have the weird impulse of telling him about *my* mess. I should, shouldn't I? My name will get out sooner or later. If I tell him now, he'll . . .

Believe that Marie—and therefore me—is a crook. Like everyone else except for Shmac. No, I can't tell him. He wouldn't care anyway.

"I have something for you," he says, the corner of his lip curving in a small smile. The back of his hand brushes mine, and my heart squeezes. It likely seems accidental from the outside. It feels anything but.

"Yeah?"

"I'll show it to you later. It has to do with your imaginary cat."

I smile weakly. "I can't wait for Félicette to puke on your keyboard."

He shrugs. "Imaginary vomit's my favorite kind." He presses his knee against mine and stands, stopping midway to whisper against the shell of my ear, "I missed you last night."

I shiver. He's gone before I can answer.

"—LONELINESS IS KILLING *me, and I must confess, I still believe.*"

Once again, everyone in the control room laughs at Guy's bellowing. The situation in the conference room is probably the same.

"That was lovely. Thank you, Britney," Levi murmurs through the mic, amused. We exchange a brief look. My heart's aflutter. I feel like I'm about to go onstage for a school play I've been practicing the whole year. But I'm an adult, and what's at stake is my professional hopes and dreams. *Which,* I remind myself, *are the only sort of hopes and dreams I allow.* "Ready to start?"

"I was born ready, baby." Guy lifts one eyebrow under the visor of the helmet. "Well. After a labor that my mother often refers to as the most harrowing forty-three hours of her life."

"Poor lady." Levi shakes his head, smiling. "You know the drill, but this is what's going to happen. We're going to start an attention task on the screen."

"I'm being paid to play video games. Excellent."

"Then we'll activate the helmet when we're ready and measure your performance under both conditions, for reaction time and accuracy."

"Got it."

"Starting in a few seconds, then." Levi turns off the mic. He and I exchange another glance, this time lingering.

This is it.

We did it.

You and I.

Together.

Then Levi turns around and nods at Lamar to start the routine. There isn't much I have to do since the protocols have been programmed and are loaded to go. I lean back, eyes on the monitor, fixed on Guy's sitting form.

I'll need to buy him a present, I think. *A bottle of something expensive. Britney concert tickets. For being so patient when I kept shooting theta bursts at his brain. For being so nice. For lying to him.* Then the task loads, and I'm too busy observing to think much of anything.

It starts like usual. Guy's job is to detect stimuli as they appear on the screen. He's an astronaut, and at baseline he performs about ten million times better than I, a regular everyday wimp, ever could. A few minutes later Levi gives another signal, and the brain stimulation protocol I wrote is activated.

Ten seconds pass. Twenty. Thirty. I eye the estimates for the performance metrics—nothing happens. Accuracy and reaction times are hovering around the same values as before.

Shit. What's going on? I squirm nervously in my seat. The lag between the inception of the stimulation and the improvement in performance is usually over by now. I glance at Levi with a worried expression, but he's calm, sitting back in his chair with his arms folded on his chest, alternating looks between Guy and the values. The only sign of impatience is his fingers, drumming on his bicep. He does that when he's focused. *Levi. My Levi.*

I'm stimulating Guy's dorsal premotor cortex—why the hell is he *not* improving—?

Suddenly, the numbers start to change. Accuracy skyrockets from 83 percent to 94. Median reaction times decrease by tens of milliseconds. The new values oscillate, and then keep steady. I swear the entire room sighs in relief in unison.

"Sweet," someone murmurs.

"Sweet?" Lamar asks. "That's *epic.*"

I turn to grin at Levi and find him already staring at me with a happy, undecipherable expression. *This*, at least, is going great. The rest of my life's a shitshow, but *this* is working. We made something good, and useful, and just plain badass.

I told you, didn't I? What's reliable, and trustworthy, and never, *ever* abandoned Dr. Curie? Science. Science is where it's at.

Until it's not.

I'm the first to realize something's wrong. Most of the engineers are talking among one another, and Levi's eyes are still clinging to me with that curious, earnest expression. But both the values and the monitors are in my line of sight, so I notice the numbers changing to values we've never before seen. And the twitchy way Guy's elbow is jerking.

"What's—" I point at it. Levi immediately turns. "Is he okay?"

"The arm?" Levi's brows knit. "I've never seen anything like that."

"It's similar to what would happen if we stimulated his motor cortex, but we definitely aren't— *Whoa*." The twitches get significantly larger. Guy's entire body starts shaking.

Levi turns on the mic. "Guy. Everything okay in there?"

No answer.

"Guy? Can you hear me?"

Silence. And Levi's deepening frown.

"Guy, do you—"

Guy falls out of his chair with a loud thud, his body at once rigid and slack. The control room bursts into chaos—everyone stands, half a dozen chairs scraping against the floor.

"Stop the protocol!" Levi yells, and a second later he's out of the room and into the lab. I see him appear on the monitor and kneel next to Guy's spasming body, taking him into his arms. He turns him to the side and clears the floor of nearby objects.

A seizure. Guy's having a seizure.

Other people barge into the room—NASA physicians, engineers— and ask Levi questions about the stimulation protocol. He answers as best as he can, still holding Guy in his arms as the doctors work around them.

It's because of Penny. Levi knows what to do because of Penny.

There's mayhem everywhere. People running in the hallways, in and out of the control room, screaming, swearing, asking questions without replies. Some are directed at me, but I cannot answer, cannot do anything but stare at Guy's face, at the way Levi is cradling him. I collapse back in my chair. After a minute or an hour, my eyes drift away.

The helmet is on the floor, rolled to the farthest corner of the room.

"—IS KOWALSKY?"

"He was driven to the hospital."

"—going to be okay?"

"Yeah, he regained consciousness. It's just a checkup, but—"

"—they gave him a fucking seizure, what is—"

"What a disaster—"

"—the end of BLINK, for sure. God, the *incompetence*."

I'm a fortress. I'm impenetrable. I'm not even here. I don't look at anyone. I try my best not to listen as I walk to Boris's office after he hissed at me to be there *stat*. It was four and a half minutes ago. I should hurry.

I knock when I arrive, but enter before being invited to come in. Levi's already inside, staring at the pretty green of the Space Center outside the square window. I ignore him. Even when I feel his eyes on me, the prickle of a glance asking for a response, I ignore him.

I wonder what he's thinking. Then I don't wonder anymore: it probably cannot be borne anyway.

"Where was the error?" Boris asks from behind the desk. He always looks tired and disheveled, but if he told me he was just run over by a truck, I'd believe him. I can't begin to comprehend the repercussions of today's events. For him. For NASA. For Levi.

"Yet unclear," Levi says, holding his eyes. "We're looking into it."

"Was there a hardware malfunction?"

"We're ascertaining whether—"

"Bullshit."

A brief silence. "As soon as we know, you'll know."

"Levi, you see me as a paper pusher—you're probably right, I have become one. But let me remind you that I *do* have a degree in engineering, plus a couple of decades of experience on you, and while I'm by no means the creative genius you are, I'm well aware that it won't take you three weeks of system analyses to figure out whether there was a malfunction on the hardware side or—"

"There wasn't," I interrupt. They both turn to me, but I only look at Boris. "At least, I doubt it. I haven't run any analytics, but I'm sure the error was in the stimulation protocol." I swallow. "On my side."

He nods, tight-lipped. "What happened?"

"I don't know. My guess is that the stimulation was too intense or too high-frequency, and either displaced or too diffuse. This caused widespread neuronal misfiring—"

"Okay." He nods again. "*How* did it happen?"

"That I don't know. We spent weeks mapping Guy's brain, and nothing like that ever happened. The protocol was tailored to him." I bend my head, staring down at my hands. I'm wringing my nonna's ring. As usual. "It won't happen again. I'm sorry."

"No, it won't." He runs a hand down his face. "BLINK's over."

There's a sharp intake of breath—Levi's. I look up. "What?"

"This is not a mistake I can tolerate. You took someone who went through years of astronaut training and had him in a puddle on the floor. Guy's fine, but what if the next astronaut isn't?"

I shake my head. "There won't be a next astronaut—"

"There should have been *no astronauts*. Especially not in front of half of NASA!"

"Boris." Levi is standing behind me. Probably a little too close. "We tested this protocol over ten times. Nothing similar ever happened. *You* rushed the demonstration when we could have waited weeks—"

"And *you* vouched for Bee when NIH sent her here, and she gave a seizure to *one of my astronauts!*" Boris clenches his jaw, trying to calm down. "Levi, I don't blame you—"

A loud knock. The door opens, and things get even worse.

No. Not *Trevor*, please. Not when I'm at my lowest.

And yet, Boris gestures for him to come in. "We were just discussing . . ."

"I heard." He shrugs darkly. "You weren't exactly quiet. So," he says, clapping his hands, "I smoothed things over with the congressmen. Told them BLINK's still salvageable."

"Wait." Boris frowns. I might throw up. "I understand there are many interests at play here, but not so fast. Clearly something went very wrong, and—"

"Someone," Trevor interrupts. The look he gives me is full of contempt. "I heard what you were saying. Clearly the problems were with one specific person, and they can be solved by eliminating the weak link and putting another NIH researcher on the project. Josh Martin and Hank Malik applied for the position, too."

"Are you an idiot?" Levi takes a step toward Trevor, looming over him. "You have no knowledge of your own scientists if you think Dr. Königswasser is a weak link—"

"Excuse me," I say. My voice is shaking. I can't cry, not now. "I don't think I'm needed for this conversation. I'll check on Guy and . . ." *Clear out my things.*

Yeah.

I get out as fast as I can. I'm not ten steps from the door when I hear feet running behind, then around me. Levi stops in front of me, a near-desperate expression in his eyes. "Bee, we can still fix this. Come back in there and—"

"I—I need to go." I try to keep my tone firm. "But you need to stay in there and make sure that BLINK actually happens."

He gives me a disbelieving look. "Not without you. Bee, we have no idea what really went wrong. Boris is overreacting and Trevor's a fucking idiot. I'm not going to—"

"Levi." I let myself reach for his wrist. Close my hand around it and squeeze. "I'm asking you to go back in there and do what you have to do to make sure BLINK happens. *Please*. Do it for Peter. For Penny. And for me." It's a low blow. I can see it in his narrowing eyes, in the set of his jaw. But when I start walking again, he doesn't follow.

And right now, that's all I want.

23

AMYGDALA, AGAIN: FEAR

REIKE WON'T ANSWER my calls, because she's finally traveling to Norway. It might be for the best: I'd just cry at her about neuronal depolarization and electromagnetic induction, which can't be healthy for me, or edifying for her. I want to visit Guy in the hospital to . . . bring him an Edible Arrangement? Offer my firstborn in penance? Self-flagellate at the foot of his bed? I'm not even sure where they brought him, if he's still there, and I doubt he wants to see me. Maybe I should text him. *Do you hate me for giving you a seizure through my carelessness and sheer incompetence? Yes, No, Maybe, pls circle.*

It's probably a good thing that I'm alone with my thoughts. Paradoxically, it allows me not to think too much. Things, bad things, are going to happen soon. My connection with WWMD will be disclosed, a community I spent years building will turn against me, and

I have no illusion that Trevor will renew my contract. It's staggering, but if I don't talk about it I can pretend it's not happening.

I eat a banana—first thing I've had in twenty-four hours—and go to my room. I pull my suitcase from under my bed, dust it off, and start folding my clothes. Jeans. Jeans. A skirt I haven't gotten a chance to wear yet. My favorite teal top. A rain poncho. Jeans.

The suitcase is almost full when my doorbell rings. I sigh and force myself to go to the door, but I suspect I already know who it is. Turns out, I'm right.

"Hey." Levi looks tired. And like he's been running a hand through his hair. And very, very beautiful. My heart knots. "You're not answering your phone. I was worried."

"Sorry, I forgot to check it. Is everything okay?"

He gives me a slightly incredulous look that I take to mean *No, absolutely nothing is okay* and follows me into the living room. Through the balcony doors, my eyes catch the hummingbird feeder. I should take it down. Pack it. But the hummingbirds . . . Maybe I could ask Rocío to hang it for me. Wouldn't want the little guy who's been coming around to find himself without dinner.

"—from Guy," Levi's saying.

I whirl around. "How is he?"

"Fine—discharged. He asked me to tell you not to freak out, and that he probably deserved it. And to thank you for the trip of a lifetime." Levi rolls his eyes, but I can see the relief in him.

"Can I— Did he say if I can go see him?"

"He's resting, but we can go tomorrow. He'd love to see you." His tone hardens ever so slightly. "Bee, he knows it's not your fault. A million things could have gone wrong, and none are exclusively your responsibility. Boris rushed the demonstration—"

"Because *I* let him rush it." I press my fingers into my eyes. "I told him I could make it. And this mess would have happened anyway, just not publicly. I must have done something wrong. I must have forgotten to account for something—I don't know. I don't *know*. I've been thinking about it and I cannot figure out what the fuck I did wrong, which means that someone else, someone who has a clue what they're doing, should be on this project with you."

He blinks. "What do you mean?"

"What I just said, I guess." I shrug. "I hope they send Hank. Josh is a prick. And you have to help me ensure that Rocío stays on—she deserves this. And could you write her a rec letter for grad school? I don't know if mine will—"

"No." He steps forward and reaches out. His hand comes up to the back of my head, spanning from my nape to the curve of my throat. It feels so . . . normal. Familiar. *He* is so familiar. "Bee, no one's going to replace you. BLINK is as much yours as it's mine. If it weren't for you, we'd still be stuck."

"You don't understand." I take a step back. His touch lingers until I'm out of reach—until he has to let go. "I'm out. Like Trevor said."

"Trevor will change his fucking mind."

"He won't. He *shouldn't*. Levi, today I endangered someone's safety. I jeopardized the existence of a project that's *your best friend's legacy*." I press my fingers to my lips. They're trembling. All of me is trembling. "How can you even want me to stay?"

"Because I trust you. Because I *know* you. I know the person you are, the scientist you are, and—" His eyes fall on my bedroom. On my almost-but-not-quite-packed suitcase, open on the floor. He stiffens, pointing at it. "What's that?"

I swallow. "I told you. I can't in all conscience stay on BLINK anymore."

He stares at me, open-mouthed, disbelieving. "So you're packing up and leaving?" The question is aggressive, in a way that makes me think that there are right and wrong answers. I struggle to imagine any besides the one.

"What else should I do?" I shrug helplessly. "What's the point of me being here?"

In the past two months, I've seen a lot of Levi Ward. I've seen him happy, focused, upset, sad, exultant, angry, horny, honest, disappointed, and various combinations of all these things. The way he's looking at me right now, though . . . that's something else. Beyond all of it.

Levi comes closer and opens his mouth, meaning to say something, then immediately turns around and paces away, shaking his head furiously. He takes a deep breath, and another, but when he looks at me again he's hardly calmer.

"Are you serious?" Icy. His voice, his eyes, the line of his jaw. Pure ice.

"I . . . Levi. My presence here was always contingent upon my role in BLINK."

"*Was.* But things have changed."

"What has changed?"

"I don't know. Maybe the fact that we've been together every second of the past two weeks, that we've made love every single night, that I know that you sigh in your sleep, that you floss like a maniac, that you taste like honey *everywhere.*"

I feel my cheeks heat. "What does that even mean?"

"Are you serious?" he repeats. "All of that—that was just . . . passing time while you were in Houston? Fucking? Is that what it was?"

"No. *No.* But there's a difference between just passing time and . . ."

"And staying. And committing. And actually *trying.* Is that what you mean?"

"I . . ." *I* what? Am speechless? Confused? Scared? I don't know what to say, or what he wants. We're friends. Good friends. Who have sex. Who were always going to go their separate ways—like *everyone* does. "Levi, this was never meant to . . . I'm just trying to be honest."

"Honest." He lets out a noiseless, bitter laugh; stares at the hummingbird feeder, his tongue roaming the inside of his cheek. "Honesty. You want some honesty?"

"Yes. I just want to be as honest as possible—"

"Here's the honesty: I'm in love with you. But that's not news. Not to me, and not to you, I don't think. Not if you're *honest* with yourself—which you say you are, right?" My eyes widen. He powers on, ruthless, merciless. Levi Ward: force of nature. Sucking the air out of my lungs. "Here's something else that's *honest*: you're in love with me, too."

"Levi." I shake my head, panic licking up my spine. "I—"

"But you're scared. You're scared shitless, and I don't blame you. Tim was a piece of shit and I want to cut off his balls. Your best friend acted supremely selfishly when you needed her the most. Your parents died when you were a child, and then your extended family—I don't know, maybe they tried their best, but they completely fucked up at giving you the sense of stability you needed. Your sister, whom you clearly adore, is constantly gone, and don't think I don't see the way you obsessively check your phone when she doesn't reply to your texts for longer than ten minutes. And I get it. Why *wouldn't* you be afraid that she'll be taken away from you? Everyone else was. Every single person you've cared about has disappeared from your life, one way or another." I don't know how he manages to look so angry, so calm, so compassionate at the same time. "I understand. I can be patient. I've tried, will try to be patient. But I need . . . something. I need you to understand that this is not a book you're writing. We're not—not two characters you can keep apart because it makes for a literary ending. These are our *lives*, Bee."

There's a tear sliding down my neck. Another, a wet splotch against my collarbone. I screw my eyes shut. "When we went to the conference? And I saw Tim?" He nods. "It was upsetting. Very. But after a while I realized that I didn't really feel anything for him, not anymore, and it was . . . nice. That's what I want, you know? I want *nice*." I've had so little of it. I was always, *always* being left behind. And the only way to *not* be left behind is to leave first. I wipe my cheek with the back of my hand, sniffling. "If *nice* means being alone, then . . . so be it."

"I can give you nice. I can give you better than nice. I can give you *everything*." He smiles at me, full of hope. "You don't even have to admit to yourself that you love me, Bee. God knows I love you enough for the both of us. But I need you to stay. I need you to stick around. Not in Houston, if you don't want to. I'll follow you, if you ask me to. But—"

"And when you get tired of me?" I'm a wet, trembling mess. "When you can't be around anymore? When you meet someone else?"

"I won't," he says, and I hate how sure, how resigned he sounds.

"You don't know that. You *can't* know that. You—"

"There hasn't been anyone else." His jaw tenses and works. "Since the first moment I saw you. Since the first moment I talked to you and made an ass of myself, there hasn't been anyone else."

Does he— He doesn't mean it. He can't mean *that*.

"Yes," he says ardently, reading my mind. "In *all* the ways you're imagining. If you're going to decide, you should have the facts. I know you're scared—do you think *I'm* not scared?"

"Not the way I am—"

"I spent years—*years*—hoping to find another who could measure up. Hoping to feel something—anything—for someone else. And now you're here, and—I have *had* you, Bee. I know how it can be. You think I don't know what it feels like, to want something so much you're afraid to let yourself take it? Even when it's in front of you? Do you think I'm *not fucking scared*?" He exhales, running a hand through his hair. "Bee. You want to belong. You want someone who won't let go. I'm it. I didn't let go of you for *years*, and I didn't even *have* you. But you need to let me."

It's difficult, looking at him. Because my eyes are blurry. Because he leaves me nothing to hide behind. Because it reminds me of the past few weeks together. Elbows brushing in the kitchen. Cat puns. Fights over what music to put on in the car—and then talking over it anyway. Kisses on the forehead when I'm still asleep. Little bites on my breasts, my hips, my neck, all over me. The smell of humming-bird mint, right before sunset. Laughing because we made a six-year-old laugh. His wrong opinions on Star Wars. The way he holds me through the night. The way he holds me when I need him.

I think of the past few weeks with him. Of a lifetime without him. Of what it would do to me, to have even more and then lose all of it. I think of everything I've made myself give up. Of the cats I won't allow myself to adopt. Of the gut-wrenching work that goes into mending a broken heart.

Levi cups my face, forehead touching mine. His hands—they *are* my home. "Bee. Don't take this from us," he murmurs. Ragged. Care-ful. Hopeful. "Please."

I've never wanted anything more than to say yes. I've never wished to reach for something as I do now. And I've never been so utterly, petrifyingly scared to lose something.

I make myself look at Levi. My voice shakes, and I say, "I'm sorry. I just . . . I can't."

He closes his eyes, staving off a violent wave of something. But after a while he nods. He just nods, without saying anything. A simple, quick movement. Then he lets go of me, puts his hand in his pocket, takes something out, and sets it on the table. The loud click echoes through the room. "This is for you."

My heart gives a hard thud. "What is it?"

He gives me a small, pained smile. My stomach twists harder. "Just something else to be scared about."

I stare at the door long after he is gone. Long after I can't hear his steps anymore. Long after the noise of his truck's engine pulls out of the parking lot. Long after I've exhausted my tears, and long after my cheeks dry. I stare at the door, thinking that in just two days I've lost everything I care about, all over again.

Maybe bad things do come in threes after all.

24

RIGHT TEMPORAL LOBE: AHA!

MIGHT BE A bit late in the game to pull my mad-scientist origin story out of its holster, but I'm sitting in the dark, staring at a less-than-flattering reflection of my splotchy face in the balcony doors, the purple of my hair nearly brown—a trick of the light. Someone just ransacked my pockets and stole my most important belongings, and that someone is me. I'm feeling very Dr. Marie Skłodowska-Curie, circa 1911, and I guess it's self-disclosure o'clock.

Originally, I wanted to be a poet. Like my mom. I'd write little sonnets about all sorts of stuff: the rain, pretty birds, the mess Reike made in the kitchen when she tried to bake a cherry pie, kittens play-ing with yarn—the works. Then we turned ten, and we moved for the fourth time in five years, this time to a mid-sized French town at the border with Germany, where my father's eldest brother had a construction business. He was kind. His wife was kind, if strict. His kids, in their late teens, were kind. The town was kind. My sister's best friend, Ines, was kind. There was lots of kindness going around.

A couple of weeks after moving, I wrote my first poem about loneliness.

Frankly, it was embarrassingly bad. Ten-year-old Bee was an emo princess of darkness. I'd quote the most dramatic verses here, but then I'd have to kill myself and everyone who read them. Still, at the time I fancied myself the next Emily Dickinson, and I showed the poem to one of my teachers (full-body cringe intensifies). She zeroed in on the first line, which would roughly translate from French to "Sometimes, when I'm alone, I feel my brain shrink," and told me, "That's what really happens. Did you know that?" I hadn't. But in the early 2000s the internet was already a thing, and by the end of the day, when Reike came home from an afternoon at Ines's place, I knew a lot about The Lonely Brain.

It doesn't *shrink*, but it withers a little. Loneliness is not abstract and intangible—metaphors about desert islands and mismatched shoes, Edward Hopper's characters staring at windows, Fiona Apple's entire discography. Loneliness is *here*. It molds our souls, but also our bodies. Right inferior temporal gyri, posterior cingulates, temporoparietal junctions, retrosplenial cortices, dorsal raphe. Lonely people's brains are shaped differently. And I just want mine to . . . not be. I want a healthy, plump, symmetrical cerebrum. I want it to work diligently, impeccably, like the extraordinary machine it's supposed to be. I want it to do as it's told.

Spoiler alert: my stupid brain doesn't. It never did. Not when I was ten. Not when I was twenty. Not eight years later, even though I've tried my best to train it not to expect anything of me. If alone's the baseline, it shouldn't wither. If a cat never gets any treats, he won't miss them. Right? I don't know. Looking at my reflection in the window, I'm not so sure anymore. My brain might be dumber than a cat's. It might be one of Reike's blobfish, swimming aimlessly in the bowl of my skull. I have no idea.

It's June. Almost summer. Sunset doesn't come early anymore—if it's dark outside, Levi must have left hours ago. I stand gingerly from the couch, feeling heavy and weightless. An old woman and a newborn calf. Wretched little me, still containing multitudes. But as much as I'd rather wallow in self-pity, this situation is a grave of my own digging. There are things I need to do. People I need to take care of.

First, Rocío. She's not in her apartment and doesn't pick up when I call—because she's with Kaylee trying to forget today's fustercluck, because she hates me, because she's a Gen Z. Could be all three, but what I have to tell her is important, and I've already hurt her chances to get into the Ph.D. program of her dreams enough, so I email her.

> Whatever happens with BLINK, get in touch with Trevor
> ASAP and ask him to let you stay on the project as the
> RA (I'd do it, but it's best if it doesn't come from me).
> Levi will support this. What happened today is my
> responsibility only and won't reflect on you.

Okay. One down. I swallow, take a deep breath, and tap on the Twitter app. Shmac's next: he needs to know what's going on with STC. That if he continues to associate with Marie, things could go south very quickly. I still don't know what the hell happened, but publicly disavowing me might be best for him.

I DM him to ask if he has a minute, but he doesn't immediately reply. *Probably with the girl,* I tell myself. After my disastrous conversation with Levi, the idea of someone brave enough to seize that kind of love, intense and eviscerating and gutting and joyful, fills me with an envy so overwhelming I have to push back against it with my entire self.

I click on Shmac's profile, wondering when's the last time he was online. He hasn't tweeted much in the past week—mostly #FairGraduateAdmissions stuff, comments on the peer-review system, a joke about how he'd *love* to be writing, but with his cat sitting on his laptop he really can't—

Wait.

What?

I click on the picture attached to the tweet. A black cat is snoozing on top of the keyboard. It's short-haired and green-eyed and . . .

Not Schrödinger. It can't be. All black cats look the same, after all. And this picture—I can barely make out the cat's face. There's no way to tell who—

The background, though. The background . . . I know that backsplash. The dark-blue tiles are just like the ones in Levi's kitchen, the ones I stared at for half an hour last week after he bent me over the counter, and even without them I can see the edge of a carton of soy milk in the picture, which Levi finds "gross, Bee, just gross" but started buying when I told him it was my favorite, and . . .

No. No, no, no. Impossible. Shmac is . . . a five-eight nerd with a beer belly and male-pattern baldness. Not the most perfect Cute Sexy Handsome Guy™ in the world. "No," I say. As if it'll somehow make everything go away—the last few disastrous days, Shmac's tweet, the possibility of . . . of *this*. But the picture is still there, with the tiles, the soy milk, and the—

"Shmac," I whisper. Hands shaking, out of breath, I scroll back up our message history. The girl. The *girl*. We started talking about the girl when I—when *did* we first talk about her? I check the dates, vision blurry once again. The day I moved to Houston was the first time he mentioned her to me. Someone from his past. But, no—he told me she was married. He said her husband had lied to her. And I'm not, so—

But he thought I was. He thought Tim and I were together. For a long time. And Tim *did* lie to me.

"Levi." I swallow, hard. "Levi." This is impossible. Things like these—they don't happen in real life. In my life. These coincidences, they're for *You've Got Mail* and nineties rom-coms, not for— My eyes fall on the longest message he sent me.

I know the shape of her. I go to sleep thinking about it, and then I wake up, go to work, and she is there, and it's impossible.

Oh my God.

I want to push her against a wall, and I want her to push back.

I did that, didn't I? He pushed me against a wall, and I pushed back. And pushed. And pushed. And pushed. And now I've pushed him away for good, forever, even though . . . Oh, *God*. He has offered me *everything*, everything I've ever wanted. And I am such a cowardly, idiotic fool.

I wipe my cheek, and my eyes fall on the object Levi left on the table. It's a flash drive, pretty, shaped like a cat's paw. A calico's. My laptop doesn't have a USB port, so I frantically look for an adapter— which *of course* is at the bottom of the damn suitcase. There's one single document on the drive. *F.mp4*. I plop down on the pile of un- folded clothes I just tossed around and immediately click on it.

I knew there were cameras everywhere in the Discovery Building, but not that Levi had access to them. And I don't understand why he'd give me thirty minutes of night surveillance footage. I frown, wondering if he uploaded the wrong file, when something small and fair slinks in the corner of the monitor.

Félicette.

The date says April 14, only a few days before I moved to Houston. Félicette looks a little smaller than the last time I saw her. She trots across the hallway, glances around, then disappears around the corner. My body leans in to the screen to follow her, but the movie cuts to April 22. Félicette jumps on one of the couches in the lobby. She circles around, finds a good spot, and starts napping with her head on her paws. Wet laughter bubbles out of me, and the video changes again—the engineering lab is semi dark, but Félicette is sniffing tools I've seen Levi use. Licking water from the drip tray of the break room's water dispenser. Running up and down the stairs. Giving herself a bath by the conference room windows.

And then, of course, in my office. Scratching her claws on my chair's armrests. Eating the treats I left out for her. Dozing on the little bed I set up in the corner. I'm laughing again, I'm *crying* again, because—I knew it. I *knew* it. And Levi knew it, too—this is not something he put together quickly last night. This is hours and hours of combing through footage. He must have known Félicette existed for a while, and—I want to strangle him. I want to kiss him. I want *everything*.

I guess this is it—being in love. Truly in love. Lots and lots of horrible, wondrous, violent emotions. It doesn't suit me. Maybe it's for the best that I sent Levi away. I could never live with this—it'd raze me to the ground in less than a week, and—

I want to push her against a wall, and I want her to push back.

Oh, Levi. Levi. *I can be fearless. I can be as fearless and honest as you are. If you will teach me.*

I sit back, let the tears flow, watch some more. She really did like my desk, Félicette. More than Rocío's. As the date changes, she nestles around my computer more often. Steps where I found her little paw prints. Delicately sniffs the rim of my cup. Chews on my computer's power cable. Scurries away when the door opens, and—

Wait.

I stop the video and lean forward. It's clear from the shift of the lights that someone is coming inside, but the video immediately cuts to new footage. Who would open the door of my office at—2:37 a.m.? Cleaners always came by late afternoons. Rocío is committed to BLINK, but not two-thirty-a.m. committed. Hell, *I'm* not two-thirty-a.m. committed.

I wipe my tears, press the space bar, and let the video run, hoping for an explanation. It doesn't come, but something else does. A segment dated two days ago, again in my office. Just a handful of seconds of Félicette sleeping at my desk. My monitor is on.

I don't leave my computer unlocked. Not ever.

I stop the video and zoom in as much as I can, feeling like a tinfoil-hatted conspiracy theorist. The video is just high-def enough that I can make out . . .

"Is that my *Twitter*?" I ask no one.

Impossible. I'd never log into WWMD on a work computer. For obvious reasons, chief among them that Rocío has a perfect visual of it. But it's right there, unless I'm hallucinating, and—it might be keychain access? But still . . .

"Félicette?" I whisper. "Do you turn on my computer in the wee hours of the night? Do you log in with my NASA password? Do you use Twitter to catfish underage kittens?" She doesn't. She would never. But it sure looks like someone *is*, and that doesn't make any sense at all. Or maybe it does. Maybe it totally does, given the weird activity from my Twitter account. *Shit.*

I paw at the table for my phone and text Levi. My fingers shake when I read his last texts, but I force myself to power through.

BEE: How do I get access to the complete security footage of the Discovery Building?

A minute passes. Three. Seven. I call him—no answer. I look at the clock—fifteen minutes past eleven. Does he hate me? No more than I hate myself. Is that why he's not answering? Is he asleep? Maybe he's not checking his phone.

Shit. I'll email him.

> How do I get access to the complete security footage of the Discovery Building? Please let me know ASAP.
> Something weird's going on.

Then I have an idea, and don't bother waiting for his reply. I slip my shoes on, grab my NASA badge with a silent prayer to Dr. Curie that it still works, and run out to the Space Center.

Something *very* weird's going on. I'm 99.9 percent sure that I am right—and 43 percent sure that I am wrong.

I STUB MY toe on the edge of the elevator, stumbling into the second floor's hallway with a loud, "Ow!"

Very suave, Bee. Perhaps I shouldn't have worn sandals. Perhaps I should have stayed at home. Perhaps I'm going insane.

Whatever. I'll go to my office, check my computer for anything weird, return home with my tail between my legs. What else do I have to do? My scientific career is over, my good name is soon to be besmirched, and I'm at once too emotionally unavailable to be with the man I love and too in love with him to deal with my own choices. I can spare twenty minutes to sleuth before I go back to browsing the Teen Drama hidden code on Netflix and wishing vegan Chunky Monkey existed.

My (former?) office looks like it always does—homey, cluttered.

No sign of Félicette. I sit at my desk, log in. Sure enough, if I navigate to the Twitter page, my password seems to be saved. My heart thuds. My stomach lurches. I look around, but the building is deserted. Okay. Okay, so someone could have conceivably accessed WWMD from this computer.

And messaged the STC guy? Yikes.

But who? Rocío? No. Not my little goth. Levi? Nah. He was in bed with me every night in the past weeks, and most of the time we weren't even sleeping. Who else, then? And why would they contact STC posing as me? To make me look bad. But *why*? These kinds of machinations require a degree of committed hatred that someone like me could never inspire. I'm too boring.

I drum my fingers, wondering if I'm a lunatic, when something else occurs to me. Something much, much bigger: if someone logged into my computer, they wouldn't just have access to my stupid social media, but to BLINK's server, too.

"Holy shit."

I navigate to the server repository. "No way." I click on the folder where the documents pertaining to today's demonstration are. "Impossible. I'm crazy. No one would—" How the hell did Levi access the logs? God, I hate engineers. They always type so quickly. "Was it—here? Where the hell did he click? Ah, yes—" I open the log for the file used for Guy's brain stimulation. The one I finalized three days ago. The one that should be locked to anyone except for me.

It was modified last night. At 1:24 a.m. By me.

Except that last night I was tossing and turning in bed.

Okay. So it was modified by someone on this computer. "Who the fuck—"

"Are you okay?"

I startle so hard, I yelp and throw my mouse across the room. It misses Guy by a few inches.

"Oh my God." I press my hand against my mouth. "I'm sorry—you scared me and I—" I laugh into my palm, high on relief, low-key thankful I didn't shit my pants. It was touch and go for a second. "I'm *so* sorry. I wasn't trying to kill you for the second time in one day!"

He smiles, leaning against the doorframe. "Third time's the charm."

"Oh, God." I press a hand against my forehead. My heart's calming down, and I remember the last time I saw Guy. He didn't look good. Because *I* gave him a seizure. "How are you?"

He gestures at himself with a self-deprecating smile. "Back to my hunky self. You don't look too good, though."

"I'm having an . . . interesting day. Guy, I want to apologize for what happened today. I take full responsibility for—"

"You shouldn't."

"I should." I lift my hand. "I absolutely should. It looks like something weird is happening—I'll show you. But that doesn't matter. With your safety at stake I should have been more careful. I take full responsibility, and—"

"You shouldn't," he repeats, his tone a touch firmer. Something about it rubs me wrong. His eyes are usually a warm golden-brown, but tonight there's an odd coldness about them.

I realize that I have no idea why he's here. Well past eleven. In my office. After a day spent at the hospital, shouldn't he be resting? I'm pretty sure he should be resting.

"Are you . . . did you forget something?" I stand to obstruct his view of my monitor, not quite knowing why. "It's late."

"Yeah." He shrugs. I'm acutely conscious that he's blocking the only exit. I'm also acutely conscious that I'm a raving lunatic. This is Guy. My friend. Levi's friend. An astronaut. I just gave him a seizure, for fuck's sake. *Of course* he looks weird.

"Are you . . . I was heading home. I'm done with . . . what I came for."

"Really?"

"Yeah. Want to leave together?"

He doesn't move. "You said there was something weird you wanted to show me?" Why is he not smiling?

"No, I . . ." I wipe my palm against the side of my thigh. It's gross, clammy. My grandmother's ring catches on the seam. "I misspoke."

"I don't think you did."

My heart skips several beats. Then it gallops, twenty times faster. "It doesn't matter." I need my stupid voice to shake less. "I gotta go. It's late, and I'm technically off BLINK. I shouldn't even be here—Boris will have me arrested." I lean back. Turn off my computer, keeping my eyes on Guy the entire time. Then I make my way to the door. "Well, have a good night. Could you let me through? I can't quite—"

"Bee." He doesn't move. His tone is slightly reproachful. "You're making things complicated for me."

I swallow. Audibly. "Why?"

"Because."

"Because . . . what? Is it the seizure? I really didn't mean to—"

"I think it would be hypocritical of me to get testy about that." He sighs, and I'm instantly aware of how much larger than me he is. He's nothing like Levi, but I'm as big as five bananas in a trench coat, which might be a . . . a problem?

"What's going on?" I whisper. "Guy?"

"What have you told Levi?" he asks, his expression a mix of

calm and irritation. A parent cleaning up after a child spilled a glass of milk.

". . . Told Levi?"

"About the security footage. Did you talk to him on the phone after you emailed him?"

I freeze. "How do you know I emailed him?"

"Answer me, please."

"H-how do you know? About my email?" I retreat until the backs of my legs hit my desk.

"Bee." He rolls his eyes. "I've been in and out of your email for a long time. Making sure Levi's messages couldn't reach you. Creating some . . . miscommunications. You know, there's a reason websites tell you to use difficult passwords, MarieMonAmour123."

"It was *you*." I gasp, trying to step even farther away. There's nowhere to go. "How did you get into my computer?"

"I set it up." He gives me an incredulous look. "You're not very good at technology, are you?"

I frown, pulled right out of shock and into furious outrage. "Hey! I can code in *three* programming languages!"

"Is one of them HTML?"

I flush. "HTML is valid, you *stemlord*. And I minored in computer science. And why the hell were you *in my damn email*?!"

"Because, Bee, you wouldn't just mind *your damn business*." He takes a step toward me, nostrils flaring. "Did you know that the Sullivan prototype should have been called Kowalsky-Sullivan? Of course, Peter had to get his head smashed—" He stops, pausing for a moment. "Okay, this came out wrong. I was sorry when it happened. But my work on BLINK was erased. By virtue of dying, Peter got all the credit, and—it would have been fine. But then Levi offered to lead BLINK out of some misplaced guilt, and they chose *him* over me. I had no control over something I spent *years* working on." His voice rises. He comes closer and I flatten against the desk. "And for so long I was sure BLINK wouldn't get done, that it'd be delayed, that Levi would move on to other things—he wasn't even doing neuroimaging anymore, did you know that? If it hadn't been for Peter, he'd still be at the Jet Propulsion Lab. But no. He had to poach my project."

"What did you do?" I murmur.

"I did what I had to. This morning I took a few caffeine pills, just to be, you know . . . excitable. And I fudged the protocols. But you put me in this situation. You and Levi. Because, Bee—oh, Bee, he was *obsessed* with you. The second NIH nominated you, he *had* to make BLINK happen. And I tried to do what I could—make you guys fight a little. Little delays. Missing files. For a while you seemed stuck, and I hoped time would run out and you'd go back to NIH." His eyes are a little crazed. "But you cracked it. And . . . I had to do it. Today had to happen. They won't let Levi stay on the project."

"On Twitter. What did you do on Twitter?"

He runs a hand down his face. "That was— I wasn't going to involve you, believe it or not. But when I found out that you weren't really married, that Levi lied to me, I was *very* upset. It didn't take long to realize that . . . I cannot believe you're fucking him, Bee. Your Twitter was on your computer, and I'd been following your online identity, so . . . I knew what to do."

"Oh my *God*."

"You were supposed to *hate* him! When NIH selected you, Levi told me you had issues in the past. And I thought—perfect!" He sighs like he's deeply tired. "And then you fell in love. Who *does* that?"

"Are you crazy?"

"I'm *angry*. Because it would have worked out great if you hadn't noticed the security footage. I guess I got a bit sloppy at editing myself out? Why were you looking at it, anyway?"

I shake my head. I'm not explaining Félicette to this asshole. "You *are* crazy."

"Yeah." He closes his eyes. "Maybe."

I look around for— I'm not sure what. A siren? A baseball bat? One of those portable transporters from *Star Trek*? "Let me go," I say.

"Bee." He opens his eyes. "You don't need to be an evil mastermind to acknowledge that I *cannot* let you go."

"You sort of have to. You can't do anything to me. There are cameras—"

"—whose footage we established I can doctor—thanks to your RA, by the way. I only got access to the surveillance circuit after catching her in flagrante."

"You still used your badge to come in—"

"—I didn't, actually. Pretty easy to clone an anonymous badge."

My fingers shake when I grip my desk. "What's your plan, then?"

He takes something out of his pocket. No. No.

No, no, *no.*

"Is that a gun?" I gasp out.

"Yeah." He sounds almost apologetic. My entire world stops.

I'm used to being scared. I live my life in fear—fear of being abandoned, fear of failing, fear of losing everything. But this is different. Is it terror? Real, hindbrain terror? Is this how the lady feels in *Scream* and *Scream* 2, 3, and 4, when she realizes that the caller is in the house? Did they ever make 5? God, will I die before *Scream 5* hits theaters?

"What— Where did you even— Is that real?"

"Yeah. Really easy to get one." He holds the gun like he hates it almost as much as I do. "NRA's crazy here."

"I guess I'm having the full Texas experience," I mumble, numb.

This cannot be happening. I'm well-acquainted with stemlords' disregard for women, but one wanting to *kill* me? A step too fucking far. "Do you even know how to use that?"

"They teach you. During astronaut training. Insert Space Force joke." He laughs once, humorlessly. "But I won't need to use it. Because we're going up to the roof. Poor little Bee. In a few short days she lost *everything*. Couldn't handle the stress. Decided to jump."

"I will do no such—"

Guy points the gun at me.

Oh, *shit*. I'm going to die. In my stupid office. Killed by a stemlord. I'm going to die without having had a cat. I'm going to die without having admitted to Levi that I love him more than I thought possible. Without a chance to show him—to show *myself*—that I can be brave.

At least Marie had Pierre for a while. At least she took a chance. At least she *tried* not to act like the stupid coward I've been and oh *God*, maybe if I beg Guy he'll let me text Levi and I'll be able to tell him, I just want to tell him, it seems such a waste not to have told him, and—

A meowing sound. We both turn. Félicette is on the filing cabinet near the door, growling at Guy. He gives her a confused look. "What the hell is—"

Félicette pounces on him with a shriek, clutching his head and clawing at him. Guy thrashes around, leaving the door empty. I sprint out of the room, running as fast as I can—not nearly fast enough. I can hear steps right behind me.

"Stop! Bee, stop, or I'm fucking going to—"

I'm at the end of the hallway. My legs are giving out, my lungs on fire. He's going to kill me. Oh my God, he's going to kill me.

I turn the corner and dart to the landing. Guy yells something I cannot make out. I take my phone out to call 911, but there is a string of loud noises behind me. Shit, has he *shot me*? No, not a gunshot.

I turn around, expecting to see him come at me, but—

Levi.

Levi?

Levi.

He and Guy are tussling on the floor, grunting and struggling and rolling around in a vicious, violent embrace. I stare at them for several seconds, open-mouthed, paralyzed. Levi's bigger, but Guy has a fucking *gun*, and when he adjusts his grip to aim at Levi I—

Levi!

I don't even think about it—I run back to where the fight is happening and kick Guy in the ribs so forcefully, I feel a zing of pain travel from my toes up my spinal cord.

I blink, and by the time my eyes are open again Levi's pinning Guy to the floor, holding his arms behind his back. The gun has skittered several feet away. It is, in fact, very close to me.

I look at it. Consider picking it up. Decide not to.

Levi.

"You okay, Bee?" He sounds winded.

I nod. "He . . . he . . ." Guy is struggling. Demanding to be let go. Swearing. Insulting Levi, me, the world. My legs feel like Jell-O—the off-brand one, which doesn't bounce very well. I could use a puke bucket.

"Bee?" Levi says.

". . . Yeah?"

"Can you do something for me, sweetheart?"

Unlikely. "Yeah?"

"I want you to take a step to your right. Another. Another." My knee hits the edge of one of the lobby couches. Levi smiles, like he's incredibly proud of me. "Perfect. Now sit down."

I do it, confused. There's something wet on my hand. I look down: Félicette is licking my fingers. "I . . . Why?"

"Because I'll need to restrain Guy until security gets here. And I won't be able to catch you when you pass out."

"But I . . ." My eyelids flutter closed, and . . .

Well. You know the drill by now.

25

ORIENS-LACUNOSUM MOLECULARE
INTERNEURONS: COURAGE

"NOT TO BE whiny," I tell the nurse with a desperate-yet-grateful-yet-really-desperate smile. "I appreciate everything you're doing, but NIH has notoriously crappy health insurance, and if I told you what a recent Ph.D. makes a year, you'd discharge me immediately." And give me ten bucks for the cab home.

"NASA will cover this," Kaylee says. She's on the bed next to me, leaning against my pillow as she shows me the wonders of TikTok. I'm clearly going to have to download this time-sinking black hole of an app.

"Or you'll sue them," Rocío adds from the guest chair. She's sprawled comfortably, a GRE prep manual on her lap and her booted feet on top of the covers. The things I let her do, just because she is, as Kaylee would put it, "my fave."

"I'm not going to sue NASA."

"What if they decide to call their next Mars rover *The Marie Curie* but they end up misspelling it *The Mariah Carey*?"

I mull it over. "I might sue in that case."

Rocío gives me a pleased *I know you* smile. My phone buzzes.

REIKE: OMG you're on the NEWS

REIKE: HERE IN NORWAY IN THIS PUB I'M AT

REIKE: Is this what stardom feels like?

I close my eyes, which proves to be a mistake. The image of Reike climbing over the counter of a Bergen dive bar and pointing at the TV is disturbingly vivid.

BEE: You don't even speak Norwegian.

REIKE: No, but the news lady said NASA and Houston, and they put the mugshot of the Guy guy on the screen

REIKE: lol the Guy guy I'm hilarious

BEE: Are you drunk?

REIKE: LISTEN MY FAVORITE SISTER ALMOST GOT KILLED LAST NIGHT I'M ALLOWED TO DROWN MY TRAUMA IN SOME NORWEGIAN LIQUOR THAT I CANNOT PRONOUNCE

BEE: I'm your only sister.

REIKE: 😊

I lock my phone and slide it under the pillow. I don't even know why I'm in a hospital. The doctors said that me passing out was concerning, and I almost laughed in their faces. I just want to go home. Stare out of the window. Think wistfully about the ephemeral nature of human existence. Watch cat videos.

"Here it says that 'abreast' means 'up to date' and has nothing whatsoever to do with boobs." Rocío stares at the vocab section of her manual. "Sounds fake."

Kaylee and I exchange a worried look.

"And 'bombastic' is a real word? This can't be right."

"Babe, I'll start tutoring you again as soon as NASA's not being sabotaged anymore."

I give Kaylee a grateful smile. She and Rocío were in the hospital room this morning when I woke up, and they've stuck around since then like the amazing human beings they are. I now know more about body decomposition *and* makeup palettes than I thought I ever would, but I regret nothing. This is almost nice.

Then Boris enters the room with a bleak expression. Closely followed by Levi.

My heart flutters. When I asked about him this morning, the girls told me he was with law enforcement in the Discovery Building. He meets my eyes, gives me a small smile, and sets a bag and a box of my favorite brand of vegan brownies on my bedside table.

Boris stands beside the bed, rubbing his forehead, looking tired, aggravated, at the end of his rope. I wonder if he slept at all. Poor man.

"I'm at an impasse, Bee." He sighs. "NASA firmly instructed me not to apologize to you because it would be admissible evidence if you decided to sue, but . . ." He shrugs. "I *am* sorry, and—"

"Don't." I smile. "Don't piss off your lawyers over this. I was right there with you, thinking that it was my error. I didn't know Guy was batshit crazy, and I worked with him every day—how could you?"

"Guy will . . . He is fired, of course. And there will be legal repercussions. We'll resume BLINK the second the Discovery Building is not caked in yellow tape, with another demonstration. I explained everything to NIH and my superiors, and of course I am begging you on my knees to return—"

"You're standing," Rocío points out, unimpressed. Levi looks away, biting back a smile.

"Rocío," I scold her gently.

"What? Make him grovel harder."

I give her a fond look. "None of this was his fault. Plus, think how good your Ph.D. applications will look when they come with a recommendation letter from the Director of Research at the Johnson Space Center." I hold Boris's gaze. After a moment he nods, defeated. He needs a nap. Or nine coffees.

"I'd be happy to, Ms. Cortoreal. You deserve it."

"Will you mention that I had sex at work with the most beautiful woman in the world?" She glances at Kaylee, who blushes prettily.

"I—" He rubs his temple. "I actually forgot about that."

"Is that a firm no? Because it's one of my proudest accomplishments."

Boris leaves a few minutes later. Levi pulls up a chair and sits next to me to catch us up. "I'm not sure what the charges are, but Guy was so high up, had access to so much information, we'll have to double-check every single chunk of code we ever wrote, every piece of hardware. It's a setback—a big one. But BLINK will be fine, ultimately." He doesn't seem too concerned.

"He has a kid, doesn't he?" Kaylee asks.

"Yeah. He had a nasty divorce last year, which I don't think helped with . . . whatever happened. I was with him a lot, but I didn't see it. I really didn't."

"Obviously," Rocío mutters. Levi and I share an amused look, and . . .

It sticks, a little bit. It's hard for me to let go of his eyes, and for him to let go of mine. I suspect it's because the last time I saw him was such a mess, and the time before an even messier mess. And now we're here, in front of this messy mess, and . . .

It's difficult to breathe.

"Well," Kaylee says, jumping up, "Rocío and I gotta go."

Rocío frowns. "Where?"

"Ah, to bed."

"But it's three in the afterno—" Kaylee drags her up by the wrist, but when they're at the door Rocío frees herself and comes to stand in front of Levi.

"I must thank you. For saving Bee's life," she says solemnly. "To me, she is like a mother. The mother I never had."

"You have an amazing mother back in Baltimore," I point out, "and I'm only five years older than you." I am ignored.

"I want to give you a token. To acknowledge your contributions."

"There's no need," Levi says, just as solemnly.

Rocío rummages in her jeans pocket and offers him an unwrapped, slightly squished red gumball.

"Thank you. This is . . ." He looks at the gum. "A thing that I now have."

Rocío nods somberly, and then Levi and I are alone. Well. With the gumball.

"Did you want it?" he asks me.

"I could never. It's your reward for saving my life."

"Pretty sure you saved your own life."

"It was a team effort." There is a small lull, a not-exactly-unpleasant silence. I find that I can't quite meet Levi's gaze, so I glance around. "Are the brownies for me?"

"I wasn't sure what the food options were." He wets his lips. "The bag's for you, too."

"Oh." I peek. Inside there's something wrapped in newspaper. I put it in my lap and start unrolling it. "It's not Guy's heart that you cut out of his chest, is it?"

He shakes his head. "I already fed that to Schrödinger."

"I—" I pause mid-action. "I'm *so* sorry. I cannot imagine how hard it must be. He's one of your closest friends, and the fact that he was so jealous of you and Peter is . . ."

"Yeah, I . . . I'll go talk to him. When it's been a while and I want to punch him less. But for now . . ." He shrugs. "You should open that."

I resume. It's about five layers before I can make out what it is.

"A mug?" I turn it around and break into a grin. "Oh my God, *Yoda Best Neuroscientist*! You had it made!"

"Look inside, too."

I do. "A bobblehead? Is this Marie Curie?" I lift it up, grinning. "She's standing in front of her lab bench! And she's wearing— This was her wedding gown, did you know that?"

"I didn't." He hesitates before adding: "I won this in middle school. Second place at the science fair. The beakers she's holding glow in the dark."

My smile vanishes slowly. I'm too busy staring at Marie's pretty face to realize that I've heard that science fair story once before. No. No, I didn't hear it. I read it. On my . . .

My arms fall into my lap. "You know. You know about . . ."

He nods. "I reviewed the security footage. I didn't notice at first, but after you wrote that text—I was jogging, by the way, so maybe next time give me fifteen minutes or so before jumping headfirst into danger *alone*—after your text I looked at the footage more closely. And saw your computer."

I stare at him. I'm wholly unprepared for this conversation. "I . . ."

"Did you know all along?"

"No." I shake my hand vehemently. "No, I— The picture. Schrödinger, was— You tweeted it. And then I . . . I had no idea. Before yesterday."

Levi just leans forward, elbows on his knees, and looks at me patiently. "Me neither." He smiles wryly. "Or I wouldn't have talked *about* you *with* you so much."

"Oh." I flush as vermillion as a cardinal male at the peak of mating season. My heart thrashes in my chest—also like a cardinal male at the peak of mating season. "Right."

The things he said.

I want to push her against a wall, and I want her to push back.

The.

Things.

He.

Said.

"Are you okay?" he asks, concerned. It's warranted: I might be in the midst of a cardiac event.

"I—I'm fine. I . . . Have you ever seen *You've Got Mail*?"

"Nope." He gives me a hesitant look. "Maybe we could watch it together?"

Yes, I want to say. I even open my mouth, but no sound comes out of my stupid, stubborn, petrified vocal box. I try again: nothing. Still nothing. My fingers clench the sheets, and I study the amused, knowing expression in his eyes. Like he fully understands what's going on inside me.

"Did you know that she used to be a governess? Marie Curie?"

I nod, slightly taken aback. "She had an agreement with her sister. Marie worked as a governess and helped her sister pay for med school. Then, once her sister had a job, they flipped."

"So you know about Kazimierz Żorawski?"

I tilt my head. "The mathematician?"

"He eventually became one—a good one, too. But initially he was just one of the sons of the family Marie worked for. He and Marie were the same age, both exceptionally . . ."

"Nerdy?"

"You know the type." He flashes a smile, which fades almost immediately. "They fell in love, but he was rich, she wasn't, and back then things weren't as simple as wanting to marry someone."

"His parents separated them," I murmur. "They were heartbroken."

"Maybe it was destiny. If she'd stayed in Poland, she wouldn't have met Pierre. The two of them were very happy by all accounts. The idea of radioactivity was hers, but Pierre helped her out. Kazimierz was a mathematician; he might not have been as involved in her research." Levi shrugs. "It's all a bunch of what-ifs."

I nod.

"But he never really got over Marie. Żorawski, I mean. He married a pianist, had children—named one Maria, which is amusing—studied in Germany, became a professor at Warsaw Polytechnic, worked on . . . geometry, I believe. He lived a full life. And yet, as an old man, he could be found sitting in front of Marie Curie's statue in Warsaw. Staring for hours. Thinking about who knows what. A bunch of what-ifs, maybe." The green of Levi's eyes is so bright I can't look away. "Maybe about whatever little personality quirk of Marie made him fall for her a handful of decades before."

"Do you think . . ." My cheeks are wet. I don't bother wiping them. "Do you think she used to cook terrible stir-fries?"

"I can see that." He bites the inside of his cheek. "Maybe she also insisted on feeding a murder of imaginary cats."

"I'll have you know that Félicette saved my life."

"I saw that. It was very impressive."

Carts roll in the hallway outside. A door closes, and another opens. Someone laughs.

"Levi?"

"Yes?"

"Do you think they . . . Marie, and Pierre, and the mathematician, and everyone else . . . do you think they ever wished they'd just never met? Never been in love?"

He nods, as though he's considered the matter before. "I really don't know, Bee. But I do know that I never have. Not once."

The hallway is suddenly silent. An odd musical chaos pounds sweetly inside my head. A precipice, this one. A deep, dangerous ocean to leap into. Maybe it's a bad idea. Maybe I should be scared. Maybe I will regret this. Maybe, maybe, maybe.

Maybe this feels like home.

"Levi?"

He looks at me, calm. Hopeful. So patient, my love.

"Levi, I—"

The door opens with a sudden noise. "How are you feeling today, Bee?" My doctor steps in with a nurse in tow.

Levi's eyes linger on me for one more second. Or five. But then he stands. "I was just about to head out."

I watch his small smile as he waves goodbye. I watch the way his hair curls on his nape as he steps out. I watch the door close behind him, and when the doctor starts asking me questions about my useless parasympathetic nervous system, it's all I can do not to glare at her.

TWO DAYS.

Two days, I'm in the damn hospital. Then the doctor discharges me with a squinty, distrustful, "There doesn't seem to be anything wrong with you." Rocío picks me up with our rental ("In ancient Egypt, female corpses were kept at home until they decomposed to avoid necrophilia at the embalmer's. Did you know that?" "*Now* I do."), and is just as squinty and distrustful when I ask her to drop me off at the Discovery Building—and to please leave the car in the parking lot.

There's no police tape inside. In fact, I meet several non-BLINK engineers in the hallways. I smile politely, shrug off their curious, intrigued looks, and head for my office. There's a Do Not Enter sign on the wall. I ignore it.

I walk out six hours later, not quite gracefully. I'm carrying a large box and I can't see my feet, so I trip a lot. (Who am I kidding? I *always* trip a lot.) In the car, I tinker with my phone, searching for a good song, and find none I care to listen to.

It's dark already, past sundown. For some unfathomable reason, the silent lights of the Houston skyline make me think of Paris at the turn of the twentieth century. The Belle Époque, they called it. While Dr. Curie holed up in her shed-slash-lab, Henri de Toulouse-Lautrec chugged absinthe at the Moulin Rouge. Edgar Degas creeped on ballet dancers and bathing ladies. Marcel Proust bent over his desk, writing books I'll never get around to reading. Auguste Rodin sculpted thinking men and grew impressive beards. The Lumière brothers laid the foundation for masterpieces such as *Citizen Kane*, *The Empire Strikes Back*, the *American Pie* franchise.

I wonder if Marie ever went out at night. Every once in a while. I wonder if Pierre ever pried a beaker full of uranium ore out of her hand and dragged her to Montmartre for a walk or a show. I wonder if they had fun, in the few years they had together.

Yes. I'm sure they did. I'm sure they had a blast. And I'm sure, like I've never been sure before, that she never regretted anything. That she treasured every second.

The solar lights are on in Levi's yard, just bright enough for me to see the hummingbird mint, purple and yellow and red. I smile and lift the large, light box from the passenger seat, stopping to coo at it. I know about the spare key hidden under a pot of rosemary, but I ring the doorbell anyway. While I wait, I try to spy into the air holes I carved on the top. Can't see much.

"Bee?"

I look up. Breathless. Not scared. I'm not scared anymore.

"Hi. I . . . Hi." He's so handsome. Stupidly, unjustly handsome. I want to look at his stupidly, unjustly handsome face for . . . for as long as I possibly can. Could be a minute. Hopefully, it'll be seventy years.

"Are you okay?"

I take a deep breath. Schrödinger's here, too; staring up quizzically at me and my cargo. "Hi."

"Hi. Are you . . . ?" Levi reaches for me. Abruptly stops himself. "Hey."

"I was wondering . . ." I lift up the box. Hold it out to him. Clear my throat. "I was wondering . . . do you think poor Schrödinger would hate us if we adopted another cat?"

Levi blinks at me, confused. "What do you—?"

Inside the box, Félicette explodes in a long, plaintive meow. Her pink nose peeks out from one of the air holes, her paw from another. I let out a wet, bubbly, happy laugh. Turns out I'm crying again.

Through the tears, I see understanding on Levi's face. Then pure, overwhelming, knee-shaking joy in his eyes. But it's only a moment. By the time he reaches over to take the box from my hands, he is grounded. Solid. Profoundly, quietly happy.

"I think," he says slowly, carefully, his voice a little thick, "that we won't know until we try."

EPILOGUE

HERE'S MY FAVORITE piece of trivia in the whole world: Dr. Marie Skłodowska-Curie and Dr. Bee Königswasser-Ward showed up to their wedding ceremonies wearing their lab gowns.

Well. Clothes. Gowns aren't really a thing anymore. Unless you're walking the red carpet at the Met Gala or . . . well, getting married, I guess. Which I was. *But.* I was wearing a Target dress—yup, *the* Target dress—which I sometimes wear at work. And I work in a NASA lab, which technically makes it "lab clothes." I guess I'm a pragmatic gal, too.

Levi and I aren't going to have a ceremony until this summer. July 26, to be precise. I'd explain why I picked that date, but it might shift your opinion of me from "quirky Marie Curie fangirl" to "dangerously obsessive stalker," so . . . yeah. I'll let you google it, if you must. Anyway, even though we're married, only a handful of people know. Reike, for instance ("Should I hyphenate my name, too? Mareike

Königswasser-Ward. Nice ring to it, huh?"). Penny and Lily (our impromptu witnesses). Schrödinger and Félicette, of course, but they didn't care too much when we told them. They just blinked sleepily at us and went back to napping on top of each other, stirring only when a dollop of celebratory whipped cream appeared.

Ungrateful creatures. I love them.

It's a bit odd, the way our elopement came about. I noticed Levi's frustration when, around the ninth time he proposed, I told him that I *did* want to marry him, but I was traumatized by the last-minute split of my previous engagement (and by the thousands of dollars wasted in security deposits). But the solution to this mess appeared to me in a dream. (That's a lie: I was plucking my eyebrows.)

I secretly applied for a marriage license. Then, on a random Thursday morning, I told him I wanted to drive the truck (he was *not* a fan, but hid it well). He thought we were heading to work (hence the Target dress), but instead I sneakily navigated us to the courthouse. In the already-crowded early-morning parking lot, while he looked around to figure out where the hell we were, I told him I'd marry him that very day. That I couldn't be afraid of him leaving me at the altar if we'd already tied the knot. That I wouldn't even make him sign a prenup to prevent him from claiming rights to my limited-edition *Empire Strikes Back* DVD, because I wasn't planning on divorcing him. Ever.

"I guess I should properly ask," I said after methodically explaining my reasoning, "will you marry me, Levi?" To which he said, "Yeah." Hoarse. Tongue-tied. Breathless. Handsome, so handsome that I had to kiss him, a little tearfully. And by "a little" I mean "a lot." And by "tearfully" I mean that snot was involved. It was ugly, kids.

And it was beautiful.

After a ninety-four-second ceremony we drove to the Space Center, made up an excuse for being late, and I had Lean Cuisine at my desk while frowning at the terrible signal dropout in the astronauts' MRI scans. I only saw Levi once, in public, and the one interaction we were able to sneak was his hand briefly brushing my lower back. Yikes, right?

It was the best day of my life.

Unlike today. Today's going to be the *worst* day of my life. It's 8:43 a.m., and I already know it.

"Are you actually going to do this?" Reike asks, staring at the "#FAIRGRADUATEADMISSIONS RACE, START LINE" banner above our heads.

"My heart says no."

"And your body?"

"My body also says no. But louder."

She nods, unsurprised. "You can probably do it. The 5K, I mean. For the love of the goddess, do not attempt the half marathon."

"That's a lot of trust from someone who has my same wimpy constitution and should know better."

"It has nothing to do with constitution and everything to do with Levi training you for . . . it's been what, eight months?"

"Eight months too long."

We exchange a glance, laughing at each other. I love having Reike here. I love that she and Levi arranged her visit behind my back and surprised me with it. I love her nagging us because we have only vegan food in the house and she's "sick of competing with the cats for a meager slice of chicken breast!" I love that she's hooking up with nose-tongue dude while she's here. I love her. I love all of this.

"Are *you* going to do the race?" I ask.

"Yeah. It's for a good cause. Not that I fully understand what a Ph.D. is, what graduate admissions are, or even why someone would voluntarily go to school, but if you say you're helping traditionally underrepresented groups, I'm on board. Rocío and I will walk and chat. She's planning to talk to me about yet-uncaught serial killers."

"Lovely."

"Isn't she? I cannot believe you let her move back to Baltimore."

"I know, but she got into her dream school, has an apartment with her dream girlfriend, and I'm pretty sure she's a leader in the local Wiccan community. I'm just glad she and Kaylee managed to be here for the 5K after putting so much effort into organizing it."

A young woman walks up to Reike with a smile. "Excuse me—Dr. Königswasser?"

"Oh"—she points at me with her thumb—"not quite the Königswasser you're looking for."

"Yep, this is actually my evil twin. I'm Bee."

"Kate. I'm a psychology grad at UMN." She shakes my hand enthusiastically. "I've been following @WhatWouldMarieDo for years, and I just wanted to say how cool this is." She gestures around herself. Three thousand people signed up for the 5K, but it feels like three million showed up—perhaps because it turned into a grad school fair of sorts. The organizing committee decided to allow universities that pledged to guarantee a fair, holistic admission process the opportunity to set up stands to recruit at the finishing lines. I glance at the crowd, spotting Annie and waving at her. We went out for dinner last night, since she flew in for the race a day early. It's not *not* strange, having a meal with your former best friend who once broke your heart, but we're slowly mending things. Plus, she helped out a lot with the logistics of the 5K.

I always thought that revealing my identity would ruin the fun of running WWMD for me, and I was frustrated when Guy's actions made it impossible for me to do otherwise. Remember when I said that I was scared of being doxxed by creeps who look back wistfully to Gamergate? Well, that happened. A little bit. There was some unpleasantness as the news spread and I went public—some awkwardness, a period of adjustment. But one day Rocío called and said, "I always suspected that deep down you were cool, but I figured it was just wishful thinking. Instead, look at you!" That's when I knew everything would be all right. And with time, it was. Being old news is such a relief.

"Thank you so much for coming all the way from Minnesota, Kate."

"You flew in, too, right? From Maryland?"

"I actually live here now. In Houston. Left NIH for NASA last year."

BLINK's demonstration was a resounding success. Well, the first was a resounding disaster. But the second one went so well, got so much positive attention—likely *because* of the botched first attempt and the publicity it generated—that Levi and I ended up having our pick of jobs. You know how I thought I'd end up living in an underpass with a pile of angry spiders? A month later I was offered Trevor's job. And when I declined, Trevor's boss's position. That's life in academia, I guess: the agony and the ecstasy. Ebbs and flows. Did I fantasize about taking the job and forcing Trevor to write me a report on how men are stupider because their brains have lower neural densities? Often. And with almost sexual pleasure.

In the end, Levi and I considered NIH. We considered NASA. We considered quitting, building a lab in a retrofitted shed, Curie-style, and going rogue. We considered faculty positions. We considered Europe. We considered industry. We considered so much, we were doing nothing but considering for a while. (And having sex. And rewatching *The Empire Strikes Back*, about once a week.) In the end, we always came back to NASA. Maybe just because we have good memories here. Because deep down, we like the weather. Because we truly enjoy annoying Boris. Because the hummingbirds rely on us for their mint.

Or because, as Levi said one night on the porch, my head in his lap as we looked at the stars, "This house is in a really good school district." He only briefly met my eyes, and I'm 74 percent sure he was blushing, but we formally accepted NASA's offers the following day. Which means that now I have my permanent lab, right next to his. A year ago, it would have been a nightmare. Funny how these things go, huh?

The two-minute warning whistles, and people start trickling to the start line. A large hand wraps around mine and pulls me toward the crowd.

"Did you come get her because you know that otherwise she'll run away?" Reike asks.

Levi smiles. "Oh, she wouldn't run. More like a brisk walk."

I sigh. "I thought I'd successfully left you behind."

"The pink hair gave you away."

"I don't think I can do this."

"I'm fully aware."

"The longest I've run so far is . . . less than 5K."

"You can start walking anytime." His hand pushes against my lower back, where my newest tattoo resides. Just the outline of Levi's house, with two little kitties inside. "Give it a try."

"You're not going to slow down your pace to match mine, are you?"

"Of course I am."

I roll my eyes. "I always knew you hated me." I grin up at him. When he smiles back, my heart picks up.

I love you, I think. *And you are my home.*

Someone blows one long whistle. I look ahead, take a deep breath, and start running.

AUTHOR'S NOTE

This book is my hate letter to standardized testing. It's also my love letter to neuroscience, Star Wars, women in STEM, friendships that hit rough patches but then try their best to bounce back, research assistants, interdisciplinary scientific collaborations, Elle Woods, ShitAcademicsSay, mermaids, hummingbird feeders, people who struggle with working out, and cats. But let's focus on the hate part!

I remember studying for the GRE about ten years ago, when I was applying for Ph.D. programs, and constantly feeling like I was a total idiot (which I probably am, but for other reasons). I also remember being really angry and really frustrated at the amount of money, time, and energy I had to pour into learning how to calculate when exactly two trains leaving from different stations will meet, especially when I could have used that time to read up on something that was actually relevant to my field. (Or to sleep. Let's be real, I would have probably just taken a nap.)

This book is, of course, fictional, but everything Kaylee says about the GRE is true, and tests like the GRE and the SATs are not only very sketchy when it comes to predicting future academic performance, but they traditionally favor people who come from economically advantaged backgrounds. Access to higher education is, as a rule, scarcer for those who aren't traditionally privileged, and standardized testing only contributes to the problem. But in the last few years there has been a shift, with more and more institutions and graduate programs not requiring these tests for admission, and that's a fantastic step in the right direction.

Thank you for coming to my TED Talk, and remember: if academia ever makes you feel like you're not good or smart enough . . . it's not you, it's academia.

Love,

Ali

ACKNOWLEDGMENTS

Publishing has very weird, very long timelines, which means that I'm writing the acknowledgments for my second book in October 2021, right after the publication of my first, and my heart is very full. Every good thing that has happened after the release of *The Love Hypothesis* I owe to my team at Berkley: Sarah Blumenstock, the best editor in the multiverse (who lets me add sex scenes till the very last minute!); Jess Brock, my fantastic publicist; Bridget O'Toole, my incredible marketer; and, of course, my most beloved agent, Thao Le, who brought me to them. Let's be real: publishing is terrifying. But the constant support, hard work, and talent of these four women made it slightly less so. Plus, through them, I got to work with the best publisher in the world. Basically: to every single person at Berkley and at SDLA who helped with my books in any capacity, thank you, thank you, THANK YOU. I'm sorry I always turn in stuff at 11:58 p.m. on deadline days. I'm sorry I ask the same questions forty times. I'm sorry I keep abusing the caps lock. I swear I'm trying to be better!! Special thanks to Penguin Creative (in particular Dana Mendelson) and to Lilith, the cover artist of my wildest dreams. And, of course, thank you to Jessica Clare, Elizabeth Everett, Christina Lauren, and Mariana Zapata for blurbing my first book (asking for blurbs is pants-crappingly scary, guys) and for the constant encouragement.

Love on the Brain wouldn't be what it is without the feedback of the brilliant Claire, Julie Soto, Lindsey Merril, Kat, Stephanie, Jordan, and, of course, Sharon Ibbotson, my very first editor. Kate Goldbeck, Sarah Hawley, Celia, Rebecca, and Victoria were amazing and let me vent to them during the writing process. The Grems, the Edge Chat, TM, the Family Chat, and the Berkletes have been crucial to my survival, and I am forever grateful to have these amazing people in my life.

And, of course, a million thanks to all the readers, booktokers, bookstagrammers, bloggers, journalists, reviewers, and fellow Reylos who supported my first book and showed enthusiasm for my second: sophomore book terrors are definitely a thing (or maybe they aren't and it's just me!?) and I spend a few hours every day worrying that people will hate mine, but everyone's excitement has been helping so, sooo much.

And last but very much not least: thanks to Lucy, for being the father I didn't know I needed, and to Jen, for holding my hand during the highs and the lows. Everybody needs a Jen, but mine is taken.

(Oh, and thanks to Stefan, I guess. But only a little.)

Don't miss *New York Times* bestselling author
Ali Hazelwood's next delightfully swoony novel,

LOVE, THEORETICALLY

Coming fall 2023!

ALI HAZELWOOD is the *New York Times* bestselling author of *The Love Hypothesis*, as well as the writer of peer-reviewed articles about brain science, in which no one makes out and the ever after is not always happy. Originally from Italy, she lived in Germany and Japan before moving to the US to pursue a Ph.D. in neuroscience. She recently became a professor, which absolutely terrifies her. When Ali is not at work, she can be found running, eating cake pops, or watching sci-fi movies with her two feline overlords (and her slightly-less-feline husband).

CONNECT ONLINE

AliHazelwood.com

🐦 EverSoAli

📷 AliHazelwood

Ready to find
your next great read?

Let us help.

Visit prh.com/nextread

Penguin
Random
House